The Whale's Footprints

A DOC ADAMS Suspense Novel

The
Whale's Footprints

Rick Boyer

HOUGHTON MIFFLIN COMPANY

Boston

1988

This is a work of fiction, and all of the characters in this
book are fictional.

For information about permission to reproduce selections from
this book, write to Permissions, Houghton Mifflin Company,
2 Park Street, Boston, Massachusetts 02108.

Library of Congress Cataloging-in-Publication Data

Boyer, Rick.
The whale's footprints : a Doc Adams suspense novel / Rick Boyer.
p. cm.
ISBN 0-395-42738-X
I. Title.
PS3552.0895W45   1988   88-14790
813'.54 — dc 19   CIP

Printed in the United States of America

P 10 9 8 7 6 5 4 3 2 1

for

JOHN MCALEER

professor, biographer, novelist,
mystery fiction's foremost man of letters,
Edgar recipient,
and Keeper of the Flame

ACKNOWLEDGMENTS

My thanks to John Boyer, Larry Kessenich, Bill Tapply, Dan Otis, and Charlotte Wade for their helpful criticisms and comments on the manuscript. I would also like to thank the following people for their professional insights and their time and patience: Frank Edwards, M.D.; Dr. Kim Klitcord and Dr. David Folger of the USGS, Woods Hole; and most especially, Dr. Richard Whittaker and his staff at the Marine Biological Laboratory in Woods Hole.

The Mexican romance is for Geraldine, of course.

THE BOY WHO LOVED WHALES

I'LL NEVER FORGET the summer Jack fell in love with the
whales. It was in 1970, when he was just six years old; his younger
brother Tony was barely three. There was a stranding of pilot
whales on the beach near Wellfleet. For reasons not yet understood, whales periodically beach themselves and die, sometimes
in great numbers. Pilot whales are particularly susceptible to this
lemming-like behavior, especially in the shallow waters of Cape
Cod Bay.

Great schools, or pods, of these twenty-foot creatures drive
themselves up onto the gently sloping beach sand inside the bay.
In the falling tide, they lie heavy on the sand and cannot move.
There they remain until they die. In the summer of seventy, we
went to see a pod of twenty-three pilot whales beached in Wellfleet. Since our cottage is just minutes away in North Eastham,
it was easy for us to visit the beach and see what was happening.

At first, Jackie was afraid of the big black monsters that lay
strewn in the shallows. No amount of coaxing could bring him
from behind his little brother's stroller, where he hid so the big
fish couldn't see him. But after a while he saw they could not
chase him and gobble him up. He heard their ragged breathing,
their strange sighing, and finally ventured to the water's edge.
He touched one tentatively, feeling the slick skin that concerned
onlookers kept wet with sea water, pouring it lovingly from buck-

ets, draping wet towels over the curious, bulbous heads and long black backs.

Jack joined the people keeping the animals wet. For two hours, he hauled water, ran among them on the wet sand, and talked to them.

"It's all right, Mr. Whale," he assured them. "It's all right!" He went up and down the entire pod, carrying the big blue beach pail that was half as big as he was, coaxing, petting, leaning over the blowholes that blew up at him like strange, faceless mouths. We could scarcely drag him away.

We returned the next day to a grimmer scene. People looked worried. Talk was hushed. Expectant whispers drifted to us over the wind. Occasional curses, exclamations of rage. People tried to push, lift, carry the whales back to deep water. It didn't work; the animals weighed four tons each. Boats appeared, their owners tying heavy lines to the wide tails. We saw the powerboats' big wakes churning out there, trying to pull the trapped animals off the sand. Jackie ran faster and faster between the long dark shapes. His coaxing grew louder, more frantic. Then, toward evening, a curious silence filled the beach. Strange and unpleasant smells grew in our nostrils. The gulls came, diving and tearing. Jackie ran and ran, shooing them off, his eyes filled with tears.

But there were hundreds of gulls, and only one little boy, waist deep in water. In the near darkness of late evening, I carried him, weeping and sunburned, back to the car. His nails dug into my raw, red shoulders. His eyelashes — tiny artist's brushes — flicked against my cheek, damp with his tears.

"Daddy! Daddy!" he wailed, "why can't they go?"

"Some will be saved, Jackie," said his mother. "Don't you worry honey, some of them will be okay."

We half believed it. Until the next day, when the stench of death drifted across the corner of the bay from Wellfleet to Eastham, and to our beach. Housebound with sunburn, silent with depression, Jackie sat at the table trying to help us with a jigsaw puzzle.

And so he discovered whales and death at the same time.

A week later, when it was apparent that the rebound we expected wasn't forthcoming, we took the boys to Sealand in Brewster to see the dolphin show. The sullen blond boy filed into the arena and sat, palms together and fingers pointed down, saying nothing. His younger brother, swarthy as a betel nut, sucked a grape Popsicle, the sticky purple juice dripping down the wooden stick onto his hands and shorts. Jackie didn't want a Popsicle. He didn't want anything. Mary and I exchanged nervous glances. Then they started the show.

The shiny gray mammals, wearing their perpetual grins, stood on their tails, wore sailor hats, shot baskets, dove for coins, wore sunglasses, went through hoops, squealed and chuckled. And when the kids clapped, the dolphins lay on their sides on the surface and, swatting the water with their flippers, clapped right back at them.

Jackie was standing up by this time. His eyes were still wet, but he wore the biggest smile I have ever seen, before or since. We had to go back to that show every other day for the rest of the month. Damn near broke me. But there was no way out.

Thus, the bond between Jackie and the whales was established — and atomic bombs couldn't have destroyed it after that. When he became a young man, Jack knew exactly what he wanted to do: go to Woods Hole on Cape Cod and follow the whales in a skiff. Listen to their songs. Watch them play and feed and mate and care for their young. Watch their endless rolling dives and chase their spirit spouts across the blue-green sea.

But the whales' footprints led him somewhere else, led him into trouble so deep that Mary and I wondered if we'd lost him for good.

ONE

ON FRIDAY, the eleventh of August, Mary and I awoke to an odd feeling in the atmosphere. The air had a lazy, leaden feel to it. I had a hunch what it was: the tropical depression that the National Weather Service had been tracking across the Atlantic for the past week was going to show its teeth. After breakfast we went down the deck stairway of our cottage to the beach and looked out across Cape Cod Bay. Gulls weren't flying; they were huddling on the shore or rafting up in the shallows, flicking their tails and squabbling. The haze was bright and fuzzy; it hurt our eyes. Our dogs walked slowly, tentatively, along the sand, pausing to sniff the air and whine softly. Distant diesel trawlers, blotchy in the haze, bounced up and down in the gathering chop, the oily smoke oozing out low from their stacks and creeping over the water as if afraid to rise.

"I feel weird, Charlie," Mary said in a low voice. "Let's turn back. I feel nervous and tired."

"It's the low pressure. That's why the birds can't fly and the smoke won't rise. There! You hear that whistle out there? Hear how close it sounds? That's a sign, too. The sounds are bouncing off the layers in the air. You feel it? I can just about feel my skin tingle."

After lunch we went back down to the beach. The sky was darker now, and the wind was picking up. Gusts blew the dune grass flat, and up on the bluffs tossed the scrub oak trees and made the pale undersides of their leaves wink at us like a million tawny freckles.

We walked back to the cottage. Inside, I turned on the big SONY short-wave. It buzzed and crackled ominously; the air was full of bad electricity. I raised a few marine stations: Nauset Beach, Point Judith, Boston. All said the same thing: the tropical depression was now a gale. The big storm was pounding the islands of Nantucket and Martha's Vineyard to the south, and moving in our direction. Gale warnings for the Northeast and to all vessels at sea. Traveler's advisory. Stay inside. Watch out.

I went back onto the deck. Now the water was glowing white-gray. The sky was darkening. Black sky, light water. The world had turned upside down.

"I'm worried about the boys, Charlie," Mary said. Our two sons, Jack and Tony, were both working at coastal locations on the ocean side of the Cape. Jack was at Woods Hole, enrolled in BUMP, the Boston University Marine Program, studying the intelligence and vocabulary of whales. His younger brother Tony was a grounds keeper at the posh Chatham Bars Inn. Both towns are on the south shore of the Cape and therefore were vulnerable to the storm's direct onslaught. Tony in particular, on the low bluffs overlooking the southeastern corner of the Cape, was in the storm's path. I didn't like it. I studied the incoming rush of the sea nervously. We would get a monster tide, no doubt about it. Would our small bluff be adequate protection against the storm surge and high waves? We'd soon find out.

"When's Jack due?" I asked.

"He said they were leaving Woods Hole around four, which means they should be here by five-thirty or six."

"Let's call them; maybe they can leave early."

"I doubt it. Jack said last night that Andy had a lab at three. I don't think he can skip it."

Andy Cunningham, a fresh Yale graduate, was Jack's new friend and roommate in Woods Hole. He was a premed doing a summer fellowship at MBL, the Marine Biological Laboratory, while Jack was working in BUMP. From our impressions of Andy during a trip to Woods Hole in July, he seemed to have everything: looks, brains, personality, and driving ambition. We'd been very struck with him during our quick visit, and now were looking forward to having them both up to the Breakers for the weekend. *If* they arrived safely, that is.

At four-thirty the storm broke. It was as if a gigantic foot came down out of the sky and stomped us flat. The sky turned black and exploded in thunder. The dogs, though accustomed to shotgun blasts, turned in tight circles under the coffee table, crying. I didn't blame them. Mary and I sat close on the braided rug in front of the fireplace. The wind shrieked through the dune grass and wailed and sobbed around the chimney. The ocean was a basso roar, and the rain crawled across the windowpanes in horizontal streaks, the way it does on the windows of a moving car. You could feel the cottage rock in the big blasts.

At six-fifteen we heard the front door open and slam; the candle flames on the mantel flickered and jumped.

"We're here!" Jack shouted above the din. "Just barely!"

We were both relieved to see them come in. They stood in the living room, dripping wet. Andy shook my hand and hugged Mary. He was a handsome kid, with black hair and bright blue eyes set wide apart. He had a strong jaw. He was almost as tall as son Jack, our blue-eyed blond who's six two and has his mother's classical Roman features but the Adams-Hatton Anglo-Scots coloring. Jack's younger brother Tony looks like his mother, with the olive skin, wavy dark brown hair, and coal black eyes of the Calabrian side of his parentage.

"When do you guys want dinner?" Mary asked. "Jeez, Jackie, you're soaked through."

"We're in for a three-day blow. Heavy-duty gale. They say maybe it's a hurricane. You been listening to the radio? Woods Hole and the Islands are swamped; it ought to peak up here sometime tonight."

"I'll put the lasagna in the oven now. I would have put it in earlier, but we weren't even sure you'd show up. God, I'm glad you're here."

"We brought some mussels with us. We could steam those up first. Did you know we saw over thirty whales yesterday? A big pod of fins, three seis, and the rest humpbacks."

"Were they singing?" I asked him.

"Oh yeah. We got their songs on the hydromike."

Just then there was a terrific crash of thunder. The window-panes and dinner plates rattled; the dogs whined under the coffee table. Mary took the mussels into the kitchen while we got drinks and stood in front of the fire. Now and then a gust would come down the chimney and send a big ball of smoke into the room.

"Last time we talked, Andy," I said, "you were still up in the air about med school, trying to decide between Harvard and Johns Hopkins."

"I've settled on Hopkins, mostly because of the financial aid package. I hope we can talk a little bit while I'm visiting, Dr. Adams. Your medical experience would be helpful."

"I'll do what I can, but I left general medicine some time ago, Andy. Now I specialize in oral surgery."

"Oh that's right. I remember Jack telling me that now. Why did you decide to switch?"

"It's, uh, rather a long story," I said, looking out the window at the rain. "Let's say it involved a family . . . sadness. But I wish I'd had your choice of schools. You can't go wrong."

I sipped my Scotch and looked at the two young men. They looked terrific. It seems, of late, that anyone under thirty looks terrific.

Mary called me into the kitchen. I left Jack and Andy standing in front of the fireplace, beers in hand, playing with the dogs. Tony was due at the Breakers the next day—Saturday noon. The sea would be kicking up like crazy in Chatham, I thought, rolling right over the outer bar and swamping the small craft in the shallows. It was storms like these that made me appreciate our protected location high on a bluff on the sheltered bay side of the Cape.

With the storm raging outside, the fire and the smell of food in the cottage, and our sons joining us for the weekend, Mary and I were in a warm, cozy mood. I cranked open a bottle of Chenin blanc and put the mussels, still in their purplish-black shells, into the steamer. I asked Mary if she wanted to hear some music, but she said she'd rather just listen to the storm. It would be another fifteen minutes for the mussels, so I went back and joined the young men in the living room.

"Okay," I said, "tell me the latest from Woods Hole. Andy, has your situation improved any?"

"You mean with my lab supervisor? Hell no; it's coming close to trashing my whole summer."

"C'mon," said Jack, "Hartzell's not that bad. In fact, I kinda like him. 'Course, I don't have to see him more than a few minutes a week —"

"*Hmmmmph!*" Andy grunted into his beer mug. "You're lucky. If you worked for the guy, you wouldn't be saying that." He paused and sipped his beer. "You know, I really and truly think the guy's a little nuts. Really. What's worst of all are his mood swings. One minute, he's okay. Next thing you know, he's hitting the roof. Like today, Dr. Adams —"

"Call me Doc. Everybody does; I don't even answer to 'Dr. Adams' anymore."

"Okay, Doc. So today, we all knew there was this big storm coming. So I ask him, can Jack and I leave early today, since we're going up to Eastham for the weekend. Well, he blows his stack. 'I want you in that lab until four o'clock, Cunningham! I've got a data run that can't wait and I've been planning it, and blah, blah,' you know. Guy's a real turkey."

"Well, what the hell, Andy," said Jack. "You know how it is with bio labs. You get the specimens all primed, the equipment all set up —"

"I know, but get this: after I get in there and start running the experiments, Hartzell leaves! I turn around and there he is in his raincoat, saying he's got an important errand to run. Guy's gone over an hour, with me stuck in Lillie Hall and the sky's getting darker by the minute. Our roommate, Tom McDonnough, says he saw his car driving past our house. So why does he get to leave when I have to stay and worry about his goddamn tunicates?"

"Tunicates?"

"Sea squirts, Dr. Adams. I mean, Doc. Sea squirts are Hartzell's babies. We go through 'em by the bushel. He's working on a way for them to concentrate silver from sea water. Gonna make himself a billion dollars —"

"What? Sea squirts? Silver? A billion dollars? What are you —"

Mary interrupted us with some hummus and pita bread, then

sat down with her glass of white, gazing at the fire and patting Danny, the yellow Lab, on his wide head.

"Sea squirts are marine organisms that concentrate various elements in their tissues," Andy explained. "They concentrate vanadium to such an extent that there's been talk of growing sea squirts for that reason alone. Now old Hartzell, my lab supervisor himself, is figuring out a way to get them to concentrate silver."

"Can he do it?" I asked.

"Well, that's the tricky part," interjected Jack. "And that's why he's so paranoid about his research data. In fact, Hartzell thinks Andy's trying to steal his secrets, doesn't he, Andy?"

"Yeah. Me or somebody. But he's convinced it's somebody our age. Some 'young punk,' as he calls us. He calls me that one more time and, so help me, I'm gonna level him."

Andy shook his balled fist in anger. I was glad I didn't have a boss. Having a lousy boss must be hell.

"Let's go back a sec," said Mary. "You say he's training these little animals to gather silver from sea water? I didn't know sea water had any silver in it."

"Sea water's got a lot of valuable stuff in it," said Andy. "They say that a cubic mile of sea water has as much gold in it as all the bullion in Fort Knox."

"No! You're kidding!"

"Well, something like that, Mom. Problem is, how do you commercially extract it? Well, old man Hartzell's got these little sea squirts —"

"Yeah, and he's watching 'em inhale that brine and spit it out again," Andy continued, "hoping that the concentrations of silver are going to build up in their slimy, stinky little bodies so that he can throw 'em into a furnace and, voila! *Silverado!*"

"Problem is, he's got you doing all the shit work," said Jack, "and accusing you of stealing on top of it all."

"Not just me. He keeps saying it's 'all you young, spoiled kids who never had to work.' Well, I keep saying to him, 'Dr. Hartzell, you may not believe this, but I'm a poor kid, too. My old man's a car salesman in Pawtucket who's worked his ass to a nub for twenty years, sending me to prep schools and then to Yale. Worked sixty-, eighty-hour weeks to pay the bills. My mom, too. What do you say to that?' "

"Really?" I asked. "All of that is true?"

"Yep. And as expensive as med school is, I'm taking no more money from them. They've done way, way more than enough. I told them I was getting a free ride all the way through, based on my past performance. Of course it isn't true; I'm in hock up to my neck. But I don't want them working like that anymore. Especially him. He had a heart attack last year; the next one's gonna kill him . . ."

He lowered his keen blue eyes briefly. "That's what sealed Hopkins for me," he continued in a low voice. "They're giving me more money."

"Why is Lionel Hartzell so obsessed with somebody stealing his data?" asked Mary.

"Because he's nuts. That's what I've come to think. Now Jack here likes the guy. But like I said, Jack isn't working for him."

Jack got up, grabbed Danny by his big neck, and hugged him. The Lab wagged his tail, batting it against a cabinet door and making a sound like a bass drum in a parade: whump! whump! whump!

"I don't really like him; I just don't hate him the way you do, Andy. And you gotta admit, you do antagonize him."

"You keep saying that."

"Well, let's go in, the mussels are done," said Mary, and we followed her into the dining room.

An hour later, just as Mary took the lasagna out of the oven, the power went out and we found ourselves in the dark except for the fire and the candles on the mantel above. We scurried around lighting lamps and candles, and soon were operational again. The low light and pounding rain made the place even cozier. Andy asked if the power outage would affect the telephone. A quick lift of the receiver proved it had not. Then we sat down to eat.

"No wine?" asked Mary, holding the bottle over Andy's glass, which he had covered with his hand.

"No thanks, Mary. I already had two beers, and that's all I should have."

"Well, he's certainly not a member of *this* tribe," said Mary, hoisting her glass.

"The reason is medical," Andy said softly. Since he did not elaborate, we let the subject drop. Dinner was just about over when Mary asked the question.

"Well, have either of you guys fallen in love yet?" she said. She asked nonchalantly, as if to make conversation. But it didn't work; a solemn hush fell over the table.

"Did I say something wrong?" she finally asked.

"Nope," said Jack, spooning lasagna into his mouth.

More silence.

"Hey. Don't everybody talk at once," she said.

As if following her advice, nobody did. Mary and I took the dishes over to the sink. She endured the unexplained silence another minute or so, then spun around.

"All right you guys," she demanded, "what the hell's going on?"

"You tell her," said Andy.

"Me? Why should I tell her? She's you're friend."

"Well, she was your friend, too."

"Yeah. Was. *Was* my friend . . ."

"Is anybody gonna tell me, or am I going to die waiting?" said Mary.

"Maybe it's private," I suggested. Mary waved me away, so I excused myself, went to my chair in the living room, and lighted a pipe, listening to the rain. I could hear them around the corner.

"Okay, what happened was, I met this girl down there at the beginning of the summer, in June, and was going out with her. Then Andy comes along and, well, takes her away from me."

"Uh-uh," I said, butting in from around the corner. "Nobody steals a woman away from you. A woman leaves because she's unhappy, but she isn't stolen away. That's a myth."

"Thanks a lot, Dad."

Mary poked her head around the corner, frowning. "When we want your opinion, Charlie, we'll ask for it."

Then I heard her voice: "Okay, tell me all about it. Everything. I want to hear it *all.*"

"Her name is Alice Henderson. She's enrolled in the SEA program — that's an ocean-going school — and cruises on the *West-*

ward. Her dad's one of the biggest commercial fishermen around Buzzards Bay. She's studying liberal arts. Maybe she'll go into biology. Who knows?"

That was Andy talking. Now Mary:

"How'd you happen to meet her, Jackie?"

"We met at the Kidd."

"Oh, we know the Kidd," said Mary, referring to Woods Hole's best-known bar and nightspot, the Cap'n Kidd.

"Let's get back to the lovely Alice Henderson," I said, walking around the corner and joining the group. "You guys still *are* friends, aren't you?"

"Huh, oh, sure," said Jack. Then it was Andy's turn to speak, looking down at the kitchen floor.

"See, when I met Alice, she'd been seeing Jack only a couple of weeks. I met her through her brother Terry, who works on his dad's boat, the *Highlander.* We were just talking one day when she came up, and we went out to get a Coke, you know —"

"And the next thing I knew," continued Jack, "she was seeing both of us. That was for about a week. Then just Andy. But hey, it's no big deal." His mouth was smiling, but his eyes weren't.

Andy continued staring at the floor. He said: "She said maybe it was a big deal, Jack. That you were kinda like real down about it. So, hey, what can I say, I'm sorry —"

"Well, she's *lying!*" shouted Jack. Then, realizing he'd betrayed himself, he spun on his heel and stomped into the living room.

"Come on now, you guys," Mary said. "I hope you don't let this thing get in the way. You're both young . . . whatever happens, you'll realize in a couple years it really isn't a big deal. C'mere, Jackie."

Reluctantly, Jack re-entered the room. I realized how young he still was in some ways. How sensitive, and quick tempered, too.

Mary diplomatically changed the subject. "We didn't tell you: the DeGroots are motoring down to Wellfleet on *Whimsea* tomorrow. Then on Tuesday we're going to do some cruising with them."

"Not in this weather we're not," I said. "Which reminds me, I better call them and see what's up."

I let the phone ring eight times with no answer. Uh-oh, I

thought, had Jim and Janice headed out despite the storm warnings? I hung up the phone and mentioned my uneasiness to Mary.

"No, Charlie. Even Jim wouldn't do that. They're probably out to eat, or at the club."

"Jim and I have been talking about some cruising," I said. "Remember last year we motored up to Portland from Cape Ann? Well, we were thinking about heading out into the Gulf of Maine later in the summer for some whale watching. You think *Whimsea*'s big enough?"

"Definitely," said Jack. "We've been out there in sea skiffs — even little runabouts, smack dab in the middle of a pod of humpbacks."

"Weren't you scared?" asked Mary.

"Well, so far nothing's happened. I think the whales like the little boats better. They seem less afraid of them. A guy we know at the MBL went out in a twelve-foot motorboat. Before he knew it, he was surrounded by a whole pod of forty-footers. Three of them were females with calves — "

"Well what I mean is, what if the whales got mad?" she said. "Couldn't they just smash a boat in half with their tails?"

"Oh yeah, in a second," said Andy.

"Well . . . jeez."

"Well then, how do you know they won't get mad and kill you?" I asked.

"You don't," said Jack. "But after a while, you get accustomed to seeing these fifty-foot shapes gliding along under your boat. Then you think: *hey!* Each one of those guys weighs fifty tons, as much as seven bull elephants! So what do you do about it? Nothing. You forget about it, and just enjoy it."

"I don't know," said Mary. "I know I'm going to be scared. You really think it'll be safe?"

"Sure. If the whales are bothered in any way, they just take off. Trust me."

"Okay," I said. "So when are you guys due back at the lab?"

"Monday afternoon. And knowing 'hardass' Hartzell, Andy better not be late, storm or no storm. So I guess we'll drive back down early Monday, which gives us the whole weekend. I'm luckier than Andy; I'm doing something I really love. My 'work' is going out in boats and watching whales, and recording their songs."

We hauled the rest of the dirty dishes into the kitchen and I washed them by hand because the power was off. Andy asked if it was all right to make a phone call. I said certainly, and he went upstairs carrying his duffel bag and clothes to use the extension in the bedroom. I assumed it was a personal call. To Alice Henderson, perhaps? None of your business, Adams.

When the dishes were done I sat back in the study corner of the living room, relighted my pipe, and looked at the cottage by candlelight. The living room has low, beamed ceilings, which go well with the fieldstone fireplace and rough plank mantel above. A wooden model of the Grand Banks schooner *Bluenose* sits atop the mantel and on each side are brass ship's running lights with red and green lenses. I love the living room at the Breakers. The wind still howled, and although the tide was ebbing, it was doing so with a thunderous fuss, as if it didn't want to leave. I smoked my pipe and listened to the storm.

Eventually, Andy returned downstairs. He looked disturbed. Jack suggested chess. Andy agreed, but seemed preoccupied. They played for over an hour, with Andy shifting nervously in his chair and glancing at his watch. Suddenly, he got up from the table and said he'd had enough chess. He threw on his waterproof slicker and told us he was going for a walk.

"In this weather?" asked Jack.

"Yeah. Just for a while. My stomach's a little upset; I think I need some air."

"Just a second, I'll go with you," said Jack. But Andy said he'd prefer to go alone, and would return shortly. He went back upstairs to the guest room briefly, then returned, all bundled up, and left.

"Gee Charlie, what's that all about?" said Mary, after he'd gone out the door.

"Well, if I were forced to guess, I would surmise a tiff with Alice. But then, it's not our business."

"I don't think he called Alice," said Jack. "She's on the *Westward* now."

"In this weather? I hope not."

"Oh, that's right . . . ," said Jack, a confused, rather hurt look on his face. I hurt for him, too. With my children, I am much too tender for my own damn good.

"Oh well, it should sort itself out."

While we waited for Andy to come back, Jack and I played chess by candlelight.

He returned, soaked to the skin, at ten-thirty. Mary had gone to bed, and Jack and I were getting concerned; he'd been gone almost two hours.

"Gee, Andy, we were worried about you," I said. "I was afraid you got struck by lightning."

"Oh. Sorry I took so long. I got lost in the dark and the rain. I missed the road and went on past it. Hey, I think I'll go up and hit the rack; I still don't feel so hot. Maybe I'm coming down with the flu or something."

I said I hoped not. That would be a helluva way to spend the weekend. He removed his dripping slicker and said good night, then struggled upstairs to the spare bedroom he would share with Jack. Somehow, he seemed a changed person, illness or no. Was it the phone call? The words with Jack over Alice Henderson?

We put the chess set away.

"It's great to have you here, guy," I said. I hugged him. I was careful not to hug him too hard or too long. It might embarrass him. But God, I lived for that.

"Dad, you okay? You crying?"

"No. I'm okay. I'm just glad to see you. You don't have any idea how much I miss you and Tony."

"But Dad, we're right nearby. We're all here in New England, right?"

"Right," I said, and went upstairs.

"I love you, Dad," he called after me.

"I love you too, boy," I managed to reply. "More than anything on earth."

I did have wet eyes after saying good night to him. And a lump in my throat, too. My little Jackie was all grown up and leaving us. He hadn't planned the departure, and maybe didn't even know it was happening. But there it was, plain as day. That huge, inexorable clock keeps ticking, swinging its giant pendulum, knocking away the years. The Great Going On stops for nothing and nobody, and there's not a thing any of us can do about it.

I couldn't wait to go out with him to watch the whales.

TWO

THE NEXT MORNING, Saturday, Mary and I awoke to the sound of heavy rain on our bedroom windows and the constant eerie wail of wind. The moaning rose and fell, rattling the windows in the gusts, but it never died away. We got up and dressed and went down to make coffee. While it was brewing, I tapped the barometer. Twenty-nine point two and rising very slightly.

"I wonder what happend to the DeGroots?" asked Mary over the rim of her cup. Her black eyes shone under the anchor light that hangs over the kitchen table. Her dark hair was pulled back in a big thick single braid. She was, having spent only twelve days on the Cape, as dark as a Tahitian.

"I don't know. With this storm, I'm hoping they never left. But I don't like not hearing from them, either. It's not like Jim to keep us in the dark."

I looked outside at the ugly leaden sky. At the foot of the bluff, the tide was coming back in, roaring and slamming every inch of the way. The sea was higher than I'd ever seen it on the bay side of the Cape. I switched on the short-wave receiver and heard the reports. We had another day, maybe two, of the heavy rain to look forward to, but the wind would abate early Sunday. Sensing that the reception was bad even for a major storm, I went outside on the deck to see that the antenna mast on the roof had blown over, the lead disconnected. We were missing a bunch of cedar shingles, too.

After coffee, we put on our rain gear to take a walk outside and assess the damage. But before we left I went to the foot of the stairs and yelled up at the boys to get up. I heard a muted thumping on the ceiling, which told me they were stirring. Then Mary and I went down to the beach, leaning into the wind and rain and shouting to each other over the roar of the surf. We found our yellow beach umbrella, which we had carefully tied shut and stowed against the cottage wall, wedged at the base of a sand dune a hundred yards up the beach. Our lounge chairs were scattered over a thirty-yard radius, having been swept off the deck in the gusts. But the most amazing and ominous sight was the water. The ocean had intruded over our forty yards of beach and was pounding against the base of our bluff. We skipped and jumped nimbly to avoid the rushes of water that followed each breaking wave.

"Charlie! There's so much stuff on the beach. Look!" I saw piles of brush, large hunks of driftwood, and even a big metal milk can, rolling and thumping in shallows. Where it had come from was anybody's guess. Had it washed ashore from some passing ship? Did it drift to our side of the bay from a dairy in Plymouth or Provincetown? Heaven only knew. No boats were out on the bay; the horizon was empty. All the sea birds were gone, hiding somewhere out of the wind. We got back to the cottage soaked, and I went into the living room to build a fire. I saw Jack coming down the stairs as if sleepwalking.

"Dad?"

"What's up? Get Andy down here; Mom's going to cook pancakes."

"Dad?"

"Hmn?"

"Dad, Andy won't wake up."

"What? What do you mean, he won't wake up?"

"I can't rouse him; I think maybe he's in a coma."

The three of us hurried up the stairs. I opened the door to the bedroom and went over to Andy's bed. He was lying there on his side, his head on the pillow, as if asleep. But as soon as I touched his head, a chill went up my spine. I probed for a pulse. I retrieved Mary's hand mirror and held it up to his mouth. Nothing.

"He's not in a coma, Jack," I whispered. "I'm afraid your friend Andy is dead."

The bedroom fell silent. Outside the wind howled, and the ocean crashed onto the beach.

THREE

I LOOKED OUT the Breakers's front window and saw Joe getting out of his cruiser in the rain. It had started up again at lunch time, stronger than ever. Now, at four o'clock, it was still coming down. How much rain had we had in the last twenty-four hours? Six inches? Eight? I had never seen it rain so heavily. As he leaned over getting out, the wind caught the back edge of his trench coat and blew it up over his head. I saw his mouth working through the driving rain; he was cussing as he threw off the coat and dumped it in the back seat. Then he slammed the door and made a beeline down our little flagstone walkway toward the front door. I let him in.

"Son of a bitch!" he said, shaking the water from his big, tan face. Its lower half was purplish-black with beard stubble. I gathered Joe hadn't had a chance to shave in maybe three hours. "Son of a *bitch!*"

"Here. Stand in front of the fire. Want a drink?"

"Do I want a drink he says. Jesus Christ. Do I want a drink. Double Scotch up, splash — now where's Sis?"

"She's over in Eastham Center with Jack. They're talking with the police up there. You believe this?"

"Yeah. Yeah, I believe it. Anything shitty like this happens, I believe it right away. Part of my job. So, I take it the boy's parents have been notified?"

"No. We've tried getting in touch with them all morning; no

answer. We're assuming they're away for the weekend. God, are they going to have some news waiting for them when they get back."

"And I guess they're taking the body back to the state lab?"

"Have to; you know that, Joe. It's an unexplained death; there has to be an autopsy. They were going to take the body back up to the morgue at Boston City Hospital —"

"Boston City? Not Boston City! Good God, I hate that place. I ever take you there?"

"Once. It was enough."

"The elevators don't even work anymore. You gotta tote the stiffs up and down the friggin' stairs, for Chrissakes. I hope they tear that —"

"Yeah, well they decided to take the body up to the forensic lab and morgue at Ten Ten. Right to your own building, Joe."

"I just left there. Left Kevin holding the bag. And know what I heard? The resident M.E. of Barnstable County just retired. They don't have an M.E. down here on the Cape. So guess what? I recommended you."

"You *what?*"

"I gave 'em your name. It's just temporary, of course. I mean, it's an appointment that's got to be confirmed and everything, and I know you wouldn't want to do it full time. But you *are* a doctor, a full-fledged physician, right? Even though you just work on mouths and jaws now? Anyway, as soon as I mention your name, Doc, everybody starts noddin'."

I sat down on the sofa to collect myself. Joe reminded me about the drink, so I went to the kitchen and made a couple. We sat in front of the fire and sipped.

"Joe . . . listen," I sighed, "I am not a good candidate for medical examiner. One: I don't want any part of it. Two: I'm not qualified. Thr —"

"Hell you're not. All I hadda do is mention a few incidents of the past couple a years. The guys are all nodding, grinning. 'Yeah, he's a good one to fill in for now. Great choice, Joe,' they're sayin'. 'Couldn't be a better one.' "

"Good God, Joe. Look: I'm not interested."

"Well, okay then. But you might think about it. It's only for a month or so."

"All right, I'll think about it. But it's hard right now to think about anything except the late Andy Cunningham."

"Jesus, doesn't this remind you of that other kid? Friend of Jack's? What was his —"

"I don't want to talk about that, Joe. I mean it. Just please shut up about that, okay?"

I realized I was on my feet, glaring right down at him.

"Okay, okay," he said softly. "I didn't realize it was so, uh, personal."

"Of course it's personal, Joe. And you know why. Allan Hart would still be alive today if it weren't for me." I took a gulp of the Scotch and let it slide down my throat, burning all the way down. Joe lighted a Benson and Hedges and leaned back in the sofa, looking at the fire.

"Know what it is, Doc? It's the goddamn curse. My goddamn curse is rubbing off on your family. That's what."

"Aw, c'mon. Don't get going on that shit again. Give it a rest."

So we sat there for maybe ten minutes, not saying anything, each of us feeling sorry for himself because he was such a jinx. We were a fine pair. The door opened and Mary came in.

"What the hell's this? What's with you two?"

We told her, and she ripped into both of us.

"Goddammit! You guys piss me off," she hissed. "I see you need the stronger sex to get you on your feet again. First you, Charlie. It was almost three years ago when I found you sitting on the pier up in Wellfleet Harbor, moaning and groaning about how you'd killed Allan Hart. Well BULLSHIT! How were you to know that there were murderers and psychos aboard that trawler? Now you did *not* kill Allan Hart. What you did was track down the guys who killed him. You set things right, Charlie, even getting that monster as he climbed up the wall to get you. Now I'm not going to go through it all again, goddammit."

Her obsidian eyes bored into mine. Her jaw came forward, and she frowned. Satisfied she had made her point, she turned on her brother.

She walked over to him and put her arms around his delicate nineteen-inch neck and kissed him on his stubbled cheek. Lucky if she had any lips left afterwards.

"Joey."

His eyes drooped like a hound dog's and he looked wonderful sad.

"C'mon, Joey." He put his big arms around her and rocked slightly. I went into the kitchen and washed my hands. When I walked back, Mary was talking softly to her younger brother, who was breathing in deep, ragged sighs.

Some vacation down on the Cape, eh?

"I know that you can't stand to think about it, Joey. But sometimes you can't help it, and it won't let you alone. If I had lost my family, I don't know if I could believe in God anymore. But it was over twelve years ago, and you've done fine. And you've got to go on, Joey. Charlie and I both need you. And now Jackie needs you, too."

"But it seems that everywhere I go I —"

"No. That's not true, and deep inside you I think you know it. You've had some real bad times. I think they'd have killed most people. But you've come through them, kid, and you're gonna be fine. Now come sit with me in front of the fire. Do you want another drink? Okay. . . ."

Before she even looked around to find me, I was there taking Joe's empty glass and going back into the kitchen to refill it. Looking out the window, I saw an Eastham Police cruiser pull into the drive. Jack and the officer got out and were heading for the house. I stopped back in the living room and gave Joe the drink. He and Mary were sitting close together on the couch, talking softly. I was outside, heading off Jack and the officer, before they reached the front door. He introduced himself as Officer David Klewski. I led them around the back way, which was the ocean side, and we went into the screened porch off the deck. Everything out there was dripping wet. I led them into the kitchen.

"How ah yah doin', Dr. Adams?" said Klewski.

"Well, not so hot right now I guess. Jack, how's it goin' buddy?"

The big blond guy didn't answer. He just stood there leaning against the counter, his arms crossed tightly against his chest, looking down at the floor. He shook his head back and forth so slightly I could scarcely notice it. I went over and put my hand on his shoulder. He didn't move. Rain dripped off his slicker. Of-

ficer Klewski accepted a mug of coffee and took off his hat, which
was covered with what resembled a plastic shower cap.

"So what's happened?" I asked. "Any more ideas?"

"We've got word that the remains have arrived at the state lab
in Boston, Doctor. What they're sayin' now, they're sayin' it looks
like a cardiac arrest. We should have definite word tomarra,
tomarra night. But then your son here told us something we
didn't know, and maybe it explains the Cunningham boy's
death."

Jack finally looked up and stared at my face. His eyes didn't
seem to see me; they looked through me. He was immensely
tired.

"Well see, I never told you this, Dad, but Andy had epilepsy.
He didn't want people to know because they're kinda like afraid
of it? So he didn't tell many people. But remember last night
when Mom offered him wine and he said no? Well he can't have
more than like a couple of beers because it interacts with his
medication. Well, I remembered that right after Mom left the
station. So now they think he might've had a seizure in his
sleep."

It was my turn to lean against the counter. Upset as I was about
the boy's death, I felt a wave of relief pass through me. For me
and for Joe. There was a pre-existing condition that had affected
young Andrew Cunningham. Apparently, he had died in his
sleep from natural causes. It had nothing to do with jinxes,
curses, or anything of the sort. I knew Joe would be relieved to
hear it. But a few stray thoughts — medical thoughts — intruded.

"So Andy had seizures? Were they grand mal seizures?"

"I don't know. He just told me he used to have seizures. You
know —"

"Yes, but did he ever describe the nature of his epilepsy to you?
I mean there are grand mal seizures, the convulsions, which
could result in a cardiac arrest. But the other forms of epilepsy
aren't violent. One of those seizures, especially in the safe confines of a bedroom, wouldn't result in a death. Which is why I —
did you say he was on medication?"

"Yes, that's why he couldn't have the wine."

I was already going up the stairs two at a time. Jack followed. I guess David Klewski was still in the kitchen. I heard Mary's heels clicking on the landing.

"Jackie? You home? Charlie? What the hell's —"

"If he was taking medication, it should still be here," I said. "Do you know where he kept it?"

"I saw him put it in his shaving kit before we left," Jack said.

As we took the kit from the dresser, I heard Mary, Joe, and Officer Klewski coming up the stairs.

"All you guys know each other?" I asked over my shoulder as I probed the small leather case. Toothbrush, nail clippers, shaving cream and razor . . . no pills.

"Yeah," said Joe, "we've just met." His voice was still weary.

"Jack, why don't you tell your Uncle Joe what the current thinking is regarding Andy's death?"

He did. Joe sat down on one of the twin beds and eased back against the big brass tubes that took the place of a headboard. I knew what he was thinking: no more jinx.

"Jack, where's the medication? It isn't in here . . ."

His hand reached past mine and picked up a long, rectangular plastic case from the dresser top. I had assumed it was a toothbrush case. But when he handed it to me, I recognized it as medication dispenser. It was really seven individual hinged compartments in a row. Each compartment had a big embossed letter on it, one for each day of the week: SMTWTFS.

"See Dad, I guess the medication is strong. He knew it would be dangerous to accidentally take more than the prescribed dose. And he couldn't forget it, either."

"Uh-huh. These are empty though, I don't — wait a sec . . . no, the last compartment has three capsules in it. So we have Saturday's dose still untouched, which means he took all of Friday's medication. Don't you assume that's what it means?"

"I know that's what it means, Dad. I watched him take those pills every night about an hour before he went to bed."

"All three pills? All three at once?"

"Yeah. See, the prescription really says take one after each meal. But they're downers, or act like downers. Andy said he liked to take them at night so he wouldn't be drowsy during the day. And at night they'd act like a sleeping pill. He'd take them and just crash."

I shook the three capsules out into my palm. They were white, with a black band around the middle of each capsule. On each side of the band was written PD 531.

"Parke-Davis. I think I know what these are. C'mon everybody, let's go back down."

So we trundled downstairs and I went over to my desk in the study corner of the living room, opened one of its large lower drawers, and drew out my *Physicians' Desk Reference*. The *PDR* is found in the office of every doctor, nurse, and pharmacist. I have three copies: one each for office, home, and cottage. Distributed by the drug manufacturers, the book describes all American-made medicinal drugs. There's even a color photo section of products, so that the pharmacist or doctor can identify medications by appearance. Under Parke-Davis, I found my capsule. As I suspected, each contained Dilantin, with a half-grain of phenobarbital added. Powerful anticonvulsant medicine. The usual dose for adult patients was three or four capsules per day. The mean lethal dose for this medication, the *PDR* said, was between two and five grains, or the equivalent of between twenty and fifty capsules.

I sat and looked out the window. Rain lashed along the glass, smearing sideways and falling down in wavy streaks.

"What's wrong, Charlie?"

"Well, I guess I think it's unlikely that Andy could have died of a convulsion in his sleep. He took his Friday's medication, and all at once before going to bed. Jack, did you hear anything in the night?"

"Nope. But I sleep pretty hard."

"Yes. And no doubt the storm outside would mask some noise. But think again, do you remember any noise?"

"No. But wait a minute. Two things come back to me now. One was that he didn't feel good yesterday; he kept having to stop on the way up here. He had to take a leak, oh, it seemed like every ten minutes. And his stomach was upset, too. Remember, Dad? The second thing is that I did hear him get up out of bed once. I think it was about two-thirty in the morning. He went into the john and came back, and I heard him like kinda groaning. I asked him what was wrong, and he said, 'I just feel shitty.' "

"That's all he said?" asked Mary. "Did he mention an aura? Did he say he felt like there was a seizure coming on?"

"No. He once told me not to worry about him — that he hadn't had a seizure in over three years."

"Then it's mighty curious," I said. "Mary, you're a nurse; you know that a seizure isn't as fearsome as most people imagine. But do you think it would go unnoticed by someone sleeping in the next bed?"

"Jackie, you didn't have a lot to drink last night, did you?" she asked.

"No. I wasn't drunk, if that's what you mean."

"Didn't think so. If Andy had a seizure that proved fatal, you would've heard something. So I agree, it's very strange. Except for the possibility of cardiac arrest. Did Andy have a bad heart, Jackie?"

"No. I'm sure he didn't; he would've told me."

"Look, we're making too much out of this thing," said Joe as he struggled out of the overstuffed chair near the fireplace. "He died. That's all there is to it. It's a damn shame, but there it is. People die. Everybody dies. He was a sick boy and his illness finally caught up with him. Mare, I'm gonna make some more coffee. David, you want a mug?"

"Love it," said the policeman, and followed Joe into the kitchen.

After Officer Klewski left, I sat at my desk, turned off the lamp, and watched the rain outside. I listened to the distant roll of thunder, saw the far-off flashes of lightning over the bay, and heard the snare-drum roll, the cozy tattoo, of rain hitting the roof and walls. It made me sleepy.

"Dad?"

"Hmmm?"

"Well? Do you think that's what happened? That he just died in his sleep."

"No. No, Jack, I don't."

I called Joe back from the kitchen, where he and Mary were cooking something that smelled terrific. My watch said six-fifteen.

"Joe, is there somebody I can speak with in the forensic lab right now?"

"Sure. Never closes. We got the day crew and then the night crew. When they're doing autopsies and forensic work, they do it around the clock because of the decomposition of tissues."

"Give me the number then," I said. "I've got a few hunches, and I want the M.E. to be looking for some substances in Andy's body."

Mary snuggled up next to me and put her bare leg over mine. I tickled her back softly and I could feel the goosebumps under my fingertips.

"Oooooooo, that feels nice," she said.

"Hey."

"Hey what?"

"How come today, when you came home and found Joe and me down in the dumps, you treated us so differently? You lashed out at me. Then you went over to Joe and cuddled him. Why?"

"Two reasons. The most important reason is this: Joe's tragedy was real. He's been permanently traumatized by it. I can't imagine anything more horrendous happening to anyone. But your moping about Allan Hart is unjustified. So therefore, I've got much less patience with you. Secondly, Joe really is sensitive underneath. The fact that all that death happened to *him* makes it all the more more unbelievable. You, on the other hand, are pretty tough inside."

"How can you say that? I consider myself pretty much of a pussycat underneath."

"No you're not, Charlie. You're sensitive and loving and nurturing and all that. But really deep down, when you scratch through your mellow exterior, you're hard as nails. When you really get mad, or when you really want something, nothing stands in your way."

I thought about this for a second.

"Bullshit. I don't believe you."

"Well it's true. Even Laitis told you that down in North Carolina. You didn't believe him, either."

"I still don't."

"Uh-huh. Well, have it your way. But I know. Laitis knows, too.

You'd make a better cop than Joey. Anyway, he needed the cuddling; you needed a kick in the ass. Because there's only one person I know of offhand who's as tough as you."

"Laitis Roantis."

"No. Me. And don't you ever forget it."

I kept tickling her back.

"I don't believe you," I said.

There was a long pause.

"Charlie? Who were you calling tonight right before dinner?"

"The medical examiner's office in the state lab. I don't think Andy died of a seizure, Mary. I think you doubt it, too. If he had skipped his medication, maybe. But he'd taken all of Friday's Dilantin-phenobarb capsules. And if by chance he *did* have a seizure, I doubt it would have been fatal. There's a chance he also had an undiagnosed weak heart — maybe a congenital defect — but it's unlikely."

"Yeah, a weak heart would've surfaced by this time."

"I think something else killed him."

"Well, what?"

"Maybe a different kind of medication. That's what the M.E. is looking for right now. For one, I suspect a strong diuretic, since Jack remembers Andy urinating almost constantly Friday afternoon. That would rapidly deplete his serum potassium."

"Ahhh . . . and cause an electrolyte imbalance."

"Right. Then maybe some kind of cardiac stimulant. Or else some . . . hell, I don't know. And I don't like not knowing."

"But why would he take the wrong meds?"

"Who knows? That's the part that's bothering me."

FOUR

IT RAINED HEAVILY for the rest of the night. Sunday morning brought a slow drizzle and lots of wind and fog. It was cold outside, a bone-chilling wet wind that went clear through you and made your teeth chatter. I sat at my desk and turned on the brass student lamp with the green glass shade.

Tony's arrival at the Breakers had been postponed a day because of the storm, so we didn't expect him until afternoon. We had not told him of the tragedy yet. He would find out when he arrived. There was no word from the DeGroots either. This we didn't like. Had Jim, in his typical Dutch hard-driving manner, said to hell with the nasty weather and decided to race down across the bay from Cape Ann in hopes of outrunning the storm? If so, there was a chance we'd never hear from them again.

Jack was down on the beach, casting bright nickel-plated spoons into the waves with a nine-foot surf rod. He needed the solitude and the peace of mind that comes with looking into the teeth of huge crashing waves, listening to the shriek of gulls overhead, and hoping for the sudden quick tugs on the line that signal a monster bluefish or striped bass. He could do a lot of hoping; the surf fishing wasn't usually much good on our side of the Cape. He had to be soaked, even with his oilskins on, but he didn't seem to mind. Joe had gone back to Boston for the morning to catch up on his mail.

I got out of my chair and went over and hugged Mary, who was cooking a big pot of clam chowder.

"Well what do you think, Charlie? Is this mess going to work itself out?"

"I hope so. Except of course for the poor Cunninghams. It sure was no fun to talk with them this morning. I haven't had to face that kind of grief since . . . since I quit general medicine."

Mary kept stirring the bacon squares with the wooden spoon. She was impassive, as if she hadn't heard me.

"Jack seems to be holding up pretty well," she said. "But I'm not sure how well Joe is coping with this. It's got to remind him of . . . of what happened."

"You think he'll ever remarry?"

"I really do," she sighed. "Joey's too much of a family man at heart not to. And he's only forty-three. He's got time."

There was a knock at the door and I opened it to see Officer Klewski standing in the rain, the water pouring off his plastic-covered hat. Next to him stood a man in a trench coat. He could have been a real estate agent or an insurance salesman. He could have been a lot of things, but since my brother-in-law is a plain-clothes detective, I can usually spot one pretty fast.

The man in the trench coat deftly slipped his hand behind the wide lapel and into his suit coat pocket, drawing out a leather folder with a badge on it.

"Dr. Adams? How do you do; I'm Paul Keegan, state detective for Barnstable County. I take it you know why we're here. Is your son Jack around?" Keegan was pleasant, but not jovial. David Klewski, who'd been almost chummy earlier, wore a very straight face.

"He's down on the beach surfcasting. I know it sounds silly in this storm, but that's where you'll find him, wearing a big yellow slicker."

"We'd like a word with you, too, if you don't mind. May we come in?"

I said sure, and soon the three of us were sitting in front of the fire, coffee mugs in hand. Mary joined us too.

Keegan had blond hair clipped short, with clear blue eyes. The whites of the eyes were bluish, too. His neck was bull-thick but not fat; you could see his Adam's apple and jawline clearly. Mr. Keegan was stocky and very strong and fit. There was no non-sense about him.

"Dr. Adams," he asked, "what's your opinion of Andrew Cunningham's death?"

"I'm curious about it," I said, shifting nervously on the couch. "Curious and disturbed. Mary and I are both medical people, and it seems a little strange that he would die of a seizure after he had taken his daily medication. My son Jack says Andy told him he'd been on the medication for some time, so the dosage was stabilized. He'd had no seizures, even minor ones, for as long as Jack knew him. If he'd forgotten his meds, there might have been a problem. But from examining the pill case we found on his dresser, he seems to have finished Friday's dose before going to bed. So all I can come up with at this point is what I've been saying all along: a fatal heart attack precipitated by a seizure seems extremely unlikely. Even more unlikely since Jack was in the next bed and heard no disturbances during the night."

Paul Keegan nodded slowly at this, staring at the oval rag rug on the floor. He cleared his throat tentatively.

"You say that it's clear the Cunningham boy took his medication Friday night. Did anyone actually see him take the pills?"

"No, because Andy went upstairs before we did. But we surmise he took the daily dose from examining the pill case."

I then briefly explained the weekly dosage case while Keegan nodded slowly.

"I think you've made a reasonable assumption here, Doctor. But nobody actually saw him swallow the pills. Therefore, it's possible that he could have discarded the medication, or taken other medication."

"Possible, I suppose, but not likely," I answered.

"I, uh, share your views on this, Doctor. I mean the part about it being curious. That's why I've got to proceed one step at a time, and why I'd like to speak with your son when he returns. I got a phone call early this morning from the state forensic laboratory in Boston. Apparently you called their office yesterday evening?"

"Right. I had a few theories and wanted them checked out."

"Uh-huh. Well, I don't have much information yet because they're not finished up there, or they weren't when I left Hyannis. But so far they've found one curious thing. The concentrations of the anticonvulsant compound ... the, uh, the two drugs ..."

"Dilantin and phenobarbital," said Mary.

"Uh, right. Well, the concentrations of those were low. So low, in fact, that the M.E. doubts the boy took his medications on Friday. That's why I wanted to know if anybody saw him swallow them."

Mary and I looked at each other for a second, not saying anything. Then I looked back at Paul Keegan, whose clear, piercing blue eyes were boring into mine.

"Well, then that could explain it," said Mary. "No meds — a seizure follows."

Keegan frowned at her.

"Excuse me, Mrs. Adams, your husband tells me you're a medical person as well?"

"I'm a registered nurse. Actually, the work I'm in, I see more of this kind of thing than my husband does."

"What kind of thing?"

"Seizures and such things."

"And you don't see them, Doctor?"

"No. I'm an oral surgeon; I specialize in surgery of the lower face and jaw."

"I see. Mrs. Adams, you agree that the death is curious?"

"Well, I did, until just now. But now we seem to have a scenario that makes some sense. Maybe Joe was right: the boy was sick, forgot his meds, had a convulsion, and died. *Sic transit gloria mundi*. Case closed."

"Sic *what?*" asked Keegan, a bewildered look on his face.

"It's an old Italian expression," she answered, heading back to the stove to turn it down. "Excuse me a second."

Keegan, still bewildered, stared back at me. I told him I did not agree with my wife that the case was closed. Not by a long shot. I asked him if he had any ideas.

"I sure don't know. You're the doctor."

"Uh-huh. Well, I've had some thoughts on this. Some bad

thoughts. I suspected, for one, that a cardiac arrest didn't fit with the circumstances. Now that we know he didn't take the . . ."

I was staring off into space. I guess some time went by.

"Dr. Adams?"

"Huh?"

"Is something wrong?"

"I was just thinking of something. He didn't take the meds. No. But he probably took the *capsules* . . ."

Keegan sat patiently, waiting for further explanation. Mary came over to my side. I asked Keegan when he'd last heard from the lab.

"Early this morning. Around nine-thirty."

"And all you got was a negative on the meds. Okay. He should have more shortly. Mary, what are you thinking?"

"I'm thinking that Joe said he would stop by the office at Ten Ten before returning here. So when he comes back here for lunch, he should know a lot more. I think I'll call his office and leave a message for him."

"Who's Joe?" asked Keegan.

"My brother, Joe Brindelli."

"Joe Brindelli. I know a Joe Brindelli. But he's —"

"You got it," she said. "A detective lieutenant. Just like you."

"And you're his younger sister. I can see it now, in your face and mouth. Jesus! Why don't people tell me these things?"

"Older sister, but thanks anyway. Listen, if you want, when Joe gets back here later, I'll have him give you a call. You want to leave me a number?"

"I'll leave two. Home and office. Both are in Hyannis; I'm only a half-hour away. Now, mind if we go down to the beach and talk with your son a minute?"

They left by the back door and clumped down the wooden stairway to the beach, their coats blowing out like capes in the wind.

Mary and I put on our slickers and walked out onto the deck in the blowing rain. We saw, far up the beach, Paul Keegan and Officer Klewski approach the big guy in the yellow slicker.

"So what do you think, Charlie?"

"I don't know. Suicide? I'd say no; Andy seemed way too upbeat for that. Choosing between Harvard and Hopkins . . . He
had everything going for him. But when he came back to the
cottage after making that phone call, he seemed real down. In
fact, it's the most amazing change in a person I've ever seen."

"Who did he call?"

I shrugged my shoulders. "Who knows? He never told Jack.
He said he was calling Woods Hole. If I had to guess, I'd say it was
his new-found love: the Henderson girl."

Mary crinkled up her nose.

"I don't know, Charlie. I mean, the relationship was new, and
Andy seemed to have both feet firmly on the ground. I sensed he
was very goal-oriented. Didn't you? I don't think he'd go off the
deep end over a girl. I just don't think it fits."

"So far, nothing in this sad story is fitting very well."

We looked up and saw Detective Keegan and Jack shaking
hands. Then Jack, who'd obviously been skunked at fishing, began to pack up his gear.

We heard the front door slam. Then the back door opened and
Joe came out on the deck to join us. He was early. We pointed at
the distant three figures who were now trudging back to the cottage, leaning forward into the strong wind.

"Who are those guys?"

"One is David Klewski, the local cop you met yesterday. The
other guy is your counterpart for Barnstable County. Name is
Keegan."

"Yeah, I know Paul Keegan. A hardass. Former marine captain. So he's here already, huh?"

The policemen were helping Jack carry the fishing gear. Joe,
Mary, and I went back inside, where Mary adjusted the heat
under the kettle. I added the potatoes. Joe poured a mug of coffee, but so far he hadn't said much. Something was bugging him;
his mood had noticeably soured since his departure earlier in the
day.

"S'matter Joey, cat got your tongue?" asked Mary.

Joe sighed and eased down into a chair at the kitchen table. He
looked down at his big, hairy, brown hands as he rubbed them
over the Formica table top.

"After I finished up at home, I went over to Ten Ten Commonwealth. You know, to check in with Kevin. So . . . So I'm in the office with Kev and who comes in but Major Mahaffey. He tells me that the M.E. has found something interesting about young Mr. Cunningham. And he tells me that it was Dr. Charles Adams, no less, who suggested certain lines of investigation regarding the corpse."

We waited for Joe to continue.

"Yeah, well?" said Mary softly, peering into the iron pot.

"And so what happened was, before I leave the building, the M.E. himself comes over to Ten Ten on his way to the D.A.'s office. So I'm standing there talking to this guy not even two hours ago. Like you two, he was thinking the cardiac arrest was curious. Even suspicious. And your phone call to the forensic lab gave them some hints, Doc, and sent them snooping again. So they went back and did more tests. And as a result, they found something else in the kid's system. They found it just before I showed up there. Another drug, along with the Dilantin."

Joe took out a pocket notebook, flipped through the pages, and read a single word.

"Digoxin."

I froze, staring down at the potatoes in the kettle. Those tan spherical shapes were beginning to move and bump around in the hot water like billiard balls in a three-dimensional game of pool. My vague hunch had been confirmed.

"*Digoxin?*" said Mary. "What the hell was digoxin doing there? He wasn't on that. Why, that would be the very worst —"

"Yep," said her brother. "That's what the M.E. told me: it would be the very worst thing for the kid to take. His parents confirmed he wasn't on it. What was it doing there? I'll tell you what it was doing: it was reacting with the Dilantin and phenobarbital. Reacting lethally, fatally, with the medication. Was what it was doing."

"I don't get it," said Mary. "How did it get there?"

Joe tapped his fingers on the counter top. "Somebody put it there, presumably by tampering with the capsules. The state M.E. told me that somebody — somebody familiar with medicine and drugs — tampered with the Cunningham boy's capsules, inserted a heavy dose of digoxin in place of the usual dose of medication."

He looked up from his notebook and wiped his hand across his stubbled chin. "That ain't all, either."

"There was another drug in there, too, wasn't there?"

"Yeah, Doc. Yeah, there was. And it was a drug you told them to look for —"

He flipped the pages of the tiny book, looking for the name.

"Lasix. That right? *Lasix?*"

I nodded. "That's right. I guessed a diuretic from what Jack told me earlier. Andy was urinating almost constantly Friday. That means, actually, that the Lasix was introduced in Thursday's meds . . . so it would take effect on Friday and deplete the boy's serum potassium."

"Well, you got it right on the button, Doc. Because according to the M.E., switching the drugs in this fashion — substituting this Lasix and digoxin in place of the Dilantin and phenobarb downers — would cause an inevitable cardiac arrest. Which is what the kid died of; it's been confirmed. So kiddies —" he looked up at us with a wide, forced, fake smile. "So kiddies, so much for the 'natural death' we'd hoped for."

There was an uncomfortable silence.

"Diabolical," I whispered. "Thursday's dose of Lasix must have been mixed with the usual drugs, so Andy wouldn't know the difference. He'd just urinate a lot and feel a little sick to the stomach, which is exactly what happened. And it would set him up for the digoxin the following night. Wham. A one-two punch. Holy Christ."

"So what did the M.E. do, Joey? Did he file for homicide with the district attorney?"

He nodded.

"Yep. And now I got to tell you this: the prime suspect in this homicide, as of right now, is none other than John Brindelli Adams."

"Joey!" Mary shouted.

"Bullshit!" I yelled at him. But his face didn't change.

The front door opened and slammed shut. Jack, dripping

wet, walked into the kitchen. The rain had matted down his blond hair and darkened it. The two policemen stood right behind him on either side. Jack's face clouded over when he looked at us.

"Hey, what's up, anyway? Why are you all staring at me?"

FIVE

"HAS ANYONE ELSE been in the house this weekend?" asked Paul Keegan, pencil poised over notebook. He leaned back in his chair near the fireplace. Officer Klewski stood behind him, while Joe, Mary, Jack, and I sat on the couch and in chairs facing Keegan. The interviews were continuing inside now, and it didn't take a genius to figure out that we were the collective object of the investigation, with Jack as its focal point. It didn't feel good. Not good at all. Keegan was a pro; his questions followed clear lines of logic and syllogistic argument. His rational methodology was inexorable, and a little frightening.

"No, just us," said Mary in a monotone. "Joey wasn't even here until after Andy died. He came down here yesterday afternoon, then returned today when you saw him."

Keegan leaned forward over the pill case and the big brown bottle of medication sitting on a sheet of clean paper on a corner of the coffee table. The bottle of meds had been found in Andy's duffel bag — his back-up supply of the important medicine. The contents, and instructions, were typed on the label. Keegan had removed them from the guest bedroom earlier, during his initial cursory examination of the room, and brought them downstairs with a pair of kitchen tongs. Now he prodded them with a pencil, using the eraser end to scoot them around on the clean paper.

"So then, whose prints could we expect to find on these items?" he asked.

"Who knows, Paul?" said Joe. The annoyance showed in his voice, even though I was sure he was trying to hide it. "Hell, Jack says there are three roommates in the house, and the medication was in the bathroom. There were parties there, too, with a lot of young people coming and going. You figure it out."

Keegan looked up at Joe as if to say something, but didn't. He looked at Jack.

"Your prints would be on here, wouldn't they, Jack? I'm not accusing you; I'm just asking, so if we find them we won't be surprised and jump to any conclusions."

"Sure, you'd find my fingerprints on the bottle, anyway, since I touched it a lot of times. So did Tom."

"Tom being?"

"Tom McDonnough, our roommate. He's another student working in Woods Hole. He works for the National Marine Fisheries Service."

Keegan held down the pill case with the pencil and flipped up the last little door on its top with the clicker end of a ball-point pen. He looked inside at Saturday's medication.

"Okay, so we're missing one capsule, which you, Dr. Adams, took out and examined in order to identify it. That capsule is here," he said, pointing to a lone capsule sitting on the paper. "Now I know that your prints will be all over that; the soft gelatin of capsules takes prints better than anything. Jack, you say that Andy took his medications each night, all at once?"

"Right. He'd take all three pills around nine or ten, usually about an hour before he went to bed. If he had to stay up late for a project, he'd take maybe one after dinner, then the other two later."

"But he didn't take them one at a time, during the day?"

"No. He said they slowed him down too much. They're downers."

"But what it says here on the label," said Keegan, peering at the side of the big brown bottle, which was a third full of the capsules, "is 'Take one capsule three times a day.' It doesn't say to take three capsules once a day."

"I know, but that's the way Andy took them; trust me."

Keegan looked up at him across the coffee table.

"No, I won't trust you. It's my job to distrust everybody."

Joe rolled his eyes up and drummed on the couch arm with his fingers. He was right; Keegan was a hardass.

"Now, you had dinner during the storm, in the dark, and then Andy went upstairs to make a phone call. What time was that?"

"Between eight and eight-thirty," I said. "He came back downstairs looking sad, or disappointed. Then he and Jack played chess for a while, and then, around nine, he put on his raincoat and left."

"He left the cottage around nine?" Keegan asked. He was writing every detail down in his notebook.

"Yes, and didn't get back till eleven. He was out in that storm walking around for two hours. We were worried about him."

"So he left soon after the phone call. Maybe then the phone call was to set up a meeting. Do you think that's possible?"

"No, I don't think —" began Jack.

"Wait!" Mary said. "When he left, he wanted to go alone. Remember Jackie, you said you'd go along, but he refused?"

"Uh-huh. He said he wanted to be alone. Dad and I figured maybe he'd had a fight with Alice and he —"

"Who's Alice?" Keegan asked, and we told him. Nothing was said, however, about Jack and Andy's rivalry over her affections. I was glad of this, and sensed that Mary was, too. It was as if the Adams family formed an immediate, unspoken alliance to protect Jack.

"We can check the phone company's records and find out where the call went," said Keegan, tapping his open notebook with his pen. "That should tell us something, since it appears that the call and the nocturnal walk could be connected. Do any of you have an idea about who he went to meet, assuming it was a meeting that took place?"

We thought for a while and drew a blank.

"How about this Henderson girl?" he asked.

"Woods Hole's pretty far away," I said. "Of course, he was gone almost two hours. Jack, who else?"

Jack shook his head.

"And now for the big one," continued Keegan. "Since it seems more and more as if we're looking at a homicide here: who would want to kill Andy Cunningham?"

Head shakes all around, and then Mary brought up the name of Lionel Hartzell, the professor who was Andy's supervisor, and who, Andy was convinced, was nuts. Keegan wrote his name down, then asked us why Andy thought this.

"Actually, I think Andy made too big a deal of it," said Jack. "I mean, it's true he's difficult at times. A real perfectionist. But then, most good research scientists are. And Andy had his difficult side, too. He was the kind of guy who'd tell you just what he thought. He couldn't stand dumb people, or people who moved too slow for him. It was natural that they wouldn't get along that well. I mean, here's old man Hartzell, who wants to go step by step, being super careful all the way. And then there's Andy, always wanting to hurry it up. But no, Mr. Keegan, I don't think Hartzell would kill him."

"But didn't Andy say something about Hartzell accusing him of stealing some research data?" I asked. "What was that all about?"

"I don't know; maybe you better talk to Hartzell after all," said Jack.

Keegan put his notebook away and stood up.

"I will do that," he said. "And I'll interview Alice Henderson and others as well. But for now, I have to tell you, Jack, that you're the one we'll be looking at most closely. I'm going on the assumption, at this stage of the game, that you won't leave the state and that you'll be available for further questioning as the need arises. We have an officer of the law who's a relative. Joe, am I safe in assuming you'll enforce these conditions?"

Joe remained seated and nodded wearily.

Right then, I started to lose it. The words 'you're the one we'll be looking at most closely' took a few seconds to sink in. The starkness of that statement. The accusatory tone of it. Directed at Jack, the kid who waded frantically back and forth to comfort those dying whales fifteen years before. My boy who'd never, ever hurt a living thing in all his life. This boy was the chief suspect in the murder of his friend.

I felt myself walking up to Paul Keegan, with his goddamn, jarhead, Marine Corps face. My legs were stiff and trembling.

"Just a minute," I said between clenched teeth. "Just a goddamn minute Keegan —"

"Charlie. Charlie!"

"C'mon, Doc, cool down —"

But the words swept by me like soft air. I was looking at Keegan, who was turning to look at me, the corners of his mouth starting to draw back. I was bearing down on him now, my hand reaching out for his face.

"You come into my house, after I've called the force to help you out in this case, you come and tell my son —"

He held his hand up, then moved it in Jack's direction. I turned quickly and saw Jack's face. The look of fear and helplessness on it. And then Keegan blew it. He turned toward Jack, murmuring something like "If that's the way you feel, maybe we'll take him in now —"

And then I totally lost it.

I remember Keegan saying something about "possible custody" and "full rights of the defendant" and approaching Jack — who was still dazed — with that thin-lipped grimace on his Marine Corps face, and grabbing my son's shoulder . . .

Then there was Paul Keegan's face only inches from mine, beet red, his eyes bugged out. I was shocked to see two hands gripped around his thick throat. Surgeon's hands that were supposed to help and heal. I saw my thumbs inch down below the cartilage of the Adam's apple to the ribbed stiffness of the trachea and press in deep, deep, trying to shut off the air supply.

I was in a dream. A slow, nasty, semisilent dream.

I could hear, from far, far away, somebody shouting. I saw Joe's big form trying to move between us. But then Keegan shot both arms up between mine and flung them outwards, breaking the hold, and an instant later I saw a tan blur cross my face, and felt a heavy blow on my cheekbone. I shook off the punch and managed to stamp my heel hard down on his instep, while bringing up a fist in an uppercut that landed right in his groin, the force of it lifting him to the balls of his feet. Then I was standing again — still feeling no pain from his punch because I had maybe a gallon of adrenalin in my bloodstream — looking down at the bowed-over Keegan. I had cocked my right hand back against my shoulder, making a hard point of my right elbow, and had jumped up high when Joe caught me from behind, snatching me right in midair. I was lucky he did, or I would have probably followed through with step three (as taught by Laitis Roantis), bringing down the point of the elbow in a smashing blow onto the nape of your opponent's neck.

Joe's bear hug from behind me, and the pain from Keegan's punch, made me come out of my nasty, waking dream long enough for Joe to release his grip and jump between us, keeping us apart until we could limp away from each other. His 230 pounds helped.

I found out later that Paul Keegan is thirty-seven. I'm about ten years older. Not bad, Adams — you stupid son of a bitch. I had a possible assault charge facing me. Assaulting a law officer, a state policeman. Great. This vacation just keeps getting better and better, I thought to myself.

SIX

"LOOK, DOC, it's not as if he's going to jail or anything. Keegan just said what I told you earlier, that Jack's the chief suspect. I mean, that's his job. He's *gotta* say that. So why you had to go and blow your stack —"

"I don't want to hear any more shit, Joe. From *anybody*, and that includes you. Far as I'm concerned, you just stood there when he was accusing him. Any cop or agency who thinks, even for one second, that Jack's a murderer is full of shit. And you didn't say anything in his defense; you just stood there."

"Listen: I talked to Paul all the way out to his cruiser to calm him down. And I kept you off the hook, too, in case you don't know it. He was ready to haul both of you in."

"If he sets foot near this place again, there's going to be a dead state cop. You tell him that."

"Look, Doc, face it; from Keegan's point of view, Jack's the one who had the best opportunity. That's just officially. I'm not saying —"

I went for him. He ducked through the bedroom door and into the hall.

"Get back in here!" I shouted. "You get the hell back in here, Joe!"

No answer. Nothing. With two fast steps, I was out in the narrow upstairs hallway. Joe was there, flattened against the wall, his right arm cocked back and his huge brown hand balled into a fist.

A fist as big as a cantaloupe. But I didn't care; I was going for him anyway. I was going to make it two dead state cops. Two in one. Why not?

"Charlie!" Mary screamed from halfway up the stairs. "Charlie, goddamn you! Stop it!"

"If he comes one step closer —" panted Joe in a hoarse whisper. I felt blood pounding in my head. Mary hustled up the rest of the way and stood between us. She put her hands against my chest and pushed me back. She was careful to do it gently. I noticed she was crying. Can't imagine why.

"Now you listen," she said softly. "Charlie, you're going out for a run. A long run, okay? I just turned on the sauna. When you get back, you can bake yourself for an hour or so. Now go in and change. Joey and I will go over Andy's things for the lab. Joe will show me what to do. There's nothing for you to do here for a few hours. You hear me, Charlie?"

I think I managed to nod, then walked back into our bedroom. She followed me, and turned me around, looking at my face.

"How is it? Jeez, it's beginning to turn already. Let me feel —"

"Nawww . . . it's not broken. Don't worry." I felt her cool hand running over my left cheekbone. "Okay, I'm changing. You can leave now."

She did. But I could hear their conversation from the next room.

"I know. I *know* he was upset, Mare. But hell, assault on a state cop. Holy shit."

"Keegan hit him first."

"Yeah, after he broke the choke hold. Jeez, you believe how fast Doc moved? Like a panther —"

"Well he's in great shape. We know that. Anybody who runs that much —"

"It's Roantis, Mary. He's gotta stop hanging around with Roantis and those loonies at the club."

"What's Keegan going to do now?"

"Go to a good urologist first, I imagine. Then he's probably going to go into Mickey Finn's in Boston and buy a steel cup. The kind hockey goalies wear."

"Do you think he was badly hurt?"

48

"Hurt? Oh Mare. You don't know. You can't know. A woman can't know just how much that hurts. And his instep, too. He nailed Doc a good one all right, but you ask me, your hubby got the best of him."

"That's why you ran out into the hallway when Charlie came for you?"

"Hell yes; I'm not as dumb as I look, you know . . ."

I was glad we'd sent Jack out to do some shopping after the scuffle. The scene was not one I was proud of. Though Laitis would've probably approved.

I laced up my shoes, pulled a lightweight nylon shell over my sweat clothes to shed the rain, then trotted down the stairs and outside.

The rain was now reduced to a blowing drizzle. I started slowly, padding up Sunken Meadow Road to the main drag. I speeded up gradually, so by the end of the second mile I was setting a pretty good clip. At the middle of mile three I doffed the nylon shell, which was making me hot and clammy, and tied it around my waist. I headed back, going as fast as I could to pump the adrenalin and the queasy trembles out of my system.

Now it looks as if Jack and I will be sharing the same cell, I thought. How cute. How familial.

Why had I done it? I wasn't sure. I certainly hadn't planned on it. One second I was the normal, concerned father, cooperating fully with law enforcement officials. The next instant, I had wrapped my hands around Lieutenant Keegan's throat and was trying to kill him. I don't get carried away when people abuse my property. I've had my house ransacked a few times, my car vandalized . . . I even had the unpleasant surprise of finding my murdered dog's head in the oven one fine morning. I can handle those things. But when somebody — anybody, even a cop — fools with my wife and kids, then the lid comes off. And the more I thought about it, the more I was willing to bet that nine out of ten men would have done exactly the same thing.

I trudged up the flagstone walk to the cottage and went upstairs, feeling much better. I stripped, put on swimming trunks, grabbed a beach towel, and went down into the sauna. On my way, I heard Joe and Mary talking in the guest room, where they were carefully arranging and cataloguing the effects of the late Andrew Cunningham. This sad task had to be completed according to strict guidelines, on which Joe was an expert.

The sauna is a little lean-to structure of redwood tacked onto the cottage. Since Mary had turned it on for me, it had been on almost an hour, so it was a cozy 165 degrees. I poured a dipper of water over the black basalt rocks and hopped up on the upper wooden ledge, inhaling the invisible, scalding, live steam before it stopped hissing. The sauna is my favorite place to think. For one thing, in that heat blood is racing through your head at practically Mach 2.

After I'd gone in and out of the sauna three times, showering and resting each time in between, wringing all the bad stuff from body and mind, I returned to the spare bedroom where Joe was labeling items prior to sending them off to the lab. I sat down on the brass bed Andy had slept in.

"Feel better?" he asked.

"Yeah. Sorry. I don't deal well with people who threaten my family."

"Ummm. You'd make a good Italian, Doc. Maybe that feeling is the result of being married to one."

"Uh-huh. Or maybe I had the trait to begin with and it's what attracted me to her."

"The old chicken and egg routine."

"I guess what's got me so upset is that I'm mostly angry with myself, Joe. There I was, hotshot Doc Adams, uncovering foul play by one brilliant deduction after another, calling the M.E.'s office and steering him in the right direction. Bravo. And where did it get me? After hearing what jar-head Keegan had to say, I'm sorry I ever made that call. If I hadn't stuck my nose in, the boy's death would have been chalked off to cardiac arrest as the result of a seizure and Jack wouldn't be in this bind."

"Yeah, right," he answered, "except that there'd be a killer on the loose. And who knows? Somebody like Jack could be next."

"So you're convinced it's murder, too?"

"Oh yeah. No problem there. Murder all right. We know the medication was tampered with. We know it wasn't suicide. We know it because to kill himself, all Andrew Cunningham had to do would be to gulp down twenty or thirty of those little capsules. Maybe wash them down with a couple of beers, then maybe have a strong highball to cap it off. Presto: into the big sleep, going quietly and painlessly. But that's not what happened. The kid was urinating all Friday, feeling lousy, not knowing why. Getting up in the middle of the night and saying to Jack 'I feel shitty.' That's not suicide; that's murder. And we both know Jack didn't do it."

"Tell that to Paul Keegan."

"I did, and will again."

"Listen Joe, I got to thinking about that dispenser case while I was out running. I knew it was significant earlier on, but I didn't put the pieces together until this morning. It was the murderer's way to determine when Andy would die."

"By picking the day?"

"Not only by picking the day, but by concentrating the lethal capsules all in one spot, namely the little compartment for Friday's meds. If you're going to doctor up some prescription meds, you've got the problem of random selection. Say there's twenty or thirty capsules in a vial; you have no way of knowing when the intended victim will take the fatal dose. The problem is compounded when it takes more than one capsule to do the job. How many do you tamper with? Half of them? All of them? No way because —"

"Because if you do that, the victim then leaves doctored capsules behind for the police to discover."

"Exactly. Or even worse, suppose he takes just one doctored capsule and another that's normal. He doesn't die; he gets sick as hell, and then calls the police himself . . . and so on."

"Uh-huh. So you're saying that the murderer slipped the doctored capsules into the Friday slot, knowing that Andrew would take all three meds on that day and then die, leaving no trace of the altered meds."

"Right. Also, the dispenser case enabled the killer to sequence the drugs for maximum effect. Thursday: Lasix and phenobarb. Friday: Lasix and digoxin. Boom. So, if Jack were the murderer, why in hell would he time it so that Andy dropped dead here? Why wouldn't he instead set the lethal dose for Saturday, and then come up here alone, say Thursday? That would give him an airtight alibi."

"And so it now seems, following this line of reasoning, that the real murderer did in fact know of Andy's visit up here in Eastham and rigged it so he'd die near Jack. That sounds like a frame as well a homicide."

"It sure does. I wonder what Paul Keegan will think of it as a working hypothesis."

"I don't know. Maybe all Paul Keegan is thinking about at the present time is how much his balls ache. And maybe about pressing charges against you."

"Do you think he's going to?"

"Actually, if I had to bet one way or another, I'd say no. Know why? Because he prides himself on being tough. *Semper fi*, all that shit, you know? Now the way I saw things, you got the better of him. How's it going to look for Paul Keegan's image if he files an assault and battery against a doctor who's ten years older? Huh? How's it gonna look? You tell me."

I was still uneasy about the incident, especially in light of how it might affect Jack.

"I think the best thing to do here is for me to apologize to him, and then go on from there. We need Keegan on this, and he needs us."

"I agree entirely," said a deep voice coming up the stairway. Footsteps came along the hallway, and there was Paul Keegan, standing there in the doorway to the bedroom, sticking out his hand. I shook it.

"How're the nuts?" asked Joe. He replied they'd recover, and noticed the bluish-green blotch on my cheek that was spreading to my left eye. There was an uneasy silence for a minute or so, then Joe began to explain our recent thinking about the pill dispenser case and the murder. Keegan thought a long time before answering.

"That could make sense. But I still have to go down to Woods Hole and interview people there. I have to talk with the boy's parents, too. There's a lot of ground to cover, and it's premature to make any theories yet."

"So you don't think this is significant?" asked Joe.

"Maybe it is. Maybe eventually it will clear Jack from all suspicion. But not now. Think of it from the state's point of view. What's the D.A. got to go on? It boils down to the same old questions of motive and opportunity. The opportunity part is obvious, no matter what our personal feelings are. Hell, Jack was his roommate. We don't have any motive. At least none has surfaced yet. But the opportunity was there, and no matter how much we don't like it, your son remains, officially, the most likely suspect at the present time."

"Yeah, well remember those words, Paul," growled Joe, " 'official,' and 'at the present time.' When you've been doing this as long as I have, you'll realize how much bullshit they are."

"I know what you're saying. I'm just advising you that, since it's official, I've got to follow this lead. Therefore, Jack must stay in touch; he can't leave Barnstable County without telling me."

"How about me?" asked Joe. "Can he tell me?"

"That's fine. That's good, in fact. But any way, any time, he's got to notify the state. Fair enough?"

Joe and I nodded.

"This crime probably does have antecedents somewhere else. I'm heading down to Woods Hole right after I interview the boy's parents in Providence."

"Well it just so happens that we'd planned to spend some of our vacation down there ourselves," I said. "We were going to sail down there and spend a few days. I see no reason to change those plans."

I saw Keegan's face cloud over with worry.

"Well, take it easy. I've seen enough of your temper to be concerned about it, Dr. Adams."

"You can call him Doc," said Joe. "And we won't go poking around where we shouldn't. I'll see to that. And I won't undertake anything in your jurisdiction unless it's okayed."

"Appreciate it," said Keegan.

As he turned to go, Joe asked Keegan if he had any theories.

"No. Not yet. But I repeat," and now he turned to me and pointed, "that you've got to be careful, Doc. I know you're emotionally involved and very upset. But if you get in too deep on this thing and you come up against somebody really mean, he won't stop until you're dead. Think about it."

Then he left.

*

Sunday evening, Anthony Hatton Adams, our Number-Two Son, was sitting next to me in my old International Scout. He'd finally arrived at the Breakers — hornet's nest that it had become — just after Keegan departed. Now the two of us were driving up to Wellfleet Harbor to meet the DeGroots, who'd pulled in that afternoon. Jim had told me over the phone that of *course* they'd decided not to make the run over the weekend. Was I nuts or something? I said they could've called and let us know, for crying out loud; we were worried. He said that Janice had tried twice Saturday morning, but the line had been busy for a long time. This figured; I had been on the blower to the state police, the local cops, the ambulance service, the boy's parents (to no avail), and a host of others. I didn't mention what had precipitated all of this; it could wait.

Tony was even darker than his mother, having been working in the sun for over three weeks. His dark, wavy hair, thick eyebrows, and coal black eyes made everyone who saw us together positive he was not my son. Sometimes, I even wondered myself. Let's see, it would have been around 1966 . . . Wasn't that the year Mary and I took that two-weeker to Puerto Rico?

"So what do you think will happen, Dad?"

"Nothing. That's what. But it's a little sticky; we can't just pretend it'll go away. I'm really glad we've got Uncle Joe in our corner; it makes all the difference."

"Who do you think did it?"

"No idea. And neither does your brother. That makes it tough, because it keeps him right in the spotlight. To make things worse, Uncle Joe just called to say that Paul Keegan, who's the chief investigator, discovered that the boy's father, who has a heart condition, was using the same medication that was used to kill his son."

"So they think the father did it?"

"No, of course not. It's just that the previous weekend, Jack visited Andy's house down in Providence. The state has pointed out that Jack therefore could have had access to the fatal medication."

Tony made a grunt of disgust, but said nothing. We went through the center of Wellfleet and down to the harbor, parking next to the little white shack that sells hot dogs and ice cream. We looked around, past all the little draggers and stern trawlers, the charter sport fishermen and "party boats," the sailboats and runabouts, and spotted a white cabin cruiser made fast to the dock. We walked down the wooden pier and saw a flurry of white in the cabin that pranced out onto the rear deck.

"Hi ho, gang!" cooed Janice DeGroot, wearing a white seersucker robe. The wind, still strong, blew her light brown hair out sideways. She grabbed at her hair with her right hand. In her left hand she held a glass with ice cubes and something red.

"How about a bloody, Doc?"

"No thanks, kid. How's tricks?"

"He's fine. Hadda leave him back in Acapulco. Damn!" Big, exaggerated wink. "Hey Jim, Doc and one of his impossibly handsome progeny are here! You coming up?"

We heard a grunt in reply, and then Jim appeared, tall, blond, and balding, coming up the shallow companionway (at least, that's what they attempt to call them on powerboats) to the main deck, where he stopped to open a beer, and then came out onto the rear deck to join us in the sun, which was trying to return after a three-day hiatus.

"Want a beer, Doc, Tony?" he asked, settling down in one of the canvas director's chairs that lined the deck. It was navy blue cloth over varnished cedar, with an embossed anchor done in white thread on the back.

"No thanks," said Tony, who was looking off down the harbor to where the smaller boats were moored. There, riding timidly at her mooring, was our sloop-rigged catboat, the *Ella Hatton*, a twenty-two-foot Marshall with a small auxiliary diesel engine. She was cute and cozy, and her shallow draft made her ideal for cruising the bays and inlets of the Cape.

"Had a nice run down here," said Jim, putting on his Ray-Ban glasses. "Still enough of a chop left to make it exciting, but the scenery was great."

"Yeah," added Janice, "I just can't wait till we get going down the — Doc?"

I looked up at her. I had been looking down at the teak planking, preoccupied.

"What's wrong, Doc? Your face looks awful!"

So I told them. It rather threw a damper on the visit.

"That's horrible," said Jim, crinkling up the aluminum beer can and tossing it into a plastic trash bag. "And stupid, too. Anybody who knows your family would know it's stupid."

"Yeah. But there it is, and the fact that the father of the dead boy took the same medication as the kind used to kill him puts Jack in a bad spot. Well, I say we leave early tomorrow for Woods Hole. I was going to drive down, but I've changed my mind. Mary and the boys can take the cars. I'll take the *Hatton* down through the canal and meet you there. I plan to stay down there until I know more about this thing."

"What about Joe? Is he still going to stay at the cottage?"

"I hope he'll spend the next week or so going between the Breakers and Woods Hole. And Moe Abramson is due down here at the end of the week, too. He's coming down for some R and R. That's a laugh, isn't it? Wait till he hears about all this."

Nobody spoke for a minute. We looked out over the harbor. Above, the clearing sky pushed along great puffy balloons of towering white clouds at a good clip. Gulls mewed and cried, circling with delicate rowing motions of their long wings, their heads darting sideways, back and forth, looking for snacks. Tony was inside the cabin, cutting pieces of Cheddar cheese from a big wedge on the bar.

"Which reminds me," I said, "I've got to call Moe tonight and ask him about the half-life of phenobarbital. It's not used that often anymore, except for brain disorders. As a psychiatrist, he'd be the one to ask."

"Why, Dad, if that's not what killed him?" asked Tony, chewing cheese.

"Because it would be good to know if many patients take their anticonvulsant medication all at once, once a day, as Andy did," I said.

"Does the offer of a sauna and shower still stand?" asked Janice. "If so, we'll close up here and ride back with you."

"That's why we're here," I said. "We'll get cleaned up and have a late cocktail hour. Then Mary's clam chowder."

So that's exactly what we did. When Janice came into the sauna bath, Mary and I got a look at her new bikini. It was rather outrageous — the two-dots-and-a-dash variety — showing a lot of bun cleavage in the rear. Mary didn't say anything as Janice pranced around, giggling. This rather surprised me, since Mary is keenly aware of my attraction for Janice's, uh . . . form. But the look on her face said a lot. I fully expected her to take Janice aside later for one of their "talks."

We had drinks on the deck, which was finally dry. Jack and Tony stood with their beers off to one side, talking low and sweeping the horizon with binoculars. Jack was holding together, from all appearances, anyway. But I sensed his inner turmoil. Tony was rallying round, as the Brits say. We let them be. Eventually, Mary and I brought the big china tureen out into the screened porch. We lighted the hurricane lamps on the long plank table and dished out bowls of the chowder. It was thick with clams, potatoes, onions, and bacon. But the broth was milky-thin, not goopy with cornstarch the way it is at most restaurants. We had the chowder with hunks of warm French bread and lettuce wedges with homemade blue cheese dressing. We had a chilled white with the meal, and were jovial by the time we had finished and poured coffee. The sun was magenta and gold over the purple bay.

I went inside and dialed Moe at his trailer.

"Yeah, yeah, I got a lot of patients wit' convulsions, Doc. Tons of 'em. I got a lot of 'em doing the Thorazine waltz, too. You wanna know about the half-life of phenobarb? Sure. It's got a nice, long half-life. Hangs around the system and stays there, like a hemorrhoid."

"And it's a common practice for patients on a multiple dosage to take them all at night?"

"Right, as long as the daily dose isn't too high. So what's this all about anyway?"

I told him.

"Hoo boy. What's going on there? Who would want to kill that kid?"

"I don't know, but somebody. We're going to find out who. When are you coming down?"

"Thursday. At least I planned on it."

"Good. If I'm still down at Woods Hole you and Joe can have the place to yourselves. Bye."

I went back out onto the deck. Mary came up and put her arms around me. She had on a low-cut Mexican blouse, with her hair pulled back and gathered, and big silver earrings I'd bought her in San Antonio. She looked like a Mexican. The sun was gone and almost all the light.

"Tomorrow I'm getting up early, running, going down to the harbor, and fitting out the boat. I want to be underway by eleven at the latest."

"Can I come with you?"

"Listen, Mary. I think it might be better to sail down with Jack and spend some time with him, considering what's happened."

"That's a great idea. I'll drive the car down. By the way, what did you think of Janice's bathing suit? If you can call something so miniscule a suit?"

"I, uh, think she's far too old to be wearing something like that, my dear."

"Good Charlie. Sometimes you say just the right thing. I'll have a talk with her and we can —"

"But with her shape she can get away with it."

Even in the fallen light, I could see her looking daggers at me.

"That won't go unforgotten," she said calmly, and we walked over to the rail to hear the tide come in.

SEVEN

NEXT DAY, Monday morning, Jack and I were up in Wellfleet Harbor stocking the *Ella Hatton*. I was glad to see that the marina had escaped major storm damage. Still, a number of small boats had swamped, and the harbor water was murky. Our little catboat had come through with flying colors, though, and now we had her made fast to a pier, ready for loading. Jack had accepted my invitation. He and I agreed that some one-on-one, coupled with two days at sea, would be just the ticket for both of us. As we packed the little catboat with supplies, I was asking him about Alice Henderson. Not trying to pry, of course. Just curious.

"Intimate?" I asked, reaching into the grocery carton that sat dockside, mentally plumbing the ramifications of the word. Like the word 'relationship,' it's a favorite of the eighties. But what the hell does it mean, really? It can mean any number of things.

"Just how intimate?" I asked, handing Jack the big chilled ham, which h.: stowed below decks in the *Hatton*'s ice chest.

"Aw, c'mon, Dad. You know: intimate."

"First base? Second?"

"Sure I kissed her. Sure. And, well, sure."

"Third?"

He let out a deep sigh. "Look, Dad, I *said* intimate, didn't I?"

"All the way to home plate?"

He suggested I mind my own business. It's a rude awakening, but sooner or later parents are forced to realize that most of the events in the lives of their children are not their business. Like maybe ninety percent of what happens in their lives. The remaining ten percent reserved for parents being mostly money and a roof to sleep under. Hey, come on, Adams; that's not fair. You couldn't have two better ones.

"Well, you could kinda call it an inside-the-park home run," he said finally, disappearing under the companionway hatch to the bows of the *Hatton*, toting a case of Poland Spring sparkling mineral water. Inside-the-park home run? What on earth did that mean? I conjured up various grotesque positions of copulation. Certain previously unimaginable circumstances of the love act.

Finally I gave up. Better not to think about it. But this brief exchange made me realize something. Much of Jack's life, and his emotions and motives, were hidden from me. And so, therefore, perhaps many of my assumptions about him were outdated and inaccurate. Somehow, it was a chilling thought, as if my son had grown a stranger to me.

Jack held up a gold-embossed cigar box. Macanudo Jamaican cigars, large palmas with dark Cameroon wrappers. A gift from Morris Abramson, M.D.

"Where do you want these?" he asked.

"Next to the whiskey and pipe tobacco, in the stow shelf over my bunk. Hey buddy, indulge your old man's curiosity for a second. What the hell does inside-the-par —"

"Forget it, Dad! I never shoulda mentioned it."

So I handed him the canned goods, the beer, the fresh pineapple, the roasted peanuts, the two New York strip steaks, the sack of potatoes and onions, an assortment of cheeses, and so on.

Inside-the-park home run. What the — ?

"Here come the DeGroots," he said, pointing with one hand and shielding his eyes from the sun's glare with the other. "Mom and Tony are with them."

I turned and saw the party trooping down to our dock. The well-wishers came up the pier, then clambered down into the *Ella Hatton*'s wide cockpit.

"Have a good sail, you guys," said Janice. "We'll be seeing you down at Woods Hole in a few days."

"Tony," I asked, "you leaving soon? When do you have to be back at Chatham Bars?"

He looked at his watch. "It's now almost ten. I'll leave at one I guess. Mom, when are you taking off?"

"Oh, around the same time," she replied. "No point in hanging around the cottage alone. Now Jackie, I can get a room key at the front desk in the dorm lobby?"

"Right. Ask for Gracie. Or Walter, the custodian. I told them everything over the phone. They know Dad and I aren't coming in until tomorrow night." Then he sighed. He didn't sigh for sympathy; he did it as a reflex. "I'm sure not looking forward to going back."

Mary snuggled next to him on the cockpit cushions.

"Now, c'mon, Jackie. You and Dad will have a nice, quiet sail down, and then we'll all be together. You'll have your family there — even Uncle Joe and Tony later on. Just remember that."

He nodded slowly, looking down at the binnacle, but sure didn't look very cheery. I knew what he was going through. Tony was idly fussing with the starboard winch, spinning the brass top of it, making a clinky metallic noise.

I broke the silence by announcing the *Hatton*'s imminent departure.

Mary took the keys to Jack's Land Cruiser and left with the gang. In the silence that followed, broken only by the whine of the bay trawlers' diesel engines, the burbling and coughing of cruiser exhaust, and the metallic *prang, prang, prang* of sailboat halyards thumping against masts, we loaded the last of the supplies into *Hatton*'s pumpkinseed hull. I started the little Westerbeke engine. Jack cast off the lines and we oozed away from the dock and headed for the harbor mouth, the little diesel grinding away beneath the cockpit, its vibration buzzing the soles of our feet. Past the breakwater, we raised the sails and cut the engine. When the self-feathering prop had folded up, like a day lily going to bed, the boat gained speed. Gone was the whine and vibration; now there was only the fresh sea breeze and the rattle and snap of taut canvas and lines. The glass hull thumped into the waves head on and the water rushed past the cockpit, hissing and foaming. The breeze sang in the rigging. *Ella Hatton* heeled to starboard ever so slightly and took the chop right in her teeth. The sea was still running high from the storm, but the sky was clear, with distant scudding clouds.

After forty minutes or so, close to eleven o'clock, the wind shifted around to the east, and was coming in over our port quarter. With the wind following, *Hatton*'s broad, shallow hull rose up and planed, and we boomed right along at a steady six knots. I was glad to be heading out, away from the Breakers and all the gloom and doom. There was nothing to do but enjoy the ocean and think important thoughts.

Inside-the-park home run . . .

I left Jack at the helm and dove down the hatch to fetch the coffee thermos, two navy mugs, and a cigar. I came topside with steaming coffee mugs, glowing stogy clenched in my mouth. Behind us, Lieutenant Island had faded from sight. Low-lying, dusky Jeremy Point was off our starboard beam. Except for a low, buff-colored ridge to the east that was the hilly spine of the Cape, none of the mainland was visible. We caught the hooter buoy at the foot of Billingsgate Island, leaving it well to starboard, and turned west. Still, skirting that eerie, sunken island, we could see bottom clearly. We were now heading straight for the opposite corner of the Bay, and the northern terminus of the Cape Cod Canal. Jack kept his eyes darting to the binnacle, continually checking our course of 273, west by southwest. I inhaled the fresh sea air and felt that things were looking up. But dark thoughts kept intruding.

"So tell me, if it's not prying," I said, "do most of the faculty down at the MBL think you and Alice Henderson were a hot item, and that you were the horrendously jilted lover, thus capable of revenge homicide?"

"No," he said without hesitation. " 'Course not. We only dated for a couple of weeks. I thought she was okay, you know. Then Andy showed up and really fell for her, so they started going out."

"Well, that's not exactly the version that came out at the cottage."

"I told you, Dad, she's lying."

"Look, Jack, any message has two parts: the words and the music. I guess the tune I heard back there is not the one you're try-ing to play now. Think about it. But you did sleep with her . . ."

"Well, yeah."

"Hmmm, well it seems you two hit the sack pretty quick for people just getting acquainted. That happen often?"

"Well sure. Usually, if you like somebody, like the second or third date."

I paused to consider this. I wasn't keen on it. I didn't like it because it cheated youth out of being young. It got the proce-dures and priorities in reverse order. And it led to rushed rela-tionships, premature commitments, bad marriages, venereal dis-ease, and a lot of other bad stuff.

"That, uh, timing seems a bit out of line," I observed.

"You're not kidding. The guys don't like it either. We really want it to happen on the *first* date. It seems like such a long time to —"

"Oh shut up," I said, and watched two gulls that were dipping and gliding in our wake. There was silence for a while, then he spoke again.

"Well, I'm not so bad about that. Really. Y'oughta see Tony."

"I have seen enough of your brother — and made the likely inferences — to have a reasonable estimate of his sexual activity. Suffice it to say that it is beyond the bounds of decency. I'd worry more, except we know he uses condoms. Your mother chanced to look inside his shaving kit this morning —"

"*Chanced* to look in? You mean snooped?"

"Whatever. Snooped is as good a word as any. Well, she was so amazed she called me in to see his collection of latex products. Keee-*riste!* — as Uncle Joe would say. The kid's got enough rub-ber in there to construct his own Goodyear Blimp."

He finished his coffee, leaned over the side, and dipped the mug into the brine to rinse it. From far off behind us came a faint *thoom, thoom, thoom* . . . It grew louder, and then we saw the boat, a big sport fisherman, hitting its hull up against the big waves at high speed. It rocketed past us, the men in the rear cockpit wav-ing arms and beer cans at us and shouting. Jack managed a tired wave back, then ran his fingers through his hair.

"Tony and I talked about it," he said.

"About screwing?"

"No. About Andy dying. And it being murder. And I told him about your fight with Detective Keegan. Anyway, he thinks it's somebody who hates me. Trouble is, we can't think of anyone who hates me."

"Well, if whoever-it-is hated you, he hated Andy Cunningham worse. Think about the people in Woods Hole. Is there anyone there you don't get along with?"

"Not that I'm aware of. Of course, somebody there could hold a secret grudge, but I haven't done anything that bad to anybody."

"How about somebody who could have hated Andy?"

"Well, there's old Lionel Hartzell, his lab supervisor. It's true that he's a little nutty, and he seems paranoid about his data; keeps thinking everybody's out to steal it. Andy told you Hartzell accused him of stealing it. But I don't think that holds water."

"Why not?"

"A couple reasons. Andy was kind of hotheaded. He had a temper, and a mouth to go with it. And while I agree that Hartzell's a little weird, I really doubt if he's violent or nasty; he's just eccentric. Personally, I kind of like the guy. He can be pretty funny sometimes when he's relaxed. As long as you respect his perfectionism and don't ride him, he's okay, at least in my book."

"And you think most people in Woods Hole would agree with you?"

"Uh-huh, I do. But you'll have to see for yourself."

"And Andy rode Hartzell?"

"Oh yeah. They clashed right away. They both had strong personalities. See, Dad, Andy was pleasant most of the time, and God knows he was bright. But he was driven and ambitious, too. Anything that got in his way or wasted his time, he had no patience for, and he'd let you know it."

"Sounds more and more as if you weren't really that close. In fact, it sounds as if you preferred Hartzell to Andy."

"No. I think Hartzell can be a roaring pain in the ass sometimes. It's just that he's not the ogre Andy made him out to be. As for Andy, it's true he's not — he wasn't — my bosom buddy. But what the hey, he was my roommate, my age, we had a lot in common . . . you know."

"Sort of a friendship of convenience for the summer?"

"Right. Exactly. And I'm real sorry he's gone. I guess I feel sorriest for his mom and dad."

"You said it. Let's get back to Hartzell for a second. Why's he so fanatical about his data?"

"Because he's a research scientist. They're all fanatical about their projects. At least the good ones. And since the labs at Woods Hole are the best in the world, they naturally attract the best talent."

"Is his data valuable? Would it be worth stealing?"

He shrugged his shoulders and cranked the winch in a few clicks. The mainsail stopped popping.

"Who knows? There could be big money in it. See Dad, some of these research jocks, they get enough data and some theories that test out in initial phases, what they do, they take their stuff and quit academics. They sell their secrets to a major pharmaceutical firm or research lab for a million bucks. Or they just borrow some money and set up their own corporation. Then the bucks really roll in."

"If they're right," I said.

"Sure. If they're right. But usually, if they're on to something, they know it. If their hunches and procedures test out, they know they've got something worth big bucks. The university can't hold them. And it can't claim title to the discovery. Now, say you work for Bell Labs, or any of the big commercial establishments. They pay you very well. But you can bet that whatever you develop there, they own it. And they won't let you take it away for your own. Most universities don't have that kind of hold on their people. If a guy hits the jackpot, the royalties are his, at least most of the time."

"And you think Hartzell is close to such a breakthrough? With his Midas-touch project, getting silver from sea water?"

"I really wouldn't know."

"Would Andy know? And if he did, would he steal the data and try to sell it on his own?"

"Naw. First of all, Andy was convinced that Lionel Hartzell was just a bunch of hot air and paranoia. Frankly, I think he under-rated Hartzell. But Andy had no respect for him or his work. But the second part of your question, would he steal it . . ."

"Well?"

"Oh, hell. I feel guilty, talking about somebody who's dead."

"Tell me, dammit."

"This may or may not figure into it, but I know that Andy had debts. He owed some money from gambling."

I was stunned at this revelation; it sure didn't fit the impression I'd formed of him.

"How do you know this? Are you sure, or just speculating?"

"I don't know the amount he owed, but I know he owed money because he told me. I don't think he was a compulsive gambler. He was just very money hungry. He wanted more than anything to lay away a nest egg for med school and take the pressure off his parents. Once when I was out running, I saw him talking to a guy driving a big white Cadillac. The kind that has an extra tire case on the back, behind the trunk? And the windows all darkened? It was on the edge of town, up near Oyster Pond Road. Andy was sticking his head inside the driver's window, talking with whoever was inside. That's just not the kind of car you see around Woods Hole very often. I asked him who the guy was and he said, 'He's an old friend from home I met after high school. I owe him a little money from loans, but he knows I'm good for it.' "

"Why didn't you tell this to Paul Keegan, for Chrissakes?"

"Why? What's it got to do with the murder?"

"Who knows? Possibly everything."

"Then we'll tell him next time we see him. But Andy said he was a friend. An old friend from high school in Providence."

"Who else in Woods Hole did you and Andy hang around with? Whoever killed Andy must have known about his epilepsy and the medication, right? So they would have to have known him pretty well."

He leaned over the side again, dragging a hand in the water. Then he brought his wet hand up and rubbed the cold water over his face. Sensing his fatigue, I took over the wheel while he stretched and yawned.

"Yeah, but see, the problem with that is, that's *me*."

"I was afraid of that. But think hard. Anybody else?"

"Well, Alice. She'd know about his condition. Then there were the rest of us living in houses around the campus. There were parties every weekend, with people coming and going in and out of our house. They'd go use the john, where Andy kept that big brown bottle of meds in the cabinet. It had the label right on it, with the drug and the dosage, the way all prescription drugs do. I suppose if they'd snooped in the cabinet, or were looking for an aspirin or something, then they could have seen the medication. Everybody there is a scientist at the graduate level; they'd be able to figure out what the meds were for. I mean, it wouldn't take a genius. Andy kept his problem quiet, like I said earlier. But I'm sure more than a few people knew he was epileptic."

"Tell me about Tom McDonnough."

"Nice guy. But he has his own private bedroom. You remember the layout of the house, don't you?"

"Vaguely," I answered. "Isn't his room upstairs, around the corner from yours and Andy's?"

"Right, and we all share the three rooms downstairs."

"Well, how did Andy and Tom get along? Any arguments? Resentments?"

"Nope. And Tom's not a good bet, Dad. He's a down-to-earth, talented professional. He's got a job next fall teaching at Holy Cross. He's engaged to be married next Christmas. Is that kind of guy going to wreck his life by committing murder?"

" 'Course not. But we know you didn't, so our inquiries will be focused outward from there. And so they'll have to include —"

"Wait a second, Dad. You said 'our inquiries.' Are you planning on making inquiries?"

I thought about it for a second. A second was all it took.

"Yes I am. I never thought about it fully until just now, but I will be digging around a bit. You're a suspect in a first degree murder case. Somebody killed Andy Cunningham in our house, probably knowing you would be put on the hook for it. Damn right I'll be making inquiries."

"Well . . . I don't know, Dad. I mean, what if people don't want to talk to you? You don't have any real authority. You're just my dad."

"One: being your dad is enough. It's plenty. Two: it so happens I do have authority. I am the temporary medical examiner for Barnstable County."

"But you told Uncle Joe you didn't want that job."

"I said I'd think about it. Well, I've thought about it, and decided. I'm going to take it."

"Medical examiner? Doesn't that mean you'll have to cut up dead people?"

"Uh . . . yes. If there are any dead people that need cutting. I'm just praying there won't be. The M.E. title will enable me to ask questions on an official basis. Remind me to inform Uncle Joe."

He sat on the cockpit cushion, head in hands, and groaned. I decided to change the subject and give the kid a break.

"We've got another three, three-and-a-half hours to the mouth of the canal if the wind holds. So say we'll arrive at around four. If we enter the mouth at four-thirty, we'll buck the current for a little bit, but it will be slowing down. Then slack water will arrive at five. Halfway through the canal, the current will turn our way."

"And how fast does it get?" he asked.

"Four to six knots. So if we add our motoring speed of five knots to the current, we'll be shooting down the ditch at nine or ten knots. That's flying."

So we sailed on, dipping and bouncing over the bay, sometimes heeling over a tad, sometimes rocking with the gentle roll of the swells. We saw pleasure craft and bay trawlers, draggers, purse-seiners, sport fishermen, and, as we neared the mouth of the canal, an increasing number of cargo freighters anxious to save the 162-mile leg around the outside of the Cape on the Boston-to-New York run. Of course the really giant vessels, especially the huge oil tankers and container ships, still went around the long way. They had to; they were way too big for the canal, even though, at over four hundred feet across, it's the widest sea-level waterway in the world.

We arrived at the canal mouth at quarter to four. Even a novice navigator can't miss the canal's eastern terminus: the three-hundred-foot smokestack of the Sagamore power plant, complete with flashing strobe lights, stands right on it. Standing off the canal about a thousand yards in a freshening breeze, I raised the canal office on VHF channel 13 and inquired about the tide currents and traffic. As I'd suspected, traffic was light on a Monday, and the keeper told me the head current was slowing. Slack water was due shortly. If we waited another forty-five minutes, we could catch the start of the westbound current. We dropped sail and motored into the canal mouth, then into a tiny mooring spot called the Harbor of Refuge. This dredged pocket of deep water within the land cut is a handy and protected stop-off point for small craft awaiting a fair tide.

We moored in a slip there, and I dove below and brought the chilled ham out from the ice locker. I'm not much on ham, frankly. But I prefer cold ham to hot, and a big chilled ham that you can carve away on at your convenience is the perfect thing to take on a sailboat cruise. We'd packed some Italian-style sub rolls, which I now sliced down the middle and packed with thin-sliced ham and Swiss cheese. I slathered Dijon mustard over the sandwiches, then spooned out Mary's cold broccoli vinaigrette on paper plates. We sat in the cockpit, fighting flies and eating our early dinner with iced bottles of Hackerbrau. I realized we'd skipped lunch, something I do regularly. But Jack was famished. He destroyed his ham and cheese immediately, and went for seconds on the cold broccoli salad. We had finished our meal and cleaned everything up shipshape by the time the tide had turned.

Engine running, we cast off and swung out into the canal traffic and kept to the right — just as on a highway — watching a Peruvian freighter dead ahead of us churning down the ditch. She was empty: riding so high we could see the violent, fountainesque wash of her screw beneath her tall, rounded stern. Behind us was a big "motor-sailer" yacht. We cracked open two more beers and sat in the dying sun. This part of the trip was delightful. We watched the shore slide by us at a rattling good clip.

There was one eerie sight: an overturned aluminum boat floating just below the surface. Undoubtedly a victim of the gale, it bumped up against our hull before we even realized it was there.

I sure hoped nobody was underneath it. Before we could grab it, it was gone, doomed to drift on its dismal journey by itself.

The Sagamore Bridge looked awfully big and high as we slid underneath it, much more impressive than it looks from on top. A light touch on the wheel was all that was needed, and I steered while Jack stripped off his shirt and lay down on the cabin top to catch the last of the sun. I lighted my pipe and reflected on how good it was to be on the water.

When we got down toward the Bourne Bridge, the canal authority turned the shore lights on, though it was still fading daylight. The big mercury vapor lamps glowed yellow on our side of the shore and white on the south side. They're spaced about five hundred feet apart. I watched them as Jack dozed on the cabin top. They seemed to be whizzing by faster and faster . . .

By the time we passed under the raised railroad bridge near the canal's mouth, we were fairly flying down toward Buzzards Bay. From experience, I knew that the easy, fun part of the sail was over. I woke Jack up and told him to get ready. He slipped his pullover shirt back on in the evening chill and joined me in the cockpit for a cup of coffee. I pointed up at the telltales, strips of bright woolen yarn and lightweight ripstop nylon that are fastened to the stays. They blow around in the slightest breeze, miniature weathervanes that tell the sailor where the wind's coming from and at what velocity. They were standing straight out now, whipping and snapping in the wind. A southwest wind, and strong.

"Okay pal, this is it," I warned as we neared the western mouth of the land cut. "The party's over. That southwest wind is driving a lot of big water up Buzzards Bay right towards us. And the canal current is blasting down towards the water. Get the picture?"

"Collision course."

"You said it. When the tidal bore meets that incoming sea, it'll raise a chop to wake the dead. So hold on. Here we go."

We shot out of the canal mouth into waves that were three and four feet high. They smacked into our little catboat head on. Since her wide, shallow hull won't slice through seas, *Ella Hatton* was thrown up and down like a steam hammer. The foredeck and cabin top were soaked, and we were continually doused with

spray. We shouted at each other over the thumping and splashing, agreeing that it wasn't fun. And we still had another five
miles to go down the dredged channel until we could veer off to
our anchorage for the night. I finally figured that the best thing
to do was cut engine speed and let the tide do the work. With
some of our forward motion gone, the chop was less intense. Still,
we kept the sails down and took turns fighting the helm.

After an hour of this thumpity-bump, we approached flasher
buoy R-4 opposite Wings Neck and bore off to port. Almost immediately after leaving the channel, we could feel the water relax.
We raised sail, cut the engine, and swept along past the point of
Wings Neck and its spooky, abandoned lighthouse, towards Pocassett Harbor. We'd had enough for one day, and were looking
for a roost for the night.

We lounged in the *Hatton*'s cockpit looking at the glowing red-
gold sky above as darkness fell. It was now nine-thirty, and there
we were, anchored in behind Bassetts Island, inside a cove in Red
Brook Harbor, in water still as a mill pond. The water slapped
and chuckled around our hull. A family of ducks paddled past,
quacking and peeping. Jack dipped up some sea water and
doused the dying embers of charcoal in the bottom of the hibachi
that was clamped over the gunwale to cook our steaks. I put the
garbage in a plastic bag, then dragged up the big oil anchor light
from the fore hatch, lighted it, and attached it to a halyard and
hoisted it aloft. It would keep other vessels away from us.

"So you're really going to go around Woods Hole questioning
everybody?" asked Jack, working a toothpick in his mouth. "Gee
Dad, that's such a drag."

"I'm not going to do that. I'm going to lurk in the shadows, so
to speak, and see what's up."

He bowed his head and didn't say anything. I could tell he was
thrilled.

"Perhaps you'd prefer Uncle Joe to do the walking and talking?"

"No, dammit! I would prefer that you all stay out of it. The
police will find out who did it, Dad; they don't need your help."

I fell silent, amazed at his naiveté.

"Don't assume that your innocence exonerates you. That can get you into deep trouble real fast."

"Okay. You and Joe can look into this. Just don't . . . just don't —"

"Make an ass of myself?"

"Right."

"That's going to be the tough part."

I pulled up the sheet and stretched, yawning. Jack blew out the little gimbaled brass oil lamp and went topside to sleep in the cockpit. I could smell the insect repellent he'd doused himself with. Darkness and quiet settled down around us like an old woolen comforter. One more time, I thought. I knew I couldn't sleep if I didn't find the answer.

"C'mon, guy. Indulge your old man's curiosity just a little bit."

"Hmmm? What?"

"You know what. Inside-the-park homer."

"You know what it means. I just meant it sort of happened fast. And inside a car. You know: *vidi, vici, veni.*"

I thought about the quote for a second. There was something out of line with Caesar's words, but I couldn't put my finger on exactly what . . .

"Good night, Jackie."

"Good night, Dad. I love you."

"Don't be a sap," I said, trying to hide my growing anxiety. I rolled over and shut my eyes.

EIGHT

WE AWOKE BEFORE SIX the next morning, Tuesday, hauled
anchor, motored out from behind our little island in the cove,
and headed back toward Buzzards Bay. Jack made coffee and
heated breakfast rolls in the galley while I minded the helm,
keeping one eye on the chart, the other on the channel marker
buoys. I estimated the distance to Woods Hole passage to be
about twelve miles. The passage is a narrow, winding channel
between Penzance Point and the islands to the south, and sepa-
rates Buzzards Bay from the open Atlantic. It's this passage, or
"hole," that gave Woods Hole its name. For the navigator, it's
very tricky, with ledges and tidal rips. To make things more difficult, the passage is buoyed and lighted for an east-to-west trav-
erse rather than the way we were headed. Therefore, to us, all
navigational aids would be backwards. It was rather like navigat-
ing through a rearview mirror, or driving in England.

Once clear of our anchorage and out on the open water again,
beating to windward in a fresh breeze, we resumed our discus-
sion of the previous afternoon.

"What about the rest of the Henderson family?" I asked.
"Didn't you or Andy mention that her father owns a fishing
boat?"

"Yeah. Several, in fact. And he has some other investments
around the foot of the Cape, too, I think. The old man's name is
Bill. William. His son is named Terry. Terry's around twenty-

four, I think. He's at most of the parties. The Hendersons seem
pretty well fixed and all, but I don't think Terry even went to
college, and he drinks a lot at the parties and is pretty crude. I
guess five or six years ago I would've been impressed by him. But
now it's like he's just kind of a drag, you know?"

"Does he have a job?"

"He works with his dad on the boats. Andy knew him better
than I do. In fact, they were kind of close. And Andy talked a lot
with Mr. Henderson, too."

"What about?"

"I don't know. They just seemed to hit it off. Andy was that
way; he could make friends at the drop of a hat."

"So we noticed. Well, I think Alice Henderson is one of the first
people I want to talk with."

"*Dad . . .*"

"Don't worry, I'm not going to get real personal. And Uncle
Joe will be with me."

"Are you sure Lieutenant Keegan wants you to —"

"I'm sure he doesn't. But that's not going to stop me. Right
about now he's probably breaking the bad news to Alice about
Andy, if he hasn't spoken to her already."

Jack gazed at the horizon, silent.

"Anything on the mother?"

"I only met her once, Dad. She didn't say much . . . just kinda
stayed in the background. I got the feeling she's not too happy,
and she seemed nervous."

"Okay, anybody else you can think of who might have been
involved with Andy, or disliked him?"

"No. Like I said, Dad, he made friends easily; he was real popu-
lar. That's what's so screwy about this."

We sailed on in silence, enjoying the sea breeze and the sounds
of the water. We entered Woods Hole Passage before eleven; the
tide was ripping through there full blast, swinging *Hatton*'s hull
sideways toward the ledges, so we finished it under power, with
sails down.

Standing off the town at the end of a short channel called "the
strait," I blew two long, two short on the air horn, and soon the
tiny drawbridge on Water Street eased up, allowing us to pass

underneath. I've never seen a smaller drawbridge than the one at Woods Hole, except the famous miniature one in Bermuda.

We crept into Eel Pond, the tiny, circular harbor on the other side of the bridge, and oozed along in a near-stall until we came to the small dock opposite a low, modern building of stone and glass. Jack pointed it out to me as Swope Dormitory, where Mary and I would be staying for these several days.

Jack climbed up onto the wooden dock toting his overnight bag, and I followed him. I got the feeling something was wrong when we went inside and the woman at the desk stared at us. Jack mumbled something in the way of greeting, took the room key, and we proceeded up a flight of stairs and down the carpeted hallway to number 215.

A man wearing a khaki uniform was sitting in front of the door.

"Jack?" he said, rising from the chair. I realized he was a maintenance man.

"Oh, hi Walter. What's going on? Where's my mom?"

"Your mother has gone over to your apartment, in the company of a Mr. Keegan," he said. Then he looked at me. "Ah, and you must be Dr. Adams. I am Walter Myles."

I shook his hand. He had an impeccable British accent and a clipped gray mustache to go with it. His face wore a worried, solicitous expression.

"I'm so sorry to hear about young Mr. Cunningham, Jack," continued Walter Myles. "And I'm afraid I have more bad news for you. It seems that in your absence, somebody broke into your rented house and burgled it. The contents are in complete disarray. That's why your mother is there right now."

Jack's jaw fell slack; he dropped his duffel bag on the carpeted floor of the hallway. "Great," he grunted.

"Somebody broke in?" I said. "Who discovered it, and when?"

"Apparently Thomas McDonnough, Jack's other roommate, discovered it when he returned there early this morning."

"Is Tom over there now?" asked Jack, recovering himself.

"I believe so. Dr. Adams, do you wish to leave your luggage inside?"

I stowed my gear in the room next to Mary's things and followed Jack over to his rented house on School Street, just on the other side of Eel Pond, about four blocks away. There was Jack's house, just as I remembered it: a gray shake-sided, two-story house. We saw Mary and Tóm McDonnough sitting together on the front porch. When she saw us, Mary jumped up and waved. She looked preoccupied.

"What's happened?" Jack asked as we walked up to the porch. Mary's smile faded, and she shrugged her shoulders, holding her palms up and out.

"Search me," she said, "but it's a mess in there."

We shook hands with Tom, who had the black hair, blue eyes, and light skin of the Irish. His skin was trying to tan, but it was mostly red and blotched from the sun. He was of medium height, and thick with muscle overlaid with a smooth layer of fat. I asked him where Lieutenant Keegan was.

"Inside," he said, "sealing everything off so the lab team can get the evidence. We're not even allowed in there; that's why we've been sitting out here waiting for you guys. How was the cruise?"

We talked about the trip until Keegan came out the front door, closing it after him. He shook hands with me cordially but, as usual, was all business.

"Tom left the house at about four-thirty last Thursday evening," said Keegan, consulting his notes. "He didn't return until this morning, at ten-thirty. From Thursday to Tuesday leaves four nights in which the break-in could have occurred: Friday, Saturday, Sunday, or Monday night. I don't believe it was a daylight job. The neighborhood's much too close and active for that."

"What did they take?" asked Jack.

"That's the weird part," said Tom. He said it like this: *weee-id paht.*

"What?"

"I can't see anything obvious that's gone. The whole house was ransacked: your room, mine, the whole downstairs. Even the cellar. But the stereo's still there. The TV, my camera, even the pile of bills and change on my dresser. All still there. We've got no silver or antiques or anything like that. So what's going on?"

"Can't I even look inside?" asked Jack.

"I'd rather you wait until the — here they are now," said Keegan, pointing to a dark green van that was pulling up in front.

Two men got out, and then Keegan opened the front door and we all filed in, letting the lab men go first with their cameras, collecting tape, and sketchbooks.

Keegan stayed with us in the front hall, just beneath the stairway. He told us that since the break-in might be connected with a homicide, he was making sure that all possible evidence would be kept. I considered the link between the burglary and Andy's death, and saw it as a positive development for us.

"Know what?" I said. "This points the finger of guilt right here in Woods Hole. And also, I think it removes suspicion from Jack. He was nowhere near here during this burglary."

Keegan turned to Jack.

"Where were you last night?"

"On board our sailboat with my dad, anchored in Pocassett Harbor," said Jack.

"And I can swear to it," I added.

"Anyone else see you two? Any impartial, unbiased witnesses?"

"No," I said. "So what?"

"We'll discuss it later. Meanwhile, let's follow the lab team from room to room as they finish up. Jack, you and Tom can help us by identifying the belongings inside. Maybe we can figure out what, if anything, is missing. Remember: don't touch anything."

We did as instructed. The team covered the downstairs first, examining doors and windows for means of entry, using their special vacuum cleaners to lift dirt and lint samples, dusting for latent prints, and photographing each room from a variety of angles. In addition, they made crude sketches showing where various objects were located in the rooms. The house had been tossed, all right, but the job appeared professional and thorough, rather than hasty. In the kitchen, the cupboards had been searched, with canned goods and bags of pasta and chips left out on the counters. In the upstairs bedrooms, the mattresses were bare, but replaced back on the box springs. Sheets and bedding were heaped in big piles in the corners. All the dresser and desk drawers had been removed and examined, and their contents apparently strewn on the floor and later pushed up against a wall, presumably to allow the intruders space to walk around. The closet doors were ajar, and the clothing pulled out and piled on the floor. Nothing appeared to be broken or ruined, but there was no doubt the search had been painstaking.

Up in Jack's bedroom, I turned and saw Mary leaning against the doorway, her arms folded across her ample front. Her head was cocked slightly to one side, her dark hair cascading down the side of her head onto her shoulder. Looked great. But her lip curled a bit in a dubious, disgusted expression.

"Well, when it rains, it pours," she said softly. "Jackie, can you tell offhand if anything's missing?"

"Not anything I can remember. Looks to me like they just searched the place."

"Looking for what?" asked Keegan.

Jack shrugged his shoulders. Keegan suggested we all go get a cup of coffee. Tom wanted to put his room back together, so he stayed at the house. The rest of us walked to the Cap'n Kidd tavern, which is down on Water Street near the drawbridge. We ordered coffee. Jack, usually hungry, had a Coke, which he sipped nervously. I repeated my observation that this ransacking of the boys' house cleared Jack of all suspicion. I was hoping Keegan would agree without reservation. But he didn't.

"Hold on, Doc," he said. "We can't assume that. Not yet. For one thing, we have no evidence that links the break-in with the murder. It could be just a random burglary."

"Aw, c'mon, Paul," said Mary. "It's not the kind of house a burglar would choose. Even *I* know that. It's student housing, and everybody around here knows it. And nothing valuable was taken. It must have been a search, not a burglary."

Keegan held up his hand.

"All that's crossed my mind. But how about this: what if somebody, like maybe a prosecuting attorney, supposes that Jack tossed the house himself on Friday afternoon prior to leaving for your cottage in order to divert suspicion? What about that?"

Mary squirmed in her chair. "That's the biggest load of horseshit I've ever heard, Paul. For one thing, he and Andy left together, didn't you, Jackie?"

"Well no, not exactly. Andy had loaded all his stuff into the Toyota at lunch time. He was in the lab all that afternoon, remember? So after my work was finished, I packed my stuff in and then picked him up at Lillie."

"What's Lillie?" asked Keegan.

"Lillie Hall. The big building right down the street. It's where the labs and offices are. I picked him up there about four-thirty."

"Right," said Keegan, "I remembered your saying that, and wrote it down. Tom left Woods Hole Thursday afternoon to visit his parents in Worcester. You were the last one to leave."

"What have you got against us?" said Mary. She was giving him a dead level stare. It wasn't friendly.

"I have nothing against any of you, believe me. If anything, I'm biased in your behalf, for two reasons. One is Doc's coming forward with the cause of death. The other is the fact that you're Joe's sister. So don't worry about my personal feelings. But remember, there are D.A.s. There are prosecuting attorneys and grand juries. These people may not see things the way you do. And speaking of that, Jack, there's a curious thing I wanted to talk to you about."

Jack looked up from his Coke. He was jiggling his legs up and down fast in his nervousness.

"The lab team checked for means of entry. Tom McDonnough says that each of you kept a key. No key was hidden under the doormat or any such place, right?"

"Right," Jack nodded.

"Tom also told me that whenever you guys left for the weekend, you always locked the doors, front and back, and you always closed and snibbed the downstairs windows. Correct?"

Jack nodded again.

"Well, when he discovered the mess, Tom looked around and saw the kitchen window left wide open, and the window screen removed and lying in the bushes below. I assume you didn't do this."

"No, I didn't. Just before I left on Friday, I checked all the windows on the first floor. They were all shut down tight. I don't know about the screen, it could have been missing. But the windows were closed and locked."

"Okay. Now the odd thing is this: there's no way the window could have been forced from the outside. There are no pry marks from tools on the sill or the bottom of the window frame. Also, the snib is intact. If the window had been forced, the fastener would be broken or pried off. Follow?"

"I guess. You're saying that the window was opened from the inside, and made to look like somebody forced it from the outside."

"Exactly. So how did they get in? We think they got in through the front door. And because there are no marks on the lock face, we're pretty sure they didn't pick the lock. Therefore, they used a key."

"Well, it wasn't *my* key."

"I didn't expect you to say it was, Jack. But Tom swears it wasn't his key, and we know for sure it wasn't Andy's key. So assuming it wasn't the landlord, my question is, who else had a key, and how'd they get it?"

After several seconds of silence, Jack admitted he had no idea.

"Think carefully, Jack. Did you loan your key to anyone, even for a few hours?"

"No. Not that I can remember. The one person I can think of that might have borrowed mine, or Andy's, is Alice Henderson."

Keegan said nothing; he just looked at Jack, whose legs and knees were bouncing a mile a minute. He wasn't a twitchy kid, so he was clearly nervous about something.

"It might interest you to know that I spoke with Alice Henderson yesterday."

Jack didn't answer, just rattled the ice around in his Coke glass, bouncing his legs so fast I thought he might become airborne. Then I saw a sheen of sweat on his lip. Oh boy —

"She, uh, had some interesting things to say about your relationship with Andy."

Jack just sat there, twitching in every muscle and staring down at the table. The lunch time crowd, swilling beer and inhaling burgers, paid no attention to our taut little group.

Mary couldn't stand it any longer.

"What is it Jackie? For God's sake, tell us!"

Jack looked back at Paul, biting his lip.

"What did she say?"

"What do you think she said?" asked Keegan. At that point I sensed danger. I don't know much about the law, but I've learned from Brady Coyne that when the water turns murky, clam up and wait for good advice. I told Keegan that the "interview" was over. The three of us got up and left him sitting at the table alone, presumably to pick up the tab. It was the least he could do. We walked awhile in silence, past the historic Candle House with its ship's prow over the door, and then I suggested we go up to our room in Swope Dormitory.

"I wanted to get you out of there before he painted you into a corner," I explained. Jack was stretched out on the bed, leaning up against the headboard, staring at his hands. "I don't think you ought to answer any more questions, for anyone, until we get a lawyer."

"Charlie! Is it that bad?"

"Hell yes it's bad. First degree murder has a tendency to be serious business. Listen, Jack, I have the distinct feeling that Alice Henderson has told Paul Keegan something that's important and perhaps damaging. Right?"

He nodded his head without hesitation. Great. Just great.

"Well?" Mary said.

"Well, what happened was, Andy and I got into a fist fight on July Fourth weekend. I'm sure that's one of the things she told him."

"Fist fight?" said Mary, getting out of her chair and walking over to the bed. "Why didn't you tell us this?"

"Why? For one thing, it was over a month ago and we'd both just about forgotten about it. Except that the side of my face still hurts sometimes, and Andy told me he had a ringing in his left ear."

I slumped over the table and let out a low groan.

"Sweet Jesus," Mary whispered. "Now listen: you're going to tell us *everything* — right here, right now."

"There's not much else to tell —"

"Who saw this fight?" I asked.

"Well, Alice did. It was kinda about her. Andy was like teasing me privately about it, and I lost my temper. Terry, Alice's brother, was there, too. Along with a few other people."

Great, I thought. Witnesses galore for the bad scenes . . . no "impartial" witnesses when we neeeded them. Great.

"So who won?" asked Mary.

"Nobody. They broke it up. For a while afterwards, Andy didn't stay at the house."

"Don't you see the position that this puts you in?" I asked. Jack lowered his head again, as if about to cry, and Mary jumped all over me for being harsh with him. I went over and joined them on the bed, putting my arm around Jack's shoulder. Then he did break down crying. He was plenty scared. Frankly, I was scared myself, and doing my damnedest not to show it.

"Seems to me that you and Andy weren't really friends," said Mary.

"That's not true. We were friends, deep down. But the thing with Alice came between us, and Andy was, you know, volatile. Sometimes he was real hard to get along with. I'm sure Alice would admit that."

"Okay," I sighed, "the first step is to get Joe down here for a day or two. I'll feel better once he's here. Also, Mary, I'm accepting the medical examiner job, at least for a while. It'll give me some clout. The best way to deal with this is to fight back. Know what I mean?"

"You? Medical examiner?" she said. "You nuts, or what?"

"Or what," I said. "Now can you try to get your brother on the phone?"

NINE

"NO, DOC. Keegan's *not* trying to blow you guys out of the water. Believe me. It's just that he doesn't want you to get an unrealistic view of the situation, is all."

"But why does he have to paint the bleakest possible picture, for Chrissakes?"

"Look, take the alibi thing. You say you were with Jack for two days aboard the boat. Fine. But you're his father; you're an interested party, a biased witness. A jury could be persuaded you're lying to protect your son. I mean, Pocassett's just a hop and a skip from Woods Hole. They could buy it that Jack went back to the house and ransacked it to divert suspicion away from him. What would be great is an unbiased witness, a casual observer. That's why it's a shame you didn't bump into some Joe Blow who could've seen —"

"Yeah, but tough shit, Joe. We didn't. And what really pissed me off was when he suggested Jack could have tossed the house himself before he left on Friday. Why did he even suggest that?"

"Why? Because a prosecutor's going to, if this thing goes that far."

"You really think it's going to? I can't believe it. You really think —"

"Look, I hope to hell not. But just don't count on being out of the woods, is all I'm saying. Where's Sis?"

"In the shower. You want me to get her?"

"No, I'll call back. And I'll be down there tomorrow, so in the meantime keep cool, and don't get yourself in troub —"

"You know I'd never —"

"Ha! I know you too well."

"Moe's coming down today. I think I'll take him with me when I see Lionel Hartzell, the loony professor with the magic silver fish."

"The *what?*"

"Never mind. Bye."

I hung up and sat back in the dorm's easy chair, uneasily, waiting for Mary to emerge from the shower. She did, dressed in a madras wraparound skirt and a white silk blouse, with big silver earrings and sandals with cork soles. She looked like a Mexican woman, only darker.

The phone rang again, and I picked it up.

"Dr. Adams? Hi, this is Art Hagstrom. I don't know if you've ever heard my name before, but I'm —"

"The director of MBL. Yes, Jack's mentioned you often, and most favorably, too."

"Well I'm glad to hear it, and the feeling is very mutual. Jack's a fine young man and a good scholar, too."

"Even though he might be a murderer."

"Aw, c'mon. Nobody here believes that. In fact, the reason I'm anxious to pay you a call is to discuss something that could be important."

"Where are you now?"

"Downstairs in the lobby."

"Well, come on up, then."

Art Hagstrom was tall, with dark curly hair, and a set of bushy eyebrows to match. Jack had told us about his national reputation. His pleasant smile and casual manner belied the pathbreaking work in gene cloning and cell replication that he was engaged in. He sat at the table with us, dressed in khaki shorts and a polo shirt, Topsiders dock loafers with no socks. He sure didn't look like a research scientist. He leaned forward, clapped his cupped hands together as if calling a meeting to order, and said: "Okay, here goes. I may slip into a shit pile for telling you this, but, as I said, it may have a slight bearing on all this craziness. I only ask that you not tell a soul. Agreed?"

We nodded.

"Good. I'm going to tell this to the police, but I feel you should both hear it too, since you're Jack's parents. Just as long as you keep in mind that it's mostly hearsay. The upshot is: I have reason to think that Andrew Cunningham, despite his charm and talent, was not the young innocent he appeared to be."

"Really? Hmmmm. Funny you should mention that. Jack had some interesting things to say about him on the way down here. So what do you know?"

"Well, first of all, I'm not trying to paint a villainous picture here. There was no denying his brilliance, or his good looks. Or his charming personality, or his drive. Perhaps it's his drive that I'm touching on here. About two weeks ago, I was visited by two gentlemen in extremely expensive, well-fitting suits. One of them was big, so big he looked like a linebacker. In the privacy of my office, they informed me that Andy owed them a lot of money in the form of an unpaid loan, and could I please set aside part of his paycheck to square things?"

"Sounds like they weren't from the local finance company," said Mary.

"Sounds like maybe they were some of your countrymen, hon," I said. Immediately, I felt a sharp kick in my shin. Cork soles notwithstanding, the pain was considerable. She leaned over close to my ear.

"Next one's gonna be higher up, and right over home plate," she hissed in a whisper only I could hear. And then, in an audible voice as demure as a newly sworn-in nun, she said, "Please continue, Dr. Hagstrom."

"Uh . . . sure. Well, it didn't take me long to realize these were underworld characters. I explained that I had nothing whatsoever to do with Andy's pay. And, as you know, the pay for graduate assistants is hardly extraordinary. Of course I didn't want to deal with them, but I was a little worried about what they might do in the community if their so-called 'loan' wasn't repaid. So after they left I called Andy, who admitted that he had considerable gambling debts from card games, racetracks, and casinos in Atlantic City."

Mary and I exchanged a glance.

"I never found out the actual amount," Hagstrom continued, "but I'd guess it was in the thousands. I hope to God it wasn't in the tens of thousands."

"But why would these guys hit you up?" asked Mary. "I mean, wouldn't they just put pressure on Andy? Maybe threaten him?"

"I don't think their visit was for my benefit, really, Mrs. Adams. Personally, I think they'd already let Andy know where he stood with them. I think their visit to me was simply to add emphasis. To make it official, so to speak. I'm pretty sure they knew I'd speak to Andy. Maybe threaten to let him go if the debts weren't cleared up. From the way they acted, and from that car they were driving . . ."

"White Cadillac Eldorado, smoked glass windows, chrome spoked wheels, continental kit?" I asked nonchalantly.

Hagstrom sat bolt upright. "Hey, that's exactly right! How'd you know?"

"Jack told me about a so-called 'friend' of Andy's from Providence. He mentioned seeing Andy sticking his head inside the driver's window of a white Caddy. I know the car. Not this particular one, but the ones like it; there are maybe two hundred of them in the East. Mary's brother's a detective and he's told me about the mob's wheels. The Wiseguys outgrew black Caddies back in the sixties. And of course, the new guys, the young bucks, don't drive Detroit iron anymore. Wouldn't be caught dead with it. They say that nowadays Caddies are for the black and Hispanic hoods. No, they want nothing but high-class kraut, the big Mercedes and Beemers. In off colors, like coffee and claret. A few choose the big Jags. But the old-time Wiseguys, they love their Caddies. Maybe a Lincoln Town Car or two thrown in —"

"Cut it out, Charlie!" Mary snapped.

"Anyway," Hagstrom continued, "they seemed to flaunt the mobster look, you know? They wanted to give the impression that if this thing with Andy weren't resolved, they were going to hang around Woods Hole until it was. Can you imagine the effect that would have on morale here?"

"I see what you mean. So they paraded around here enough to tarnish the kid's image, then split?"

"Uh-huh. They drove off in the afternoon, around three. Back to Providence, I guess. The car had Rhode Island plates, but it was one of those custom-made plates. What are they called?"

"Vanity plates."

"Right. I'll never forget the name on it: SLINKY."

"Slinky? Like those kid's toys?" said Mary. "Those springy things that walk down stairs?"

"Uh-huh. SLINKY."

"And what did Andy have to say about this?"

"Well, he didn't deny it. And he said that he wasn't gambling for the love of it, either, but because he was hoping to turn his meager savings into big bucks."

"Did he say he planned to pay them back?" asked Mary.

"Oh, he assured me there was no long-range problem. Of course, in light of what's happened, I felt I had to tell you."

"Why haven't you gone to the police?" I asked.

"You mean before now? Why? When I first heard of the boy's death, it was presented as an accidental overdose of medication. And by the way, it was medication for a condition that I — and most of the staff — was unaware of. But a state detective called me early this morning —"

"Paul Keegan?"

"Right. So you know him. He wants to talk with me later today, and over the phone he filled me in on Andy's death. I thought it was a good idea to talk with both of you first."

"And for that, we thank you," said Mary softly. "We might need all the help we can get on this thing."

I left the chair and paced slowly to and fro on the carpet. A large vessel must have been entering Woods Hole's Great Harbor; I heard the faint deep blast of her whistle. The windowpane rattled.

"Andy was a poor boy, you know," said Mary, and then proceeded to explain his background to Art. I was uneasy, and continued to walk around the small room. I lighted a pipe and puffed and thought. Finally, I spoke.

"I don't think the mob killed Andy," I said. "For one thing, no matter what he owed them, he was small-time. The mob only kills big shots, and Andy wasn't one. Secondly, when we consider the way the murder was done, the ingenuity behind it, we can rule out the Wiseguys. When they make a hit, there's nothing subtle about it. We've all heard about the bloated, stinky corpses found in car trunks. There are stereotypes about the mob, but like many stereotypes, they have some basis in fact. No: whoever killed Andrew Cunningham knew him intimately, knew of his illness and medication, his schedule, everything. The murderer even had access to his pill case."

Hagstrom shook his head and furrowed his bushy black eyebrows. "Son of a bitch. Then no wonder it looks bad for Jack."

I turned, stunned at these words. Mary sat frozen, looking helplessly at Hagstrom. We both knew he was right. Our optimism brought about by the sacking of Jack's house was fading. Facts were facts: in the eyes of the law, Jack was the most likely culprit.

Hagstrom sensed our distress, and made a valiant but futile effort to comfort us. We thanked him, and he rose to go.

"If I can be any help, just come over to my office in the Candle House any time. It's right on Water Street. By the way, though, I won't be here the next several days. Four of us from the MBL are going to a conference at the Jersey shore. You can get the number from my secretary. Goodbye, and best of luck."

Ah-OOOOOOOOOOOOOOOOOO-(weee).
  OOOOOO (wee)!
  OOOOOO (wee)!
One long, two short. The ship crept ahead, scarcely raising a ripple at her prow. Her whistle blasts meant "keep clear; restricted in maneuverability." The ship eased up to the WHOI dock. She was the research vessel *Knorr*, operated by the Woods Hole Oceanographic Institute. It was the same vessel I'd seen from the motel window minutes earlier.

"Did you see that current kicking up on her beam out there?" said Jack. "Jeez, that tidal rip hits a two-hundred footer sideways, it's a bitch to get her moving right. Did you know she doesn't have a prop? She's got directional hydro jets. She can —"

"Jack, where's Mom?"

"I don't know. I saw her walking down Water Street a little while ago. I think she probably went shopping up the way."

"Thanks. I'm going to go looking for her."

I found her in a boutique looking at batik blouses. But she wasn't really looking at them; she was picking them up and flinging them down again.

"I'm so scared, Charlie. I'm so scared all over again about Jack. I mean, look: here's Arthur Hagstrom, a trained, educated professional, who's known Jackie for two summers now. Trusts him like a father. And what does he say right off the bat? 'Whew! No wonder it looks bad for Jack!' Good Christ, Charlie!"

She was looking down at the pile of cloth. Dark spots were appearing all over it. I lifted her face up and dried her eyes with the cuff of my sweat shirt. "Sorry hon," she said, and sniffed. She was talking with that hiccuppy, squeaky high voice that women have when they're crying, and blinking away a lot of tears. Well, it melted me, just like that. Always does.

I gave her a hug, right there in the store, and kissed her.

We glided out of there and down the street. At the little drawbridge on Water Street she drew me close and hugged me hard. I could feel her chest shaking as she cried.

"It'll be okay," I whispered.

"Charlie. Promise me you won't quit the medical examiner job. Promise me you'll keep it."

TEN

ONE GLANCE at Alice Henderson and it was easy to see why the guys were attracted to her. She was lithe and athletic, a tall blonde with dark skin and eyes. And only a few minutes with her convinced me of her mental agility and powers of recollection. We were sitting on the forward hatch cover of the barque *Westward*, the most beautiful sailing ship I'd been on in years. A beautiful woman on a beautiful ship. I was surrounded by beauty. But it didn't keep me from the business at hand, and I'm afraid, looking back, that I put Alice Henderson under a lot of pressure that summer afternoon. I had to; I wanted to find out the truth, and the digging was bound to be painful.

She wiped her eyes again and lighted another cigarette, her fourth in the short time we'd been talking. Between drags, she was winding her long hair around in her fingers, chewing on strands of it, shaking it back over her shoulders, and fidgeting in general.

"Look, I mean what *is* this, Dr. Adams? I told you already. I am *not* trying to frame your son. I am not trying to put Jack in the hot seat. He's a nice guy. I like him a lot. So why —"

"Hold on. I never accused you of that, Alice. I know you had to answer the questions Lieutenant Keegan asked you, and answer truthfully. You did that. And I admit Jack showed very poor judgment in not coming clean about the fight earlier on. Having Keegan discover it later makes him look . . . uh . . . doesn't make him look good."

"It's all been so . . . terrible . . ." she said, heaving. Her words came in short, hiccuppy gasps, that ragged breathing that comes after a lot of sobbing. Yes, I did feel sorry for her. I was feeling sorry for a lot of people these days. Including, probably, me.

"You loved Andy, didn't you? I'm so sorry."

She looked down at the deck, biting her lip and nodding, the tears pouring out of her eyes. Behind her, the sky was deep, dark blue. So blue and dark that you thought you could stare into it. But right away it hurt your eyes. The sea breeze blew her hair out, and she wiped her tears away and looked up again. A gorgeous girl, and this was no way for her to have to spend her summer.

"Do you want us to drive you down to Providence for the funeral tomorrow?" I asked.

She shook her head.

"Terry and I are going to drive down. Thanks anyway. I'm not sure I'd feel . . . comfortable . . . riding down with Jack."

"Because he might be a murderer?"

"No," she said after a second's hesitation. I didn't like the pause; it was as if she had to think before answering. "I'd just feel awkward, and he would too. He probably thinks I betrayed him."

"I doubt that. Have you talked with Terry about all this? What does he think?"

"He doesn't think Jack did it, if that's what you mean. We sat around for a couple of nights trying to figure out who could've done it. What we came up with, we decided it wasn't anybody here in Woods Hole."

"How about Lionel Hartzell? They didn't get along, and Hartzell's training would qualify him for the method."

"Yea!, but we just didn't think it fit. Hartzell's strange, but he's not that mean. Haven't you talked with him yet?"

"No. I've called him, but he refuses to see me. I know Lieutenant Keegan's talked to him at least once. But I'll see him one way or another. Right now, I'm waiting for a friend of mine to come down from Boston and interview him with me. He's a psychiatrist."

"Well, Terry and I don't think he killed Andy; we think it's somebody out of Andy's past. Somebody we've never met."

I thought a second and decided to go out on a limb. I began to describe the white Cadillac to her. But before I could finish, she waved me off.

"Oh, no. Eddie wouldn't do that, Dr. Adams."

"Eddie?"

"Yeah, Andy's friend from Providence. Andy said his name was Eddie. I met him once."

"And?"

"And what can I say? I know he's in some racket or other. Probably gambling and dealing dope or something. Or maybe playing the numbers, or whatever. But he liked Andy; he wouldn't kill him."

"Andy owed him money, Alice."

"I know that; Andy told me. But still, I don't —"

"What's Eddie's last name?"

She shrugged her shoulders.

"How can I get in touch with him?"

Another shrug. I sat there on the hatch cover, looking at her. It was something a man could do for a long time without getting bored. My son Jack had been in bed with this girl-woman. Did I envy him? Hell yes.

Stick to the business at hand, Adams.

"Alice, the police have determined that whoever broke into Andy and Jack's rented house used a key. Did either of them ever loan you a key to the front door?"

"I'm . . . not sure I should tell you."

"Well, you just have. Was it Andy, or Jack?"

She bowed her head. "Both. And when Andy loaned me his key later on, I made a copy at the general store."

"Can I see it?"

"No, because I don't have it with me; I left it at home. Why would I need it now?"

She looked at me with a questioning look, which turned sour and pouty, and then she was crying again. I moved next to her and put my arm around her. Nobody else was on deck. The *Westward*, majestic even in her berth, was all ours. She cried into my shoulder, saying she was sorry about Jack, sorry about Andy, sorry about everything, and that maybe everything was all her fault. Finally her sobbing ebbed and we got off the hatch cover and walked over to the cutaway and down the gang-plank.

We walked along the big pier towards town. The giant hull of the *Knorr* loomed up over us.

"I just can't . . . I just can't . . . seem to stop crying, Dr. Adams."

"Don't try. Just keep on crying until the pain cries itself out. If you need me, call me or Mary at the Swope Dorm, okay?"

She nodded.

"Who could have taken your key or made a copy of it? Terry?"

"Sure. Terry or . . . or any number of people I guess. But what would he want with a key?"

"Who knows? But somebody went in there looking for something. And they had a key."

Joe was waiting for me in his cruiser outside Swope Dormitory. After we pulled out of town and were on the highway to the clinic in Hyannis, he pulled something out of his coat pocket and hand-ed it to me. A brass badge: a shield with the Commonwealth of Massachusetts state seal on it. Above the seal were the words DEPARTMENT OF PUBLIC SAFETY. Below the seal it said SPECIAL POLICE. I turned the heavy shield over and over in my hands, trying to get used to it.

Joe grinned at me out of the side of his mouth.

"I know you're excited, Doc. Try not to wet your pants."

"What does this entitle me to?" I asked.

"You ready for this? It's a license to kill. Anybody you don't like, or that pisses you off, POW! Blow 'em away."

"I mean seriously."

"Seriously? Okay, try this then: it allows you to be abused, ver-bally and physically, with almost no right to fight back or defend yourself. It gives you the right to be called out at four in the morning to scrape the corpse of a teenaged hooker off the rail-road tracks beneath a viaduct . . . the right to expose yourself to constant danger, including getting shot at. The right to drink half a bottle of booze at ten in the morning to stop the shakes from seeing your partner's brains blown out while he's standing next to you on a dark street. The right to be called a motherfucking honky pig by blacks, and a nigger-lover by whites. The right —"

"Hey, you want this back?"

"Do I want it back? Hell no I don't want it back. Carrying one is more than enough. It's yours now, pal. You're stuck with the fuckin' thing."

He reached into the coat again and pulled out a worn leather folding case the size and shape of a wallet. He tossed me the badge holder.

"This was Joe Kenny's; he retired last fall. You can have it. When he left he told me he never wanted to see it again."

"What can I say? Words fail me. I'm overjoyed."

"You've got to read the code of conduct, and memorize it. You've also got to memorize a bunch of legal stuff, and you've got to sign some forms and be photographed and fingerprinted. You've got to take a set of polygraph tests and some personality profile tests for mental soundness."

"Mental soundness, eh?" I said, fingering the badge. "Well, it was fun while it lasted . . ."

"We need copies of your diplomas and all that stuff. Some letters of recommendation and other — hell, that can wait. Right now you're going to take a short tour of your new work place."

"Can't wait."

"And for this, you'll be paid the smashing salary of eighty-five hundred a year."

"What can I say? I'm over —"

"Plus an hourly fee for your lab time. Plus expenses."

We exited for Hyannis and headed for the small clinic that was also the forensic mortuary for Barnstable County.

"I'm thinking that this appointment — should it go through — is a godsend," said Joe as he pulled the cruiser into a parking slot outside the low brick building. "Because as of now, you are officially a state cop, of sorts."

"So?"

"So you figure it out. We cops stick up for each other. Your son's in trouble; we stick up for him. Get it?"

"Yeah, I get it. Now I see what Mary was getting at. Have you ever noticed how smart your sister is?"

"Or how brilliant her brother is? C'mon, let's get this over with, and hope to Jesus you don't have a 'customer' waiting."

Joe and I followed Carl Blessing through the hospital corridor and down a flight of stairs. He opened the second door on the left and flipped on the light.

The big drain table caught our attention first. Stainless steel, with a molded gutter around its perimeter. To catch what is euphemistically referred to as "bodily fluids." Then there were the enameled steel cabinets on the walls, filled with dark brown bottles, cotton swabs, balance scales, and photographic equipment.

"Here's where you'll be working, Dr. Adams," said Blessing. "Actually, it isn't used all that often. By the way, there are three death certificates I'd like you to sign off on before you leave: a drowning victim and two motor vehicle fatalities. Fortunately, none required autopsies because in each instance the cause of accidental death is clear. The report of the attending emergency room physicians is sufficient."

Blessing pulled out a wide, silent drawer filled with bright steel tools.

"And here, of course, are your postmortem instruments," he said in a weary tone, picking each one up and naming it as he did so.

"These are the rib shears, as you must remember from med school: Bethune rib shears, Semb rib shears, Saurbach serrated rib shears . . ."

Get me out of here, I was thinking to myself. Just get me the hell out of here —

"The rib spreaders are these: Finochietto rib spreader here, Sweet rib spreader, Giertz rib guillotine . . . here are the hand retractors . . . a Charriere bone saw there . . . here are the cranial drills . . . Satterlee bone saw . . . Smollett geared retractor . . . Meyerding bone chisel — that'll go through anything! — your mallets are here, these are the suction tubes —" he said, pointing to a tray of neatly arrayed hollow steel probes with holes in them, "and of course your motorized surgical saw. Howard used this one for cranial cutting prior to removing the skull cap —"

I took an involuntary step backward. Joe was staring, transfixed, at the gruesome array of implements. Torquemada would have loved to get his mitts on them. Nothing delicate about them: they were massive, with gear-driven mechanisms for shearing, clipping, tearing, crunching through the stoutest chest cavity, the thickest femur, the heaviest skull and jaw. And no concern whatsoever for pain . . . of course.

"Thanks, Carl," I said, trying to catch my breath, "you've been most helpful. I think we can be going now. I —"

"Wait. I've got to show you the chem lab and radiology."

"Do we hafta?" asked Joe, holding a hanky up to his mouth.

"Carl, uh, how often are autopsies performed here?"

He thought for a second, hand on chin, his white lab coat flopped open. "More in the summertime, of course. I'd say a total of eighty to ninety annually, which isn't much, really. Increasingly, they're done up in Boston. Remember though, the rate's two hundred an hour. Comes in handy," he said with a wry grin. "Of course, it's not much fun working with a floater, but then we —"

"Floater?" said Joe weakly. "You mean like . . . a *floater?*"

"Uh-huh. Not a drowning victim . . . a floater. Mostly decomposed. Hard to tell if they're male or female, or even human. And definitely aromatic. But like I was saying, every job has its drawbacks."

We left the hospital and got back into Joe's cruiser. We both had our windows open all the way back, trying to suck in the sea air.

"I quit," I said. "In case you haven't realized by now, I quit."

"Now, c'mon, Doc. There aren't that many. Carl himself said —"

"Listen, it was the only part of med school I hated: cutting up the cadavers in gross anatomy. I swore I'd never do it again. And I'll tell you this, too: the only floater I'm having anything to do with is the *Ella Hatton.*"

"So you're quitting? Before you even start?"

I thought again about what Joe had said about cops sticking together, protecting one of their own. Jack needed all the protection he could get.

"No. I'll stay on and sign the death certificates and things like that. The title gives me some authority and I want it. But I've still got my practice, and it just won't leave me time for autopsies. Sorry about that. So the first heap of stinky meat that comes in, waiting for the knife, it's *goodbye Doc.* Get it?"

"Okay, okay," he said. "Can't say I blame you."

Joe dropped me off in Woods Hole on his way back to Boston.

"I'll be in touch with the lab people who've been examining the evidence from the Breakers and the stuff from the boys' rented house here," he said. "We should have a clearer picture of what took place. The funeral in Providence is tomorrow?"

"Uh-huh, at three. Just can't wait. You going to be there?"

"No. Paul and I are meeting with the D.A.'s office in Boston. So now you're going to try to see Lionel Hartzell?"

"Yep. First thing tomorrow when Moe gets here. I want his diagnostic expertise."

"Well, good luck. Remember, though, you still can't make him see you. How's our boy doing?"

"Jack? He's doing pretty well, considering. Yesterday he went out whale watching with Tom McDonnough, so things can't be that bad."

"But they could be better, right?"

"You said it. Hey, and don't forget to run that car through R and I, okay?"

Joe pulled out his notebook. "White Caddy Eldo. Rhode Island vanity plate, SLINKY. Guy's first name is Eddie. Gotcha. So long."

I found Mary up in our dormitory room, resting after a day of shopping and sightseeing. We poured drinks and relaxed. I showed her the badge.

"Hmmmm. This mean you're going to start wearing a uniform, Charlie? I like uniforms on men. I go to pieces."

"Well, bad news. I stay in civvies."

"You gonna carry a big gun? Huh?"

"You know me, Babe. I'm always packing a big gun."

She sat down on my lap and sipped.

"C'mon now," she said. "Let's not get arrogant."

ELEVEN

I WAS FIRST UP, so I was elected to go down to Water Street and fetch two big cups of coffee back to the dorm. Mary propped herself up on one elbow and looked out the window at the sun.

"Oh, Charlie! I feel great today. I think I'll go running up along Oyster Pond Road with Jackie. It's a good feeling, having grown-up kids when you aren't even old yet."

"Well speak for yourself. For me, fifty's just around the corner."

"You're not old. You're very, very young. You've proved that twice in the past —" she glanced at her watch "— fourteen hours. You hot shit, you."

I sat down at the foot of the bed while she got up. "You mean it wasn't just a dream?"

She had just pulled on her panties. I like that word: panties. They were hip-huggers, of some yellow, slick material that felt good when you ran your hand along it. She leaned over and rubbed my shoulders.

"But the reason you're so good is because *I'm* good. Isn't that right?"

"Sure is. And you've got the press to prove it, too. Didn't I tell you what I saw written over the urinal in the bowling alley last week?"

"Let me guess: 'For a great fuck, call Mary at three-six-nine, eight-four, six-oh.'"

"That's it! Verbatim. Done in red spray paint. And only two misspellings. You're attracting an increasingly literate following, my dear."

"Ahhhh. Good news travels fast." She climbed back on the bed and reclined lazily, stroking her bare thigh and licking her lips, yawning.

"I wish they'd hurry up and get here," she whispered.

"Who?"

"Those bikers. She palmed her hand behind her ear and cocked her head toward the open window. "I can almost hear the rumble of those Harleys now . . ."

"Well, hate to break the spell, but we've got a funeral to attend this afternoon."

She froze, lowered her eyes, and got up and put on her bra. Mary is a knockout. She's also a nurse, a potter, a cook, and a wife and mother. But mainly, she's a knockout. Always will be. That's the part I like best.

"Where are you going?"

"Outside to wait for Moe. I'll be back to take you to lunch before we change and leave. Bye."

I kissed her and left. Ten minutes later I saw Morris Abramson's faded 1974 lime-green Dodge pull into the parking lot. What a car; the blow-lunch special. He hopped out, dressed in khakis and a freshly ironed shirt. Moe can surprise me; he looked almost legit.

"Well, Doc, here I am, ready to meet this nut case."

"How do you know he's a nut case? You haven't even met him yet."

"You told me he was and I believe you."

"Why?"

"Takes one to know one."

We rang the bell at Lionel Hartzell's house. No answer. Three doors down was Jack's place. I couldn't see anybody stirring there, and since it was almost nine, I supposed the boys were out on the briny deep or in a lab somewhere. We rang again, then knocked on the door. Still no answer. I knocked extra loudly.

"Who the hell is it?" said a crusty voice.

"Dr. Charles Adams," I said. And then I added: "With the state police."

"Go away."

"Dr. Hartzell, I'm here on official business. I have to see you about the murder of Andrew Cunningham."

"I already talked to somebody. Go away."

We heard footsteps retreating from the door.

"Now what?" said Moe.

I shrugged, looking down at the badge I'd been waiting to flash. Not having opened the door, Hartzell hadn't even seen it. The badge wasn't worth diddly-shit.

"Let's go wait for him in the office building. It's called Lillie Hall."

So we hoofed it back down Water Street and found Lillie Hall, where we located his office and waited around the corner, sitting on the corridor floor. People walked to and fro, scarcely giving us a glance. After almost an hour I heard quick footsteps coming down the linoleum that stopped where we knew his office door was. I heard a key make its beady metallic noise as it was inserted into a lock, and when the lock clacked I was up on my feet and around the corner, forcing my way through the open door into Hartzell's office, right behind him.

He spun, muttering and throwing his hands up. The man who looked up at me was short and gray-haired, with half-moon, tortoiseshell glasses. His head was large and bulbous at the top, tapering to a small mouth and chin. His eyes were large and dark gray. His face looked a little like the actor Peter Lorre. It was full of fear and rage, the eyes intense, the jaw set. Hartzell looked past me toward the door. Moe had come in right behind me, gently shutting the door and establishing his angular presence between us and the way out.

"Who are you?" he said, panting. "Get out!" For added emphasis, he shoved his attaché case into my gut, as if trying to force me back. No such luck, you little twerp, I thought, and deftly removed the badge from my pants pocket and held it up in front of his face.

"We'll leave shortly. Right after you answer our questions truthfully."

"Were you at my house earlier? I told you then —"

"I know what you told us. Now I'm telling you something; I'm telling you we're staying here until you answer my questions."

"I talked with the police already."

"I know you spoke with my colleague, Lieutenant Keegan. Now you're going to talk to us."

I had used the word "colleague" inadvertently; it just seemed to leap from my mouth. I hoped Keegan wouldn't get wind of it.

"Who's he?" Hartzell asked, pointing to Moe.

"I'll ask the questions for now, Dr. Hartzell. I'm Charles Adams, Jack's father. I'm the interim medical examiner for this region. Since Andy Cunningham died in my house and was my son's friend, you can see my interest in this case, professional and otherwise."

"Jack's father? You're not a cop."

"Oh yes I am," I said quietly. "Now this won't take long, I promise. You can cooperate and we'll be out of here fast. If not, we can only view your failure to cooperate in the worst possible light. Do you understand what I'm saying?"

I could see that he did, and he didn't like it at all. Still glaring at both of us, he turned and walked stiff-legged toward his desk at the far end of the room. The desk was located behind a lab table covered with equipment, including a rack of laboratory glassware that acted as a tall trellis, shielding his work area from view of the doorway. Moe and I followed him into this tiny, encapsulated area. He sat and we stood; there wasn't room for three chairs. I set my badge down on the tabletop and leaned against a cabinet. Hartzell immediately lowered the blinds and adjusted them so that he could see out to the waterfront, but nobody outside could see in. He crossed his legs tightly and crossed his arms over his chest, staring balefully at us.

"Hurry up then. You know, your son is a nice kid. It's a shame I could never say the same about Andy."

"It's well known that the two of you did not get along," I said, staring at him levelly. I wanted to try and unnerve him a bit, to catch him off guard. All I got from him was a shoulder shrug.

"Andy Cunningham was a kid who charmed people, Dr. Adams. But underneath he was spoiled and greedy. I happen to know he stole a major portion of my research notes."

Hartzell pointed to a series of shelves along the near wall. All of them except one were full. He pointed at the empty shelf.

"There! Right there was my folder of rough notes from two-and-a-half years of experimentation. It's now gone; it disappeared two weeks ago. I don't know if you've heard about the nature of my project —"

"Andy mentioned something about extracting precious metals from the ocean by means of a little organism."

He nodded shortly, looking down at his stomach with a frown.

"Yes. Most people here know the general nature of the research," he said. He pointed to a marine tank on the counter whose bottom was covered with small brown bulbous shapes resembling Milk Duds, the caramel candy.

"These are the tunicates called sea squirts," said Hartzell, rapping the glass softly for emphasis. "They have the ability to extract and concentrate various elements from sea water. But exactly *how* they're going to do this for a selected metal is extremely complex . . . and . . . very secret."

"Why are you so certain that Andy took your notes?" I asked.

"Why? Because only he had access to the folder. As for me, I can get along fine without it; I had the raw data transcribed, and it's safe in my possession. That is, I think it's safe. I hope it's safe."

"And so Andy's access to the data makes him automatically guilty," I continued. "Just as, supposedly, Jack's proximity to Andy when he died makes him a suspect." I paused to wag my finger right in front of Hartzell's nose. "I don't like that kind of thinking, Hartzell. I don't care for it at all. Now Andy might have had some character flaws, but he wasn't stupid. Even you would have to admit that. He would certainly realize he would be suspected of the theft immediately. Therefore, one could argue that he didn't take it. Someone else probably took it knowing Andy would take the heat."

"Your reverse logic insults my intelligence, Dr. Adams. I knew the boy well enough to know that underneath he was venal, greedy, and ruthless. Also, he was rude and disrespectful to me."

"It appears, then," I said after a silence, "that you had the strongest possible motives for killing him."

For a second or two, he seemed about to explode. But then he let out his breath in a low hiss and fiddled with the blinds, prying apart the metal slats and peering outside at the people in the street.

"Don't think that I don't know what's really going on," he said. His tone was hushed and menacing. "I know what you're all after."

He sat there looking smug, clasping and unclasping his thick hands.

"What?"

"You know. You all want the fruits of my labor. The results of my research, which will be worth not millions but *billions*. Don't think for an instant I don't know this. The proof of its value is that kid's stealing my rough notes, the crude beginnings of this project, which I was going to discard. It's a shame I didn't. I was careless . . . so careless."

He removed his glasses and rubbed his eyes wearily.

"Professor Hartzell, I want you to know a few things, if you don't already. First, it was I who figured out exactly how Andy was murdered. He was cleverly killed by someone with an intimate knowledge of drugs. He was killed on a day chosen by the murderer, who is somebody in this town. He was killed, you might say, by remote control. The police didn't know this until I told them. I know some more things, too. That's why I'm going to be watching you, Dr. Hartzell, watching you every —"

"Stop it!" he shouted, jumping to his feet. "I won't put up with this anymore. I'm sick to death of having everyone against me. Why should brilliance be hounded, eh? This is supposedly the best laboratory of its kind in the world. So why am I hounded just because everyone wants to get rich off my efforts, eh? Answer me that!"

"Nobody's trying to get rich off you, or steal your research either."

"Don't say that. Don't you ever say that! What do you know about what goes on here? Believe me, I know. I have ways of knowing about the people here, and I won't put up with it. I'm sick to death of this eavesdropping —"

He poked at the blinds again, peering outside, sweeping his eyes back and forth at the people on the sidewalk and the lawn.

"Dr. Hartzell, I've got one more question to ask you," I said, leaning against a counter.

"I may answer it; I may not. And I don't care what you try to do to me. I'm tough, in case you haven't noticed."

"Before he died, Andy mentioned something curious that's just come back to me. He said that last Friday you insisted that he stay in the lab and finish up a project, despite the storm warnings and the fact that he and Jack were going to drive up to Eastham. You recall that?"

"No," he said shortly, with a half-smile on his face, obviously wishing to terminate the interview.

"Let me refresh your memory. You insisted he stay in the lab, but you left for an hour on what you called a 'personal errand.' What was that errand, and where did you go?"

"The boy lied; I didn't leave the lab."

I leaned back and crossed my arms over my chest.

"You stick with that statement? Under oath?"

"I'll do what I damn well please. Now leave."

"Because I have a witness who saw you driving around during the hour in question. You were seen driving toward Andy's house."

"I was not! I was going home!"

"So you *were* on an errand."

"Get out. Get out!"

Sensing the interview was at an end, Moe and I departed. As we left, the door slammed behind us and we heard the bolt slide into place.

"Whew!" said Moe as we descended the stairs and went outside into the fresh air. We walked down to the little beach right in front of Lillie Hall and watched a big black Lab frolicking in the shallows. He ran up to us with a stick of driftwood in his mouth, wagging his tail and flipping water everywhere.

"You big dummy," I said. He sat down and pawed at my leg, his tail carving a shallow crescent in the sand as it wagged. I threw the stick out as far as I could and he dove in after it. I turned to Moe, who was picking up shells.

"Well, Dr. Abramson?"

"Well, I think da guy's a classic. A textbook case: paranoid schizophrenic. At least from the outward signs. It's unprofessional to make a thumbnail diagnosis like dat. But he's got the signs.

Notice the office? The lab tables all pushed up around the desk, as if to protect it? The drawn blinds? The peeking out at the people who he says are spying on him? And the delusions, the feelings of persecution? They're all there. I'd say he's the one to watch. By the way, was that true about his leaving the lab last Friday?"

"According to Andy. And you heard him admit it. Tom McDonnough was the witness, and it'll be easy to check with him. Now wouldn't an hour be enough time to go to the boys' house, find the pill dispenser, and switch the capsules? Hartzell knew where Andy was at the time, and he knew Jack was out on the ocean. Tom saw him from his car on the way to somewhere. Hartzell could have found the house empty and made the switch, knowing Andy would self-destruct over the weekend, leaving him in the clear —"

"Yeah . . . and protecting his precious research data from prying eyes."

"Notice how it scared him?"

"Uh-huh. By the way, Doc, you were ruthless in there. You seem to have caught on real quick. Does carrying a badge change a guy dat fast?"

"I guess so, I — hey! Oh shit!"

"What's wrong?"

"I can't find my damn badge, Moe," I said, feeling around in my pockets. "I must have left it in Hartzell's office on the table."

"Well, something tells me you're gonna have a hard time going back in there and getting it back. No?"

I said nothing, watching the black dog pumping back through the water, stick in mouth and panting hard.

"I think you're right," I said finally, catching a glance over my shoulder at the impressive brick bulk of Lillie Hall, "and I think Joe's going to be pissed."

An hour after Moe left for his office back in Concord, our sorry little procession wound its way down to Providence for the funeral of Andrew Cunningham. The Adams family went in Mary's Audi. Behind us, Tom McDonnough and Terry and Alice Henderson rode in the Hendersons' big Buick. There are many in-

stances on life's bumpy road when I wish I could push a button
and magically advance the time by two or three hours. Most of
my patients tell me that's the way they feel about visiting me. Gee
Doc, they tell me, when I've got an eleven o'clock appointment
with you, I just wish all of a sudden it would be twelve-thirty. You
know?

Sure I know. That's what gets me down so much about my job.
And going to kids' funerals isn't exactly my idea of a high time,
either. We found the church, parked, and walked up the stone
steps together. Andy's parents, Paula and Boyd Cunningham,
were standing up at the top to meet us. There they were, standing up near the door, their faces blank with grief. Ohhh, boy.
The position I never, ever want to be in. I kept looking at Boyd
Cunningham all the way up those steps. Gray, pale, and thin.
The very life knocked out of him. I remembered hugging Jack
the night Andy died. Hugging and crying a little because he is so
precious to me. And the Cunninghams, busting their asses all
these past twenty years for their only kid. Good God . . .

The service ended at three-twenty. The forty-odd people filed
out of St. Joan of Arc Church and went to their cars for the ride
to the cemetery and the burial. Hey, folks, the fun never stops.

The burial was mercifully brief. But then came the part I really
dreaded: the home visit. And for us it was obligatory, of that
there was no doubt. Now where's my magic button? Just push it
and pow, it's five-thirty and time for cocktails.

Both parents were still in shock, and sat immobile, eyes un-
focused, their skin ashen gray. Boyd, as handsome as his son had
been, drummed his fingers on his forehead and temple.

"So hard to get used to. I still can't believe it. So hard —"

Then he swallowed fast several times, and started to break
down again. Mary hugged him tight and talked to him. I stood
around like a heron in the Sahara, hating myself and not knowing what to do about it. Hating myself because I had two sons,
and they were both alive, and his only son was dead, and it wasn't
fair. I was so glad my boys were fine, but it was so unfair I
couldn't help hating myself, as if I had cheated at a game and left
poor Boyd Cunningham in ruins. I found it terribly hard to face
him. Jack consoled Paula, and I went back and forth between the

stricken parents, doing the best I could. My patients tell me I've got a good bedside manner. The bedside manner I can cultivate; it's the graveside manner I'm not so hot at.

Finally, it was time to go. We walked down the modest front stoop and went over to the car. Boyd had walked us out. He summoned Jack and me to stand on each side of him. He put his trembling arms around us and said in a low voice: "I heard it was murder. The detective told me he thought it was murder, and that you, Dr. Adams, discovered it. Is this true?"

"Yes. We think so, Boyd," I said.

"Well, that's awful. Who could have done that? The detective said he was sure it was somebody at the laboratory. Is that right?"

"We just don't know at this point. Jack's even a suspect."

"We all know better than that," he said. "And listen, I'm going to keep my eyes and ears open, all the time. And if you hear anything about who might have done it, you let me know, hear? Because I just can't —"

He couldn't continue, so we all hugged him again, giving our word we'd stay in touch and help in any way possible, and left.

So we rode back in the car, watching the green world slip by, not saying a word. Tony — a.k.a. the Condom Kid — was driving. Nice of him, and appropriate, since he was less emotionally wrecked than the rest of us. Mary and I sat together in back, holding hands in silence.

"Tony, can you turn the air up a notch?" I asked. He flipped the switch and the cool air came rushing over me. I leaned my head back and closed my eyes, trying to doze. It didn't work.

"Hey Jackie," said Mary, "who was that tall kid with glasses who came up to you after the service? Is he from Woods Hole, or what?"

"Him? Oh, I kinda forget. He's some nerdy guy who works over at the USGS warehouse, I think. I was surprised to see him there. I didn't even think he knew Andy. Is that cool enough for you, Dad?"

I said it was fine. Then Mary asked for music, and Jack put on a Handel tape. I let my mind wander then, and didn't wake up until we were back at Swope Dorm.

"Look Charlie, the DeGroots are here," said Mary, shaking me gently out of my sleep. We walked up toward the dorm and saw them both sitting on the grass, waiting for us. We hiked to the room, Jim carrying a jug with a spigot on the bottom of it.

"You want a G and T, Doc?"

"Do I ever. And so does Mary. How long you guys been here?"

"About an hour. We heard you were all down in Providence for the funeral. Too bad. Joe's here too; we saw his car pull in here a while ago. He's out walking around somewhere. Said he'd be right back."

So we went up to our room and wrapped ourselves around big gin and tonics. The DeGroots reported on their cruise, and we talked about places and harbors we knew. Joe entered shortly afterwards, looking glum. He made himself a drink and went over and hugged Mary and Jack.

"Hey," she said. "Weren't you coming down tomorrow? Why so early? An extra day off, or what?"

"No. I have to tell you something. Doc too. So let's sit down and get comfortable for a second."

I didn't like the vibes I was getting from him. First of all, why was he walking around while waiting for us to return? Joe doesn't like to hike; he only paces around when he's upset or nervous. And then telling us he had an announcement to make. Uh-oh . . .

I saw Joe "freshen up" his drinkie. The way Joe makes his G and Ts, it was a little like "freshening up" Lake Erie. He wasn't smiling, but was doing his level best to look happy. Something was up. I didn't know exactly what was headed our way, winging its way toward us like a poisoned spear, but I knew I wanted to jump out of the way, and fast. We all sat down, and then Joe came forward and spoke softly.

"What it is, is I just came from the D.A.'s office with Paul Keegan —" He looked at Jack. "The lab reports all came back, from your room at the Breakers and from your house in town here. The upshot is, Jack, that your prints are all over Andy's pill case and the bottle of meds. But we knew that . . ."

We all shifted around in the silence.

"The bad news is, there are no other prints there, except Andy's."

"Well so what, godammit!" cried Mary. "Who else was up at the cottage, anyway?"

Joe held up his hand and continued in a soft voice, with a tone that was soothing and words that definitely weren't.

"Mary, the D.A. just thinks he can't let it go, that's all. He says we've got to take Jack up there for a statement."

"And what else?" I said, getting to my feet.

"And see . . . and see if they want to call a grand jury."

We all sat, stunned.

"And, uh, so Paul and I had a little talk, and we —"

"I'm sick of hearing about Paul Keegan, that son —"

"No Mary, he's in our corner, believe me. I know. We all discussed it, Paul, the D.A., and I. I told them if it was okay with your mom and dad, Jackie, I'd take you up with me tonight and have you stay with me at my place, and then we can go in there early tomorrow and get it over with."

Mary, fighting tears, said we were all going together. Joe went over and put his hand on her shoulder.

"I know that's what you want. But believe me, it'll be easier and quicker this way. They just want a statement, that's all, before the judge. I'm sure, as sure as I'm sitting here, that day after tommorrow we'll all be back down here together with Jack off the hook, okay?"

Okay? *Okay?* What the hell did he mean, okay?

I went over to the window and opened it wide. The cool, tangy sea breeze wafted in. I breathed in deep to steady myself. From over behind the buildings of MBL, from Great Harbor, I heard a familiar sound from a ship I couldn't see.

Ah-OOOOOOOOOOOOOOOOOOOOO (wee)!

One long blast. In ship talk, it said: *I am about to depart . . .*

I looked over at Jack.

"God help us," I whispered to myself.

Mayday . . . Mayday . . .

TWELVE

I SAT UP IN BED. Mary was purring away beside me. I leaned over and pecked her on the cheek. She didn't stir, and I could smell that sweet vapor of beverage alcohol. My watch said three-thirty. In the company of the DeGroots, we'd really put down the Destroyer after Joe and Jack had pulled away in Joe's car. The party didn't end until after one, if such a glum gathering could be called a party. I sighed, tasting the dry, metallic taste of old booze and pipe smoke. Not good. I smacked my lips. What did I want? First of all, to brush my teeth. And I was hungry. I thought about that cold ham aboard the *Hatton*. The iced Hackerbrau. And what about the coffee I'd ground fresh before we'd left the dock up in Wellfleet? And those Jamaican cigars Moe had given me? They were probably getting stale by the minute. A ham and cheese sandwich with plenty of Dijon mustard, with ice-cold beer, followed by a cup of strong, steaming java. And a cigar to top it off . . .

In the near darkness, I scanned the small dormitory room. Nice beds and bathroom, but otherwise none of the creature comforts. And the dock at Eel Pond was just outside the back door of Swope. Barely thirty yards away. I crept out of bed, went into the john, and brushed my teeth. Massive improvement. Massive. I slipped into shorts, a knit shirt, and sockless dock shoes. I left a note on the bathroom counter telling Mary I was down at the boat. In all likelihood, I'd return before she woke up. But if I didn't, she'd worry. And when Mary worries, she frets. And when she frets, she steams. And so on.

I left the room, went down the silent carpeted hallway, downstairs, and out into the dark. Tiny droplets of cold dew stung my ankles as I walked over the grass. Light danced faintly on the dark water of the pond in shimmers and wavy lines. A pair of mallards, hearing my footsteps on the wooden dock, muttered and splashed out in the middle somewhere. The sailboats with their tall masts appeared still; there was no metallic pranging of halyards. The powerboats, cruisers, and lobster boats sat hunkered down low in the dark. Out toward the middle of Eel Pond I could see the bright topsides of Jim DeGroot's sport fisherman, the *Whimsea*. I walked onto the dock and out to the end, where the *Hatton* was made fast. After jumping down into the wide, shallow cockpit, I unlocked the companionway hatch and crept inside. Flicking on the cabin light, which temporarily blinded me, I took an iced beer from the cooler and retrieved the hunk of ham, which I sliced thin and piled onto chewy rye bread. Rather than light the alcohol stove in the galley, I decided to make the coffee with the tiny camping stove we use in the cockpit when the boat is berthed. I set this up in the cockpit, turned out the cabin lights, and sat in the darkness with my beer and sandwich, watching the stove's bright blue flame underneath the percolator, which was beginning to purr and buzz with the heat.

I heard the ducks coming closer, quacking softly. Then they were right alongside the boat, begging. I went below and got some bread, which I broke up and dropped on the water for them, their bills clacking and sputtering as they ate.

Funny, but I thought I heard another faint sound behind me, a sound like a screen door shutting. I turned, listening intently, but all was quiet. So I returned to the percolator, now bubbling merrily away. At my back I heard a faint splash. Turning around again, I saw nothing. I finished my beer and poured the first cup of coffee. No, I wasn't imagining it; there was a measured muffled splashing, a regular flip of water approaching from the middle of the pond behind me. More ducks? Perhaps a lone swan? Who knew what the —

"*Pssst! . . . Doc!*"

I turned again to see a long, pale shape sliding through the dark water toward my boat. As it grew closer, I could see the rhythmic stroking of the arms, and heard the raspy sputter of the swimmer's breath.

"Jim? Jim, is that you?" I called in a whisper. But he couldn't hear me because his head was underwater. So I'd just go below and get another mug for him. Or did he want a beer? Knowing Jim, it would be a be —

"Hiya, hunk," said a soft voice at the gunwale. Not Jim.

I looked over the side at Janice as she flipped her head, sending spray from her long hair to get it out of her eyes. She was wearing a light-colored bathing suit. Was it one piece, or two?

"What are you doing here?" I asked.

"Going for a swim; what's it look like? I was sitting out on deck — couldn't sleep — and I saw your cabin light go on. Permission to come aboard, Captain?"

"Well, I don't know. I think maybe —"

But her hands came up with another splash and grabbed the cockpit combing. Her grip slipped a bit, and she held one hand up and waved it.

"C'mon muscles, give a hand."

I took her hand and pulled her halfway up. She put one leg over the combing, and was perched for an instant, half over the boat, half over the pond, and I got a good look at her in the faint light. Uh-oh.

"Janice!"

"What? Oh, c'mon, Doc. Don't tell me you've never been skinny-dipping."

"Yeah, but not with strangers."

"So I'm a stranger, huh? Well I like that."

"You know what I mean. Look Janice, I don't like this. I mean, what if somebody came along and —"

"Oh bullshit," she said softly, and began to ease over the gunwale, heading for the cockpit. I released my grip on her arm, and she fell back into the pond with a loud splash.

"Thanks a lot!" she sputtered.

"Shhhhhhh! You'll wake everybody up," I said in a hoarse whisper.

"C'mon. It's four in the morning, who's gonna know?"

"Jim, for one. Mary, for another. There's two good ones for starters. I'm not taking you aboard, Janice; I'm afraid of what might happen."

"Fraidy cat, fraidy cat," she teased in a soft, purring voice. "Doc is a fraidy cat —"

She treaded water, right off my transom. I could see her arms fanning out, and the pale, squiggly lines of her legs working to keep her head up.

"Gee, Doc, this makes me feel so young. Makes me feel like I'm back in high school or something. I jus — hey, what's that?"

"What's what? I don't hear anything."

There was silence, broken only by the sputter and quacking of the feeding mallards. Then a soft voice sang out:

"*Chaaaaarlie?* Charlie, are you out there?"

My blood froze in my veins. Then I was half-standing, half-crouching in the wide, shallow cockpit, looking down the dock and past it to the dimly lighted dormitory building. A dark figure was padding across the grass . . . coming out onto the dock now. Oh Jesus . . .

"Charlie?" came the calling whisper again. I was wishing I were someplace else now. The Ross Ice Shelf would do nicely.

I heard Mary's cork-soled sandals on the wooden pier, thumping closer and closer.

Janice stopped treading water. "Oh shit —" I heard her say to herself. Then she took in a deep breath, like those women in Japan who dive for sponges, and went under. In the dim light, I could see, for a millisecond only, the sight I had so longed for all these years: her round, luscious, plump rump, wet and shiny, as it broke the pond surface. After her dive, I saw a faint luminescence, a long pale shape, sliding beneath the water toward the middle of the pond. I then turned to see Mary approaching the *Hatton*.

"Couldn't sleep either, I see. Is there any more coffee?"

"Sure. Almost a whole pot. You want a sandwich too?"

"No. I want a beer too, I guess. And do you have any aspirin aboard?"

We sat together on the cushions, sipping the hot, strong coffee.

I lighted a cigar and, between puffs, kept glancing back over the stern. No doubt Janice had already surfaced for breath a few times and was now back behind *Whimsea*, out of sight, climbing back aboard. Close call.

"What was that splash a second ago? A fish jumping, or what?"

"A fish for sure. Place is lousy with fish."

"Why was it so loud? Must've been a big fish, huh?"

"Very big. This pond holds some of the biggest fish around."

"Then why do they call it Eel Pond?"

"Eels are fish. Long, skinny fish."

"Are you nervous, Charlie?"

"Huh? 'Course not." I glanced around again. Boy, she was a quiet swimmer. I had heard no noise at all.

"Charlie, I know the reason we're not sleeping. We're thinking about Jackie up there. Is he in a jail cell?"

"No. Remember what Joe said? He's under the direct recognizance of an officer of the law. He's in Joe's safekeeping. They're up in Joe's apartment right this instant, sawing logs after a big home-cooked meal. I bet Joe cooked lasagna. Or maybe manicotti."

"I just hope Jackie's all right. Charlie? Do you think the judge will be satisfied with Jackie's statement? Or will he call a grand jury? And if he does, do you think they'll . . . *puthiminjail?*"

The last four words ran together fast, in a tiny voice that squeaked with fright. Mary clenched her teeth and made the strangled throat sounds of a bursting sob. I put my arms around her and held her tight while she cried.

But after about thirty seconds I let her go, my gaze looking skyward. Why had I let her go? What was . . .?

. . . no noise at all . . .

I jumped up, leaving Mary stunned on the seat cushions. I stood up and looked over the pond. All was still and dark. The water showed not a ripple in the night.

"Janice?" I called.

No answer. No noise at all.

"Charlie! You'll wake them up! What the —"

"Janice!" I shouted. "Janice!"

I kicked off my shoes and dove in, skimming the bottom, looking for her.

THIRTEEN

BRIGHT AND EARLY next morning I was down at Eel Pond aboard the catboat, going over NOAA Nautical Chart #13230, *Buzzards Bay*. I had the big chart spread out on the cabin top and weighted down against the breeze with smooth beach rocks.

I was going out for a day cruise. I wanted be alone, away from Woods Hole and especially Swope Dormitory. It would be evening before we heard any word from Joe up in Boston, and Mary was on the warpath. I was irritable, uneasy, and in a bad temper generally. I don't like being blamed for things I haven't done.

As it turned out, Janice DeGroot, the Midnight Mermaid, had been in no danger of drowning the previous night. She was fine, having swum back to the *Whimsea* silently as a wraith after her surface dive into the dark pond. But I thought she was in trouble, and so jumped in after her. And so spilled the beans. And so got in Dutch with Mary, and so on.

And now Jim and Mary were furious with both of us, mainly because Jim discovered his wife's bathing suit was bone dry and made the logical inference. I even got a little lecture from Tony on sexual mores. *Tony*, mind you. The guy who toted around enough rubbers to supply the Brazilian navy. Is there no justice?

Nope. Hard cheese, old chap.

And soon, my son Jack was going before a judge to make his statement. It was now eight-thirty. I'd be back by one or two at the latest.

"Where you going?" asked a voice behind me. I turned and looked up at Tony, who was standing on the dock watching me.

"Over to the Vineyard for an hour or so, then back. I just want to get away from here for a few hours."

"Yeah. Don't blame you."

"There really was nothing going on, you know."

"Yeah, I guess. But see, Dad, Mom caught you with Mrs. De-Groot before. Remember that time in the phone booth when we had that big party and —"

"Yeah yeah yeah yeah. I remember. Who could forget?"

"You left that time, too. You went all the way to North Carolina."

"Uh-huh. Well, events have a way of, uh, snowballing sometimes. All I'm going to do now is just slide over to Vineyard Haven for the morning until your Mom cools down a bit."

"Aren't you even going to say goodbye?"

I shrugged my shoulders. "Who knows? I'll tell you, sport, I don't like being accused of things I haven't done. And I don't like Mom not believing me. And I don't like Janice getting me into trouble. I guess with this mess Jack's in it's just . . . it's just too, too much right now. Know what I mean?"

"Uh-huh. Can I come along?"

"Well, sure. But, hey! Don't you have to work?"

He jumped aboard and joined me on the cabin top.

"They just called me and said they were laying me off. The place was damaged in the storm and they're having to close part of the inn for repairs, so they don't need a full staff."

"Well," I sighed, "ordinarily, that wouldn't be good news. But the way things have been shaping up here, it'll be good having the family as close as possible."

"That's what Mom said. Deep down, does she believe you? Does she believe you weren't skinny-dipping with Janice?"

"Who knows. I hope she does. But let's face it, chum, it doesn't look good. I seem to have a knack for getting myself into messes like this one. I hope that neither you nor Jack have inherited this unseemly quirk."

"Naw, don't worry. We're not *that* stupid."

I did my best to ignore this little barb, hunkering down over the chart and pretending to study crosscurrents, eddies, and tidal rips. But the little sucker stung, that was a fact.

"And I hate to admit it, but you're right, Tony. Mom's having trouble believing me because Mrs. DeGroot and I have been in this situation before. The phone booth episode, as you have correctly recalled. So you see, I've queered my reputation with her, and now I have to pay for it. You listening to this? Okay. There's a lesson to be learned here, son: don't get a bad reputation. In sex, in financial matters, in sportsmanship, business, or — hey! Where're you going?"

He had jumped back up onto the dock. Looking past him, towards the campus road, I saw a succulent young thing in faded cutoffs and a cotton sweater strolling along the pond walk. From behind, she looked wonderful. Tony called to her, and she turned. Even better. Her eyes lit up in a smile and they walked off together. Oh well, I thought, you can lead a horse to water . . .

"Be right back!" he yelled as they walked off together.

I plotted a tentative course in my head and started the little diesel engine and let it warm up, staring down at the chart. I'd better be careful there around East Chop, I thought to myself, and before that, watch myself around Great Ledge.

"*Going someplace?*" said a husky voice above me that was cold as ice. Gee, who could that be?

I looked up to see Mary standing there with her hair pulled back, dark glasses on (those French mountain-climber jobs that cost seventy bucks), snug white canvas shorts, and a small white halter. The white clothes looked positively iridescent against her deep brown skin. Looking good. But not so hot in the personality department.

"So where the hell do you think *you're* going?" she repeated.

"Tony and I are going over to the Vineyard. I assume it's a stupid question to ask if you'd like to come along?"

"You're going over to the Vineyard with our son in custody on a murder charge? Swell, Charlie. Just terrific."

I could tell by her tone that this promised to be an extended engagement. I wished Tony would come back so it would end.

"You really going over to the Vineyard? You were going without me, without even saying goodbye?" She hopped down into the cockpit.

"No, I guess I was going to say goodbye, directly or indirectly."

"Well you'd better be back by three. That's when Joe's calling."

I nodded. She propped up the sunglasses on her head and looked at me hard and level with those big obsidian eyes.

"Tell me, Charlie, and no screwing around. As God is your witness, did you touch Janice last night?"

"As God is my witness, and on my immortal soul — if, by remote chance, such a thing exists — I swear I did not touch her."

She leaned forward and planted a wet one on me. Felt great.

"And how about any other time? Did you tou —"

"Uh! Uh! Uh! Uh! You only get one question."

"Bullshit; I get all the questions I want."

"If you tell me about the Old Days, I'll tell you everything. Deal?"

She pondered this awhile, and shook her head sadly. "No, Charlie. I mean, it's very personal, and happened a long time ago. It's true Mexico was involved. And those gold trains and cattle drives. The men coming down from the mountains, riding those stallions, their spurs jingling. Saddle lean, rock hard, and dark. And very, very horny . . ."

"Mary!"

She gave her shoulders a big shrug. "Hey, sorry. What can I say?"

She went back up onto the dock and began walking back. She walked with a soft, swinging glide. Saddle lean . . . rock hard . . . dark . . . and very, very —

"Where are you going?" I shouted after her.

"Well," she said without turning around, "I was thinking of Mexico. But I guess I'll stay here until you two get back." She walked to the end of the dock, then turned and faced me.

"Remember: three o'clock."

A few minutes later, Tony returned and said he was ready to depart. We cast off, and within minutes, we'd cleared the tiny drawbridge and were out in the passage again. Then we left Juniper Point behind and were heading out to West Chop, the island of Martha's Vineyard a big, purplish mound on the horizon.

"How do you think Mom's doing?" I asked the young, bronzed helmsman as he took the *Hatton* into a slight heel, the spray breaking over the gunwale on the leeward side. "Your mother, otherwise known as Tampico Belle?"

"Huh? Tampico Belle?"

"Just a joke," I said, adjusting the jib sheet. "I *think*."

Despite the good southwest wind, it took us over an hour to get to Vineyard Haven. We were bucking the tail end of an ebb tide running against the wind off West Chop and the water was "lumpy," as they say. So we scooted around between the dual lighthouses at West Chop and East Chop, fighting all that fast water, then going into the inner harbor and looking for a roost behind the breakwater. There was none; the place was filled. So we tacked back out past the breakwater and anchored in the wide outer harbor, where the wash from ferryboats and big yachts kept us gently pitching.

Tony said he was hungry and asked me if I'd ever been to the Black Dog Tavern. I said no, observing that it sounded like something out of *Treasure Island*. We decided to go there for lunch, motoring over to the beach just north of the steamer wharf. We hit the sand running, centerboard up, and jumped out, hauling *Hatton*'s bow up onto the beach as far as we could. As we landed, I had a vision of myself as a high school kid up in Frankfort, Michigan, sailing with luscious Patty Froelich over to the far end of Crystal Lake and beaching the sailboat on a deserted stretch of sand near the town of Beulah. There was nobody there but us. The sand was hot in the sun, but cool underneath the pines and sumac bushes. We gave each other back rubs, then she took down the top of her one-piece, black Jantzen suit — the kind with the flap of cloth called the modesty panel in front, so her good, Catholic crotch couldn't be seen — so I could rub her better. Which I did. Then we were both naked. I remembered how white her skin looked where her tan stopped. And how cold her skin was where the wet suit had been. I got on top of her and kissed her . . . Seventeen years old . . .

"What's going on?" asked Tony as we walked up the bluff to town. "Why are you grinning like that?"

"Oh . . . nothing. I was just thinking about something that happened a long time ago, when I was around your age."

"Yeah? *Must've* been a long time ago."

Shut up, kid, I thought as we padded up the beach toward town.

Tony and I had a fun time on the island. We rented bicycles and rode the slow, tree-lined curves of the quiet place. It sure was a refreshing change from the clogged highways of the Cape, which are nearly bumper-to-bumper all summer long. I wore a happy face, but inside I was anxious. I had a bad feeling about what was happening up in Boston at the courthouse. I regretted we hadn't gone up there with them, but Joe had been adamant in saying that it was a private affair, and we weren't allowed into the chambers no matter what. It was just a sworn deposition in front of a judge and stenographer. I would feel better after his phone call. A little after one we returned to the boat, hoisted sail, and started back.

Mary must have been watching Eel Pond because she was at the dock to meet us as soon as we tied up.

"I wanted to say I'm sorry, Charlie, for getting mad at you. I guess this thing with Jackie has me on edge. I had a long talk with Janice after you left. She swore on a stack of Bibles that nothing happened."

"'Course not. I told you the truth."

"I know you did. I remembered something. You wrote me a note last night and left it near the bathroom sink. That's how I knew where to find you."

"Uh-huh."

"Well, I figure if you had planned that meeting with Janice, you wouldn't have left me a note telling me the meeting place, would you?"

"I wouldn't think so, Mare. That sounds even dumber than usual."

"Oh, honey, I'm so sorry."

"This mean I can come back into your room now?"

"Yes. And I — hey! I forgot. Look what I found in our room when I came back before lunch time —"

She took a manila envelope out of her handbag and handed it to me. I opened it and out slid my badge and wallet. I looked at them in disbelief. The badge had been mutilated, struck repeatedly with, it appeared, a ball-peen hammer. The state seal and the lettering, which were done in enamel, were all chipped and cracked. The badge had been ruined, deliberately. And the leather folder had been burned. I turned it around and around in my hands. Somebody had soaked the leather in a flammable substance, maybe lighter fluid, and then set it ablaze.

"You didn't tell me you'd lost it," said Mary. "And what do you suppose happened to it?"

"What happened? Lionel Hartzell was angry with me and he mutilated it, that's what. Oh boy, wait till Joe sees this. And Keegan, too. If this doesn't incriminate him, I don't know what will. You found it in our room?"

"Uh-huh. After I saw you off I went for a drive, then returned to the dorm just before lunch time to shower. It was right there on the carpet inside the door."

"Hartzell must have slid it under the door. Good God, Mary, he's a sickie, all right."

But that wasn't the only treat in store for us that Friday. Joe and Jack showed up before three, when the phone call was supposed to come through. As they got out of Joe's cruiser, I knew right away the news was bad. Joe stood solemnly, his eyes on the ground in front of him. Jack wore the face of the condemned. Mary ran out with me, her hands clutched into pale fists. Joe let us get up close to him before he shook his head. And then we knew for sure.

"No, no, Doc. Your going up there wouldn't have changed anything, believe me. It was over in a minute, and not a goddamn thing we could have done about it. Jake Schermerhorn, the guy your pal, Brady Coyne, found for us, is the best attorney around, too. It's just that it's murder one, Doc. Hell, the judge said he just didn't have a choice but to call the grand jury. He had no out, and I realize that now . . ."

Mary thumped her fist on the roof of Joe's car, then rested her head on the fist, crying.

"And will they indict?" I asked.

"Probably," he said in a deadpan voice. "They'll indict and set a trial date. Which means we've got to come up with another lead or suspect pronto to keep Jack out of the hot seat. I'm sorry."

"You knew, didn't you?" said Mary, looking up at her brother with tear-stained cheeks. "Goddamn you, Joey, you knew before you even left —"

He shook his head, slowly and sadly.

"No Mare. But I had a feeling. The evidence — the evidence at this point anyway — is just too overwhelming. I thought if you were there you might have, well, blown your cool and the judge would have —"

"You're goddamn fucking right I would have blown my cool! What do you think I —"

I put my arm around her, trying to steer her back to the dorm. But it was like trying to steer a mustang. Her emotional fit proved one thing, if nothing else: Joe's instincts about her being anywhere near the courtroom were correct.

The Adams family sat together for an hour in the room. Jack said that on the way up to Boston his uncle had prepared him for the reality of the situation.

"But everybody knows and likes this Jake Schermerhorn, Dad," said Jack, sitting on the edge of the bed, opening and closing his hands, trying to be upbeat. "Everybody's got a lot of respect for him. You remember what Brady Coyne had to say about him."

"I'm not doubting any of that. It's just the ... whole thing. Hey, I forgot —"

I hauled out the mutilated badge and folder and showed them to Joe, who's face wore a look of horror as he examined it.

"Holy shit. Have you touched the metal?"

"Not much."

"Let's get it dusted for prints, then," he said, carefully folding it up and putting it back in the envelope. "This might be the break we've been looking for. I think old Hartzell's just given himself away. You say Moe was on the interview with you? That's good. That's great, in fact. We can use a witness, especially a practicing shrink."

"That's why I took him along."

"Has he seen this?"

"No. But he's going down to the cottage tomorrow; we loaned him a key. When we go up to meet him there let's take it with us."

"No, we'll just tell him about it; I want this in a lab right away. By the way, Paul and I have located our friend in the big white car. Slinky's real name is Edward Falcone. And he is connected. A low-echelon Wiseguy from Providence. We do a lot of work with the Providence law enforcement people, as you can imagine. We'll have Slinky up here before long to question. But what you and I are going to do right now is find Lionel Hartzell."

We left the dorm and went over to his house. Not there. Went to his office. Same result. Asked for his whereabouts at the administration office in the restored building on Water Street called the Candle House. Drew a blank. Nobody knew where Hartzell was hiding. And Art Hagstrom, we remembered, was out of town, gone to a conference at the Jersey Shore.

"Let's go back to his place," said Joe. "I might even pick the friggin' lock. I know he's hiding somewhere."

"But where? Remember what the lady said: he's a loner. He could be anywhere."

"We'll track him down. Hey, are you sure you left the badge in his office?"

"Positive."

"You couldn't have dropped it on the way out?"

"I don't see how; I missed it right after the interview."

"Hmmn. Well, maybe it's God telling you that you shouldn't have done that interview, Doc. I know Keegan will be pissed."

"Fuck Keegan."

"Hey, don't say that. You should have seen him in the chambers. He's on our side. Hard to believe sometimes, but true. Boy oh boy, I wonder what Joe Kenny would think."

"Who's Joe Kenny?"

"The retired cop who gave me this badge folder. Remember? I wonder what he'd think if he saw it now."

"I know what he'd think. He'd think Lionel Hartzell is a weird, vindictive son of a bitch who should be locked up."

We went back to the Hartzell residence. Joe decided not to pick the lock.

"Anything against regulations could blow the whole thing," he said. "Let's try again tomorrow. We'll find him sooner or later."

So we returned to the dorm and girded our collective loins to make the best of a bad situation. We went to dinner at a nice restaurant up the road, the Coonamessett Inn, and it buoyed our spirits. With Jim and Janice gone back to Boston, we had a pleasant, if subdued, family evening. The next day was Saturday, and we were heading back to the Breakers.

"Doc? Moe."

"Jeez, what time it it?"

"Seven-thirty. I'm here at the cottage."

"Already? What time did you leave?"

"Five-thirty. You told me it was the best way to beat the traffic. Listen: hold tight; I've got something to tell you."

Good Christ, I thought to myself, not again. Why is this bad tape playing over and over again? Can't somebody switch it?

"Doc?"

"Yeah, what is it?"

"Your cottage has been broken into. I opened the front door and walked into a total mess."

I rolled over in bed, holding the receiver to my head.

"Doc?"

"I'm still here."

"Sorry to have to tell you this."

"Next to the other news I've been getting, it's not too bad. Does it look as if they took a lot of stuff?"

"If you mean stuff like televisions and appliances, no. It looks more like somebody was just searching for something."

"Who is it, Charlie?" said Mary, who had her eyes open and was propping herself up on her elbow.

"Moe. The cottage has been burglarized. Ransacked, just like Jack's house."

"Sweet Jesus," she moaned, and pulled the pillow over her head.

"Listen Moe, stay there and don't touch anything. Call the Eastham police and ask for Officer David Klewski. You won't have to give him directions; he knows the way by heart."

Within twenty minutes we were heading back up to Eastham. Joe followed us in his cruiser. Since it was Saturday, the traffic on Route 6 was a perfect horror. Still, I was remarkably at ease. For one thing, the news didn't involve a family member directly. Secondly, I couldn't help but think that this second break-in, clearly committed while we were all away, would divert some of the heat away from Jack. Joe agreed. But be careful, Adams, a voice in my head said, every time you think things are looking up, another bombshell arrives.

A little after ten we rolled into the driveway of the Breakers to see Moe coming out the front door with Officer David Klewski, who I bet was sick of visiting the Adams cottage. The cop came forward and leaned into my driver's window.

"When it rains, it pours, eh Dawktah?"

"Do tell. Moe, give us a tour."

It was not a happy one. The crooks had come in through the back door, on the ocean side, where they would be invisible from the road. They'd smashed a pane in the door and reached in and unlocked it. No room had been spared, including the crawl space beneath the cottage where the beach furniture and Sunfish sailboats were stored. All the bedrooms, the kitchen, and the living room were tossed. Debris and our prized possessions were all over the floors. We had a good fix on when it happened, because our neighbors who take the mail in for us had checked the place Friday morning, and it was still intact. It was my initial suspicion that this was the handiwork of the same thugs who'd trashed Jack and Andy's house in Woods Hole, but it certainly was not as neat a job. Simply looking at the kitchen, with the strewn pots and pans and broken crockery, told me the search had been quick and noisy.

"Well, dat figures, Doc," observed the sagacious Morris Abramson. "I mean, in the center of town, dey hadda be pretty quiet, ya know? But here on the beach, wit' nobody around, they could be as crude as they wanted."

"At least they didn't slice open the sofas and chairs like they did a couple years ago," said Mary, referring to a previous episode in our lives.

"Thank the Lord for small favors," I said, surveying the wreckage. I made the comment in irony, but the more I looked around, the more I realized we'd gotten off lightly. Mary agreed, reluctantly. After two hours of cleaning and straightening up, she agreed more readily. The seven of us sat on the deck with fresh coffee, watching the bay kick up into a green and white froth. It was a clear, blustery, high-pressure day, with puffy white clouds racing across the dark blue sky in the high wind. Gulls mewed and dove over the water; waves thundered onto the beach as we sipped the coffee from giant steaming mugs and raised our voices to be heard over the surf.

"I can't see anything missing, Charlie," said Mary. "What do you come up with?"

"Your binoculars, for one. Mine I took with me on the boat. But yours are gone. Also your Nikon."

"No!" she shouted, leaning toward me, her dark hair blowing straight out behind her, like a storm pennant. "I've got my camera with me. It must be Jackie's camera —"

"Well, whatever, Hon. That spare Nikon we kept hidden under the old clothes in the hall closet . . . and my radio's gone, too. Dammit!"

"No it isn't. I turned it on when we —"

"Not the stereo, the short-wave. The big SONY. It's gone."

It wasn't just the high cost of this item that bothered me, it was the fact that model 6800 W was no longer made. But I had no gripes; I was counting my blessings. Things could have been a whole lot worse.

Joe said, "I bet Keegan's going to be interested in this. Seems like somebody's been looking for something of Andy's, wouldn't you say?"

"Yep. Or something Andy had that he shouldn't have. Like Hartzell's papers, maybe?" I suggested.

"Hey, right! He searched in Woods Hole and came up blank. So then he tried here."

"But whoever killed Andy set the deed in motion earlier," I said, "several days before the break-in of the house."

"Before, or roughly the same time," said Joe. "The odds are overwhelming that the killing and the burglaries are related."

I nodded to him, then turned to Jack.

"Can you think of anything Andy might have stolen that somebody would want badly enough to kill him for?"

"No, Dad. And listen: he didn't take old Hartzell's papers. I would have seen them if he did. Besides, Andy didn't take Hartzell seriously enough to steal his stuff, believe me."

"You think Hartzell's nutty?"

"Sure. A little, anyway." He shrugged.

"Is he mean?" asked Joe, sitting down next to Jack.

Jack shook his head. "A little gruff and nasty sometimes, but only professionally. I don't think he's really mean, like a killer."

Joe hauled out the envelope, sliding the badge and wallet carefully onto the plank table without touching it.

"Remember this, Jack? Your dad showed it to us last night, but maybe you were so upset you didn't take a good look. Your 'nutty-but-nice' friend, Lionel Hartzell, did this. He pounded it with a hammer and burned the wallet. What do you say to that?"

"Yeah, well, I guess he could be mean, then. But he was never mean to me."

Moe studied the ruined shield with interest, remarking that it showed a lot of hostility.

"Before we get all worked up," said Joe, replacing the evidence, "let's not forget we've got no proof. And unless I find Hartzell's prints on this thing, which I doubt I will, we've still got no proof. Besides, destroying the badge doesn't make him a killer. It means he was irritated at having been cornered in his office by two *unauthorized* persons."

"I'm an official cop now."

"Uh-huh, but not authorized to do Keegan's job. Moe, you think this makes him dangerous?"

"In one sense, as an act of disrespect for what Doc and I put him through, it helps him. It shows he has nothing to fear from us, knowing he did nothing wrong. Follow?"

We nodded.

"On the other hand, I mentioned to Doc dat I think Lionel Hartzell shows the classic signs of paranoid schizophrenia. This diagnosis is admittedly based on a thumbnail sketch. But, if forced to say yea or nay, I'd say yea. Which means —" and he sat down at the table and swept his gaze over all of us to emphasize his point, "which means dat if he *is* paranoid, den he views all his actions as totally justified, as divinely ordained, if you will."

"So he'll stop at nothing?"

"Right. The true paranoid schizophrenic has no conscience, and therefore no telltale guilt feelings, either. He can lie under oath wid'out a twinge. He can lie under a polygraph, too."

"Gee Moe, that's scary," said Mary.

"Scary because he's hard to corner. He acts innocent because, in his mind, he *is* innocent; he's acting with total justification."

"Whatever happens, Jackie, I want you to promise me you'll steer clear of Lionel Hartzell."

"You know that's impossible, Mom. Hey, I think maybe everybody's jumping to conclusions here."

We spent the rest of the day at the Breakers, taking time out for yet another lab team to go over the place. Mary said if she saw one more lab team she'd pitch a fit. Joe called Paul Keegan and filled him in about the episode of the badge. Joe said he was "less than pleased," but would try to get Hartzell fingerprinted, nonetheless.

Around four Moe and I set up the chessboard on the low table between the easy chairs in the study corner and began to play, listening to the surf crash outside and Mozart's Concerto in A for clarinet on the stereo. The soloist was Benny Goodman. I got skunked, as usual. Am I a closet masochist? I wonder . . . Of course, if I were and Moe suspected it, he'd never say boo; he enjoys whipping my ass too much.

At six I lighted the grill for the halibut steaks, then Joe and I relaxed on the deck, each with a balloon glass of white wine. Since we were alone for a few minutes, and temporarily free from the hustle and tension of the past week, I thought I'd ask him about something that was bugging me.

"Aw, hell no, Doc," he said, answering my question. "Sure, she was in Mexico once when she was in college, during the summer. I think it was right before she met you."

"I know about that. I mean before."

"Naw. She just says that shit to push your buttons when she gets steamed. She's just yanking your chain is all."

"What about those horsemen, coming down out of the sun-parched hills with gold? Guys that she says were dark, saddle lean, and horny? How about them?"

"Pure bullshit, is what. I just — hey! Hey, where'd you get that line?"

"From her."

"I'll be damned. It's kinda good, don't you think? I mean, maybe she could write one of those romance novels; I bet she'd be good at it."

"She says she's always wanted to try writing. But I don't know . . ."

"Well, it might keep her busy, take her mind off all this shit that's been coming down around your ears. Maybe I'll speak with her. More wine?"

The sun went down in glows of gold and purple. The ocean talked to us, thumping and hissing, throughout the dinner on the porch. Overhead, gulls, silhouetted black against the glowing sky, winged their way up and down the beach, mewing and honking. If Jack weren't in the hot seat, it would have been the perfect end to a summer's day. But things weren't resolved, and I felt a vague uneasiness.

FOURTEEN

THE NEXT DAY the fair weather held; we spent all day Sunday at the Breakers, enjoying the sea and sun. The convening of the grand jury, which Joe assured us would happen shortly, hung over us like a dark cloud. But we did our best to ignore it and have fun.

Mary insisted that the family stick tightly together during this trial (no pun intended). It didn't take the rest of us long to see the wisdom of her stance, which was just as well, because once Mary makes up her mind on a family issue, there is no budging her. Accordingly, early Monday morning found us back down in Woods Hole, settling back into our home-away-from-home room at Swope. We would continue this back and forth trek from Eastham to Woods Hole until the matter was laid to rest, Mary announced. While she unpacked our clothes, and Moe and Joe did likewise in their room, which adjoined ours, I drove both boys back to Jack's rented house over on School Street. As we pulled up I could hear Jack sigh; undoubtedly this would be a tough time for him, and my heart ached. Thank God the storm had freed Tony to be with his brother.

Jack unloaded his bag, and I saw him staring into the trunk of the Audi at the navy and tan canvas duffel that had belonged to the late Andrew Cunningham. The contents having been duly inspected by the local police and the state lab team, the bag had been returned to us with the expectation that we would return it to the boy's parents at the funeral. This we had forgotten to do, and now Jack lifted it out of the trunk and held it in his other hand, walking toward his quarters.

"I'm going back to Providence to visit Andy's folks again," he said. "I promised I would. They'll need it. I might as well take this."

"That's nice of you," I said. "Why don't you take Alice along?"

"Maybe. If she's up to it. But wait, where's the rest of his stuff?"

"That's all I know of. That's what Keegan handed back to us. He didn't have a garment case or anything, did he?"

"No, I mean in here," Jack said, glancing down at the canvas duffel, which he hefted up and down in his left hand. "I remember lifting it out of my Land Cruiser when we got to the cottage. This bag was heavy — much heavier than it is now. I asked Andy what he had in there and he said some textbooks. So where are they?"

"I don't know, did he leave them in your car?"

"Yeah, maybe. Let me check."

But a quick search of the Toyota truck revealed nothing.

"How much heavier was the duffel, Jack?" I asked.

"Lots. Like maybe twice as heavy as this."

"Well, that's what Keegan gave back to us. Anyway, have a good day, you guys; Mom and I will pick you up for dinner about six."

I drove back to the dorm. Finding nobody there, I walked over to Water Street and along it until I came to the old Candle House, a stone building where, in the old whaling days, candles were manufactured from whale oil and beeswax. Over the front door is the bow of a model whaling ship. It's sticking out of the building prow first, with only its front half visible, and gives the impression that this miniature vessel has just crashed through the stone wall from inside, as if trying to escape from the building. Beneath the ship, Moe was standing in the doorway chatting excitedly with a stocky, red-faced, white-haired guy in a fisherman's bill cap and rubber hip boots. It was Wayland Smith. Jack had introduced him to us as Smitty. He was skipper of the collecting vessel *Gemma* and in charge of supplies. Supplies as in fresh creatures from the ocean. When I saw Moe's excited face, like a kid at his own birthday party, I should have realized what was about to come down. I should have been forewarned. Moe was bending Smitty's ear like there was no tomorrow. They looked up when I approached them.

"C'mon, Doc — you oughta see what Smitty's got around the corner. Follow me."

He hotfooted it around the corner of the Candle House and headed for a low wooden building with wide, garage-type doors that sat in the middle of the MBL's cluster of buildings. The sign over the big double doors said DEPARTMENT OF MARINE RE-SOURCES. I walked with him; I had to trot to keep up. Then I took a good look at what Moe was wearing. Roman-style sandals with leather thongs laced up his calves. Balloon-fit canary yellow shorts with elastic waistband, and a Hawaiian shirt in shades of lime green, purple, scarlet, and electric blue, all on a field of deep black. Reminded me of those Elvis paintings on black velvet. Only worse.

"Where'd you get that shirt?"

"Filene's. Why?"

"It's the worst thing I've ever seen, is why."

"What's wrong wid it?"

"What's wrong with it? Everything. Every possible thing. Nothing horrendous has been left out."

"Oh yeah, well look again."

"I can't; I'll get a retinal hernia."

To save the old blinkers, I looked straight ahead, saw Joe inside the building, leaning over a big circular brine tank that sat on the concrete floor. His wide rump stretched out the seat of his slacks as he bent over. Moe and Joe; what a pair. We walked inside, where the smell of brine and that heady, muddy, fishy smell of sea creatures was overpowering. I left my gaily hued friend — who resembled a bird of paradise in heat — and joined Joe at the wide tank, which was about four feet deep. A cascade of fresh brine entered the tank from a four-inch pipe two feet above it, filling the shed with the constant, echoing sound of splashing water. The building was cool, dark, and damp. I looked inside the tank and saw a mass of thick, snakelike creatures thrashing a hula dance around the perimeter in a counterclockwise circle, like lifers in the exercise yard of the pen. I almost felt sorry for them, but I didn't; they were too damn ugly.

"Eels," said Joe, with horror on his face. "Holy shit; remind me never to eat eel. Aren't they gawdawful?"

"You bet. I had an eel sandwich once in Holland, before I ever saw one close up. I'll never do that again."

"While you were dropping Jackie off, I called Paul over in Hyannis. He's getting our friend Slinky up here this week, he thinks. I said you could come along for the interview."

"Thanks. I'd appreciate it."

"He also traced the call that Andy made from the Breakers the night he died. Not much help, unfortunately; it's a pay phone sitting all by itself on a stretch of road."

"Tough luck. But maybe we can —"

"Doc! Oh Christ! Look!"

Eyes wide, Joe pointed at the brine pipe over the tank's lip. I was amazed, and horrified, to see a big, blunt-headed eel emerging from it. The monster wriggled, thrashing its primitive head from side to side as it slid from the pipe and plopped into the tank.

"Surprised ya, huh?" said Smitty, who had walked over to join us. "They'll do that, eels. They're programmed to swim up estuaries and rivers, since they're all born in the sea. Our pipe takes water from Eel Pond, and the eels there just naturally like to swim up the pipe. Neat, eh?"

Joe looked as if he'd swallowed a scorpion.

"Neat? It's about as neat as a bucket of maggots."

He stomped off, hand held lightly to his mouth. I saw him cross Water Street and walk over toward the beach, facing the sea, breathing deep. Smitty, stung by this comment, ambled out onto the rear dock. I heard excited jabbering in the corner, and turned to see Morris Abramson holding out a plastic bag, into which a lab attendant was busy scooping things from the briny deep. Nasty things. Slimy, flipping, wriggling, horrid things.

Lord, say it ain't so . . .

"Hold it!" I said, interjecting myself between the two. "Stop right there. Moe, what do you intend to do with these, uh, specimens?"

He beamed a broad smile at me. The biggest smile I'd seen on him in ages.

"I'm gonna put 'em in my fish ta —"

"No. No you are not."

His face fell.

"Why not?"

"Because I will not allow it. Because it's against the rules. Now behave yourself and put down that plastic bag and follow me outside. Let's take a walk in the nice weather. Come on . . ."

"What is dis? Smitty said I coul —"

"He was mistaken. I've checked the rules, Moe, and the answer is no. These cost a lot to get, and you can't have them." I took his plastic bag full of writhing bad dreams and handed it back to the attendant. "If Smitty makes more mistakes like that, I'm sure they'll fire him. We wouldn't want that now, would we?"

He just stood there, stunned, so I left him and joined Joe on the little beach out in front. Joe had his eyes set in the direction of the big docks, gazing at the lofty spars and rigging of the barque *Westward*. As we stood admiring her, I glanced back into the supply shed and was dismayed to see that Smitty had returned and was standing at Moe's side. Both men were talking and glancing my way. Moe was angry, pointing at me, then the tanks. Oh well, one does what one *can*.

"Dammit, Joe, I never should've brought Moe down here. I should've known better. I forget about that damn fish tank of his for a few days and look what happens. He's like a kid in a candy store in there. This lab's got every repulsive sea creature known to man. And then some. And now the guys in there who keep the monsters alive, who've got to feed 'em and clean up their shit, they've found a guy who appreciates their work. Know what's gonna happen now? Put two and two together."

"I know. They're gonna lay every blow-lunch critter from Davy Jones on him for *free*, that's what."

"You got it," I groaned. "Our whole office wing is going to turn into Barf City."

"Know what, Doc? This place is givin' me the creeps. I liked it when I first got here, but now, I mean, shit. Eels comin' outa pipes, for Chrissakes. Who needs it? I mean, you get inna bathtub, turn on the faucet, a friggin' eel slides out. Who the fuck needs it?"

"Uh-huh. Know whatcha mean."

"I mean, cut me some slack."

"I'm with you, pal."

"And I'm thinking, looking at the old Cap'n Kidd bar up ahead, or rather, dead ahead. Isn't that what they say on boats? Dead ahead?"

"Uh-huh."

"— that after what I've been through, what with taking Jackie up to face the judge and all, and what with eels in the plumbing and all, that I could use a drink."

"I'm with you, pal."

"Yeah, you're with me, but are you *buyin'*?"

Off to my left, I heard Moe in the supply shed.

"No. No, not dat one. Over dere, inna corner, dat big guy. Yeah, that's it! That fat *juicy* one —"

Dear God, I thought to myself as I made my weary way to the swinging doors. Cut me some slack.

FIFTEEN

THE NEXT DAY, on Tuesday morning shortly before noon, Detective Lieutenant Paul Keegan and a local Falmouth cop came to get Lionel Hartzell. They presented him with his marching orders in his office in Lillie Hall, where, Keegan later told me, they found him crouching defiantly behind his heavy work counter in the little protected niche he'd hollowed in the corner of his office for his desk and himself.

Joe and I heard the commotion on the stairway as soon as we went inside the building. There was shouting and cussing and Paul Keegan's voice giving the old guy warnings. He was a crusty old coot, I'll give him that. The three of them came fumbling down the stairs, the young uniformed cop and Keegan flanking old Lionel Hartzell. The guy was strong, as well as obnoxious. I mean, it took both of them to hold him until they got him into the cruiser's back seat. The back seat that was full of surprises, like no inside door handles or window cranks, with a heavy wire mesh between it and the front seat. But Keegan had said no cuffs. It would look bad, at the laboratory and all. I guess I would agree, but the commotion they made getting the old professor to the car wasn't worth it. If it were me, I'd have cuffed the guy, and maybe gagged him too. Joe agreed.

The crime lab had found no prints at all on my mutilated shield. But old Hartzell had made a fatal slip: he'd been careless with the manila envelope, allowing his thumb to rest momentarily on the gummed flap before sealing it up. And, Joe gloated, the

only thing that takes a fingerprint better than a gummed envelope flap is an inked plate at the police station, for Chrissakes. So
after they'd fingerprinted the old buzzard and found a twelve-
point positive make, or perfect match, they'd issued a warrant for
his arrest. We all knew the grounds were tenuous at best. But it
was an arrest, which meant another suspect was on deck, and at a
crucial time. Keegan had orchestrated it. Any doubts I'd had
about him were gone with the wind; it was now clear that he was
our friend.

Just before they pulled away Hartzell stuck his oddly shaped
gray head up against the closed window and started cussing at
Jack, who was standing next to me. He cussed me, too, for being
his father. He was wearing his tortoiseshell glasses with the thick,
half-moon lenses. With those distorting his eyes, which were
large to begin with, he looked like a huge, enraged toad.

"And I trusted you," he yelled through the glass, wagging an
accusing finger at Jack. "You! Of all the spoiled kids . . . you were
the one I trusted most. You idiots can't match my brilliance, so
you stole my secret. And then you got the police to take me away
so I couldn't finish it! But I'll get back at you! Don't you worry —"

The car went off into the distance, and with it, the old man's
screams and threats.

"That guy's scary," I said.

"Yeah. I've never seen him like this," said Jack. "What's going
to happen now? Will he have to give a statement?"

"Uh-huh," said Joe. "But let's not get our hopes up premature-
ly. It may result in a probable cause hearing or a grand jury and it
may not. God knows it's no crime to deface a police badge you
happen to find in your office. But the act does show hostility and
the desire for retaliation. And the fact that Hartzell repeatedly
denied any connection with the act will show the court he lied,
that his word's no good."

"It shows something else more important, Joe. It shows he's
sneaky. The kind of guy who would mutilate a personal belong-
ing and slide it under your door is the same kind of guy who
would slip fatal medication into your shaving kit when you're
running his lab. Get it? In both cases he avoids direct confronta-
tion; he retaliates indirectly by cunning."

"That's good, Doc. That's real good."

"Moe thought it up."

"Well, in any event, you guys, this should act as a diversion. It should take some of the heat off us a while."

"Can we get Moe up there on the stand as an expert witness?"

"Eventually, if it comes to trial. Certainly Moe's pretty convinced, based on his observations and this incident, that Hartzell's a good bet for this murder."

Thus concluded Paul Keegan's five-day investigation in Woods Hole. He had uncovered not only motive, misplaced and misguided as it was, but means as well.

Motive: Lionel Hartzell, who in Moe's judgment was a classic paranoid schizophrenic, was totally, unshakably convinced that his data detailing the processes governing the concentration of silver in marine organisms were being stolen by Andy Cunningham. Who else but this rude and greedy boy would be so eager to steal his valuable secrets and sell them to a giant pharmaceutical firm? Of course, to a person in Hartzell's frame of mind, any revenge was justifiable and necessary.

Means: Lionel Hartzell was himself taking Lasix, one of the medications used to kill Andy. This was not surprising, as a large percentage of older men are on this or similar medications. In addition, a quick survey by Keegan revealed that no fewer than eight of Hartzell's contemporaries in Woods Hole were on digoxin, the other component of the fatal medication that stopped Andy Cunningham's heart. Therefore, the proximity and availability of these drugs to Hartzell, and his background in physiology and chemistry, provided him with the means for the murder, the means nobody else had.

"You gotta admit, Doc, Keegan did a helluva job. Comes down here, solo, and in less than a week's time has collared a suspect that looks very, very good for it."

Joe and I were sitting on the concrete quay adjoining the Coast Guard station, watching jellyfish pulsating through the water below. They looked like clear plastic Baggies sprung to life, rhythmically contracting and dilating their parachute-shaped bells, squeezing their way through the brine. Inside the bells lurked some dense material that resembled cloudy cauliflower. Disgusting. I prayed Moe wouldn't see these. No doubt he'd want one — or maybe eight — for his aquarium.

"Well?"

"Well what?" I answered. "What can I say? I think Hartzell looks like a good bet on this thing, the old fart. I always thought so. Question is, can Keegan make anything stick?"

"That's the hard part," he sighed. "In fact, the only thing Keegan's got sticking, at this point, is his neck out. If he can't get an indictment, his case falls apart real fast, and he's got his ass in a sling. I'm sure he's taking this chance for Jackie, Doc; he's convinced Jack's innocent. But for what it's worth, I like Hartzell a lot for it. Every piece fits. And know what? Basically, it's a psycho killing, which fits best of all. Here we were, lacking a motive and trying to figure out if the mob enforcers could have done it. Well, we all suspected the mob would never kill a kid for gambling debts. And we knew they'd never do it in such a sneaky way."

"I was the one who first said that, remember?"

"Uh-huh. And it's true. If the mob had done it, it'd be a straight hit, clean and fast. Something like this: a knock on Andy's door, the fake delivery man holding a bulky package, and when Andy turns around to set the bogus package on the table, out comes the twenty-two auto pistol —"

"Right. That's more their style. Our late friend Carmen DeLucca would have loved it."

"So with the kid's back turned, the button man leans over close, holding the piece, say, half a foot from the head. The pistol, of course, is hot from across the country, with serial numbers filed off, disposable silencer in place, bore of the barrel mutilated with a jeweler's rat-tail file to nullify the ballistics tests, and no prints."

"Yeah, right —"

"Then *thufff-thufff!* two quick pops in the back of the head. Before the kid even hits the floor, the delivery man's dropped the piece in the wastebasket and is out and gone, hoofing it back to the car before the kid's even stopped twitching. Now *that's* a mob hit. Hey, what's wrong?"

"What's *wrong?*" I answered, almost falling off the quay in a fit of dizziness, "what the hell do you mean, what's *wrong?* You've just described the cold-blooded murder of a kid and you ask me what's wrong? Sweet Jesus, Joe. And what if the mob did set out to kill Andy, and just by accident got his roommate, Jack, instead?"

"Oh yeah. See what you mean, Doc."

"But finish what you were saying. Why does a psycho killing fit so well?"

"Because nobody could figure out a motive that was strong enough. Who would want the kid dead? We couldn't find anybody who hated him, and he wasn't rich, so that eliminated the personal gain motive. So we were stuck. Until Keegan put the pieces together. Now it all fits."

"So this nutty professor, who's convinced the effort of a lifetime is being taken from him, thinks up a way to kill Andy while he's away from Woods Hole. He knows he won't get caught because one, he was nowhere near the scene of death and two, everyone will assume the boy died of his epilepsy."

"Uh-huh. It was almost perfect, and it shows that a crazed mind is still capable of rational thought and painstaking planning."

I sat and thought a minute.

"And so it was Hartzell who tossed the kids' house and ransacked the Breakers?"

"Yep. Look: Hartzell's convinced the kids are stealing his stuff. He confronts them, accuses them. Of course they deny it and tell him to kiss off. So he sits and steams over it. And from what you've said about Andy — the way you and Jack and Mary have described him to me — I'd bet that he was very direct with old man Hartzell. I bet he told him exactly what he thought of him."

"That part's true for sure; Jack told me as much."

"So Andy was the first victim. And I'd say we're lucky Keegan nabbed Hartzell when he did. Because, you ask me, Jack was next."

I gave an involuntary shudder.

"Well, I hope they commit him for life. But still, I have doubts about the burglary thing. Why would he break into Andy's house, then go up alone to Eastham and do the Breakers?"

"He was searching for the data he was convinced Andy took."

"Listen Joe: Jack's told me more than once that Andy didn't take Hartzell's notes; Andy thought the old guy was wacko and that the project was, too."

"So what? We're talking from Hartzell's point of view: Andy stole the data. So, one, Andy had to die for it. Two: the place to look for it was Andy's house."

"And when he didn't find it down here, he assumed Andy had taken it with him up to our cottage."

"Right. And when he had a chance, he went up there and tossed the Breakers, trying to recover it."

"That's interesting, Joe. Because just yesterday Jack hefted Andy's duffel bag and said that it was a lot heavier on the way up to Eastham. So maybe Andy did rip off old man Hartzell. And maybe he did hide the stuff in the cottage."

"And maybe Hartzell recovered it. Lot of good it'll do him in the slammer."

"Even though Jack's convinced Andy didn't take anything of Hartzell's."

"Well, considering the circumstances, Doc, maybe Jack should keep his mouth shut about that. Savvy?"

"Gotcha. Hey, here they come now. This is what I've been waiting for."

We watched the thirty-foot sea skiff round the point and head toward us. Built for offshore expeditions, the *Mola Mola* was powered by twin stern-drive Volvo engines, each over a hundred horsepower. It resembled a cross between an open, deep-water lobster boat and a big Boston Whaler. As an open boat, it had no cabin, instead relying for shelter on its high, wide bow with lots of flair. The bow was kicking up a nice wave with two pretty fans of spray. Jack was at the wheel, with Tony and Tom McDonnough on either side of him, sitting at the big center control console. On the boat's side was the Department of Commerce logo and the words NATIONAL MARINE FISHERIES.

"You sure you don't wanna come along?" I asked Joe.

"I'm sure. You ask me, you guys are nitwits, going out to look at whales in that thing. Hell, they're twice as long and thirty times heavier than that little boat. They get the slightest little bit pissed off, it's all she wrote."

"Yeah, but they won't get pissed off. They're nice. They love people."

"That's what Jonah thought," he said, getting up and brushing off the seat of his pants. "And poor old Ahab, too. When you get back, let me know if you'll be needing a wooden leg."

"It was an ivory leg, not a wooden one. And besides, Moby Dick was a sperm whale, a toothed whale. These are humpback whales, baleen whales that aren't aggressive . . . I think."

"You hope. *Arrivederla.*"

And so he sauntered off toward the docks with that rolling, elephantine shuffle of his.

We were out there. Way, way out there, riding the soft, slow swells of the big water. We'd raced over the waves for an hour, and were almost thirty miles offshore, in the neighborhood of the treacherous Nantucket Shoals. Tom worked the helm, keeping his eyes on the horizon and on the console compass, while I watched the chart that was stretched over my knees, the corners of the paper rattling in the wind. Together we would keep a rough estimate of our position. No land was visible; we could have been in the mid-Atlantic. This is an unsettling feeling, especially in a thirty-foot open boat with nothing over your head, not even a mast and sails. Jack and Tony glassed the ocean with marine binoculars, searching for that telltale puff of breath vapor, the spout that signaled a surfacing whale. So far, we'd had no luck.

A tuna boat came chugging into view. Jack told me it was what's called a "stick boat," meaning a harpoon boat. It had a long bowsprit and high spotting tower that gave it a rickety, insectlike appearance. Its diesel engine gave off a faint *rhum-rhum-rhum-rhum* that came to us over the slick, oily-smooth water. The tuna boat rolled in the big swells, the high tower swaying in a ten-foot arc, the spotter sitting Indian fashion on the tiny plywood platform eighteen feet above the deck, gripping the stays with his crossed legs. He wore big, wrap-around dark glasses, and his nose and cheekbones were painted mime white with zinc oxide ointment. He held a huge pair of naval binoculars. When he spotted the Marine Fisheries logo on the side of the *Mola Mola*, he pointed northeast, making a dipping, diving motion with his flattened palm.

"He's telling us there are whales further out," said Tom as he spun the wheel, heading us over to the fishing boat. The tuna boat was old, its planked sides flaking paint chips and stained with rust streaks. Two of the cabin windows were cracked and the smokestack was solid rust. Guy wires ran from the long bowsprit pole back to the bow, and also up to the tower from the deck and topsides, and then down to the bowsprit tip from above, much like the standing rigging of a Grand Banks schooner. But the wire was old, tightened and repaired with turnbuckles, bolt clamps, and wound coils. The entire vessel had a frail, rickety appearance, resembling a giant, splayed cricket, or perhaps a water strider that ticked and groaned its way through the sea. It looked as if it would come apart any second.

There were three men aboard: the skipper, the lookout, and the harpooner, who was busy coiling lines into plastic tubs on the foredeck. Two harpoon shafts were braced against the cabin sides, and three old beer kegs, spray-painted Day-glo orange for visibility, stood in a crude rack. Reminded me of the movie *Jaws*.

"You see whales?" shouted Jack to the lookout.

"Yeah!" shouted the man with the binoculars. "Fins and humpbacks, about four miles up the line. Maybe six miles by now." We thanked the men and headed on, looking back to see the vessel's name on her wide, low transom: the *Auk*.

We saw the tuna boat grow small in the distance, then disappear over the southern horizon. I thought of that frail machine crawling over the wide ocean and shuddered. How presumptuous of man to head out over the deep in crafts like that. Down below us, in the several hundred feet of cold darkness, giant forms pushed through the water, six or seven times the mass of the biggest African bull elephants, moving soundlessly, gliding through the black, steep-walled undersea canyons. Huge slimy things lurked on or near the bottom, with gnashing beaks, poison spines, sucking mouths. Razor-toothed sea-raptors prowled the blackness, too, waiting for a chance to attack animals of all sizes and engage in silent combat, with billowing, red-brown clouds of blood and shivering, trembling masses of injured muscle and severed nerves . . .

There was a whole lot of bad jazz down there. Oodles of it, including a spiny fish the size of a toad that can kill a horse with its venom, and a stomatopod as long as a cigar, called a mantis shrimp, that can crack your skull with a flip of its forelegs. And here we were in our little skiff, crawling our feeble way over the top of it all.

It was almost two o'clock when we saw the first pod of humpbacks. Following my sons' pointing fingers, I saw the occasional cloud of vapor coming up from the surface of the ocean, but no whales were visible. Accustomed to old whaling prints showing breaching whales leaping over whaleboats, with the terrified occupants scrambling for their lives, I expected at least to see a lot of animal. Instead, when we drew near, I saw a dark, slick mass rolling gently over on the water, perhaps two feet high at its tallest point. A section of blacktop highway, sliding over. Big deal.

But then the surprise: after twenty feet or so of this slick macadam came the tail. The tail was horizontal, with flukes set wide like the wings of a jet, each the size and shape of a small dingy, measuring nine feet from tip to tip. It was jet black and shiny, gently serrated along its rear edge, maybe two feet thick in the center, tapering to mere inches at the tips. It moved with absolute grace, lifting a few feet, standing clear of the water, dripping at its drooped edges like a fresh-plucked lily pad, and then sliding under, without a sound and with scarcely a ripple.

Great God almighty . . .

"Dad? Dad, you okay?" asked Jack, who was bending over to speak urgently in my ear.

"Yeah, I'm okay," I answered finally, as soon as I could work my jaw, "I'm fine."

"How big was he?" asked Tony. The boy's tone was hushed, reverent.

"Maybe fifty feet," said Tom, leaning over the starboard bow and trying to peer into the deep. "And, it might be a girl. We won't know until it surfaces again."

We motored along, cut to a crawl, and waited and watched.

ffffffffffffoooosh! . . . *ffffffffffoooooshh!*

Two whales surfaced in unison, blowing enough air between them to last a man a day and a half. I saw their heads: from above, the taper in front resembled a blunt gothic arch. The tops of the heads were relatively flat, and were covered with patterned bumps several inches across. These bumps, which Jack told me later were enlarged hair follicles, looked almost exactly like rivet heads, making the whales' heads look like the blackened metal boilerplate sides of old steamships. They looked, in fact, like the Disney rendition of Captain Nemo's *Nautilus*.

We watched the two whales roll forward, tucking their heads and letting their long, wet-asphalt backs slide forward, then there was a repeat vision of those beautiful tails, each powerful enough to smash our thirty-foot skiff into splinters with one swipe.

Picture yourself walking out of the African scrub onto a parched plain on which forty huge elephants are feeding. Think of walking out into this herd, standing in front of, behind, underneath them as they feed, hearing the muted grinding of their molars, the loud, damp plats of their bowling-ball-sized droppings, the sound of their stomachs and bowels rumbling wet . . . perhaps the rough rasp of their trunks as they slide past you . . . seeing the dusty, dry flap of their billboard-sized ears. And you're out there on that parched plain totally exposed. There's nothing but you and all of them — no trees to climb, no place to hide. And all you can do is stand there amazed and awed, and hope like hell they don't get steamed and stomp you into grease, or maybe skewer you with one of their tusks.

That's the feeling of being in the middle of a pod of whales in an open skiff thirty miles offshore. Except that each whale weighs forty or fifty tons, not six or seven.

The two tails slid under. We waited about forty seconds to see the animals surface again. They reappeared, puffing great gray clouds of vapor, then slid under again. At no time were the tops of their backs more than a few feet out of the water. But the third time they surfaced they showed their heads clearly as they came up. Their giant puffy breathing was louder, and after their front halves went under, their backs had a much more pronounced arch.

"See them hunching up like that, Dad? They're getting ready to sound. That's how they got their name: humpback."

The tails came up, up, towering ten feet above us, spread out and dripping, like the wings of an airborne manta ray. Then the entire stem and tail of each whale stiffened straight up and shot downward with a speed and finality that meant we wouldn't see them for a while. I couldn't say anything, not even gee or golly. I just sat there dumbfounded, amazed that a creature so gigantic could surface, breathe, and dive within twenty yards of us and do it with such grace, and, except for the big puff of blowing air, in total silence.

"Did you see the markings on the underside of the tails, Dad?" asked Jack.

"Well, I saw a lot of white, with black blotches, if that's what you mean."

"That's what I mean. Those markings are different for each animal, and it's how we tell them apart. The one on the left was Churchill, the guy on the right was Roy."

"You mean you know each whale? You've given them names?"

"Oh sure. There are several pods in these waters. Most of the whales come back each year and we know them intimately. Now Churchill's been around for years, but Roy's a rookie. Churchill got his name for the V-shaped notch on his flukes. Look here . . ."

Jack went to the bow and leaned over, pointing at the water. Where the two whales had sounded was a pair of swirling depressions in the sea, two whirlpools as wide as living rooms.

"The whales' footprints," he said triumphantly. "When they sound, whales always leave footprints."

I stared at the gently swirling, shallow conical depressions on the ocean's surface. They remained perhaps half a minute, then disappeared.

"Footprints, eh? What good are footprints that disappear?"

"Everything disappears, Dad, given time."

I pondered this metaphysical tidbit while we waited for the pair to come back up. They stayed down over thirty minutes, then surfaced two hundred yards off our port bow, spurting those gray plumes of vapor and sliding their black, slick shapes forward and under. We were so busy watching the antics of Churchill and Roy that we forgot the water right under us.

"*Ooo, wow!*" said Tom McDonnough, "look below us. We got company."

Well offshore, the ocean is quite clear, unclouded by river run-off. In strong light, you can see thirty or forty feet down with no problem, especially if what you're gawking at is as big as a pair of hitched locomotives. Below us was a whale, perhaps thirty feet directly under the boat, hovering there in the wavy green shimmer. It was my first look at the whole thing at once, rather than its various parts exposed to the surface in sequence. It took my breath away. I noticed how really long the humpback's flippers were. They were whitish gray, in contrast to the black of the body, and were about eighteen feet long, swept back in a crescent. The animal looked almost like a deformed jumbo jet, with its streamlined, fat body and rear-swept flippers that seemed way too big for flippers, way too small for wings. . . .

Then it came up. It rose without effort or apparent motion; we simply saw it getting bigger and bigger, closer and closer, until at last there it was, right alongside us, floating motionless next to the boat, its exposed portion about as large as a black, shiny, bumpy, shuffleboard court. My heart was doing the shimmy-shake, and seemed to want to leave my chest and dance around on the gunwale awhile until it calmed down.

"Let's get the hell out of —"

"Wait a second, that's Crystal. HI CRYSTAL!" shouted Jack, leaning over the rail and waving. It was the dumbest thing I've ever seen, and I told him so. But then, lo and behold, if the whale, Crystal, didn't do the most amazing thing. She rolled on her side and swatted the ocean with her port flipper. Whap! Whap! Whap! It wasn't a hard swat, but rather a gentle patting, though I'm sure you could have heard it a hundred yards away.

"Why's she doing that?" asked Tony.

"*He*, Dad. Crystal's a guy. He's glad to see us. I can recognize Crystal from front and top by his barnacles. See those three huge growths on his lip? That's Crystal. Of course, when he sounds, we can always tell him by his tail markings, too. Now watch! He's gonna open his mouth for us."

Lucky us. The huge creature rolled over again, making the skiff pitch and roll, and then the enormous upper jaw opened.

It resembled a giant car hood and gave the impression that the animal was upside down. It wasn't of course. Jack explained it was just the shape of the baleen whale's mouth. The flat, pointed, black top of Crystal's head lifted up, revealing rows and rows of hanging baleen plates inside. His mouth looked large enough to hold ten or twelve men, which meant that while a whale couldn't actually *swallow* Jonah, it could sure as hell hold him in its mouth with no problem. The baleen plates, all seven hundred of them, were triangular, fringed and fibrous, and colored brownish black. They looked more vegetable than animal. It looked as if poor Crystal had tried to swallow a dozen rotting palm trees. Or maybe two tons of dead eucalyptus bark. The mouth was wondrous, amazing, surrealistic. It was also disgusting.

The odor that issued forth was nothing to brag about, either. As an oral surgeon, I'm an expert on halitosis, and believe me, Crystal the humpback was in the running for the Bad Breath of the Universe award. In fact, with his warty, rivet-head hair follicles, his bumpy, grayish white clusters of barnacles, and his weird, otherworldly appearance, it was difficult to call Crystal handsome, and I told Jack so.

Jack frowned in my direction. "Handsome is as handsome does," he said. And he continued to talk and coo to his enormous friend, telling us what a rotten shame it was he hadn't brought the hydrophone, so we could all hear the whales talking underwater. I leaned way over, almost touching the animal, and saw his tiny eye, two feet under the surface, staring at us.

"His eyes are sure small; they're out of proportion to the rest of him," I said.

"Uh-huh. Horses' eyes are bigger. Whales don't use their eyes a whole lot. So long, kid . . ."

Crystal eased forward and down, thrashed his immense flukes against the sea, and was gone.

"Wow!" said Tony softly.

"Yeah," I agreed, as Tom throttled up. We saw fourteen more whales that afternoon, including a mother with her calf. It sure beat the hell out of anything I'd ever seen before, or have seen since.

On our way back to Great Harbor I asked Jack if he remembered that summer back in 1970 when the whales died on the beach and he cried for a week, and then we went to see the dolphin show up in Brewster where the dolphins clapped their flippers on the water just the way Crystal had done. He said he didn't remember it. I asked him again, just to make sure, and he said the same thing. I guess maybe he'd repressed the painful memory. For some reason, it made me very sad. A powerful, shared experience had crumbled with time.

SIXTEEN

JOE'S KNOCKING at our door woke us up a little after eight. It was Wednesday morning, the day after the whale watch. I was tired after our day on the water, still feeling stunned by the experience. I had been dreaming about the whales sliding along through the swells, their dripping tails following behind . . .

"C'mon you two — get up. I just got a call from Keegan. He says Slinky and company are on their way up here from Providence. Mary, you keep saying you want to see a real mobster —"

"I do, I do," she said, bounding out of bed bare-ass.

I still can't get used to the way these two siblings parade around naked in front of each other. We WASPs frown on such impropriety.

"Keegan's a wonder kid," I said. "How'd he manage to collar Slinky anyway?"

"Let's just say, diplomatic pressure applied by our Rhode Island counterparts. But I think the kid's cooperation makes him look pretty good, frankly. Although Keegan warned me Slinky will have his mouthpiece with him. I'll go down to town and get coffee and rolls. You guys hurry up and be ready when I get back."

Keegan joined us over coffee, and the four of us were waiting on the steps of Lillie Hall when the big white Caddy slid up Water Street and came to a halt in front of us. It was a Mafia wagon all right. The windows were so dark you couldn't see inside. I noticed two fancy antennae riding on the rear deck, right in front of the continental kit holding the spare tire. The spoked wheels were all shined up. The driver's door opened and a huge man got out, walked across the street, and positioned himself nonchalantly on a bench overlooking the beach. Nobody would notice him, of course, just your average 270-pound chauffeur wearing shades, a cream-white tropical wool sport coat, burgundy slacks, and alligator shoes so shiny they gave off sunbeams. He didn't stand out in Woods Hole. Nooooo. Not any more than the Colossus of Rhodes . . .

"He's packing iron," whispered Joe to Keegan. "Only reason anybody wears a friggin' coat in the summertime is to hide artillery. There! See the bulge?"

Keegan nodded, chewing his gum slowly, keeping his steely gaze fixed on the car. The back doors opened and two men got out. Right away I knew which one was Eddie Falcone, a.k.a. Slinky. He was young, with thinning black hair, and was wearing white, pleated, baggy pants, a blue silk shirt with no tie, and a stone-washed denim jacket. Right out of Ralph Lauren's latest catalog. His shoes were Mexican huaraches of woven leather. He wore shades, too, and a lot of gold. With the dark glasses on top of the smoked glass of the car, how the hell could they *see*, I wondered. The man with him carried a brown attaché case and was dressed in a plain brown summer suit, with white shirt and tie. That would be the mouthpiece Keegan had mentioned; he had lawyer written all over him. I was surprised he wasn't carrying a pair of scales.

"Mr. Keegan?" said the man in the suit. "I'm Marshall Brooks, representing Mr. Falcone. We have come here voluntarily to see if we can help you in this investigation."

"Thanks, we do appreciate it," answered Keegan. "But does your heavy think it's necessary to carry a piece with him? We've got a strict law against handguns in this state."

Brooks glanced over his shoulder at the big man sitting on the bench, who was watching our every move from behind those shades. I could tell.

"My client's assistant is fully licensed to carry a firearm to insure the safety of my client," said Brooks, snapping open the latches of his brown case. "If necessary, I can produce the authorizations for Rhode Island and the Commonwealth of Mass —"

"That won't be necessary," said Joe, holding up his hand. "But you might tell Boris Karloff over there that he needn't be so obvious about it. We can see the bulge under his arm from way over here. Now, you must be Mr. Falcone, right?"

He shook hands with the kid, and the rest of us shook hands all around. Eddie Falcone's eyes lit up when he came face to face with Mary. I suppose it was a compliment to both of us, but still, it pissed me off.

"Can you take a ride with us, Eddie?" asked Keegan. "We'd like to show you something."

"My client is here voluntarily, on a goodwill basis only," spouted Brooks, "he is not here for an interrogation or —"

"It's okay Marshall, I'll go for a ride. My car or yours, gentlemen?"

"Ours," said Keegan.

"Why not his?" said Mary. "Can I ride in his car?"

Keegan and Joe glared at her. Sensing the predicament, I quietly told Mary it would be better to go in Joe's car.

"But we can't all fit in, can we?" she said.

"We'll let them follow us then," said Paul.

"I'd love you to ride with us," Eddie said to Mary. "I really would. And we can watch TV on the way."

"Thanks, Eddie, but my sister would really rather —"

"That's okay Joey; I'll ride with him."

"Mary!"

I yanked her aside, away from all the onlookers.

"What the hell do you mean, 'I'll ride with him?' Don't you know he's the enemy? He could be responsible for Andy's death, for Chrissakes, what do —"

"Aw c'mon, Charlie!" she hissed, flinging my arm away. "You guys think you're so tough, threatening him like that. Can't you see he's only a kid?"

"Yeah, a punk kid. A *connected* kid —"

"Listen: I bet I find out three times as much from him as you guys do. There's more than one way to get information, you know. Or maybe you guys *don't* know . . . "

"I think it's a dumb idea."

"What's he going to do, attack me in his car while he's got a police escort? Look, I want to get to the bottom of this and clear Jackie just as much as you do. Remember that. Now *lay off!*"

I knew I couldn't change her mind, so I stood and watched while she and Eddie Falcone tripped down the stairs and along the sidewalk to the Cadillac Eldorado, followed by lawyer Brooks, who hurried ahead of them to open the rear door and see them safely inside, then got in the front seat next to Baby Huey, who was starting the engine.

"Sis is a pain in the ass sometimes," growled Joe. "Paul, where are we going, anyway?"

Keegan directed us out of the center of town onto Sippiwissett Road, which we followed almost a mile, past some of the plushest real estate in New England, until we stopped at a quiet intersection. There, standing solitary as Minot's Ledge lighthouse, was a phone booth. Keegan pointed to it.

"There, Doc. That's the phone we traced the number to. That's the phone Andy placed the call to the night he died, just before he went out for his two-hour ramble in the rain."

"Well hell, he couldn't have come all the way here on foot."

"No. He called somebody who was here, waiting for his call. Then that somebody drove to your cottage to meet him. How's that sound?"

"It sounds as good as anything else we've come up with," said Joe. We got out of the cruiser and met the party of four as they emerged from the Caddy. The two helpers stood back. Mary and the kid were talking to each other a mile a minute. Then Joe, who wasn't pleased, drew her aside.

"Well, did he give you an all-day sucker?"

Mary told him to lay off the sexual innuendoes. Joe, taken aback, murmured to me that he hadn't intended any. Then she approached me.

"Jeez, Charlie, you ought to see it inside. He's got a TV and even a VCR. He can watch movies and everything while he's riding. There's a bar and a phone, too."

"I'm terribly impressed. Are you planning on spending the rest of the day with him, or what?"

"C'mon, Charlie . . . Joe."

"The guy's a mobster, Mare," said her brother.

"He's also not much older than Jackie. And I don't think he's mean."

"Good. I'm glad you're such an expert," said Joe. "Too bad his rap sheet doesn't agree."

"*Shhhh!*" she said, as Falcone walked up with Brooks.

"Eddie," asked Keegan, "have you ever taken a phone call in that booth?"

"No sir. Besides, I don't need a booth. I got a phone in my car."

"You told me it's broken," said Mary, looking reproachfully at the kid.

"Well, yeah. Not workin' too good right now."

"You never took a call here? Not a week before last Friday? Think carefully, Eddie."

"No sir."

"Because that's where Andy called the night he died. You have any idea who he could have called here?"

"Maybe his girl friend, Alice. She lives not too far from here, up in Falmouth."

"When did you last talk with Andy?"

"About three or four weeks ago. Dr. Adams, your son saw us talking. It was up on the road north of town."

"And what did you talk about, Eddie?" pursued Keegan.

"Things."

"Things? You mean money? We know you loaned him money, Eddie. Andy told Jack Adams about the loan. And Arthur Hagstrom, the director of the MBL, told us. Well?"

"Yeah. I loaned him money."

"How much?"

"Excuse me," interrupted Marshall Brooks, "my client is under no obligation to answer that. He is here voluntarily, in a spirit of cooperation in the investigation of a friend's murder. The loan was consummated across state lines. Moreover, no record of the transaction was made, as it was a gentlemen's agreement. Furthermore, I advise —"

"Yeah yeah yeah yeah. No record made, Eddie? How many loans you make without records?'

"Not many."

"Not many, eh? We beg to differ with you. We've got —"

"Lay off, you guys!" said Mary, leaning up against Joe's cruiser with her arms crossed. "C'mon. He didn't have to come up here, did you, Eddie?"

The two men stared at her, dumbfounded and angry. Paul Keegan flipped his pocket notebook shut with a loud flap, jammed it into his inside breast pocket, and grunted that the interview was over. He and Joe climbed into the cruiser. I looked at Mary.

"You riding with us?" I asked.

"No, Charlie. You're riding with us. C'mon."

Before I could decide, Joe and Keegan pulled off, in a huff, no doubt. So Mary and I got inside the big white car, which, I quickly noticed, was not new, and settled ourselves in back, with Slinky sitting between us. A stereo system with fuzzy speakers played the theme from *Mondo Cane*. The car's shocks weren't in the best of shape, either; we bounced along the road like a pogo stick. Eddie Falcone was a good-looking boy, and he was doing his damnedest to be polite.

"Would you care for another ginger ale, Mrs. Adams? My, you look ravishing this morning . . ."

"Thanks, Eddie," she answered with an amused grin. I could tell she was enjoying herself.

"Dr. Adams?"

"No thanks," I said, not wishing to taint myself with his hospitality. Slinky leaned forward and spoke to the driver.

"Take it easy on these curves, eh Vinnie? We wouldn't want Mrs. Adams here to get nauseous."

The big man nodded. He had a crew cut, and a neck that spilled out over his collar in enormous wrinkles of fat. His neck was much bigger than his head. He seemed competent, though. He understood spoken commands, for starters. He was probably even toilet trained. Marshall Brooks, the mouthpiece, sat with hands folded on top of his attaché case.

"Isn't this lovely weather we've been having lately," continued the kid. You should go on a talk show, I thought. Mary opened a small cabinet attached to the back of the front seat. I saw her flipping through stacks of videocassettes. Eyeing her, Eddie Falcone grew nervous. I saw beads of sweat on his upper lip.

"Mrs. Adams, I don't think you should —"

"Aw, Charlie! He's got skin flicks in here. So *now* I know why you've got the VCR, Eddie. So, you take your girl friend for rides with you? Is that the reason for the darkened windows? Huh, Eddie? Where's the curtain for the front seat then? Oooooo, these look good. Do you have *A Hard Man Is Good to Find*? It's my fav —"

"Mary! Can it."

The big Caddy oozed to a stop right in front of Lillie Hall.

"Who killed Andy?" I asked Falcone.

"I don't know, Dr. Adams. I swear on the cross I don't know," he said, fingering the gold crucifix that dangled on his hairy chest.

"And the last time you saw Andy was a month ago? I doubt that, Eddie."

He looked at me, panic-stricken, and said nothing. Marshall Brooks and Vinnie both turned around in the front seat, looking at me. Eddie Falcone gave me a nervous, boyish grin and stuck out his hand.

"Dr. Adams, it's been ever so nice to meet you and your charming, lovely wife."

I climbed out of the mob-mobile. Joe and Paul were aloof as I walked up to them.

"So, you too," said Joe.

"For Chrissakes; you guys didn't give me a choice, you just pulled off."

"We have a big dinner most Friday nights," Mary was saying as she leaned into the rear window.

"Well, what do you think about Mr. Falcone?" I asked them.

"I think he's a smooth-talking punk," said Joe.

"Yeah? Well tell that to Mary," said Keegan.

"So come on up, Eddie; we'd love to see you. And bring Carla. Except, you get into those flicks on the way up, you won't have much energy left for dinner."

"Good God, Sis is a pain in the ass."

"Runs in the family I guess," said Paul. "Let's go get some coffee."

"Oh, and here's my ginger ale can —" said Mary, leaning in and giving Eddie Falcone, a.k.a. Slinky, a hug and a kiss on the cheek. Then she hopped gaily up the walk and met us. The white Caddy pulled away in silence. All three of us descended on Mary, giving her hell for fraternizing with the enemy. I thought we were pretty impressive, myself. Apparently, she didn't.

"Okay, okay, *okay*," she said, her arms crossed in defiance. "I *know* he's connected. I *know* he's a crook. Okay? You happy now? But I also know, based on my feelings, my instincts, that Eddie's telling the truth when he says he didn't kill Andy. I just know he didn't. Charlie, you said yourself the Wiseguys didn't kill Andy, remember?"

"Well, yeah, but —"

"That's it!" she said, throwing up her hands, "Now let's shut up and go back to the Breakers. I'm sick of all this male bullshit."

The three of us puffed out our chests and looked at each other, trying to think of something forceful and penetrating to say. But we couldn't. So we went back to the cars for the ride up to the cottage.

"I'm not being belligerent, Joe. I'm just saying that I don't think it covers all the facts," I said. We were just pulling into the gravel parking space at the Breakers. The three of us had driven up after our bout with the Sicilian Connection, leaving Paul Keegan and the boys in Woods Hole for the nonce so we could get some R and R at the cottage. Then Mary and I had to return to Concord for a few days to catch up on work and errands. Moe met us at the door and we went out on the deck.

"You have no respect for the way law enforcement works," said Joe. "Either of you."

"Shut up, Joey." said Mary. "You're just sore because I think Eddie Falcone's an okay guy. And because Charlie doesn't think old Lionel Hartzell's the guy who broke in here."

"So? Who's he like better for it?"

"Nobody," I said. "But the lack of a better suspect doesn't make Hartzell guilty . . . anymore than it made Jack guilty. If Hartzell had ransacked the Breakers, he wouldn't have stolen my short-wave radio."

"Sure he would, to throw us off, make it look like a routine burglary."

"C'mon. It just doesn't fit. Look: nothing was taken from the guys' rooms in Woods Hole. Jack says he can't account for anything missing, and there was a lot of stuff there that a burglar would want. So that was a genuine toss; somebody was looking for something they didn't find. But up here, hell, they took my radio, a camera, and some jewelry they must've thought was valuable. Little did they know."

"Yeah. Little did they know poor Mary doesn't own any genuine ice. Or hardly anything . . ."

Joe looked over at his forlorn sister. Poor Mary Adams.

"Yeah, right. Except poor Mary Adams is gonna fix all that with her new book, right?"

Mary beamed and blushed, and turned in her canvas director's chair to gaze off over Cape Cod Bay.

"What book?" I said.

"Your wife's writing a novel, Doc. Remember the book we talked about?"

"Mare, is this true?"

"Well," she blushed, "Joe mentioned to me yesterday that I had a gift with words, and that maybe I could put my . . . some of my past experiences into a romance novel."

"What past experiences?"

"Oh, you know, just experiences. The title's great, isn't it, Joey?" She spun her head toward me. "I'm calling it *Hills of Gold, Men of Bronze.*"

"*Hills of Gold, Men of Bronze?* Christ almighty."

"I tink it's great, Mary." piped Moe, looking up from his book, "I tink it —"

"Nobody asked you," I said, turning back to Mary. "What experiences?"

"*Hmmmph!*" she sniffed, snapping her head away from me. "You wanna find out what experiences, you gotta read the book, right Joey?"

"Right."

"Well, when am I going to get a chance to sample this masterpiece?"

"When I start writing it. Right now, what I'm doing is, I'm just thinking about it. You know, getting ideas."

"Oh I see. Moe, when did you hear about this?"

"Just now. And you know, Doc, Mary's got a creative mind. Her pottery proves that. I tink dis is a great idea. And who knows? She could be very successful at it."

It figured Moe would like the idea. Good old Moe, who wouldn't say shit if he had a mouthful. I gazed out at the bay. The water was a deep turquoise, with occasional whitecaps.

"Okay, Doc, so Keegan's having trouble making the charge stick. That's no surprise. But Hartzell's been arrested and detained on the charge; the whole thing will hinge on the probable cause hearing."

"Moe, do you think Lionel Hartzell killed Andy, searched his rooms, and then sacked the cottage?"

"I think it is possible, Doc. Perhaps, given the lack of other suspects, it is even probable. Joe says a hearing, wid a cross-examination, could reveal or disprove it."

I rose from my chair and paced the wooden planks. I wasn't satisfied. I turned back to Joe.

"You think the two break-ins are related or just coincidence?"

"C'mon! They were related, of course. To call it coincidence is lunacy. But they weren't similar. For instance, the burglary in Woods Hole wasn't forced. The burglar went right in the front door. But Hartzell could have used a key he had taken and copied, something he could have easily done, sharing an office with Andy. But he couldn't get a key to the cottage, so he forced the rear door."

"Yeah, I'd say he forced it, Joey," said Mary, opening a bottle of nail polish. "He smashed the window."

"No. No, he didn't smash it. He didn't have to. Here, let me show you something."

We joined him at the kitchen door, which had a cracked pane of glass nearest the lock and a hole in it big enough for a hand to go through. Joe took a pointed can opener — the type you used to use to open beer cans — and placed the point on an unbroken corner of the shattered pane of glass.

"I know you installed shatterproof safety glass in all the doors facing the ocean, Doc. Maybe it was smart, since you're worried about flying objects during storms. But watch what happens when I press this point against it."

We saw three tiny lines ooze out from the point of the tool as Joe slowly pressed it against the glass.

"Keep watching," he said.

The cracks grew longer, and four others joined the original three. After half a minute, we could see a spider-web pattern of shatter marks. Another minute and the point of the can opener pushed through the pane with a soft crunch. Joe then pulled out the squarish glass fragments with his bare fingers, leaving a hole exactly like the one already in the pane.

"See? No fuss, no muss, no *noise*. And no cut fingers, either. Safety glass *is* safe. It can also be pressure fractured in total silence. I tell ya, crooks love it."

"Good God! What do we do now?" asked Mary.

"What you do is nothing. Except replace the safety glass — on your door anyway — with wire-impregnated glass."

"Wait a second, Joe. You mean to tell me that old Lionel Hartzell, the wacko professor who's trying to grow silver in sea squirts, is up on the latest burglary techniques? And you think he also lifted the valuable stuff in this cottage too, just to make it look like a regular B and E, when he was really searching for stolen papers that were never stolen?"

Joe leaned back against the wall and tapped the can opener idly against his palm.

"There are some problems with it. I never said there weren't problems."

"Too many problems. I agree the two break-ins are connected. We can start there. But I think the burglars were looking for something real, not imaginary. And when they didn't find it in Woods Hole, they came up here."

"Looking for what?" asked Moe, joining us in the kitchen. "And did they find it?"

"If we don't know what they're looking for," said Mary, "then how do we know if they found it or not?"

"Right," said Joe. "Except you ask me, Andy could have buried it in the sand, the whatever-it-was. Then we'd never find it."

"And what about Lionel Hartzell?" I asked.

"What about him?" answered Joe. "He's our new suspect."

"You still think he did it? All by himself?"

"Look: he *is* a suspect. It's always good to have a suspect and a bunch of leads you're following. You don't have these, the public thinks you're just screwing around. Know what I mean? So, as I say, he *is* our suspect at this point in time. And also, if you haven't forgotten, it's looking better for Jack. And how do we know that Hartzell's papers *weren't* stolen, eh? He may be a goofball, but Andy was no babe in the woods, either. He could've waltzed into that lab, stolen some valuable research stuff, and waltzed out again with nobody the wiser. And what was he gonna do with it? Sell it, a ' course, to some pharmaceutical company or something. He can't leave the goods there, so he brings it up here with him for safekeeping over the weekend. And, hey! That could also explain the phone call."

"You mean he was trying to make contact with a buyer or something?" asked Mary.

"Sure. Hell, maybe there's a third party who knew about Hartzell's research beforehand, and just hired the kid fo lift it. There you go —"

"Sounds like the pieces fit to me," said Moe. "That's as good an explanation as any."

So Moe and I went for a search-run along the beach. Joe said he'd stay home and guard the bar and help Mary cook.

We decided to jog and walk, and went at it for two hours, going first up and down the beach three miles in either direction and scanning the scrub and grass-covered bluffs as we went. At every blowing plastic garbage bag, container, overturned boat, or pile of debris or driftwood, we stopped and poked around. We searched for curious-looking disturbances in the sand. There were none, and of course we both knew that ten days of Cape wind and weather would have obliterated them anyway. Moe suggested we find cottages or buildings that were vacant and look inside. Good idea, if we could've found any. But we didn't, and took to the back roads, sweeping our eyes everywhere for likely hiding spots that Andy could have found in the dark.

"Zip?" Mary asked as we trudged, sweat-soaked, up the bone-colored wooden stairs from the beach to the cottage deck. We nodded, and she said that at least we'd worked up good appetites. We went in and out of the sauna for another hour and emerged, showered and starved, at six, ready for food and drink.

We sat at the deck rail, sipping wine, feeling the cool bay breeze blow over us, and watching the sky turn yellow-gold. Then it was time to tuck into Mary's calamari.

"Well, whoever they are, they found what they were looking for," I announced as I sat down.

"What makes you so sure?" asked Moe, peering at me over his wine goblet.

"Nothing. I'm just sick of worrying about it. Pass the pasta."

SEVENTEEN

Poor Maria! She curled up on her pallet of fur and animal skins inside the tent. She could hear the hoof beats of the horses as the riders came and went in the night. The mountain air was cold, and her flimsy garments were scant comfort. She shivered and wept.

She thought of their leader, Fuente. A head taller than the others, he was magnificently strong. And, yes, she admitted to herself, sinfully handsome as well. It was Fuente who had beaten the ruffian called Pablo silly, then thrown him into the palmettos, to the laughter and ridicule of the others . . .

Maria knew she was to be Fuente's woman now. She rolled on the skin and fur floor of the tent, gathering her scanty rags about her shoulders. But as she thought of the tall dark one, the man with the features of an eagle, the feeling of liquid fire was spreading in her.

"Oh for Chrissakes," I said to myself.

— and she could not stop this feeling, this wonderful sensation that the sisters at the convent school had never mentioned. Who could have ever thought that she, Maria Teresa Perez, the pretty girl who, since the tragic death of her parents and the loss of La Sombra, the huge family ranch in the steep, cool mountains of Durango, had studied to be a nun, pure of heart and body, should be degraded so terribly! She shuddered at the recent memory of that terrible day when the bandits had ridden down from the high hills, shooting their carbines in the air, singing and shouting drunkenly, burning the ranch buildings and killing the shepherds. And then, then they had found her, hiding like a frightened rab-

bit in the tiny chapel . . . And yet, as she saw the light of the campfire flickering on the wall of her rude tent, and heard the coarse language and rough laughter of the bandits outside, she somehow felt a strange, wild release . . .

"Good God . . .," I groaned.

But what was that? What was this sound, coming closer to where she lay shivering? It was a clinking of metal, and the sound of slow, strong, footsteps approaching. Then Maria drew in a sharp breath of fear as she looked underneath the tent flap and saw the shiny leather boots . . . the gleaming silver spurs that jangled and rang with each strong step . . .

"Maria! Maria, my little pumpkin! Are you ready for me?"

Then the tent flap jerked aside, and she lifted her weary head, trembling, to gaze up helplessly at the dark, aquiline face of Fuente, red-brown in the firelight, his dark eyebrows and fierce mustache setting off his gleaming eyes, his fine, white teeth. He looked the brutal bandit, the iron-hard revolutionary, born of the injustice and poverty of the Mexican hills. And yet . . . and yet, she did see a sensitivity there, an inner gentleness that spoke through the sad eyes and full, soft mouth. What was he like, really, she wondered? Could he ever love? Was he capable of more than mere lust? Would she ever truly know him?

"So there you are, my little mountain warbler! My little vixen of the hills . . . you are rested I hope?" said Fuente in a hoarse whisper. He strode into the tent, clad in rough leather and metal. The cartridge belts across his wide chest gleamed gold. He cast them off, threw down his sombrero, and grabbed her in his iron talons. Too weak and frightened to resist, she let herself be raised up, and he took her in his powerful arms.

"Iron talons? *Iron talons?*"

Maria smelled the raw tequila on his breath, and beneath that, the male smell, the rough, salty-sweet drift of his man sweat. She felt herself growing weak, a strange dizziness sweeping over her. Fuente forced his lips on hers. She tried to struggle, but it was no use. She felt herself melting into him, yielding herself into his rough strength. The night noises of the wind and crickets, and the laughing, cursing ruffians around the fireside grew faint as a new sound rose in her ears, a warm, rushing sound like a million molten waterfalls —

"For crying out loud," I moaned, "spare me —"

Truly, this was a man who had known many women, who knew far more than the simple peasants he rode with. Maria felt herself blush with shame. Yes, she admitted to herself, yes, it was pleasure. She could no longer deny it.

She moaned aloud as the heat within her grew. A wet, liquid, burning fire, like the lava from a young volcano.

She could not speak, but buried her face in his massive chest, then raised it to seek his mouth again.

What would the mother superior say? Maria Teresa Perez, turned into a common slut, a slave of the passions of the flesh, by this brazen bandit!

The feeling of liquid fire returned now, with renewed force and fury. Moaning and writhing on the animal skins, she realized sadly that she was powerless in passion's grasp.

"Oh, yes . . ." she moaned, through trembling lips. Her brown eyes were half closed as she reached out and drew him on top of her. "I know I am to pay the price, Fuente. I am yours. You may do what you like with me . . . now and forever . . . !"

I put the manuscript down on the end table. What I wanted to do was, I wanted to throw it down the toilet.

But I was afraid of the steam.

So I went from my study desk, through the hallway that leads to Mary's pottery workshop and the greenhouse, and into the kitchen, where I proceeded to make a Dewar's and soda at the sideboard. No, better make that a double. Jeeeez . . . *Hills of Gold, Men of Bronze . . . Ay, carrramba! Sangre de Cristo!* Gimmie a break already. Actually, better make that a triple. The bottle gurgled softly, soothingly, as I poured in the Destroyer. Who did she think she was? I mean, get serious. Then I heard Mary's fast footsteps in the hallway, and she joined me in the kitchen.

"Well?" she said, eyes blazing with excitement. "Whadduyuh think, Charlie?"

I sipped, leaned back against the sideboard, and ruminated about phraseology. How to put it delicately.

"Well?"

"It's uh . . . certainly uh, *descriptive* . . ."

"Uh-huh. Go on . . ."

"And it's uh, sensual. Very sensual, Mare. That's for sure."

Her eyes lit up. "You bet. That's what Moe said down at the cottage. It's good, isn't it? You like it, don't you?"

"Uhhhhh. No. No, I can't say I'm too wild about it, hon."

Her face fell. Her jaw crept forward a quarter inch into a bull-dog pout. She crossed her arms over her bosom and worked her clay-covered fingers back and forth, letting fragments and powder sift to the floor. She looked at the floor, shifting her feet back and forth.

"Why not? What's wrong with it?"

"What's wrong with it? Everything, that's what. I mean, it's just a trashy, cheap story is all."

"Oh yeah? Well shit, then. Why did I ever ask you, anyway? You just haven't read any of the best sellers lately. Moe likes it. And Janice loves it."

"Of that I have not the slightest doubt. But the fact remains, Mare, that the story is simply a vehicle for cheap sex scenes."

"You catch on fast. So what's wrong with that?"

"Mary, in literature, portrayals of love, sex, and intimacy should be subtle and refined, not gross and animalistic. And while sex is a good thing, and enhances affection and love, it should not be the end in itself."

"Says who?"

"Says everyone. So say all the critics. People like Clifton Fadiman, for example. In short: art is supposed to elevate, not denigrate."

"Oh lighten up, Charlie. You don't really believe that, I hope. It's just your WASP training showing through. Every day I thank God I'm not a WASP. Now take that poker out of your ass and read the next chapter."

"I'd rather read it after you've gone through it again and cleaned —"

"Listen, Charlie: I don't want it to be great art. I want it to be fun to read. And I bet I sell it to a publisher."

"I doubt that."

"Oh yeah? Then put your money on the table; a hundred bucks says I sell it."

Something told me not to take that bet.

Trying to be diplomatic, I made a final, futile attempt to explain literature as defined by Aristotle, or what I remembered of him, which was scant. Her response to this well-meaning lecture was unappreciative. She suggested I take Aristotle and Clifton "what's-his-name" and shove them up my nether orifice. I replied that this was clearly impossible since, according to her, a poker was already residing therein. With a crisp "Fuck you, Charlie!" she departed, slamming her workshop door behind her.

Sensing that our dialogue had reached an impasse, I opened the door cautiously, peered around, and saw Mary at her work table, working a big hunk of wet clay, strangling it with her incredibly strong hands.

"Listen, Mary, I didn't mean to sound harsh. All I was trying to say was —"

She turned fast, her mouth drawn up in a sour look, her cheeks wet. Her right arm swung back and snapped forward, doing a dynamite imitation of Roger Clemens on the Red Sox mound. I ducked behind the door.

Wham!

The wad of wet earth stuck to the door for a second before it came unstuck and plopped softly on the tile floor behind the closed door. It was safe to assume she was upset. Chances were, if I stayed around, she'd lose her temper. So I beat a hasty retreat into the study again. Just as I sat down behind my desk, the phone rang.

"Is this Dr. Charles Adams?"

"Yes it is. How may I help you?"

"My name is Marvin Isaacson, Dr. Adams, and I run a pawn-shop down here in New Bedford. Tell me, Doctor, have you lost any valuable articles recently? Say, within the past week?"

Instantly, I knew the purpose of the call.

"Yes I have. They were stolen from my cottage down on Cape Cod."

"Ah! The pieces seem to fit. Listen: my sons and I have been trying to reach you for the last four days —"

"Well, we've been down on the Cape the whole time. We just came back here to Concord last night to get the mail and mow the lawn and things. I'm glad you caught us. Do you want me to describe the articles?"

"Please."

So I did, paying particular attention to the SONY short-wave. I told him I'd removed the back and fastened an I.D. plate inside, containing name, address, and phone.

"That's how I found you," said Isaacson. "One of my sons took the radio in pawn when I was out. When I saw it, and thought there was a chance it might have been stolen, I removed the back and checked for any sort of owner identification. You were smart to put your name in there. So you want to come down and get it?"

"Uh-huh. Tomorrow. How much will it cost me?"

"We gave the kid two hundred on pawn. So if I can get my money back, I'm happy."

"I'll get your money back and then some, for your honesty. And I'm also thinking you can help us identify the kid. You say he is a kid, a young man?"

"Yes, my son says maybe between twenty and thirty."

"That's interesting. If he comes back to reclaim it, stall him and phone the cops."

"I know, but he won't. The whole thing smelled so much of stolen goods I began searching for a name as soon as I saw it. I been in this business a long time."

We rang off and I called Joe at the cottage.

"Hmmmm. And so you think this supports your feeling that it wasn't Hartzell who was behind it?"

"I sure do. What do you think?"

"I don't know yet. I think maybe Hartzell could've gotten some young punk help for the break-ins. But that poisoning job, Doc, that was clearly done by somebody extremely knowledgeable and cunning. The poisoning certainly doesn't fit with a young punk kid. You read me?"

"Yeah. I hear what you're saying. Well, I'd like you to come down to New Bedford with me tomorrow and interview Marvin Isaacson."

"Can do."

"How's Moe?"

"Fine. He's off down the beach looking for whatever's washed up in the night."

"Figures. See you tomorrow."

So I hung the phone up again and spent the next hour psyching myself up to go out and trim the hedges.

EIGHTEEN

MARY AND I rolled out of the sack at seven, made a quick pot of coffee, drank half and bottled the rest, and drove down to New Bedford. We rolled into town off highway 140 and met Joe at a small shopping center we all knew about. He was leaning against his cruiser munching on a doughnut, a tall plastic-foam cup of coffee sitting on the roof.

"'Bout time," he said, his mouth swollen with dough. He climbed aboard the Audi and off we went.

New Bedford made her name in the last century as the world's premier whaling port. It remains one of the most historic and colorful towns in the east, and one of my very favorite Massachusetts towns.

Gloucester, her sister city to the north, is like New Bedford in many ways. The biggest resemblance lies in the maritime flavor they both have. When you visit either town, you smell fish and see fishing boats, fish markets, fish processing plants, fish piers, marine supply houses, and so on. And they both have strong ethnic communities with roots in the fishing industry. Up in Gloucester, it's the Italians. In New Bedford, the Portuguese.

We were now heading down Pleasant Street toward the historic south end and the whaling museum. Nearby is the famous Seamen's Bethel church on Johnny Cake Hill, the church with the unique pulpit in the shape of a ship's prow, where Ishmael heard the sermon delivered by Father Mapple in the beginning of *Moby Dick*. It's all still there, virtually unchanged since Melville wrote about it. And having been "a-whaling" — in a manner of speaking — and seen the beasts close-up, I felt as if I almost belonged there. We followed Marvin Isaacson's directions and found his pawnshop just a hop and a skip from the old church, on the edge of the historic district with its brick buildings and cobbled streets.

There weren't three gold balls hanging over the doorway, but the window was filled with the usual items one finds in pawnshops, namely firearms, musical instruments, cameras, and watches. Marvin, a white-haired guy of about sixty, welcomed us warmly, but was slightly taken aback when Joe introduced himself as the fuzz.

"Don't worry, Marvin. I've come here as a brother-in-law as much as a cop. But we all are interested in how you came into posssession of this radio." And he briefly related the story of Andy's death and the subsequent burglaries. Marvin drummed his fingers nervously on the glass case he was leaning on, then ran his fingers through his ample white hair.

"See, we've been in this business now four generations. We run a good shop. Believe me, I'm familiar with the new laws about fencing stolen merchandise, so you see, we're real careful. Darryl looked all over the outside of the radio for an I.D., but couldn't find any. But when I came back and saw the radio, and when I heard a kid had pawned it, well, naturally, I had my doubts. So that's when I took off the back cover."

Joe took out his notebook and sat in the corner with Darryl Isaacson, the son who'd taken the radio in pawn, while Marvin placed my SONY on the counter. I wrote him a check for his money, hoping I could get at least part of it back from the insurance company. Joe requested that the young Isaacson go up to Boston and cooperate in a computer-generated composite reproduction of the young man who came into the shop.

"It takes maybe thirty, thirty-five minutes," Joe said. "What you do is, you sit in front of a screen, and they flash up faces with different types of eyes, nose, hair, facial shapes, and so on, and all you do is tell them to change this and that until you see a face that resembles the guy as closely as you can remember. Remember that toy called Mr. Potato Head? Well, that's what it's like; you just keep playing with parts of a face until you get it."

The kid wasn't really eager, but the elder Isaacson assured us that both of them would go up to Ten Ten Commonwealth Avenue and do it. We thanked them and left, arriving back at the Breakers, as planned, in time for lunch. The three of us met Moe, who was already there, finishing up his little vacation. We all changed into bathing suits and sat on the deck.

I'd bought some of that spicy-hot red sausage the Portuguese call *linguiça* in the north end of town on the way back. This Mary and I cooked quickly in a wide iron skillet, then added marinara sauce. Then I cut three long pieces of a French baguette, put in the sausage, covered it with the sauce, and sprinkled on a lot of Parmesan cheese and some hot peppers. Sausage subs. I took them out onto the deck, where Joe dove into his with his usual fury: eyes glazed, chin shiny with grease, low moans of ecstasy punctuated by chewing and gulping.

Moe, who'd been reading and beachcombing, had his usual lunch. He brought out three big plastic bags of dried fruit and nuts, and sat munching on these items, washing down the health food with blue milk. Moe never has any fun. I was only eating lunch because I'd had no breakfast, but the subs were good. We sipped beer and looked at the far, hazy horizon. Joe wiped his hands and took out his notebook, flipping through the pages and belching softly.

"This was a lucky break," he said. "Besides getting your radio back, we've got a description of the kid who pawned it."

I eased back in my deck chair, feeling the warm sun all over me. "So have your thoughts about Hartzell as the culprit changed any?"

He shrugged. "Somehow, it seems a little less likely, but I can't say why. It's just a feeling."

"Uh-huh. I share it. And I think the reason is, we're remembering that Hartzell hates young guys. So why would he enlist the aid of a young kid in a burglary? So the pieces just don't fit very well."

"So? So what do *you* think?"

"If the two B and Es are not connected, then the break-in here was done by some young druggie, or druggies, strung out and needing quick cash. That's what I think."

He nodded and stretched out his huge, hairy legs, which, for him, were deadly pale. "Yeah, fine. But because a strange little voice keeps telling us, we've been assuming that the B and Es *are* related. This little voice that won't go away keeps saying that the same person or persons did both jobs, looking for something that wasn't a radio, that the stolen radio was just an afterthought."

"That's what I think, too."

"And you're also saying it might not be Hartzell. And I'm beginning to agree. So where do we go now?"

I shrugged, chewing. "Who knows? Maybe back to the Henderson family."

"Why them?" asked Mary.

"Because they're the link that fits best. They, at least Alice, seem to be in the center of this whole affair. Terry is roughly the same age as the kid who pawned the radio. I'm not saying that he did it; I'm saying that he's the right age, in the right place, at the right time, and he knew Andy."

"But you've already talked to Alice, Doc. And Keegan's interviewed Terry, too. In depth."

"Then I guess it's our turn."

"You have no authority," said Moe, trying to remove a bit of apricot skin, or bean sprout, or some damn thing, from his teeth.

"I do have authority. I am the interim medical examiner for Barnstable County. So there."

"Big deal," Moe sniffed. "Dat doesn't cut any ice wid me."

"Well I'm not interviewing you. So go eat your steamed grass and shut up."

NINETEEN

Eye — eeeeeee! . . . Eeeee-yonk! . . . Yonk, yonk, yonk yonk!

The big herring gull glided in over us with delicate rowing motions of its long wings, then fanned them forward against the air as it stopped its flight above the trawler's mast, extended its oversized, ducklike feet, and settled down there twenty feet above the deck, moving its head around in little jerks, looking out over Penzance Point.

Joe and I were standing on the afterdeck of the *Highlander*, the sixty-foot stern trawler owned by William Henderson, father of Alice and Terry. The vessel's hailing port, listed under her name, was Falmouth. But now she was berthed in Woods Hole, at the fishing docks west of the MBL. The senior Henderson was ashore at the moment, but Terry was sitting on the engine housing near the big winch drums, looking up at us nervously. I took my eyes off the noisy gull and looked down at the boy.

"I know Lieutenant Keegan already talked to you," said Joe softly. He has a great bedside manner when he wants to turn it on. Usually he begins an interview in this fashion, resorting to the tough cop routine only when he meets resistance. Clearly, we had Terry Henderson's attention.

"What we want to find out now is, who would want to break into Andy and Jack's room, and maybe also into the Adams's cottage up near Wellfleet?"

The kid shrugged and bit his lower lip lightly, nervously. "I don't know. I kinda thought that old man Hartzell was a good shot at it, you wanta know. But see, I'm not really with that group at the labs; I work for my dad on the boats and stuff. I don't really know what's going on there; the only time I see those guys is at some of the beach parties."

"What guys?"

"You know, Jack, Tom McDonnough, the younger guys at the lab. We see each other at some of the parties. My sister helped get us together, kinda."

"Where is Alice now?"

"She's out on the *Westward* again. We haven't seen her in two days."

"And you have no idea at all who would've wanted to kill Andy?" I asked.

"No. Like I said before, knowing Andy, I can't believe it was anybody in their right mind, you know? So that's why, when they tagged that old nut, I thought he might be the one."

We heard a thump from the *Highlander*'s bow, looked up through the wheelhouse, and saw a big, ruddy, white-blond man walking aft with heavy, deliberate steps. He glanced in at the three of us and frowned.

"Something wrong? What's this?"

"Dad, these guys are asking about Andy Cunningham again," said Terry.

"Oh really now," the big man said, setting down a cardboard carton on the engine housing. "Well gentlemen, that's nice and all, that you're so concerned, but I've got a business to run. That boy's been dead now going on two weeks. We're all sorry, but life goes on."

He offered his hand and we introduced ourselves. Bill Henderson was the owner of the *Highlander* and apparently several other boats as well. He was half a head taller than I am, which made him at least six four. And he was solid, too. His hands were big, rough, warm, and dry. After we shook hands, Henderson returned to the carton, taking out a can of grease, prying it open with a wide screwdriver, and scooping out big globs of the greenish-brown jelly, which he smeared on the winch axles.

"Goddamn salt air is pure hell on metal," he grunted. "Even

the new alloys that are supposed to be — *ummmph!* shit! — supposed to be corrosion resistant. Terry, go into the wheelhouse and start this up," he said, almost under his breath. But before he'd even finished, the boy, so casual to most people, was on his feet and making a beeline for the wheelhouse. We heard the twin diesels rev up and watched the drums turn, then reverse. Bill Henderson made minor adjustments, primed the axles with more slick goop, and ordered the winches switched off.

"I think I heard a strange thing about this Cunningham kid," said Henderson as he lighted a cigarette, then tapped the grease can's top back in place with the screwdriver's butt. "Somebody happened to mention to me — was it you Terry? — that the kid owed some money. Or something like that. What was it anyway, Terry?"

The kid shrugged his shoulders, and his old man squinted at him. There was the look of interrogation in that squint. Terry just shook his head vaguely.

"Wasn't it you who told me? Goddammit! Who the hell was it?" *Bap! Bap! Bap!* He tapped the can harder in his frustration. His son's jaw fell slack, and again he shrugged.

"Well anyway, I heard this scuttlebutt, and it could be pure bullshit, that the kid was in hock. Pretty deep in hock, and that he —"

"Can you remember where you heard it?" asked Joe. "This could be important."

"Well, I'm trying. I thought it was Terry, or Alice, or one of the kids. Hell, Dr. Adams, it coulda been your kid. Naw ... no wait —" He rose, grabbed the can of grease, and went forward to stow it in a locker. He came back almost immediately, leaving scarcely a lull in the conversation. For such a big man, he moved with a lot of speed and grace. But as he sat down, he was breathing faster. "Aw hell, I can't remember, but it was somebody. Anyhow, it just made me think that the kid wasn't what he —"

Henderson was looking past us; something had momentarily caught his eye. But in a flash, he seemed to wave it off and kept muttering about "outside elements."

"You know what I'm saying, right Lieutenant? I mean, it seems like everybody's questioning all of us in the community. And you're all wondering why it doesn't make too much sense and you're not getting anywhere. You ask me, you're not looking far enough away from home. But shit, what do I know? I'm just another one of life's chumps, tryin' to rub two nickels together — excuse me a sec —"

He hustled down the *Highlander*'s gangplank and across the dock, moving with that same driving speed I found so remarkable for a man his size. Looking beyond the docks, I saw that a big navy blue Mercedes had pulled up into the asphalt parking area. The driver, a plump, well-dressed, white-haired gentleman, leaned against the door, facing us. He was dressed in what I'd call rich-casual. I saw him flip his left arm up, brush back the sleeve of his blazer with his right hand, check a gold watch on his wrist, and lower the arm again. Bill Henderson came up to the man and they started talking without shaking hands. That meant they knew each other well, or had seen each other often. I turned around and saw Joe busy watching two young women padding along Albatross Street in bikinis. By the time I turned around again, the Mercedes was rolling away and the senior Henderson was trudging aboard his boat again.

I went aft and stared along the ramp cut into the *Highlander*'s rear deck that sloped down to the water's surface. The nets were played out and hauled in right up the stern. Hence the name: stern trawler. We Americans finally got the hang of building these efficient boats after spending twenty years watching the Koreans, East Germans, Russians, and Japanese use them to slurp up all our fish. We were catching up, slowly but surely. Even so, the two-hundred-mile limit — excluding foreign craft from our rich coastal waters — hadn't come along any too soon.

"No, I tell ya I can't remember," I heard Henderson saying to Joe. He said it like this: cahnt. I swept my eyes around the big boat. I didn't want to ask permission to go below, but I knew there would be berths there for four, five, maybe as many as eight crew members. And then there were those big twin diesels, and all that navigation gear: radar, Loran, SATNAV, ASDIC, sonar depth sounders, sonar fish finders. Two-way radios ... the works. What was I looking at? Half a million? Eight hundred thou? A mil and a half? What?

"No," Henderson continued in his boomy baritone. "Seems to me somebody saw a Mafia wagon around. Aw hell, don't lissen a' me Lieutenant. What do I know?"

I went up to where the two men were standing near the wheelhouse. Joe was putting away his notebook. He stuck his hands into his pants pockets and shrugged. Then Henderson leaned over and pointed a big finger at his chest.

"Hey. Not to get nosey or anythin', but I thought that other guy was workin on this thing."

"Paul Keegan? Yeah, he is. But we're helping out. And I'm not sure the suspect he's got is going to pan out."

Henderson looked up to the wheelhouse. He shouted for his son to start the engines. Again we heard the rising crescendo of the big diesels beneath us. The steel deck vibrated under our feet as Henderson went forward to cast off. Time to leave. Joe and I thanked Henderson for his time, waved to his son up behind the glass in the wheelhouse, and disembarked, walked along the dock toward the MBL.

"Why not stop in the Kidd first for a coupla cold ones?" suggested Joe. So we did.

The pretty girl behind the bar handed us two St. Pauli Girl beers as we leaned on that unique and curious marble rail in the Cap'n Kidd. Never seen one like it before or since.

"So what are you thinking, Doc? You seem awfully preoccupied."

"I'm wondering where Henderson sells his fish. It can't be here in Woods Hole. And Falmouth's harbor hardly deserves the name."

"I asked him that very question. He sells fish in New Bedford. Where else?"

"That makes sense. I've heard New Bedford is the biggest commercial fishing port in America. Bigger than Gloucester. Bigger than San Francisco, Seattle . . ."

Joe chewed a handful of peanuts and scuffed his size thirteen shoes along the floor of the bar.

"I been thinking; there may be a new angle on this thing. Suppose the mob was in on the hit. Not necessarily that kid Slinky, but somebody else in the organization not so wet behind the ears.

We know they never woulda killed Andy the way it was done. But supposing they bumped into old Hartzell and discovered he hated Andy too. Why then wouldn't they make a deal with him and —"

"Naw. C'mon, Joe, even *I* know the mob would never do a hit like that."

He chewed some more, nodding philosophically.

"Okay, try this: Andy has done something really major to piss the Wiseguys off. A lot of times, you owe the mob money and can't pay, and they know you haven't got the scratch, they ask you to do them a favor. So maybe he undertook the favor — whatever slimy thing it might be — and totally blew it. That would get him wasted."

I swiped a couple of peanuts. After one, I couldn't stop. There was a ring of truth to Joe's theory. It seemed to fill in a lot of blank spots.

"What kind of favor would this be?" I asked.

"A common one is courier, or bagman. They ask the guy to carry something hot for them. Or maybe carry a big load of dope across the border. Something like that."

"Well, we know the favor had to be in this region. What's most likely here?"

"Well, keeping to the dope idea, maybe the mob asked him to borrow one of the official small craft from here, say like that skiff you guys used the other day. Where was it from? The National Marine Fisheries Service? Anyway, asked Andy to borrow a boat for half a day and run in a load of coke or grass from the mother ship. Just zip out there, take on the goods, and zip inland in a —"

The hair on the back of my neck stood up.

"*That's it!* Joe, it fits perfectly. These labs and the boats they use are the most respected things around here. You *know* the Coast Guard wouldn't stop and search one of those vessels. Never."

Joe swirled the beer around slowly in his glass and smiled. He was pleased with himself.

"Yeah, Doc. It does fit together nicely. Not bad for a cop on vacation, eh?"

"But it still leaves the question of the murderer."

"Okay, the mob wants Andy out, so they either have Hartzell

do it, or else find out from somebody like Hartzell how to do it . . ."

I felt we were getting off base there, as if riding a crosscurrent. I shook my head.

"One thing the mob connection could explain is the break-ins," he continued. "If Andy held out on them, you know, kept part of the shipment for himself to sell, then they'd kill him and go looking for the stuff."

"That fits. That and the part about smuggling. But the method employed . . . that does not fit."

"Let's go eat, and think about it some more."

"How's Keegan coming with Hartzell up in Boston? You heard anything?"

"Not lately. But if Hartzell's a washout, we'll tell Paul about this mob theory. Hey, let's go up to the Coonamessett for dinner, huh?"

TWENTY

SEVERAL DAYS LATER, the last day of August and twenty days after Andrew Cunningham was found dead in our cottage, Mary, Joe, Moe, and the boys and I were all at sea. In more ways than one, I suppose. We were aboard the MBL's collecting vessel the *Gemma*, the forty-foot trawler skippered by Wayland Smith. We were collecting all right, but sounds, not creatures. In the boat's high, broad bow stood Smitty and Moe, leaning over the hydromike that had been lowered into the sea to record the songs of the humpback whale.

Jack sat in the wheelhouse hunched over a console filled with electronic gear. He peered intently at an oscilloscope as the sounds picked up by the mike made sine curves and pairs of snaking, wavy lines. Wearing earphones, he fiddled with knobs and dials while his brother Tony minded the helm, keeping us at a steady four knots.

PPHHEEEEEWWWWW!

"Thar she blows . . . ," said Tony softly.

Thirty feet off our port bow three whales surfaced, spewing big clouds of vapor. Then they began their slow forward somersault back into the deep. Farther off, another whale smacked its tail down flat onto the surface; it sounded like a rifle shot. Sheets of water shot out sideways from under the big flukes. We'd been out three hours, and would shortly head for home. We had collected a lot of whale songs, those curious clicks, grunts, squeaks, and low, bass-fiddle groans that were so strange and haunting.

But Joe and Mary weren't talking about the whales; they were discussing a subject more dear to their hearts.

"And the part where she's sold as a slave girl is great," said Joe. "I really hate that what's-his-name —"

"Raoul Estevez?"

"Yeah. That guy. Wow Mary! You've really got some great characters going."

"Charlie says it's too shallow and sex-ridden."

"What does he know? Doc, what do you know?"

"Nothing, I guess. What's Moe's opinion?"

"He loves it, Charlie. Loves it."

I shrugged my shoulders and looked straight down. Twenty feet below the boat were a mother whale and her calf. The calf was swimming along her left flank, never leaving her side, exactly like a heeling dog. The calf was small, perhaps twenty-some feet in length. I called attention to them, and everybody looked over the rail at the touching sight. Jack said the little tyke was growing, though — gaining weight at the rate of a hundred pounds a day.

When they disappeared, diving down into the shimmering green, getting smaller and smaller and smaller until at last they were out of sight, Joe stepped back from the rail and lighted a cigarette, taking out his ever-present notebook and flipping through the pages.

"Can we talk?" he said in a low voice. "I've got some stuff to tell you, and with all the rushing around I haven't had a chance until now. Okay?" We went and sat down on a bench next to the engine-room bulkhead.

"Got some more stuff on Slinky," he said. "He's older than he looks. Twenty-eight. Divorced; no kids. Lives in Pawtucket. Five priors, mostly stuff on the low end, and nothing that stuck. Not employed . . . by anything straight, that is. Claims he's in the construction business. In the organization he might be what we'd call a junior vice president. What he's been brought in for is strong-arm extortion, loan sharking, gambling, bookmaking, small-time stuff. So far, there's nothing to indicate he's into drug dealing. If he was, then the NEA could come down on him."

"Seems to me you're going to have a hard time getting anything on him."

"With connected guys like this, even the low-level ones, it's damn hard. They can come up with witnesses, pay off or threaten prosecutors, you name it. The only success we've had, especially at the federal level, is making deals with stoolies."

"The Witness Protection Program?"

"Right. The feds wait till they've got a live one in the net . . . a high-ranking mobster who's nailed dead to rights and faces life without parole. They cut a deal with the guy: we'll let you entirely off the hook if you testify against the mob. In return, in addition to letting you walk, we'll set you up under different cover and protect you for life."

"That really works, doesn't it?"

"Oh sure, *if* you've got the guy nailed. But I don't think we're ever going to get enough on Falcone — a.k.a. Slinky — to nail him to the barn door."

"So what you're saying is, chances are he'll walk anyway."

"Unfortunately, yes. That's what it comes down to."

"Well, too bad. Because I really think that drug-running scenario of yours makes sense. It explains just about everything."

"Yeah. I heard from Paul Keegan this morning, too. He admitted that things up in Boston were looking bleak. Hartzell remains a suspect, but Paul will come back here without an indictment unless something dramatic unravels."

I said nothing, but my gaze fell. If Hartzell got out of the hot seat, I knew Jack would be back in.

Just then an enormous humpback, not more than twenty yards off our beam, hunched its back up in a tight curl, rolled forward, and sounded, leaving behind its curious "footprint" of swirling water. I pointed at the whirlpool, the inverted cone of swirling brine and foam.

"Know what that is?" I asked Joe. "That's the whale's footprint."

He leaned over the rail skeptically. "The what?"

"The whale's footprint. It's the whale's calling card he leaves when he sounds."

"*Hmmmph!*" he muttered, blowing smoke into the sea breeze.

There was a few seconds of silence while Joe smoked, watching the footprint on the water's surface disperse and fade.

"Some footprint, Doc," he said. "Now you see it, now you don't.

That's what this Cunningham case reminds me of: the friggin' whale's footprints. Leads keep appearing and then disappearing. Driving us nuts. I'm going inside."

"Why?"

"To read the next chapter of *Hills of Gold, Men of Bronze*. Why else?"

"You've gotta be kidding. You'd rather do that than witness this spectacle?"

"Yep. That book's great. Can't put it down."

"Thanks, Joey," cooed Mary, who'd overheard the tail end of the conversation. "By the way, I'm thinking of changing the title. I'm thinking of calling it *The Men*."

"The men what?"

"Just *The Men*. Whadduyuh think, Joey?"

"Great."

"Please," I said. "How about *Maria Makes Matamoros*? You know, kinda like *Debbie Does Dallas*?"

She told me my humor was not appreciated, and they both went below to discuss the magnum opus — or is it magnus opus? Isn't that second declension?

TWENTY-ONE

OUR VACATION was due to end with the arrival of September, which rolled in with some surprising hot and muggy weather down on the Cape. This unusual heat was another incentive to return to chez Adams in Concord, where at least there was air conditioning. So on Saturday, September 2, we called it quits and headed back toward Boston after breakfast. Mary and I were in her car followed by Joe in his cruiser. Moe, driving his twelve-year-old lime green Dodge, brought up the rear. Moe had made a rather mysterious trip down to Woods Hole and back early in the day, and it had me thinking. I had a theory about why he'd gone down there. But what Joe had to tell us when we stopped for coffee in Wareham drove it from my mind completely.

"Just before we left, I phoned Keegan at his office in Hyannis," said Joe, lighting a cigarette and sipping from the steaming cup. Mary, Moe, and I leaned forward intently. "The D.A.'s letting Hartzell walk. Sorry, but that's it. No indictment, mainly because there's no hard evidence. They admit he appears to be unstable — that's the word they're using — but the fact that he was away on a three-day conference with Art Hagstrom, the MBL director, right when your cottage was burgled didn't help the case at all —"

"What?"

"Apparently, Hartzell was one of the people who went with Hagstrom down to the Jersey shore. Weren't you the one who told me Art Hagstrom was down there?"

"Good God," whispered Mary. "He went down there with Art."

I recalled Art mentioning his imminent departure in our dormitory room. He said he was going down there with 'several other scientists.' And now it turned out Hartzell was one of them, which meant that Hartzell had not — couldn't have — ransacked the Breakers. He was in the clear and could not be detained any longer.

"What's Keegan say about all this?" I said, trying to hide my disappointment and fear.

"Not much, obviously. Now he's got his ass in a sling with the brass for moving too fast; he should've checked Hartzell's whereabouts more carefully before he collared him. And Art Hagstrom's mad, too. This is off the record: Art's mad because he wanted Hartzell removed from the MBL's roster of visiting fellows. He can't stand him, and he told Keegan that everyone else in Woods Hole is fed up with his temper tantrums and paranoia. It's ironic that it was Art's own statement that let the air right out of the case."

"I must say it doesn't surprise me much," I said. "What's the latest development on Slinky and the Rhode Island police?"

"I'll find out more next week. I wouldn't be surprised if we have a joint meeting with the state guys from Rhode Island about Falcone. They want to use Andy's death as another means of leverage against him and the families. They're thinking if they throw enough stuff at him, maybe they can shake something loose."

"Eddie didn't kill anybody," said Mary. "You guys are looking in the wrong direction there. Trust me."

Joe and I were not pleased to hear Mary defending Slinky but we just eyed each other, neither of us in the mood to cross swords with her on the subject. We arrived home at one-thirty. Mary and I made a cold lobster salad, which we served in heated sub rolls along with chilled white grapes and a hunk of Vermont Cheddar. Before lunch, I noticed Moe slip away and walk back to the driveway. The second time he excused himself, I went into the living room and watched through the window. I saw him go to his car, lift the trunk carefully, and peer inside. I had an ominous hunch what was in the trunk. My suspicions were heightened when I saw him take a coiled electric cord and snake it from the trunk over to our outdoor wall socket on the side of the house.

Sneaking out of the house and around the lawn, I crept up behind him and peered over his shoulder. I spied three big cardboard cartons resting in the trunk. Each was filled with a big plastic bag. The tops of the bags were gathered with wound rubber bands and plastic tubes snaked into each bag. I heard the purring of an electric pump and the muted sounds of bubbling. Moe didn't know I was behind him.

"We're almost home, kids," he whispered lovingly to the cartons. "Then Daddy's gonna give you all a *big* lunch. Yeah . . . "

You tell me this guy's not wacko? You wonder why he's allowed to practice psychiatry? It's possibly crossed your mind?

"Okay Moe, what the hell's this?" I said.

He spun around fast, gulped, and tried to close the trunk. But the extension cord was in the way and it wouldn't shut. I stepped around him and raised the lid, then leaned over the nearest carton and peered into the cloudy bag. A pair of hideous beady eyes glared back. Fanning around the eyes were waving fins and speckled, blotchy tendrils of undulating flesh. Spare me.

I turned and looked at him. He had on his bird-of-paradise outfit again: Roman sandals, Day-Glo Hawaiian shirt, yellow shorts. Unbelievable.

"Moe, you're a living monument to nausea."

"C'mon, Doc, shut dat trunk. The light's not good for 'em. They could die."

"What a shame."

He disconnected the cord and slammed the trunk lid down.

"Know why the sunlight's bad for them?" I asked. "Because they're bottom feeders. Every last one of 'em! You got those plug-uglies from Smitty, didn't you? You sucked up to him and his staff so they'd let you have all the sea slime you could carry home." I pointed at the trunk. "Every fish in there is a dropout from God's plan."

"Not so," he sniffed. "You're just narrow minded."

"Look: I don't know where you managed to hide those, but I —"

"Ha! You admit it! I knew you and Joe were sneaking into the supply shed to try to find these and dump them. But I hid them in a lab in Lillie Hall. So there!"

"What's going on?"

We turned to see Mary coming from the front door. I explained. She told me it was none of my business. That I should leave Moe's hobby entirely alone. And so on. And on.

But then she went and looked.

"Sweet Jesus, Moe, *dump 'em!*"

So Moe left in a huff. As he got behind the wheel, I told him not to reappear until he had dumped the fish and changed his clothes. He leaned out the window and loudly thanked Mary for the hospitality. Then he glared at me silently, rolled up the window, and left. His old Dodge snorted, backfired, and blew clouds of blue smoke. The shocks were gone and at the foot of the drive, the back end jumped up and down, scraping on the road.

"Poor Moe," said Mary.

"Don't give me poor Moe. That guy can afford a brace of Porsches annually."

"No he can't. You know he gives all his money to charity. That's why he drives that old car and lives in a trailer."

"And buys his clothes at K Mart. No, wait. It must be Western Tire and Auto."

"You shouldn't be so mean to him, Charlie."

"I'm the one who's gonna have to look at those fish, Mare. Right in our office suite. The place where people come to get well, not sick. C'mon, let's go inside."

We found Joe on the phone in the sun porch. He nodded and grunted into the receiver, then rang off.

"I'm going to be meeting with Keegan Monday. We've got the composite computer-generated sketch furnished by the Isaacsons. He's been showing it around Woods Hole with no success. We'll try New Bedford next. Then the towns in Rhode Island."

"I just might spook around myself on Monday," I said, "I've only got a couple of patients."

"Where are you going?" Joe asked.

"Maybe New Bedford."

"Why? Don't you think Keegan and I can do our jobs?" he said with a touch of belligerence.

"Look Joe: the spotlight is shifting away from Hartzell back to my son. Three guys in the field are better than two. Besides, I said *maybe*."

Sobbing, Maria tugged at the cruel chains that bit into her flesh. Her cries were in vain, and with tears streaming down her face, she accepted her fate. She sank down onto the straw-covered floor of her cell and wept bitterly.

Later, she heard footsteps in the dreary stone hallway outside. Then there was a brassy rattle of keys, the sound of the thick iron bolt being pulled back, and the heavy, iron-bound oaken door crept open on groaning hinges. Flickering torches that smelled of pine pitch shot golden light on the stone walls. The two men entered.

"Hah! There you are wench! Come! On your feet! The auction begins!" said the coarse jailer. He stank of ale, and as she staggered to her feet, he pulled her forth roughly by her chains. As he pulled her up the gangplank, she bit her lip to keep from cursing him and crying out . . .

"Is it getting any better?" asked Mary. She asked nicely, and she was lying on her side, rubbing my back. We were naked in the heat.

"Much better." What else could I say?

"Where are you?"

"At the auction."

"Mmm. Wait till you see what happens next."

"I've got a pretty good idea. I mean, she mostly gets laid right and left. And I have also observed that she doesn't put up too much of a struggle, either."

The hand stopped rubbing my back. Uh-oh. It started again, working down below my waist this time. A skilled hand at that . . .

"Keep reading, Charlie."

There were four women on the auction block. But it was clear to Maria from the way the men were leering at her that she was the most desirable. A pretty blonde next to her was weeping. Maria swayed on her feet from hunger and thirst. Through clenched teeth she offered up a prayer, and her eyes clouded over with tears. The auctioneer came up on the block, pacing from one slave girl to the next, turning them around this way and that, so that the bidders could get a good look.

"Oh Virgin Mary! Save me! Save me!" she cried, and she closed her eyes in terror.

Through her delirium, she heard the sound of rifle shots off to her left. There was too the pounding of horses, many horses, galloping closer at high speed. The shots grew louder, and mingled with the surprised shouts of the crowd below her. Opening her eyes, she saw a black stallion, wild-eyed and covered with foam, leap up to the auction block. The rider was clothed in black, his face hidden by a wide sombrero. The auctioneer, plainly fearing for his life, tried to flee. But a rifle butt swung around over Maria's head and knocked him senseless. She half swooned, and then felt the iron arms reach down and pluck her from her shame . . . the iron arms she recognized instantly as they swung her up onto the saddle. They leaped off the platform in an instant and she heard the ring of silver spurs as the rider, who gripped her tightly from behind, drove his steed through the dazed crowd, who fled before them, screaming.

In her half-conscious state, she was aware that they rode long and hard. Then the pace slowed; she opened her eyes and recovered her senses. The horse trotted along the high plateau, and stopped at a winding brook, gleaming gold in the setting sun. Nervously, Maria turned her head. Was it him? Or was she foolish to even hope for it? She dared not look! What if it was the evil Raoul Estevez! Oh God! She couldn't —

"So, my little desert flower, you thought could run away, eh?" came a familiar voice. Maria turned her head; she was looking up into the cruel, coal black eyes of Fuente. She gasped, and offered her mouth to his. They kissed passionately, and then Fuente dismounted, pulled her down, and kissed her again as he threw his coat onto the ground. Kneeling with her, his voice grew rough as he panted in his desire. The stars shone brightly in the golden air. The night birds sang. "I love you," she whispered. "I love you, Fuente . . ."

"You will forgive me, my love, if I cannot wait. There is so much to do . . . so little time . . . " And he pushed her down on the coat, a love bower in the wilderness —

"How's it coming?"

"I think somebody's about to," I said, turning the page. "That happens a lot in this book."

"Art imitates life," she sighed. Her voice was soft and purring. She was rubbing my legs now. I lowered my head on the pillow and closed my eyes.

"So? Whadduyuh think?" she asked. The rubbing was more intense, and I was beginning to feel the effects of the book and her hands. Good thing I was lying face down.

"It, uh, has its moments, I guess," I admitted, trying not to hurt her feelings.

"Zat all?"

"Yeah . . . it's uh, pretty good in spots."

Suddenly she grabbed my hip with her right hand and spun me over on my back.

"Ha! I thought so, Charlie. You can't fool me."

Then she was kissing me, the way only Mary can kiss, and I couldn't talk. But leave it to Mary to throw a twist on it at the end. Just before she plunged over that warm, wet waterfall into the scarlet mists, she cried out.

"Ohhhhhh, Fuente! . . . Fuente, I'm yours!"

TWENTY-TWO

MONDAY MORNING I got up early, went into the office for two patients back to back, then returned to the house before ten to change clothes and grab a cup of coffee before heading out.

Mary saw me off at the front door; we walked down the steps onto the flagstone walk. I noticed she carried a parcel under her arm wrapped in brown paper. In size and shape, it resembled a giant cigar box.

"My manuscript," she said, patting it proudly. "After last night, I *know* it's ready to send off. You know, Charlie, I bet this is the only romance novel that's actually been field tested." Then she grabbed me.

"Hey, not out here in public, Mare —"

"Nobody's looking, dummy. God, it must be hell being a WASP. Anyway, be careful down there in New Bedford."

We kissed, and I hopped into the car for the eighty-minute drive. Once in New Bedford Center, I parked and walked to the Seamen's Bethel Church and Isaacson's Pawnshop. It was the pawnshop incident that kept sticking in my head. The kid who'd swiped the radio had gone to Isaacson's to hock it. Of course, pawnshops are a natural place to fence stolen stuff, but why this one?

Maybe because it was near his home, or on his way home. And I thought if I just hung around the neighborhood long enough, something might suggest itself. I sauntered down to Isaacson's, looking casually in the window but not going in. I noticed a nice Martin D-18 guitar in the window, and wondered how much they wanted for it. Probably a grand. I looked around. On the next street over were a whole raft of antique and curio shops. Some sold junk, but others sold things like mounted elephant tusks, Ming porcelains, ship's figureheads, and other neat things. It reminded me of Charles Street in Boston, or Royal Street in New Orleans. Isaacson's street was a notch or two lower, though definitely respectable. There were also two small grocery stores, the kind that stock imported beers and fancy foodstuffs. A coin-op laundromat. A paint store. Ho-hum . . .

A block up was Water Street, the main drag of the historic part of town, just as Woods Hole's Water Street was. A block away in the other direction was the waterfront. I ambled down there and surveyed the fish piers, seafood packing houses, fish brokerage offices, and marine supply houses. All the elements of Gloucester Harbor, its sister city to the north, were there, except that the harbor was huge and spread out, as opposed to the forest of masts and spars, hawsers and packed hulls of the crowded confines of Gloucester's inner harbor.

As I walked along the asphalt and cyclone fences bordering the piers and factories, sunburned men with red faces, wearing wool and flannel jackets, hooded sweatshirts, corduroy pants, and waterproof boots passed me, smoking, cussing, and laughing. The clothes were the tip-off that these were fishermen. Nobody goes about dressed for fall in midsummer. Nobody but deep-water fishermen, who must work round-the-clock in the chill sea breeze and soaking spray. And they had those lobster hands. You could see that each time they raised them up to drag from their cigarettes, every time they lifted a Styrofoam cup of steaming java — those swollen, scarlet, baseball-glove mitts of theirs. The hauling of nets and line soaked in brine does that. It's a dead giveaway.

I sat for forty minutes looking out across the water, then walked back north to the maritime museum, with its moored lightship *New Bedford* and other preserved vessels. I skirted the museum and continued walking north another five or six blocks. Then I walked back inland a few blocks and turned south again. I didn't know what I was looking for; I was getting the feel of the neighborhood, hoping something would catch my eye. I circled back in on the historic area, returned to my car, and drove south down Rodney French Boulevard, which circles around the promontory that holds old Fort Rodman. On the way I passed the gigantic rock hurricane barrier, which the town finally erected after several hurricanes almost destroyed the city. When bad weather threatens, huge steel floodgates can be closed along the barrier, sealing the harbor from tidal surges. I was willing to bet they'd been shut during the recent storm, too.

All during this meandering I'm thinking to myself: a guy who's burgled my house hocks my radio on New Bedford's waterfront. He could simply be an out-of-work fisherman, or a guy on the lam who happened to pass by. But I don't think so; the location was too inconvenient for a casual thief.

As things stood, the most obvious connection between New Bedford and Woods Hole was Bill Henderson's big stern trawler, the *Highlander*. So far I had not seen her. And it could be a long, long wait; a vessel that big could stay out on the Banks almost two weeks.

I drove back into the center of town and resumed my walking tour. It was another hour and a half, past noon, when I found what I wanted: a guard shack at the gate of Fairhaven Fisheries, Inc., just inside the high cyclone fence of the plant's parking lot. It sat on a rise right over the harbor with a bird's-eye view of everything. I knocked at the heavy glass window of the shack. The pockmarked young man in the guard's uniform looked up from his magazine. I looked closely and saw that the magazine was the *National Enquirer*. Will Victoria Principal return to *Dallas*? What are Vanna White's views on quantum reality? Is the chewing gum diet for you? Will Michael Jackson go "all the way" and undergo surgery in Stockholm to become a blonde starlet? How does your license plate number affect your health? *Inquiring minds want to know!*

"Yeah?" he managed, leaning down to speak through the metal air vent. Obviously a verbal chap. I pulled out my new county medical examiner's badge and flashed it.

"I'm on business for the Commonwealth of Massachusetts," I said in a low, confidential half-whisper. "I am investigating a series of burglaries and a murder. Follow?"

"Uh, shuwa. Yeah, I follow." His eyes bugged out; he

drummed his fingers fast on a two-page color photograph of Madonna, wearing a leather corset, eight-inch heels, net stockings, and a bowler hat. They've got nice pix; you've got to give them that. The *Wall Street Journal* can't touch them there.

"It's absolutely imperative that I have somebody on my side who's reliable and smart. Frankly, you look like that kind of guy."

"I *do*?" he said, amazed.

I stepped back, a confused look on my face. I shuffled my feet, became reluctant. "Well, don't you think so? Maybe I misjudged you."

"No. No. I can help. Who are you?"

I explained I was a private physician on state business, and told him what I was looking for. I didn't lie, even a little bit. I didn't have to. The kid was all ears. To top it off, I took a twenty and slid it under the glass.

"Consider this a personal gift, from me," I said. "But you go blabbing around and wreck everything, I'll be very disappointed. In fact, I'll be downright pissed off."

"No prawblem, no prawblem."

I said he was to keep a sharp eye out for the stern trawler *Highlander*, and call me the second she pulled in. Furthermore, without being seen by the boat's crew he was, if possible, to keep track of whoever came and went.

"And just maybe you could remember what direction they go, okay?"

"No prawblem. You gawt it."

"And one more thing, Melvin," I said, reading his name off the badge on his shirt, "if we bust this thing wide open, do you have any objections if your name and picture appear in the newspapers?"

"You kiddin'?" he said, practically wetting his fresh-pressed, gabardine guard's slacks. "*No prawblem!*" I handed him four phone numbers: my home, office, cottage, and Jack's number in Woods Hole. He told me to have a nice day, and I left for home.

"Okay, pal, what's up?"

"Nothing's up. What do you mean?" It was the next morning, and we were having breakfast together in the kitchen.

"I mean you're fidgeting around, Charlie. I know the signs."

One of the things that's so maddening about Mary is that she always knows; she always finds out. I told her briefly about bribing the kid in the guard shack. She was less than elated.

"What are you doing?" I asked, seeing her make a beeline for the phone.

"Telling Joe. What else? Somebody's got to make sure you don't get killed."

I protested that it was just a routine check, but she dialed anyway, and I went off to work.

The call came at ten forty-five, just as I was suturing a third molar extraction on a comely twenty-year-old co-ed named Jo Anne Fleming. The call was taken by an assistant who fills in for Susan Petri when Susan's helping me with surgery. "We're in surgery, so tell him to hold," said Susan through her gauze mask. In her right hand she held the bloody suction tube, in her left, spare sutures.

I finished the suture and shot Jo Anne with a hefty dose of penicillin, then picked up the phone.

"Dawktah Adams? Melvin Combs, down at New Bedfid?"

"How you doing? See anything?"

"Yeah. The *Highlandah* pulled in a few minutes ago down at the fish dawk. She'll be theah maybe six, seven howahs anyway —"

"Good. Keep an eye out. Can you leave the shack?"

"No. Nawt on duty. But I get a lunch break at eleven."

"Good. Skip lunch and spend the time watching the boat and who comes and goes. Try to remember the people, and where they came from and where you think they're headed. And act casual and stay out of sight. I have a patient at one, but I should be down there by four."

"No prawblem. Have a nice day."

I pulled into the asphalt area near Melvin's guard shack at four-fifteen. I wore a fisherman's long-billed cap, aviator glasses, jeans, and a dark-blue canvas pullover. Even if Henderson and son saw me from the *Highlander*, they wouldn't recognize me. Melvin's guard shack was occupied by a stranger. I skirted the tall cyclone fence and went down to the water. There was Henderson's big sixty-foot stern trawler, pulled up to the fish dock at Bertelsen's freezer warehouse and market. There were a slew of boats there, but the big, new *Highlander* stood out, white and sassy, against the other boats. I sat down on the concrete of a neighboring pier and leaned my back against a giant piling there and watched. I could've seen better with binoculars, but they'd attract attention. I pulled out my pipe, loaded it, and lit up. To all appearances I was just a waterfront hanger-on idling away a summer afternoon.

It didn't take me long to find Melvin. He was standing, in his guard's uniform of course, flat against a wall of the warehouse, arms spread out and stuck to the wall, like a ledge clinger about to jump. Every so often he'd peep around the corner at the boat, then snap back behind the wall. Sweet Jesus.

I circled around and came up on him from behind.

"Melvin —" I said in a whisper.

He screamed and jumped out of his skin, twirling around like a majorette in full view of the pier. I crooked a finger at him and motioned him in. "Great job, Melvin; I'll take over now. What did you see?"

"A bunch of 'em walked off the boat and headed up theah," he said, pointing south, past the giant freezer warehouses.

"How many, and what did they look like?"

"A big white-haired guy. I think he must be the ownah. And two youngah guys. They been gone, maybe hahf an howah."

I slipped him another twenty, thanked him, and told him to walk casually back to the guardhouse as if nothing had happened.

"I'll be in touch if I need you, Melvin. As you walk back, please don't look around.

"No prawblem. Have a ni —"

"Same to you. So long."

The big white-haired guy would be Bill Henderson. Probably one of the younger guys was his son Terry. And perhaps the third guy a crew member. I ambled south, taking care not to appear to be in a hurry or have any definite destination, glancing toward the water. More warehouses, two fisheries offices, another dock, a marine tackle shop, and a repair shed. Another office attached to a hangar-type building and supply yard, another pier . . . and that appeared to be about all. I sat down on a clump of turf at the foot of an earthen rise that led back to the streets behind me, and puffed my pipe and sat. My gaze wandered from building to building. Nothing was unusual. Nothing seemed out of place. And also, I bet that *Highlander* did indeed have a hold full of fish. And so the crew, faced with several hours' wait until they could unload the catch, went up the line for a smoke and a gam. So what?

I rose and walked still more, all the way past the big docks down to where Rodney French Boulevard began snaking its way down the peninsula toward the hurricane gates. Not seeing a soul down that way, I turned and headed back, idly kicking at stones, tin cans, and other junk. I passed a series of sheds, and then walked opposite the office that was attached to the hangar. Then I stopped in my tracks. Along with a pickup truck and a compact sedan, a big blue Mercedes was parked at the office building, and damned if it wasn't the same one I saw pull up near the Woods Hole dock the previous week. I was sure of it, and I knew it hadn't been there ten minutes before. So it had just arrived, which suggested its owner knew the *Highlander* had just arrived and had come to meet it.

I looked at the office building. There was a blue and white logo on it showing a stylized Neptune with trident set against wavy blue lines. In a way, it reminded me of the logo of the Cousteau Society. Under it were the letters OEI. What the hell was OEI? Then I saw three words underneath the logo, but I was still too far away to read them. I had to get closer; I wanted the license plate number of the Mercedes, too.

Ambling to and fro, stopping now and then to throw rocks into the water and watch the gulls, I got close enough. Hoping nobody inside was looking out, I read Oceanic Enterprises, Inc., on the side of the office building. I read the Mercedes's plate number and kept repeating it to myself until I got downrange far enough to write it down. I had also seen that the hangar-type building and office were joined together. Furthermore, there was a large work boat moored next to the hangar, which had been

invisible from where I stood earlier. It was almost the size of the
Highlander, but much older and rather beat-up. It was a western
rig, which meant cabin and wheelhouse forward, with a long,
wide deck aft and a very heavy-duty crane. She was built along
the lines of a coastal trawler, with a high bow, pronounced sheer,
and low freeboard aft. I also saw a big air compressor rig on the
afterdeck, which I figured could be used to power air tools, or,
more likely, air hoses for "hard-hat" diving. The yard was untidy,
littered with marker buoys, oil drums, geared machinery, and
long, canvas-covered mounds of something, perhaps pipe or
reinforcing rods. Thus, I reasoned, OEI was some sort of marine
engineering or salvage firm. I then tried to think what possible
connection a firm like this would have with the murder of young
Andrew Cunningham. My conclusion was: not much.

I walked up past the guard shack, buttonholed Melvin, and
said that regrettably the lead didn't look too promising, but that
I'd let him know.

"But nevertheless, don't mention this to anyone, Melvin.
There has been a murder; there could be a lot of danger to you.
Know what I mean?"

"No prawblem. Have —"

"Goodbye, Melvin."

Driving back I realized that nothing much had come from my
surveillance of New Bedford. I had a tag number and the name
of a firm. Also, perhaps, I had the knowledge that the Slinky connection, however tenuous, was much more promising than this
one.

"Well, it's no surprise to me, sport, that you didn't bump into
much down there" said Joe, making himself a giant G and T in a
half-liter beer stein. Whenever he shows up at my house, either
house, his first act is to see how big a dent he can make in my
liquor cabinet. "While you were farting around in New Bedford,
Paul Keegan and I were following up in Providence. Guess what?
It so happens we stumbled onto a connected guy being held on
other charges, i.e., possession with intent to sell. Name's Evans,
nicknamed "the Drugstore." This guy's a prime candidate for the
WPP —"

"Witness Protection Program?"

"You got it. And boy, is he gonna need it. See, the state guys nailed him sitting on four kilos of pure, uncut Columbian coke. Naturally, this puts a lot of pressure on the poor baby. So next thing you know, he's implicating several leading families of Providence, and who else but Falcone, our friend Slinky. Seems Slinky's been in on the nose-candy trade, despite his earlier cover-up. And it looks like we'll be getting enough evidence and testimony to put him away . . . maybe for good.

"So Slinky *was* involving the Cunningham kid."

"Yep. Yep, yep, yep. I think the pieces are just about in place. And think about it, Doc, Mary: between Slinky and the Drugstore, don't you think they'd know enough about drugs to doctor up a capsule to do the kid in?"

"Possibly."

"At least possibly. More like probably. You ask me, my original thinking on this thing is on the money: Slinky needed a safe cover to help run coke in from a mother ship. The Cunningham kid was in hock to him, so he'd be the likely bagman, using Woods Hole research vessels, which wouldn't be stopped and searched. It's perfect."

"If it's so perfect," said Mary, "then why did Slinky go to Arthur Hagstrom last month and tell him the kid owed money? Huh?"

"Good question, Mare," I said. Leave it to her to cut through to the meat.

"Okay . . . you wanna know why? Simple: the kid refused to play ball. So Slinky went to Hagstrom as a last resort. And finally, he had to kill Andy because he wouldn't budge."

I rocked my open palm back and forth. "Iffy, Joe. There it gets kinda iffy . . . For example, how does your theory explain the two burglaries, huh?"

"Simple: Andy had the coke and held out, planning to sell it himself for a fortune."

"And you think this kid, smart enough to get into the best med schools in the country, and having grown up in the mob's home town, is gonna do that?"

"Well, it's better than your research."

"You mean you're not going to run down those items?"

"Oh, sure. I'll humor you. In fact, that should be coming in this afternoon. Hell, the new computer networks are amazing. We plug into a phone line here, we get everything on companies. We plug into another line, we get everything we want on cars, trucks, vans, coast to coast. We can now contact the FBI's master fingerprint files via modem and get visualizations of prints on computer screens in seconds. Same with mug shots. You believe it?"

Joe and I were sitting out on the brick terrace nursing our drinks while Mary pan-fried filet mignons in butter in a very hot skillet, searing the meat so the juice would stay in. We were going to eat them with gobs and gobs of béarnaise sauce. If you're going to go with cholesterol, go all the way. As Mae West said: "Anything worth doing is worth overdoing." Fortunately, we were downing massive quantities of alcohol to cut the fat and keep our arteries clear.

I mean, hey: your health is important.

The phone rang for Joe, and he got up with a grunt and walked inside for it, doing that slow, rolling shuffle of his. It's like the walk of a big bull elephant. You see an elephant sauntering along and you figure he's dawdling, but in fact he's doing eight miles an hour.

Joe was in there awhile, which told me my information might be coming in. I was correct; he came back holding his notebook.

"Okay . . . here we go. First the car. The Mercedes Five-twenty SEL belongs to a Mr. Hunter Whitesides. Actually, H. V. Whitesides, the Fourth. Pahdon me . . . Whitesides has no priors, no record of any kind. So what we do with guys like this is, we go to the second tier. You know, run a check on financial standing, medical history, other personal stuff."

"You can do that? I thought that was illegal."

"Right you are, my boy. It's against all the invasion of privacy statutes. Nobody's supposed to run this kind of check unless it's voluntary, like for a handgun permit . . . or, if a guy wants to apply for insurance, or a fancy credit card or something similar. Then he signs a slip *authorizing* people to check him out. You tell anybody we're doing this, it's our ass."

"I'll keep mum. So what about Hunter Whitesides the Fourth.

Shit, with a moniker like that, you'd think he was an old Yankee blueblood."

"And you'd be right. Financial standing is triple A, gilt edged. Two addresses: a P.O. box on Nantucket Island, and a residence on Tuckernuck Island. Top dollar. No lien on the car, and it's about sixty K. Went to Princeton, class of forty-six. That means he avoided the draft in the big one. Thanks no doubt to daddy's big bucks, and friends in high places. Got something on his old man, in fact. The Whitesides were big in banking in the twenties and thirties. Daddy, Hunter the Third, was in tight with Governor Alvin Fuller. Remember him?"

"Oh yeah. The friend of the working man."

"Count on it. Anyway, Whitesides headed up the banking commission and a lot of other commonwealth stuff. You ask me, it was the old man's state connections that got Whitesides off the hook in World War Two. But I'm only theorizing."

"Any occupation listed? Married?"

"No occupation. Probably doesn't need one. Married and two boys — nothing on them, though we could look. Wife died twelve years ago. So know what I think?"

"What?"

"Tell you after I tell you about OEI. Oceanic Enterprises, Inc., was founded and chartered in nineteen seventy-three. Its purpose, as stated in the charter, is to 'locate, acquire, and develop the resources of the eastern continental shelf for commercial and humanitarian ends.' Quote, unquote."

"Sounds nice. Too nice."

"Yeah. Sounds to me like an underwater mining company or something. But interesting point: one of the main financial backer is, guess who?"

"Hunter Whitesides."

"Uh-huh, he's one of them. Then there's a Dr. Michael Chisholm. I suppose it's a doctorate in geology or something. And finally, William A. Henderson, Falmouth, Mass."

"Ahhhhhh . . ."

" 'Ahhhh,' *what?*"

"I dunno," I shrugged, "just 'Ahhhhhh.' "

"Well anyway, OEI is in trouble. Deep financial trouble. I can't understand why they're not in chapter eleven already. All Cochrane told me over the phone was that there's a ton of overdue notes with a lot of banks and lending institutions. OEI's been on the skids for the past four years."

"So Henderson's hurting, possibly desperate. Maybe Whitesides was brought in to bankroll the company at the beginning, or maybe brought in later as a corporate sugar daddy to help bail the firm out of debt."

"Possible."

"But then again, maybe not. Maybe Hunter Whitesides, despite his gilt-edged pedigree, is experiencing some hard times, too. Maybe he's worn out three pairs of scissors clipping his daddy's coupons."

"That had crossed my mind. So you've hit on the Henderson-Whitesides connection, Doc. But so far, despite financial reversals, everything concerning OEI appears to be aboveboard."

"I'm just wondering why Bill Henderson would form a company like OEI. Wouldn't a mining and explorations company be against the interests of fishermen? If you had to guess, wouldn't you think so?"

"Uh-huh. But that's the beauty of it, Doc. Everybody in this state knows how off and on fishing is, right? So what does Henderson do about fifteen years ago when he's got some extra cash? Buy another boat? No. He diversifies."

"So when the fishing's off," I said, "he can make money on the other side of the table. Wait a minute; we were aboard *Highlander* for the better part of an hour. That boat isn't four years old yet. If he's hurting so bad in his investments, how'd he afford her?"

"Good question. We can check around the edges on that one. But I'm beginning to think Bill Henderson is more clever than he lets on."

"Dinner's ready, guys," called Mary, appearing on the terrace working a wire whisk in a stainless steel bowl. She was putting the finishing touches on the béarnaise.

"Ahhhhh," sighed Joe, following her inside, "once more into the breach, dear friends . . ."

TWENTY-THREE

ALL OF A SUDDEN it was Labor Day. On the weekend of September 9, we realized it had been a month since the unsolved murder of Andrew Cunningham. Time sure flies when you're having fun. But I had just completed a full week of postvacation work and it seemed to cheer me up. Work is good for that. It seems, in my case especially, that idleness breeds boredom, and boredom leads quickly to depression.

What was new? Well, Jack called from Woods Hole to tell us that the MBL and Lionel Hartzell had mutually decided that he would terminate his stay at the lab. According to Jack, that was good news for a lot of the folks at Woods Hole. Another ray of sunshine on an otherwise bleak horizon was that Morris Abramson's precious cargo of hideous marine bottom-feeders met with a mysterious malady that killed most of them off. Take out your handkerchiefs. Moe was downhearted, and couldn't figure out what had decimated his beloved menagerie.

Since we're on the subject, I'll inject something I once heard: if someone drops iron — even an old-fashioned cut nail — into a marine tank the results can be disastrous.

Hey, I know what you're thinking, and it wasn't me. In fact, it wasn't even iron. Moe hired a guy from one of Boston's leading pet fish suppliers, and he did all sorts of chemical tests but couldn't find the cause. It must have been Divine Intervention. So with that in mind, I promised to go to church at least three weeks in a row.

Joe and Paul Keegan continued to hammer away at the Providence mob connection, and even succeeded in hauling Falcone in for tough questioning. Joe didn't tell Mary about this; she'd think he was picking on the poor, sweet kid. Anyway, they still couldn't make anything stick, even with the help of Howard "the Drugstore" Evans, who was growing more scared by the second and wanted nothing more than to be off the stand and shipped out to Steamboat Springs, or wherever he was to begin his new life under the Witness Protection Program.

The month or so that follows Labor Day is a pleasant time in New England, and it's especially nice on the Cape. The ocean is warm, the days are crisp and clear, it's chilly at night, and ninety percent of the tourists are gone and the roads actually work.

And so Friday evening of that Labor Day weekend found Mary and me down at the Breakers, spiffing up the place after all the houseguests and partying of the summertime, getting it ready for the cozy family weekends that we would enjoy throughout the fall. Joe was due to come down and spend a quiet weekend with us. The boys were wrapping up their summer in Woods Hole, apparently determined to squeeze another week of fun out of the season before all their friends either returned to school or went elsewhere for jobs.

Mary was carrying a special letter in her handbag that she wouldn't let me see. I had retrieved it from our mailbox in Concord just before we left. All I knew was, it wasn't for her; it was addressed to a Ms. Candace Lockewood.

"Do you still have Ms. Lockewood's letter?"

"Yes," she said. I saw that her jaw was trembling.

"What's wrong? Is she in trouble or what?"

But she didn't answer me. She walked back to the dining room table fast, snatched the letter out, and tore it open with shaking hands.

"Hey, you can't open other people's —"

"It's for me, dummy. That's my pen name. My *nom de plume.*"

"Candace Lockewood? What the hell's wrong with Mary Adams?"

"Get serious, Charlie —" she broke off and read the letter, her eyes zipping over the page. *"Yippee! Yippee! They like it!"*

"They *do?*"

"Yes, they do!" she cried, holding the sheet of paper to her breast with a look of ecstasy. And if the paper were human, it would have been wearing an ecstatic look as well. No doubt the expression was similar to Maria's on seeing Fuente's face in a crowd. I picked up the envelope and saw that it was from a New York outfit called Fountainhead Press. Never heard of it.

Mary wouldn't show me the letter. She said I could see it later.

So we returned to vacuuming and dusting and straightening up. Joe said he'd be down in time for a late dinner, and he'd promised to bring the raw materials. Mary remembered she had to change the sheets, so she hustled upstairs while I finished vacuuming. Then I unloaded the dishwasher and took out the trash in big black plastic bags. When I came back inside, Mary was calling me.

"Charlie? Help me move this bed!"

She was in the boys' room, tugging at the far brass bed, which had been stripped.

"Well, you had no trouble with the other one," I said, pointing to its freshly made twin.

"Yeah, but this one seems heavy, and I don't want to leave a mark on the floor." So I grabbed the head of the brass bed while she grabbed the foot, and we lifted and yanked the bed far enough away from the wall that she could get behind it.

"Gee, I think I left some marks on the new varnish anyway," she said, looking down at the floor. Sure enough, there were faint pale streaks where the feet had dragged across the finish. I hefted the bed out of the way and rubbed the floor. Then we made the bed and went into the third bedroom, the guest room, to get it ready.

Halfway through making that bed, I stood up and stared out the window.

"That bed's too heavy," I said, and we went back into the boys' room. I approached the far bed and lifted the foot. Then I went to the head and lifted it. No wonder Mary had had trouble; the foot of the bed was much heavier than the head. Went to the other bed and lifted the foot. Not particularly heavy. Lifted foot of far bed: heavy. What gives?

The beds were brass, not antiques, but well made and handsome, with vertical ribs of wide brass tubing at head and foot, the head being much higher, with a gently curving brass rail on top. The foot had two big end posts at each side, and a horizontal rail of brass joining them.

On top of the end posts were big brass finials, shaped like the "onion domes" of the churches in Bavaria and Russia. I unscrewed one of the finials, which was fastened firmly. Then both of us were peering down into the hollow brass post. We saw paper a few inches below the lip.

Mary took hold of the paper and pulled, but it wouldn't budge. She pulled harder, and it tore. No good. I unscrewed the ornate brass cap on the other side and looked in. Same thing. And the paper wouldn't budge there, either.

"There's something in there besides paper, Charlie," said Mary. "Just gotta be."

So then we eased the mattress, complete with clean sheets and comforter, off the box spring and onto the other bed. We put the box spring on the floor on the far side of the room. The late afternoon sun streamed in through the gabled windows. Mary and I got on one side of the bed and gently turned it up on its side, then, walking around to the other side, gently lowered it until it was upside down. We were both breathing a little hard; the brass was quite heavy. Then I grabbed the underside of the foot of the bed frame and jerked up. Nothing. I jerked up again and again, and finally a paper-wrapped cylinder fell onto the floor with a loud thump. Then another fell out. Then two more. We checked the other side, and with a little pulling and prying, Mary got three out of that side as well. Seven bundles of . . . what? Mary picked one of the cylinders up and began to peel the paper off. I rushed over and grabbed it from her.

"Don't, Mare! We don't know what it is. How do we know they aren't explosive or something?"

Well, we watched them awhile and they just sat there, so we took all seven cylinders out onto the deck and placed them on the picnic table under the yellow beach umbrella and stared at them. I noticed Mary was drumming her fingers, her eyes bugged out with curiosity. I wanted to wait a minute or two, at least, to see if they started ticking or humming. As a diversion, I asked to see the letter from Fountainhead Press. She went and got it:

Dear Ms. Lockewood:

We have now read the four sample chapters of your book, *Hills of Gold, Men of Bronze.* I am pleased to inform you that the reaction from our staff so far has been quite favorable! We look forward to seeing the completed manuscript as soon as it's available. Meanwhile, don't hesitate to call us and keep us informed as to your progress.

Incidentally, we urge you to overcome any shyness you might have in writing your love scenes, Ms. Lockewood. While quite descriptive, we feel they certainly could go a lot farther in conveying the physical passion that obviously plays so key a role in your fine novel. Quite frankly, we're asking you to be more explicit with the sex, Candace. After all my dear, these *are* the eighties. As they say on the street, let it all hang out!

Sincerely,
Louisa Latour,
Managing Editor

I put down the letter.

"More explicit? Did I read that right, Mary?"

"Yep. Well, I guess I better stop pussy-footing around, so to speak. No more beating around the bush. Get right to the meat of the problem . . ."

"Louisa Latour? I bet that's not even her real name."

"So? Candace Lockewood's not my real name, either."

"This whole operation is downright tawdry, Mare. You've already got a novel that's just this side of X-rated and what do they want? More sleaze!"

"Can do," she murmured, smiling implishly. *"Caaaaaaan dooo . . ."*

I returned to the picnic table and carefully hefted one of the paper-wrapped cylinders. I don't have an extraordinary fondness for paper-wrapped cylinders. My mercenary-commando buddy, Laitis Roantis, carried one with us during the Daisy

Ducks' escapade in the mountains of North Carolina. It was packed with extra-high-grade plastique, or cyclonite, and was powerful enough to blow a mountain apart. Still, it wasn't nearly this heavy . . .

I pulled the paper softly. It unwrapped, and I realized the paper was folded over several times. I unrolled all of it and found myself staring at a hunk of grayish rock in a perfect cylinder, two inches in diameter and maybe nine inches long. I was almost positive I knew what it was.

"Huh? Is it rock? Granite?"

"It's rock. I remember when I was a kid in high school my parents had friends who lived in central Indiana. He was a part-time oil prospector, and he had pieces of rock exactly like this. It's a core sample, from a special drill bit that carves out these cylinders deep in the ground."

"What are they for?"

"They tell what kind of rock there is at various levels below the earth's surface. By the color and texture, I'd say this is limestone. And I know a way to find out, too. We have white vinegar, don't we?"

While she went into the kitchen, I carefully unwrapped another cylinder. This one had a dab of flat gray paint on one end, and some numbers written on the gray in heavy black ink. The rock looked different, though; it was tan colored and softer. Sandstone? Caked mud? I sure couldn't tell. Mary came back with a bottle of white vinegar. I spilled a little on the gray rock. Instantly, there was a fizzing and bubbling.

"Wow, Charlie!"

"It's limestone. That's the acid test, as they say. Limestone is pure $CaCO_3$: calcium carbonate. It reacts strongly with acid, just like the old soda-acid fire extinguishers. I learned that trick back in high school chemistry."

"What about the others?"

"I don't know. I think if Joe takes these to a lab he can —"

"Charlie! Look!"

She had unfolded one of the wrapping papers, revealing faint squiggly lines inside. We unfolded it still more. It unfolded and unfolded, like a road map. When we were finished, we had a piece of paper a yard wide and almost eight feet high. We took it into the porch out of the wind and spread it on the table.

"What the hell . . ."

"Beats me," I said, looking at layers and layers of wavy graph lines in ink.

"Looks like an EKG, only . . . only . . ."

"Yeah, only far more complex, with maybe six or seven different types of recording."

"What're you two doing, wrapping presents or what?"

We turned to see Joe standing in the porch doorway. His arms were full of groceries and bundles wrapped in white paper. He put the food in the kitchen and joined us, examining the pieces of core and the strange graph closely, clucking his tongue and smoking intently. His face looked serious. Deadly serious.

"Where'd you find all this?"

We told him.

"What do you think it all means?" asked Mary.

"I don't know what it means in and of itself," he said, turning the rock samples around and around in his huge, plump, brown hands, "but I am sure that they're the reason Andy Cunningham was killed. *This* is the stuff they've been looking for. Right here is the reason for the burglaries. And as we were beginning to suspect, they've got nothing to do with Lionel Hartzell. And maybe even nothing to do with Eddie Falcone and his friend the Drugstore."

"I'm calling Jack," said Mary, turning quickly to go inside. Joe grabbed her hard by the elbow.

"Not so fast, Mary," he said softly. "I came down here on another bad errand, I'm afraid —"

"Oh Joey! Did the grand jury —"

"Yeah. Handed it down. Murder one. At three-thirty today. Sorry."

There was an awful silence in the air, filled with fear, surrounding us like bad electricity. And a bitter, sick taste in my mouth, like an old tin can. Then I recovered, or did my best at it.

"C'mon everybody," I said softly, "we were expecting it anyway. With Hartzell off the hook, it was just a question of time."

"Two quick things, both good," Joe continued, putting his

arms around us. "One: bail is set for fifty grand. That's nothing for murder one, so that shows you how they're really viewing this thing. And two: this new evidence. Hey! It points the finger away from Jack."

He looked at each of us in turn, wearing a smile that was too forced. He then turned his gaze back to the littered table.

"I don't know where the hell it does point," he said, "but it's pointing *away* from Jack."

Walking into the house, I wanted more than anything to believe him.

And then we were standing around under the lamp inside. I looked at Mary, staring down at her letter, crying, not believing that good and bad news could come so close together.

TWENTY-FOUR

MARY, JOE, AND I sat opposite Ronnie Henshaw. We had drawn up folding chairs, and were sitting under the stark glare of the fluorescent lamp that overhung the kid's desk. He studied my face, then spoke.

"I remember you from somewhere," he said. "And your wife, too."

"It was at Andy Cunningham's funeral," said Mary. "I remember seeing you there. So you knew Andy."

"Sure, I knew him. I knew Andy well, in fact. He used to come and study here. Said it was nice and quiet, and there was nobody else around to distract him."

He was right about that; the USGS warehouse was a regular tomb. Sitting there in that single-story building on the Quissett Campus, we could have been inside the Great Pyramid.

"When did you guys meet each other?" I asked. "One of the beach parties, maybe?"

Ronnie scratched his dirty brown hair and squinted in concentration behind his thick lenses. "No. I don't go to the parties. Nobody invites me. I never hear about them until the next day."

This didn't surprise me. Ronnie was wearing scuffed old wing-tip shoes over orange and black argyle socks. Baggy corduroy pants — in July mind you — that he wore so high they were practically tucked up under his armpits. A baggy, short-sleeved seersucker white shirt with a plastic pouch in the breast pocket crammed with writing instruments. A gangly, nerdy kid, he didn't look like the kind of guy Andy Cunningham would associate with, and he sure didn't look like anybody Jack had ever brought over to the house.

"So how did you two meet, then?" Mary asked.

"He kind of showed up here one afternoon and asked to take a look around. It's not open to the public. In fact, unauthorized personnel aren't allowed beyond that door there —"

He pointed to a black steel door with a small glass window in the center. The glass inside was wire-impregnated. Same kind of stuff Joe wanted me to get for the Breakers's back windows.

"He said he just wanted a quiet place to study. He was sick of all the noise in town, and asked if he could set up a small desk here in this office, or even just a chair where he could read. I said it was against the rules, but then I found out he was a student at MBL, and a premed and everything. So I let him sit at my desk when I went out for breaks. With him here, sitting in for me, I could take longer breaks, too. We got to talking sometimes, you know, and pretty soon we were friends."

"What's behind here?" asked Joe, rapping on the metal door with his knuckles. He rapped backhanded, facing the kid.

"Well, a lot of valuable equipment, mostly. And our core samples. Those are pieces of rock. And then we've got our SRPs there in the back, in fireproof file cases."

"What are those?"

"Seismic reflection profiles. They're kinda like graphs. In fact, they *are* graphs. They're — *hey!* — that's one in your hands! Where did you get it?"

"I found it," I said, handing Ronnie Henshaw one of the folded pieces of huge paper we'd found wrapped around the rock and stuffed into the bedpost of the day before. "That's why we're here."

"You're not supposed to have this," he said after unfolding it all the way and reading the data under the wavy lines. "This is property of the U.S. Geological Survey. It's not in public domain yet. In fact it's —"

"We kinda figured that," said Joe, holding up his palm to shut the kid up. He flashed his badge and cocked a thumb in my direction. "We're police. We're assisting in the investigation of Andy Cunningham's death, and we're pretty sure he was in possession of this profile thing just before he died. We just wanted you to identify it. And what we'd like you to do now, Ronnie, is go back behind this off-limits door, walk around the warehouse there or whatever it is . . . ," he paused, resting his hands on the desk and leaning over it until his face was only a foot from the kid's, ". . . and tell us if anything's missing."

Ronnie said he needed to call his superior first. We said fine. Thirty minutes later a bald, graying man of fifty-five or so came in and introduced himself as Calvin Beard. We told him our story, and he opened the black steel door and led us into the big room, which had three long aisles lined with wooden bins. Our little procession snaked up and down the rows of bins, with Beard darting his eyes right and left as we walked the aisles. He stopped halfway down the second row and rapped the edge of the bin with his fingers.

"Here," he said. "Core samples from the Nantucket hole are missing."

"What's the Nantucket hole?" I asked.

"In eighty-one we drilled a hole on Nantucket Island for a ground water study. You said you live here on the Cape?"

"Part of the year," I answered.

"Well then you know firsthand that we've got an increasing water shortage here, and on the islands, too. I mean, the population's increased tenfold here in the past thirty years. The demand for fresh water has increased maybe twenty times. And geologically speaking, places surrounded by sea water suffer from saline intrusion when their water tables are depleted."

"That's nice," said Joe. "What the hell's it mean?"

"What I'm saying is that when you pump a lot of water out of the ground in a place that's surrounded by sea water, pretty soon the sea water starts creeping into your aquifer and your water tastes salty. It can get so bad the water's undrinkable. So what we did in Nantucket was, we drilled a deep hole in the center of the island to determine the status of the water table, and to see if we couldn't dig new water wells there in the future."

"That's it?"

"Yep," replied Beard, peering into the recesses of the bin. "And I sure wish to hell I knew where those cores went to."

We said we thought we could help out on that score, and took him and the kid out to the car where we'd stowed them and the rest of the big graphs, or seismic reflection profiles. We carried the stuff back inside, where Beard set them on the big table in the back room, confirming that these indeed were the missing pieces.

"But why would Andy, or anybody else, want these?" asked Mary, leaning over the table and staring at the rocks and the large graphs.

"I have absolutely no idea," said Calvin Beard.

I tried another tack, filling Beard in on Andy's murder, and asking him if he could think of any economic value the things on the table before us could have.

"Well," he said, almost absent-mindedly, "both the cores and the profiles reveal the presence of rift basins. These are known to have hydrocarbon potential."

"Hydrocarbon potential. Then you mean —"

"Oil, Dr. Adams. High-grade crude petroleum."

"I've heard that before, it seems to me," said Mary.

"Uh-huh," said Beard. "We've known about the oil for over twenty years. In the mid-seventies, if you'll recall, there was big debate about whether or not to exploit the rift basins under Georges Bank. There was a lot of concern that such development would endanger the fisheries. In the end, the environmentalists and fishermen won, and the Bank was declared off limits."

"So what's the big deal with this?" asked Joe, nodding his head down at the rocks and graphs.

"I don't know, except that it's not Georges Bank; it's Nantucket Island."

"Tell me what you see here," I said, sweeping my hand over the table.

"Okay, first of all, these core samples . . . This is how they'd stack up, roughly," explained Beard, as he quickly arranged the cores one above the other, "which reveals a limestone cap on top. Underneath it is a series of conglomerate sandstone formations — which are these cores, here — each with high hydrocarbon yield and good permeability. Permeability in the rock is essential for the petroleum to seep through it. Otherwise, oil wells wouldn't work. So in a nutshell, what we have here is a classic example of a site that could be very feasibly exploited. If it weren't for the fact that the environmental impact studies ruled it out."

"Who knows about these samples, and the test well?"

"Just us. The USGS. And the people at the Oceanographic Institute. We work together on these profiles."

"Who did the drilling?" I asked. "You, or WHOI?"

"Actually, neither. We contracted the drilling out to a private company."

"Whose name is?"

"A firm called OEI. It's out of New Bedford."

"Oceanic Enterprises, Incorporated," I said.

"How'd you know?"

"Calvin, can we use your phone a second?"

"But you still don't have a direct tie-in, I don't think," said Paul Keegan over the phone. "I mean, sure, the cores and charts show that Nantucket's sitting on a pool of oil. So what? They're telling you that no development can take place there."

"No legal development. Obviously, OEI wants to sink an oil well *sub rosa*. That would explain everything, Andy's murder, the break-ins, the New Bedford connection with the hocked radio, everything."

"I'll be up around three, Doc. Hold tight till then. Where's Joe?"

"Up in Boston meeting with people at the D.A.'s office. He gave me your number just before he left. Listen Paul, we really appreciate all you've tried to do for Jack. But now that the indictment's handed down, we really need you more than ever —"

"I hear you, and I agree that this latest development is important. It could even be what clears Jack. But let me tie up a few loose ends down here first. Joe and I have indirectly succeeded where the state guys from Rhode Island failed: we've got Eddie Falcone sitting in the hot seat, finally."

"Did that guy, the Drugstore, take the stand?"

"Oh yeah. And Slinky's squirming. He motioned me aside privately and hinted that he's willing to plea-bargain. That's no surprise, since he's facing a federal rap from the DEA on this one. What we're talking here, we're talking five to ten in a federal pen, like Atlanta. The Atlanta pen. It's the modern day version of Andersonville. If you were facing five to ten in that hellhole, wouldn't you want to plea-bargain?"

"Sure would."

"Well, that's what we got here. Now, being out of state, Joe and I are about through down here in Providence. But the federal thing, the drugs, that we can serve up on a platter to the federal prosecutors in Boston."

"I'll meet you up here around three."

"Fine. By the way, Doc, has the senior Cunningham been calling you?"

"Boyd Cunningham? Andy's dad? Once."

"Uh-huh. Well, he keeps callling us. Wants to know if we've got the people who killed his son."

"That's what he was asking me. And he keeps calling Jack, too. I kept quiet. What are you telling him?"

"That we're following some promising leads, and that we'll have the killer, we hope, before too long. He keeps asking about old man Hartzell — keeps asking where he can find him. He sounds dangerous, like he's got blood in his eye."

"Well, it might be wise to explain to him, next time he calls, that it seems less and less likely that Hartzell had anything to do with Andy's murder."

"Right. Now, sit tight. I don't want you and Joe poking around up there and blowing the whistle before the time is ripe. We'll plan a stategy. Maybe pick up some of the people from OEI for questioning separately — see how their stories jibe. But what we don't want at this time, we don't want them to get the slightest hint we're onto them."

I told him not to worry, just to meet us at the cottage at three so we could plan it all out.

Calvin Beard accepted the chilled glass of white and brushed the crumbs of fresh baguette off his sweater. He was sitting on our deck, bathed in the red-gold light of the dying sun. Sitting next to him was the trim, athletic Paul Keegan, replete with crew cut and square jaw. He was probably thinking to himself, "We're looking for a few good men . . ."

Joe was talking with Mary next to the porch door. I was cutting cheese, pâté, and bread and pouring wine. After the appetizers, while waiting for Mary's onion soup, we convened in the porch where Calvin Beard spread out a seismic reflection profile on the table and weighted it down with beach rocks so it wouldn't blow.

"Now these reflection profiles are graphs of echo soundings through rock," he said, tracing his hand along the wavy lines. "The sonar pulser works like a sonar depth finder, or a fish finder. The echoes that are reflected are put on this paper. Different types of rock and mud have different echoes, and these appear on the graph paper as different types of wavy lines. To the trained eye, they reveal the type of rock and the thickness of the layer. This base line here is the ocean floor. Okay, and here, you can all see the differing densities and layers of rock underneath it. The location is Nantucket Shoals. The other profiles you found in the bedposts are of the same general area."

"And these are worth a lot of money," said Joe, leaning over the table, "they're worth killing for?"

"I would hope not, Lieutenant. The value of the reflection profile is that it lets us get a peek at the ocean floor without drilling for core samples. As I told Dr. and Mrs. Adams earlier, it's incredibly expensive to drill from a ship. The cost seems to expand geometrically with the depth of the water. And, if you add shifting currents and strong winds and tides, the cost is soon prohibitive."

"So what these do, they tell you where to drill and where to forget it."

"Pretty much."

"So let's put the package together, then. Core samples from Nantucket hole, dug in eighty-one. These reflection profiles from Nantucket Shoals and surrounding ocean areas, which show — what? Promising sites for oil drilling?"

"Precisely. A virtual guarantee of connecting with high-grade crude."

"But it's illegal," said Joe. "And, even if legal, incredibly expensive to undertake. Which is why our friend Doc here has thought out a neat little scenario to explain it all. Haven't you, Doc?"

All eyes stared at me.

"It's just a theory. But here goes. Back in the mid-seventies Henderson and Whitesides — and this professor Chisholm, or whoever the third partner is — start up Oceanic Enterprises with the full expectation of reaping the rewards of undersea exploration. But the enterprise gets bogged down by the ruling against oil exploitation of the fishing grounds. The company does odd drilling jobs, but makes no big scores. Recently, things get so bad that they look around for other avenues. Maybe Chisholm, since he's the full-timer at OEI and presumably the undersea expert, remembers the core samples they took from the Nantucket hole and gave to the USGS. These apparently all but prove rich oil deposits. Also, the partners at OEI are aware that the USGS has other data — namely these seismic reflection profiles — that show rich fields underlying the ocean throughout the area. If they can get their hands on these proofs, they could attract full-scale development of a small well or two in the area."

Beard shook his head.

"I don't see how that would be possible, Dr. Adams. Any exploitation of the shelf couldn't go unnoticed. And what company, legitimate or otherwise, would undertake such a costly venture when they'd be certain to be intercepted?"

"You're right. No company would even think of undertaking it. But what if the venture were land based? And what if it were legal?"

Beard twisted up his face as though he'd just swallowed a lemon. He cleared his throat.

"Wait a second. The key to any mineral exploration is the Minerals Management Service, a federal agency that is in charge of offering drilling leases for sale at auction. The continental shelf is part of the exclusive economic zone set up by the president in eighty-three. It's the same zone, incidentally, that extends U.S. fishing rights offshore for two hundred miles. The government has regulatory power over it. Follow me?"

"You're saying that the feds regulate the whole shmear," said Joe, "and people can't sneak around drilling for oil on the shelf without getting caught."

Beard spoke up. "That's exactly what I'm — did you say *land based*?"

"Land based, on privately held land on Tuckernuck Island."

Beard stroked his chin and looked up, staring off over the ocean.

"I still don't think they'd allow it. The state, I mean. The Commonwealth of Massachusetts, or any other state, has the power of injunction against anything that threatens a fragile environment. Now, I know that mineral rights in this state are reserved for landowners. So I don't see how it would be illegal initially. But I'm sure that eventually they'd go to court and close down the well."

"I'm sure they would, too. Don't you see?"

He thought a second before replying.

"You mean that's why they're being so secretive?"

"Sure. That's why they hired Andrew Cunningham to befriend that — what's his name?"

"Ronnie Henshaw?"

"Yeah, make friends with Henshaw, be his best buddy, so that he'd have access to the core samples and profiles, and could sneak them out of the USGS lab so that the strapped partners in OEI could get the backing to start drilling. Tell me something, Calvin. On a land-based operation like this, over the kind of field we know exists down there in these rift basins, what would the cost be?"

"Minimal. And also, you'd have minimal risk of a dry hole. Maybe no risk at all. All you'd need is a forty-foot derrick and some pipe. When the well came in, you could take down the derrick and install a small-bore boom to the beach to load shoal-draft barges with the crude. I can't say how long you could operate before you were found out. Tuckernuck's not that widely visited. I know the commuter planes fly over it daily, but then again, part of it is wooded. If the ships were loaded at night, it might be a long while before anybody even caught on. But assuming only a few months, you'd still make a lot of money."

"And how long before any legal action would be effective?" asked Mary.

Calvin Beard shrugged. "Maybe just a few months. Maybe a year or more. Hell, maybe they could fight the injunction in court and keep the well going indefinitely. But I doubt it. I think secrecy at the outset would be vital. And the people they'd contact to come in on the venture would be wildcatters, not major oil companies."

We all looked out over the water, not saying anything.

"It's a good thing Jack's not here to hear what could happen to his whales," Mary said.

"You're not kidding," I said. "Or Art Hagstrom, or any of the other people at Woods Hole. So . . . what do we do now?"

"What we do," said Joe, "is make a plan to get these guys in the net, and at the same time charge them with first degree murder. I think the link is going to be Alice Henderson, or maybe her brother. Either one of them, or perhaps both, are the link between Andy Cunningham and OEI. As for the oil venture, we're going to need some evidence. And for that, I'm going to call the Coast Guard."

TWENTY-FIVE

TWO DAYS ELAPSED before Joe showed up in Concord for supper and flipped an envelope marked PHOTOS — DO NOT BEND! onto the kitchen table.

"You wouldn't believe the rigamarole bullshit we had to go through to get those," he said wearily, shuffling over to the sideboard. He uncorked the square bottle of Bombay gin and held it, gurgling, over a huge art-deco–style martini glass. The bottle gurgled long and hard, reminding me of the travelogue film I'd seen of Murchison Falls. He threw in an ice cube and, almost as an afterthought, a twist of lemon peel.

"Let's not forget the vitamin C, eh Doc?"

I opened the manila envelope and withdrew the photos. There were six of them, ten-by-fourteen full-color glossies of aerial views of Tuckernuck Island and watery environs. Excellent resolution; you could see footprints on the beaches.

"So what took so long? People didn't buy our hunch?"

"Partly that. But we had to go through the attorney general's office to get to the Coast Guard. Then we had to get special clearance. They had to wait till a plane was free and they could get a staff photographer. And so on. Hell, next time we need something fast, let's just go do it on our own. Whadduyuh say?"

"I agree. When the chips are down, circumvent the bureaucracy. That's what Roantis says. Now I assume this bit of shoreline off to the right here is Nantucket?"

"Yep," he said, leaning over me, "that's Nantucket's western shoreline, right around Eel Point. That's what they told me, anyway. Take a look at the next one."

I was looking at a direct view of Tuckernuck Island, taken overhead from the south, showing North and East ponds on the top. The shot was exactly the way the island appeared on the nautical charts. Joe rapped his finger on a clump of trees between the ponds, near the northern shore.

"There's where Whitesides's house is. See the little brown speck? That's his house, stuck away all by itself, maybe a quarter mile from the nearest neighbor. See the road?"

"Barely. It's hard to see anything with all those trees. And I sure don't see any preparations for sinking an oil well."

"Right. So the pilot was smart enough to do a low-level flyby so he could get his lens under the trees. Look at the next two."

These were oblique shots made with a very long lens. In these pictures, Hunter Whitesides's rambling frame house was clearly visible in the left side of the frame, with tall pine trees looming over it. On the far right side was a lattice steel tower. On the tower's tip was a large three-bladed propeller.

"Wind machine for a generator. Whitesides has installed a windmill."

"Look again. A windmill, or a drilling derrick?"

I studied the photo closely. But the more I looked at it, the more the tower resembled a windmill. I know windmills; I grew up with them in the Midwest in the 1940s, before they were replaced with electric pumps.

"Yeah, it could be a drilling rig, but is it?" I said, squinting at the photo.

"Frankly, there's no way to tell from a distance. Take a look at this last shot. It was snapped from low level off the north side of the island."

This shot, from the opposite side of the island, showed the rear of the Whitesides mansion. It was impressive any way you looked at it. The steel structure was partially hidden by scrub oak and pine trees. But what was interesting was the low, tarpaulin-covered bundle that sat behind the house. It looked, judging from the scale of the rest of the things in the pix, about thirty or forty feet long. It made me think of similar bundles I'd seen in the yard at OEI, and I told Joe so.

He went back to the first high-altitude shot of Tuckernuck and pointed at the ocean north of the island. The water was gray-brown, fading to light tan.

"Shallow. Very shallow, Joe."

"That's what the C.G. says, too. And your charts, they'd say the same thing. This is called Tuckernuck Bank, and it's shallow as all hell. Sometimes just a couple of feet deep. Shit, you could wade it. And we now think this is why OEI needs financial help from and oil company before they can realize any gain."

"You mean to dredge some kind of channel into the shore?"

"Either that, or construct a retractable floating boom to pump the oil out to ships. Look here, see that darker area? That's been dredged already, probably so the *Oceanic* could get in there and unload the pipe."

"*Oceanic* is the name of that work boat I saw in New Bedford?"

"The very same. So you called this one right on the money, Doc. How would you write the script, judging from what we've got in hand at this point?"

"The script? Well, as I was saying the other night, it starts maybe a couple months ago. The guys at OEI, realizing their firm is going down the tubes, recollect the well they dug earlier on Nantucket, and the rich cores it yielded. They figure the crude can be exploited without an ocean drilling platform by simply setting up a small operation on their partner's property. But wouldn't it be great to get the core samples and those seismic reflection profiles as hard evidence so they can rope in a wildcatter for money and equipment?"

"And Bill Henderson, skipper of the *Highlander*, with connections at Woods Hole through his kids, volunteers to sneak the evidence out of the warehouse, using his daughter's boyfriend, Andy Cunningham, as the conduit."

"Bingo. And Andy was to get a small cut for taking the risk. But once he's got the cores and realizes what he's sitting on, Andy gets greedy and tries to hold out for more money. Maybe a lot more money, to pay off Slinky, among others," I said.

"Uh-huh. But the three partners refuse, and when the kids are gone for the weekend, they break into their house in a frantic effort to recover the stuff. They come up empty-handed, and figure he's taken the core samples up to the cottage with Jack."

"Right," I continued. "But even before this happens, they have realized that Andy Cunningham is a thorn in their side and has to be dealt out. Earlier in the week, they doctor Andy's meds with the knowledge that he'll die over the weekend away from Woods Hole, leaving them free of suspicion, and free to keep searching for the cores. Which they don't find in the cottage because Andy hid them so cleverly."

"That's good, Doc. That's real good. You oughta be a cop."

"I am, remember?" I said, going to the refrigerator and returning with a bottle of Bud and a bottle of Guinness Stout. I mixed these together in a big English dimpled glass tankard, in approximation of a pint of "bitter," and sipped. Finally, I shook my head.

"Whatzamatter?"

"It doesn't seem quite right, Joe. I just keep thinking that what Andy did wasn't bad enough to get him murdered."

"Not bad enough? Listen: extortion and blackmail tend to piss people off. Especially people as tough as Bill Henderson, who could be facing bankruptcy and a jail term because of this greedy kid. I just got the feeling, Doc, watching him stomp around his trawler, that he doesn't put up with any shit. Know whudda mean? And it just so happens, to support my point, that we just uncovered a prior on Henderson: aggravated assault. It happened in a bar in Fall River a few years ago. Henderson got off on a plea of self-defense. But it wasn't pretty; the other guy was hospitalized for ten days."

"Well then, cleared or not, he's certainly capable of violence. I keep thinking about Andy's phone call to that isolated booth on Sippiwissett Road, just before he took his strange walk outside in the storm. If it was to meet somebody, then who was it?"

More than a minute went by in silence while we sipped.

"Hunter Whitesides," said Joe finally. "And I'll tell you why. After Andy realizes he's being chased, that Henderson and company won't go along with his raised ante, he makes a last-ditch effort to cut a deal directly with Whitesides, leaving out the other two partners. Get it?"

"Because Whitesides owns the land —"

"Sure! The mineral rights go with the land. So if any money is to be made, it's Whitesides's, by law. The derrick's in place, ready to go. Who needs the other guys? It would mean more money for both of them. So Andy calls Whitesides, who's staying somewhere on the Cape, and arranges to meet him on your beach. Maybe Whitesides promises to come, but he doesn't keep the promise because he knows Andy will be dead in a matter of hours. So Andy spends two hours waiting in vain to make his secret deal. Disappointed and angry, he returns to the Breakers, takes the fatal dose, dies in his sleep. *Finito.*"

"It's fitting together, Joe. Just like a Swiss watch. So what happens now?"

"What happens now is, we get all the evidence in hand. We get all our witnesses lined up, which includes the two of us, Mary, Jack, and Paul Keegan. And there'll be others, too, like the Isaacsons, and that Henshaw kid who works in the warehouse. We get all our paperwork done beforehand so everything will go without a hitch. Then we collar everybody at once: Henderson and his kids, Whitesides, and this guy Chisholm. We get them all in the net and tell them they're looking good for murder one."

He dabbed his mouth lightly with a napkin, a hint of a grin forming on his lips.

"Then, you watch. The shit's gonna fly, with everyone scared, and trying to clear himself by blaming the others. We'll interview them separately, so they won't have time to make up a story, and see how each person's version fits with the others. I promise you, Doc, when we get finished, at least a couple of them are going down. Count on it. And Keegan and I are gonna owe you. Because we're gonna be heroes, nailing Slinky and the OEI outfit both at the same time."

"Sounds great. But there's just one thing still unresolved," I said, tapping the photograph on the table with my finger.

Joe's face clouded over.

"Yeah . . . ," he said wearily, "I know: the damn tower. Is it a drilling rig, or a windmill? We just don't know."

"And if you get your master plan in motion, Joe, with you and Paul nabbing all these suspects, and it turns out to be just a windmill . . ."

"Yeah, right. We're gonna look dumb. And Paul's already in trouble with the brass for his 'premature' arrest and detention of Hartzell."

"But we need to know, Joe, and soon. Jack's officially out on bail for murder one. Know how that feels? To have your son *out on bail on a murder charge,* for Chrissakes?"

"I guess I'll work on getting a warrant. But Christ, it'll take days to actually —"

"I know a short cut," I said softly, moving toward the phone.

"It's got to be legal. If it's not strictly in accordance with —"

"Cover your ears, pal," I instructed, punching in the number to the Boston Young Men's Christian Union. The phone rang twice before a male voice answered.

"I want to speak to Laitis Roantis," I said. "It's urgent."

"Roantis!" said Joe, jumping up from the table. "Look, I said legal, Doc, and that lunatic —"

"You're not covering your ears, Dumbo. Naughty, naughty."

TWENTY-SIX

"LAITIS IS BUSY NOW," said the voice. "He's giving a demonstration in kick-fighting."

I heard a man scream in the background. Some unlucky sparring partner was getting a dose of Roantis's uncanny skill at the lethal arts. The scream was followed by wailing and moaning. Whoever it was, it *wasn't* Laitis Roantis. You could bet your virginity on that.

"I assume he'll be finished sometime tonight. Please tell him Doc Adams wants to talk to him."

"What's it about? Can I tell him?"

"Uh . . . just tell him Doc says the Daisy Ducks are taking wing. He'll know."

"Daisy Ducks? Are you one of the Daisy Ducks?"

"Right, and it's important he return my call, okay?"

There was silence. Maybe three or four heartbeats worth, and then the voice came back.

"Uh . . . I'll get Mr. Roantis right away for you, sir. Sorry you had to wait."

I was impressed with the rep the Daisy Ducks enjoyed at the BYMCU. Of course, I'd failed to mention that I was only an honorary Daisy Duck. I wasn't one of the original eight — the guys who fought deep behind enemy lines in Southeast Asia. Who dove out of planes in the dead of night and strangled armies with piano wire in swamps. But I was with the Ducks in North Carolina. Oh yeah . . .

The moaning offstage diminished. Were they toting the guy away to the dying room, or what?

"Yeah."

"Laitis, it's Doc."

"Hey, Doc boy. How is everyt'ing with you?"

"Everything is iffy right now. I need help on a little midnight prowl. Amphibious. Can you come along?"

"You want killing, Doc? That's not like you."

"No killing, just some nighttime recon and photos."

"You said ambiguous. That usually means —"

"No. I said am-FIB-ious." Laitis's English still isn't so hot.

"Tell me about it."

"That's not an old beat-up Dodge, Doc; that's a goddamn *van,*" said Jim DeGroot, peering at the parking lot through his marine glasses.

It was dark aboard *Whimsea*; we wanted to remain as low key as possible. We were sitting up in the flying bridge, out under the stars in the dark. There were some low, puffy clouds playing tag with a half-moon up there. Enough light for ultra-speed film and no flash? Or would we have to go with the infrared? Maybe just use the thousand-speed film and push the hell out of it in the tank, I thought. My mind was racing. I looked at the big white van in the marina parking lot again.

"Wonder where he got that?" I whispered. "Probably stole it. Hey, there's somebody with him. Good Christ, is he big."

The two silhouetted figures walked across the lot, approaching the dock where *Whimsea* was tied up with a lot of other cruisers. We could only see their outlines, but the stranger looked two heads taller than Roantis, which put him over six six, with shoulders that weren't quite as wide as a flight deck.

"*Psssst!* Doc!"

"Over here," I said, in a voice just loud enough so he could locate us. He spotted the *Whimsea*, then saw us up on the bridge. He walked up the dock opposite our boat and looked up.

"Help us with the Zode," he said.

"What?"

"We need help carrying the Zode. C'mon, both of you."

As we walked across the deserted parking lot in the dark, Roantis introduced the man with him as John Smith. We shook hands, and a horny sheath of muscle and bone engulfed my hand. John Smith nodded to us, but didn't say boo. He had blue eyes, a deep tan, and white-blond hair. I noticed the eyes. They had that same flat look as Laitis's eyes. The low-affect look. The pit bulldog stare. John Smith my ass.

It was a little after one in the morning. We were at a marina in Lewis Bay, which is right next to Hyannis, on the Cape's southern shore. Our destination, Tuckernuck Island, was about twenty-five miles due south, right across Nantucket Sound. A two-hour run at moderate speed. I had Jim bring *Whimsea* down here on short notice, but I convinced him it was important. Even so, he wasn't overly eager.

"I feel uneasy around this Roantis guy," he whispered to me as we followed the two men to the van. I told him that was understandable.

"Is it really true he once ate a chunk of two-by-four to win a bar bet?"

"Oh yeah. He did that. But he cheated."

"Cheated?"

"Uh-huh; he covered it with whipped cream first."

"Look, I don't have to do this you know —"

"Come on, we've got to unload this Zode, whatever the hell it is."

We heard the back doors of the van open softly as we approached it. Then Roantis and Mr. John Smith hopped inside and heaved a large, very heavy bundle halfway out the bed of the truck. The four of us hauled it over to *Whimsea*'s foredeck quick and quiet. Roantis instructed us to lash the bundle down, which Jim and I did while they returned to the van for two duffel bags and a large outboard motor, which Mr. Smith carried back to the boat under one arm, as if it were a camera bag.

We started the engines and cast off, purring out of the marina and into Lewis Bay. In short order, we were clear of land and heading out over Nantucket Sound, with only the running lights on. I doubt anyone saw us, which was just fine. The water was calm and inky black, with big soft swells. We would get to Tuckernuck about three A.M. Perfect.

Below us, in the forward stateroom, the light flicked on. Roantis and John Smith were talking. The language was one I'd never heard before. It wasn't Lithuanian, which was Roantis's native tongue. This speech sounded like a cross between Swedish and Japanese. Or maybe Apache.

"Pssst! Hey Doc," whispered Jim, his eyes on the console. "You think that guy's name is really John Smith? I say, if he's John Smith, I'm Pochahontas."

"Could be. There's a remote chance —"

"And I say he's a foreigner, too."

"Good going, Jim. You could be a candidate for Mensa."

He told me to go fuck myself, put his big hands on the twin throttle knobs, and shoved them forward. The engines revved, and I felt *Whimsea's* hull rise up and plane. We were clipping along, the silver gray wake spreading out behind us, faint in the moon glow. There was the cozy hum of the engines, and the slight pitching of the deep V hull, cutting through the black water of the Atlantic.

I heard the clank of metal, and knew that the guys below were unpacking their toys. Then Roantis would slip into his jetblack neophrene wet suit. The one with faint purple and gray swirls on it. His "Black Widow" outfit. Mr. Smith was probably donning his mask and cape . . .

"God, I'm nervous," Jim said, wiping his palms of his pants and peering ahead into the darkness. "Cross Rip Shoals dead ahead. Graveyard of the Atlantic. Then we've got to sneak up there . . . What if we're seen? What if they've got —"

"Hey," I said, shrugging my shoulders and lighting a small Brazilian cigar. "Don't think about it till it happens."

"Well I hate this, Doc. I don't mind telling you, I fucking hate it."

"C'mon, Jim; you *like* boating . . ."

Naturally, I felt the gut-wrenching rush of adrenalin, too. But I don't suppose it would do any good to tell him how I really felt.

I loved it.

TWENTY-SEVEN

AFTER NINETY MINUTES of churning along, we cut speed and crept up on Tuckernuck slow and easy, at one-third throttle, Jim watching the echo sounder carefully. We had used dead reckoning for most of the way, relying on compass heading and speed over time for a rough fix. Now we used the RDF to catch the radio beacons at Brant Point, Chatham, and Woods Hole to pinpoint our position. At two-fifteen, the water shoaled fast: our depth reading going from twenty-some feet to less than eight in under a minute. We knew then we had reached Tuckernuck Bank, and Jim stopped *Whimsea* dead in the water, saying he wasn't going to risk a cracked hull or a stranded vessel in these tricky waters.

"Sure t'ing, kid, that's why we brought the Zode," said Roantis, going out onto the foredeck with John Smith. I lowered the bow anchor, which seemed to bump the bottom immediately, even though we were still two miles off the island. Jim threw a hook off the stern as well, to keep the cruiser pointing toward Tuckernuck. We doused the running lights, keeping only the tiny anchor light going. Working by flashlight, Roantis undid the big bundle and we all unfolded the heavy-gauge rubber with metallic coating. I saw the word ZODIAC on the side. So that's what the mysterious "Zode" was: a Zodiac rubber boat, just like Jacques Cousteau's. John Smith attached an air tank to the valves of the boat and inflated it in three winks, the rubber making a hollow, pneumatic echo as the raft flumped and stretched into shape, resulting in a hardness and rigidity that left me, well, envious. I was wondering if I could hook that bottle up to my —

"C'mon Doc, let's get her launched," said Roantis. And we put the Zode into the sea, with John Smith handing down the huge Mercury motor as if it were a hiker's day pack. He wasn't wearing the cape after all, but a black wet suit with matching hood, a nylon pack on his broad back, and a black knife as big as a machete strapped to his calf. I was wearing cutoffs, a sweat shirt, a navy-blue wool sweater over the sweat shirt, and a woolen black watch cap pulled down low over my head. I put on a pair of high-top sneakers and laced them tight. I threw my waterproof camera bag into the Zode. Roantis was crouched in the bow, holding an illuminated compass. He wore his .45 in a shoulder rig made of nylon. Mr. John Smith, in the stern, secured my camera bag between his feet. You couldn't even see Roantis or his big friend in the dark. No kidding.

The friend, Mr. Smith, intrigued me. Except for a few foreign phrases to Roantis, he hadn't spoken in two hours. Probably shy.

The outboard motor had been altered with a special blackened shroud and an exhaust pipe that extended down below the surface. The purpose of these modifications was immediately apparent when John Smith started it. It was slightly louder than a Mixmaster. Circling *Whimsea* in our silent craft, allowing the engine to warm up, we told Jim we'd return within an hour.

"But if we're not back by five, raise the Coast Guard on your radio," I said. "See ya, guy. Don't take any wooden nickels . . ."

And we were off, bouncing over the swells in the dark with the big motor purring at our backs. In the bow, Roantis kept his eyes riveted to the compass, indicating course changes to John Smith by waving his arm. The warm sea breeze blew over us as we crouched low in the boat. I suppose our speed was about ten or twelve miles an hour. Not fast, but we didn't have far to go. Just to be on the safe side, I'd brought by Browning Hi Power, which I now took out of the waterproof camera bag and shoved into the nylon Bianchi shoulder rig Roantis had loaned me. The automatic rode right under my left armpit, thirteen hollow-point rounds in the magazine and one up the spout. God, I hoped we wouldn't have to use any of the hardware.

In a little while I heard surf. The muffled motor was a double boon: it enabled us not only to travel in silence, but to hear as well. We crept up to the beach, which was a faint pale line stretched out before us. Then we were riding the surf with the engine off . . . we skidded into the sandy shallows with the motor tipped up. Jumping out, we towed the boat through the calf-deep water. The water was warm on my legs. We slogged up to the wet sand at the water's edge, then dragged the Zode across the beach to where the trees and scrub began. We stood there for a second on the sand in the dark, listening to the gentle surf, looking up and down the beach for a landmark. I felt the delicious thrill of being somewhere I shouldn't be.

Roantis snapped the compass shut and put it away, saying that according to his calculations, we'd landed a half-mile west of Hunter Whitesides's mansion. So we followed him, walking single file, thirty feet apart, up the beach.

The problem was that Tucknernuck Island was so sparsely settled it was practically deserted. Consequently, landmarks were nonexistent; all we had to guide us was water, sand, and trees. But Roantis left the beach after a few minutes and started cutting diagonally up the sloping sand, headed for the woods. Sure enough, after struggling through thick brush, trying to be as silent as possible, we saw the faint dark outline of a big, big house. Roantis's sense of direction and skill at tracking defies belief. But then, he's had a lot of practice sneaking around in the dark.

Roantis scanned the place with his night glasses and pointed. I followed his arm and saw the steel tower forty yards away. It was much bigger than it had seemed in the photos — at least sixty feet high. We began to creep toward it but were stopped by a barbed wire fence. Barbed wire? On Tuckernuck Island? Surely this, if anything, was a dead giveaway that Whitesides and company were up to something shady. Roantis handed me the glasses. John Smith also took out a pair from his rucksack. The big house was dark. The large clearing between the house and the woods where we crouched would be a lawn. I saw a group of Adirondack chairs and a wooden table. Then I looked at the steel latticework of the tower again. I recalled the things that geologist Calvin Beard had told me to look for, things that were a dead giveaway for a drilling rig: crown block. Traveling block. The turntable and the "kelly." Drilling motors . . .

Great, Calvin. But from where we sat, I couldn't see shit. For one thing, the base of the tower was hidden by a small rise on the other side of the fence.

I felt a tap on my shoulder. Roantis whispered close.

"The fence means dey're up to something. To cut it is a trespass. Just t'inking about it from the legal aspect, you know . . . for later on . . ."

I nodded and thought. Maybe we could get some long-range pix of the tower. Would that be good enough?

No it wouldn't. That's why we had come all this way in the dead of night: to get close. Again, I heard Calvin Beard briefing me on the wharf at Woods Hole. Look for pipe lying around. Look for the mud hose. Above all, *look for the mud,* he'd told me. They can't hide the damn mud. The drilling mud, the slurry that's pumped down the pipe as it rotates, is what cools the bit, keeps pressure on the well head, and drives the broken rock back up the hole.

"Let's go on through," I said. "Even if the photos won't stand up in court, we can use them to pressure the OEI boys." Roantis nodded and soon I heard the *crink, crink* of John Smith's wire cutters. Then he held the wire clear for us to enter. We went through the breach and crawled up the ridge just above the spot where the base of the structure was. We made no noise. Gazing upward, I could see the pale, linear shapes of the propeller blades sixty feet above. Seeing the whole thing from that distance, I was pretty sure the propeller was fake. It was clever, there was no denying that, because wind machines are now common in coastal New England. But clearly, this was not one of them. For starters, the tower was too massive.

I crept over the ridge and went down to the tower's base, with Roantis and Smith waiting behind me in the bush. I took out my waterproof flashlight and swept the ground around the place. There it was: mud. Gray-brown drilling mud, caked on the tower frame, spattered on the corrugated tin housing of the drilling motors, set hard in pools and frozen rivers at my feet. Mud everywhere, even a big reservoir of it dug into the ground. And it looked old, as if the drilling had stopped weeks ago. At the tower's base was the turntable which drove the "kelly" and turned the pipe and the bit at its terminus. Above it was the caked end of the mud hose, and the traveling block, which raised and lowered the sections of pipe. I shined the light beam straight up and saw the crown block way up there, right underneath the bogus propeller. As I watched, the blades turned lazily in the breeze. They would turn easily, I thought since they were free floating, unconnected to anything.

It was all there. Every bit of the evidence we needed.

I took shots of the apparatus and the muddy surroundings, including stacks of pipe and worn-out bits. None of this was visible from the air, the sea, or even the beach; all of it was hidden by the trees and the hill. And people couldn't get over the hill because of the fence. I took the pictures using a small tripod, taking exposures at four, six, eight, ten, and twelve seconds. Roantis was up on the hill behind me, shooting with a Leica loaded with infrared film. He was no stranger to this kind of work.

Everything I saw gave the strong impression that the drilling operation had been abandoned for some time. Why? Easy: OEI had run out of money. Unless Hunter Whitesides was willing to mortgage his fine mansion and hock his big Mercedes, there wasn't enough cash on hand to continue. And that's why they so desperately needed the cores: to attract outside help.

It was when I was getting a closer shot of the drilling machinery and the small shack in the clearing that we saw the lights go on inside the house. Seconds later, two floodlights snapped on outside. I heard a door open and shut. Then Roantis scurried down the slope to me.

"The wires, Doc," he said in a hoarse whisper. "They must have been carrying a charge. When the circuit's broken an alarm goes off inside.

"Give me another second; I've got to get a shot of the pipe under the tarps —"

I didn't care how much noise I was making now. Circling around to the end of the long bundle, I saw the four-inch circles of exposed pipe ends visible underneath the canvas cover. Three more shots and I was finished.

"Doc!" Roantis shouted. No whispers now, and I wondered why. Then I heard the rapid patter of feet, and a rising growl.

I doused the light and headed up the slope as the big dog spun to a stop at the clearing's edge. I heard him down there, woofing and turning in tight circles, trying to catch a scent. Then there was a commotion at the edge of the clearing, a clump of bushes swishing back and forth. The dog made for the bushes, snarling and raising a ruckus. Somebody at the house yelled, and then there was a gunshot.

It seemed to me it was time to depart.

The dog leaped at the waving bush and was met with something that made him sit down in a hurry. I heard a flat crack and then saw the dog stretched out as if asleep. By this time I was back at the wire, hanging onto the camera bag with one hand and trying to find the hole in the fence with the other. While I was groping, an arm reached out and grabbed me by the elbow, yanking me through the fence. Then John Smith came barreling through behind me, sheathing his giant black knife. Gunshots were coming faster now. Twice I heard the slugs strike tree trunks above us. We made for the beach and sprinted along the sand, staying close up against the covering trees. We heard buzzing over our heads, which meant whoever was shooting at us was using a pistol, not a high-powered rifle. And we doubted he could see us, but that was scant comfort.

Roantis huddled us together under a low, spreading pine bough about two hundred yards from the boat. We crouched together on the cold sand, looking up the pale stretch of beach into the darkness beyond. And damned if I didn't think back to that time at Crystal Lake, Michigan, with good old Patty Froelich peeling off her swimsuit. Cold sand does it every time. Damn!

Roantis took out his pistol and covered the beach behind us. I knew exactly what he was thinking: if we were caught in the open carrying the boat back into the sea, or in open water, we were fish in a barrel.

So we waited for about ten minutes. When nobody came up the beach after us, we went to the boat, slinking low and slow at the edge of the trees.

Hauling the heavy Zode and its motor back down the beach took under five seconds. It's amazing what you can do when you're pumped up. We waded into the ocean, shoving the rubber boat along, ready to duck under at the slightest noise from behind. But there was none, and soon we were all aboard, with Mr. Smith starting the big Mercury, and the boat jumping forward, thumping against the incoming breakers, heading back out to where *Whimsea* was waiting for us.

Jim had the anchors up and the engines running by the time we bumped up alongside *Whimsea*'s hull.

"Everything go okay?" he asked, reaching down to help us aboard.

"Didn't you hear the shots?"

"Yeah, right, Doc," he said, laughing, "you're a born bullshitter."

Exhausted and elated, I let it pass. As soon as the boat and motor were hauled aboard, Jim gunned the engines and we were off. John Smith stowed the motor while Roantis and I opened the valves to deflate the rubber boat, then stretched its wet skin out on the foredeck to dry off in the breeze. We all changed into warm, dry clothes, and then I filled four plastic mugs with Scotch and water. Mostly Scotch. We sat in the wheel house sipping the whiskey in the dark, absorbing the cozy hum and vibration of the big engines going full bore as we shot homeward.

I felt a warm glow growing in me. It wasn't just the booze, but the afterglow of the adrenalin rush and the knowledge of a job well done. There is no better feeling. Roantis lighted a cigarette and let it dangle from his mouth, the end glowing red in the darkened cabin. He blew the smoke out of his nostrils like a dragon. He was looking very fit these days, having abandoned his suicidal lifestyle for one that was merely horrendous. I saw before me a lean, whipcord-hard man, with short grayish hair and crinkles around his Mongol eyes. Roantis is over fifty, maybe five feet seven or eight, and a hundred sixty-some pounds. Not very big or impressive looking. But then, neither is a wad of plastique. Jim sipped his drink and minded the helm, wearing a huge grin. He couldn't hide it if he tried.

"Feeling better about all this?" I asked him.

"Feeling great, Doc. Feeling just great. I'll never forget to-night. Can't wait until we do it again . . ."

"We'll see if you say that when the time comes, sport."

"Did Mary buy the story?"

"That I was going fishing with you? Seemed to. If she didn't, you can bet I'll hear about it."

An hour later we purred into Lewis Bay and slipped into the marina and up to the dock. The Zode was folded and bundled and whisked over to the van along with the special outboard. We all stood at the van while Roantis and his mysterious comrade prepared to take off.

"Who owns that stuff, anyway?" I asked.

"The Tenth Group, if you really *must* know. If this van and boat aren't back tomorrow, Mr. Smith here goes to the stockade. I go to the guillotine."

"So who is this guy, really?" I asked, nodding in John Smith's direction.

"Timo Pekkalla. Finnish national training with the Tenth Group out at Fort Devens. But that's very confidential, Doc, if you haven't already guessed."

The big man laughed and nodded. "Sssank yeeew, so much."

"Yah, sheeuuuurre," I said. Finns. They make the world's finest knives and rifles, live in places no sane person would even consider, and are not people you want as enemies. If you don't believe me, ask the Russians. I've met some Finns in my time, mostly in northern Minnesota. I love every one I've ever met. Just don't get them mad. We all shook hands goodbye, but not before I laid several large bills into Laitis's hand.

Jim and I went back to the boat. I looked at my watch. Five-thirty; dawn was breaking. I went below into the bow bunk. The day would be busy, busy. Go to Cambridge to the small photo lab in Kendall Square and have the film done. Pray to God some of it came out. Go to the fish pier in Boston and buy a couple whole bluefish so Mary and Janice would believe our little white lie about the fishing trip.

Thinking back on our little escapade, I was glad Timo didn't kill that dog. I'd thought he had, but Roantis explained he'd smacked it on the noggin with the flat of the blade and stunned it.

I had the inescapable feeling that Timo Pekkalla, a.k.a. John Smith, had been in tough scrapes before.

The afterglow wouldn't go away; I felt warm and tingly all over. I lay in the bunk, watching the dawn come through the fore hatch skylight. This is why we're alive, I thought, feeling the boat rocking under me. Country clubs, bank accounts, and fancy cars don't cut it. Falling in love, having kids, looking out for one another, and having adventures do. Especially the adventures . . .

The cabin cruiser swayed and sighed in the current. Her hull squeaked and whined against the dock fenders. And I slept.

TWENTY-EIGHT

JACK'S TRIAL DATE was set for October tenth. It was hanging over all of us like the sword of Damocles.

Within four days of our little nighttime jaunt to Tuckernuck Island, Joe and Paul Keegan had sprung the trap. Armed with the necessary evidence, including my photos, they collared Bill Henderson and Michael Chisholm as they emerged from OEI headquarters on the docks of New Bedford. At the same time, both Henderson kids were detained in Woods Hole and Falmouth, while Hunter Whitesides was intercepted on Nantucket as he went to his post office box.

They were all advised of their rights and taken separately to Boston, where each was interviewed by Joe and Paul. They all refused to talk, which slowed things down for a few days until the state attorneys met with counsels for the defense and waved the evidence in their faces, whereupon the defense attorneys returned to their clients and huddled, long and silent. Joe had a hunch they were advising their clients to cooperate in hopes of a deal being struck, suggesting they might be packing their toothbrushes for Walpole or Deer Island if they didn't.

I felt sorry for the Henderson kids, who, according to Joe and Paul, were plainly scared to death. Olivia Henderson, their mother, stayed close to them and spent much of her time cursing her husband and urging them to tell all. So much for Bill Henderson's standing with his family. I've noticed that many "successful" men have this problem.

Paul told me the kids broke down first. Alice swore she knew nothing of the operation. Her brother Terry backed her up, admitting that he was the one who sneaked Jack's room key during a party and had it copied, on his father's orders.

"When was this?" I asked Keegan.

"Shortly before the first burglary," he said, looking through his notebook.

"And Terry helped ransack the place?"

"Not according to him. We assume it was his father, maybe with help from his partners. But the older guys aren't talking yet."

"And who did the break-in at the cottage?"

"Oh, we got that one in the bag. The Isaacsons made a positive on Chisholm's kid. Didn't Joe tell you?"

"No. They identified Chisholm's son as the one who pawned the radio? Jeez, I bet he's steamed at the kid."

"I would assume so. But he's not talking. All three partners are still silent. But just you wait: with a murder one rap out on them, they'll get scared and start pointing at one another. It won't be long."

The break came early the next day. Joe called me from Ten Ten Comm. Ave., where they were interviewing Hunter Whitesides, who was out on bail, thanks to a good lawyer and a hefty bank account. Joe said Whitesides wanted to talk and requested my presence also, since I was pressing charges for B and E.

"I thought it fitting that you be in on it, Doc, since you cracked the thing open. Whitesides is coming across pretty straight, I think. Either that, or he's a master liar. See you in an hour?"

"Thank you for coming, Dr. Adams," said Hunter Whitesides, who was dressed in subdued good taste, including a tropical-weight wool-and-silk jacket I might have killed for. And I don't particularly go in for clothes.

His lawyer, John Higgins, sat in a blue three-piece slightly behind him and off to one side, ready to interrupt at the faintest hint that his client was treading on thin ice.

"I am here to admit in full candor that I am guilty as an accessory to breaking and entering," said Whitesides. "That, and that *only*. I have no knowledge whatsoever of the events or circumstances surrounding the unfortunate death of Andrew Cunningham."

Having given this opening statement, he sat at Joe's desk, hands clasped before him, ready for questioning. Which Joe and Paul proceeded with. There was a tape machine running, but no stenographer. Question: did he know Cunningham? Had he met him? Yes, briefly, to arrange for him to take the government cores and seismic data from the USGS warehouse on the Quissett campus. Had he been in contact with the Cunningham boy since then? Yes, once, aboard the *Highlander*, during a brief exchange in which Bill Henderson threatened to kill him unless he handed over the stolen data as agreed.

"And what was the agreement, Mr. Whitesides?" asked Keegan.

"That Cunningham was to deliver to us, in secret, the core samples and profile graphs for the sum of two thousand dollars."

"Which was paid to him?"

"No. To be paid when we received the data."

"The purpose of which was to attract investors and raise cash?"

"Yes. And Cunningham refused to give us the data as agreed, stating that the price was too low. He demanded ten thousand."

"Which you and your partners refused to pay him, is that correct?"

"Yes. Because it wasn't part of the deal. And frankly, we couldn't afford it anyway."

"What was the nature of the threat issued by Mr. Henderson?"

"It wasn't specific, just that Andy could wind up dead if he held out."

"And what was Mr. Cunningham's response to this?"

"He left the boat, saying we know where he could be reached if we changed our minds."

"And that was the last you saw of Mr. Cunningham?"

"Yes."

"You are certain?"

"Absolutely."

"May I ask a question?"

"Go ahead, Doc."

"Mr. Whitesides, you're certain that the last time you had contact with Cunningham was aboard Henderson's trawler?"

"Positive."

"You didn't even have as much as, say, a phone conversation with him afterwards?"

The man stared at me, his silver hair immaculately parted far down the side of his ruddy head, his fine clothes evidence of his status and upbringing in the highest circles. And yet, I saw him twitch slightly, saw his eyes lose a bit of their keen focus. He was coming a little unglued at the question.

"I, uh, might have. I don't remember."

"You don't remember. That's mighty unlikely. I say you did. I say you did because Andy called you from my house on the Cape. He called you the very same night he died."

"Hold it!" snapped Higgins, springing to his feet and approaching his client's side. "You don't have to answer that, Mr. Whitesides. We've agreed to —"

"I'll answer, goddammit!" said Whitesides, shifting his ample bottom around in the chair. "Don't forget, Higgins, the charge is murder one, and I know I didn't do it. I feel suckered enough by those other two. I'll be damned if I'll face a charge like that alone. For all we know, they're talking right now, making up a story to put me away. Yes, Dr. Adams. Yes, I got a call from Andy Cunningham the night he died. But I was nowhere near him; I couldn't have had anything to do with his death."

"The murderers didn't have to be near the boy," said Paul Keegan slowly. His voice was full of menace. "It was a murder done by remote control. Doc, I think that was your expression . . ."

"Okay, so where *were* you that Saturday night?" I asked.

"I was home, on Tuckernuck."

"Do you have any witness to swear to that?"

"No. I don't think so."

"We could check the phone records," said Joe, looking at Paul. "See if a call was made from Doc's place that night to the island, to the number of the Whitesides residence. That sound like a good idea to you, Whitesides? Or, for some strange reason, does it maybe bother you?"

Whitesides got up and shuffled around the room, breathing

heavily. He was almost all the way unglued now, but still, he didn't talk. Then Joe spoke.

"Mr. Whitesides, we've checked the records of the phone company for the night in question. The call Andy made was to a phone booth. We know where that phone booth is . . . and we think you know, too. Is there anything you'd like to say now?"

"Okay," he said in a hoarse whisper, "I wasn't on the island, I was in Woods Hole. I said I was home because . . . well, you know . . . because it's farther away from where the kid was that night. You know . . ."

"Okay, now we get a different version," said Keegan slowly, using his inquisition whisper. "You were on the Cape that night, in Woods Hole. Where?"

"The Forrest House. It's a little guest house out on Sippiwissett Road. A private home with rooms. I keep a room there year-round so I can stay there anytime I miss the ferry, or when I want to be on the mainland."

"Who saw you there? Anybody?"

"I don't know. Somebody, probably. I hope to hell somebody."

"Wouldn't matter," hissed Keegan. "Woods Hole's not that far from Eastham. At night, with light traffic, maybe an hour's drive, right Doc?"

I nodded. "But let's get back to this phone call. What did he say to you?"

"He said he wanted to give me the stuff he took from the Geological Survey. Give it to me alone, and then we could be partners together. He said he'd give me the stuff for free if I'd cut him in on the well, and leave the others out. He told me the other two were cheating me, since it was my land the well was on, so why keep them in?"

Joe and I exchanged a quick glance. The phone call was exactly as we had predicted. And of course, I had confronted Whitesides about the call without the slightest proof that he was on the receiving end of it; it was just logic and luck working in our favor.

"And what did you say?"

"I said no. Absolutely no way. We were a corporation, and that was that. And I warned him that he'd better keep his part of the deal or he'd be sorry."

"What was that supposed to mean?" asked Keegan.

"Nothing specific; just a warning. Bill Henderson is nobody to mess with, let me tell you. You heard he put a guy in the hospital six years ago? In a bar fight in Fall River?"

Whitesides's attorney, Higgins, sat on the very edge of his chair, his eyes beginning to bug out.

"If you want to know, Cunningham's offer sounded attractive," continued Whitesides. "I knew I was sort of being taken for a ride. But frankly, I was a little afraid of Henderson. No way was I going to try and leave him out, and have him come after me."

"You say you were afraid of Henderson. What about Dr. Chisholm?"

"Not really, He's kind of bookish, even though he's a big guy. I think he's under Bill's thumb, too."

"Is Bill Henderson capable of murder, Mr. Whitesides?" asked Joe.

Higgins jumped up and objected, saying the question was speculative, and that his client shouldn't be put in a position to answer it. He added quickly that, of course, it was obvious that his client was certainly *not* capable of such an act. Keegan growled that the jury would determine that. Both Higgins and Whitesides grew pale at this. I had to credit Paul Keegan. He was good at intimidation, he knew how to keep the fire going under Whitesides's feet. Seeing him squirm, and recalling the success of my earlier bluff, I decided to try another.

"Mr. Whitesides, now that you've apparently come clean on the phone call, how about telling us about your meeting with Andy later that night? Was it on the beach? On Sunken Meadow Road? Or did you pick him up near our cottage in your big blue Mercedes and go somewhere to talk it over?"

"*What?* What meeting? There was no meeting later on. I swear it. I swear it on a stack of Bibles. As God is my witness, there was no meeting; I stayed in Forrest House the rest of that night."

"Be careful, Mr. Whitesides. We're talking murder one here. Murder *one*."

But Whitesides, panicked, swore up and down he wasn't there. That it must have been somebody else. That the other two were out to frame him, et cetera, et cetera. Seeing his client's distress,

Higgins called an end to the interview, and Joe, Paul, and I left the building shortly after they did.

The three of us were sitting over in the Greek's across the street from state police headquarters at Ten Ten Comm. Ave., having subs when Kevin O'Hearn, Joe's office mate and partner, came in.

Joe and Paul read over their notes while I attacked my half of a steak and cheese sub. That's a sandwich made with grill-fried shaved beef, lots of provolone cheese melted on top, oil, spices, tomato chunks, vinegar, and crushed hot peppers, all in a big Italian roll. It is the finest sandwich ever invented. But since I go light on lunch, I was only having half. Joe was eating the other half, along with a sub of his own: jumbo meatball and sausage.

"So . . . ," quipped O'Hearn, "don't leave me in the dark, fellas. What does everybody think?"

There was only the muted sound of grinding molars in reply.

"C'mon, you guys. Fill me in. I'm shittin' pink."

Joe raised his eyes at him. "That is *not* dinner table talk," he said.

"Oh. Well *ex-cuuuuuuuse* me."

"You may do a lot of things, Kev, but shitting pink isn't one of them," I said. "What'll you have? I'll buy."

"Thanks Doc. You're the only gentleman here. I'll have a lobster salad sub and a large Sprite."

He said lobster like this: *lawbstah*. I took out the money and started to get up from the table.

"Don't put yourself out, Doc; I'll go up and get it."

He slid off the slick red vinyl of the booth seat and waddled up to the counter. Joe saw him and swallowed fast.

"Hey Kev! As long as you're up there would y —"

"Fuck you, asshole."

Cops.

Kevin quickly returned with his food and slid into the booth.

"So what do *I* think?" said Joe philosophically as he wiped his mouth and blew over the top of his coffee cup. "I guess what I think is that poor Hunter Whitesides is telling the truth."

"Same here," said Keegan.

"Doc?"

"I agree. Joe, why don't you try and get a detailed financial background on him, see what his motivation was for getting mixed up in the scheme? Still, no matter how desperate he's been, I don't think murder is in the cards for him."

"I'm putting my money on Henderson," said Keegan softly. "He hates to be crossed, he's got a bad temper, and he's done violence in the past."

More chewing and blowing on coffee. Then Kevin said: "How about the drugs business? The lethal pills that killed the kid? How'd Henderson the fisherman have the savvy to pull that off?"

Keegan said, "Doc's the expert on that. Doc?"

"Well, since they roped Andy into stealing for them for a price, it's reasonable to assume that Henderson knew Andy pretty well. He made contact with the kid shortly after Andy arrived at Woods Hole and started dating his daughter. I mean, would Henderson walk up to Cunningham, introduce himself, and right off the bat say hey, we want you to steal something for us?"

Headshakes all around the booth.

"'Course not. Therefore, the deal they finally struck suggests that they saw each other often, and knew each other well. We thought old man Hartzell was a good bet for it because he's a biologist. But would he know about Andy's epilepsy? Not too likely, since the kids hated him and didn't talk with him more than they had to. But Henderson was in a perfect situation to learn of the illness. Why? Because Andy told Alice, his lady love, and Alice might easily have let it slip at home."

"Hey, that's good, Doc," said Joe. "Isn't that good?"

Nods all around the booth.

"Of course it's good; I'm the medical examiner for Barnstable County. You guys forgetting that?"

"You're a regular genius, Doc," said Keegan, picking his fine, straight teeth with a matchbook cover. "Joe, how come you never mentioned Doc's past adventures to me?"

Joe shrugged and sipped his coffee. O'Hearn was grinning at him.

"And another thing, Joe, speaking of past adventures. Why aren't you married? I'd a thought you'd be quite the family man."

"Forget it, Paul," said O'Hearn quietly. He'd felt my kick under the table.

"Huh? Aw, c'mon. I know he's not gay. Joe, you're not gay, are you?"

"No," said Joe. "I'm not gay."

"Paul. I said forget it, okay?" said O'Hearn. He'd lost his smile. Keegan looked dumbfounded at all of us.

"I say something wrong?"

"It's a long story, Paul," I said. "Maybe we'll talk about it some time."

I looked at Joe. He hadn't moved. Just sipped his coffee. But I noticed that a shiny curtain of sweat had formed on his lip and his hands shook a bit. Keegan mumbled some kind of apology and nobody said anything. There wasn't much talking after that, and we got up to leave the Greek's. I left the tip. Keegan was making a beeline for his cruiser parked down the street. O'Hearn and Joe were walking back to Ten Ten. Kev had his arm around Joe's shoulder and was trying to tell him a joke. Good old Kev. Joe seemed to be walking okay, and when he turned to give me a quick goodbye, I could've sworn he was smiling.

TWENTY-NINE

WELL, IT SEESAWED back and forth with the gang from OEI. For a corporation with such a lofty name, and with stated objectives and ideals as fancy as those that appeared in the company's charter, it sure sounded strange to hear the partners arguing — secondhand, as Mary and I were obliged to hear it from Joe — about who really killed Andy Cunningham. Whitesides seemed to us to be mostly in the clear, since his chances of financial gain seemed to remain constant whether Andy lived or died. Henderson remained the best suspect, not only because of his forceful personality and fierce temper, but because he was most financially strapped. And if Andy had indeed convinced Hunter Whitesides to dump the other two and strike a deal on his own with Andy's help, then he'd be left utterly out in the cold.

Michael Chisholm was the mystery man, a mild-mannered, bearded guy with a doctorate in geology who seemed at first blush immune from greed and financial pressures. But life is full of surprises; in addition to the Isaacsons fingering Chisholm's son, Jim, as the young man who came into their shop to pawn my radio, Chisholm's estranged wife, Barbara, established that he was a cokehead and a wife beater. Barbara was more than eager to document his drug dependency, fits of temper, sullen depressions, and random violence, not to mention his woeful financial situation.

With each passing day, the state guys up in Boston tried to

tighten the noose by playing one suspect against another. Every day, more accusations and "proofs" were hurled at each defendant by the others. But whenever the prosecutors thought they had a chance to close the net, the defense lawyers intervened and left them with nothing.

So while things got stickier and stickier between the three erstwhile partners, definite tie-ins to Andy's death were not established. Nobody on our side dared admit it, but it was becoming clear that while we had them dead to rights on the oil scam, the murder charge wasn't going anywhere. And Jack's trial date was fast approaching. Mary was very down. So was I, but doing my best to hide it.

Mary and I were down at the cottage that third week in September, trying to have fun. Jack, who was still at Woods Hole with his brother and Tom McDonnough, was keeping busy and trying to get through life one day at a time. Still, we knew he was watching the days slip by, and watching the dreaded date approach. Joe was coming down to stay with us about every other night. He was growing more tired and fidgety with each visit.

"I don't know, you guys . . . ," he sighed as he sipped his afterdinner cappuccino, "I just don't know anymore. I was so sure we had 'em. Now, I just . . . shit, I don't know . . ."

This was Friday night, September 22, six weeks to the night since Andy Cunningham died. We were sitting out on the porch, treating ourselves to yet another glorious sunset. "I'm beginning to doubt we'll ever put them in the bag for it," Joe continued wearily. "We're so close. And God knows we've got the lawyers jumping through hoops, each guy busy trying to incriminate the others. Christ, you'd think something would shake loose pretty soon."

"You don't think they planned it together?" asked Mary.

"We all thought so at first. But then came Whitesides's voluntary confessional Monday, and his story seems to be holding together. We did find a witness at Forrest House who recalls him there most of the night in question."

"Mmmmm. But remember, it's only a little more than an hour from there to here," I said. "That doesn't necessarily clear him."

"No. But let's face it, Doc: it helps him."

"Sure does. I don't think he's the killer, anyway. Never did."

Joe finished his coffee and looked skyward, stroking his stubbled chin.

"But this leaves an interesting blank," he mused. "If not Whitesides, then who? For all their motivation, it wasn't Henderson or Chisholm. They have an airtight alibi for that Friday night; they were seen together in a bar in Falmouth until after midnight. They may have killed the kid by doctoring his pills, but they weren't up here the night he died. So if it wasn't them, then who was it Andy met outside in the rain?"

"Maybe it was nobody," offered Mary. "Maybe Andy was just so pissed off and upset he went out for a solo walk in the rain."

"Yeah . . . shit," said Joe, lighting a Benson and Hedges.

"And then you thought the other two must've cooked it up together," I added. "But now, even that seems shaky. If they'd acted together, there'd be a trip-up by this time, wouldn't there?"

"Sure would. There'd be a catch in their stories. Or more agreement in their stories. You know, something to indicate that they'd worked out an alibi in advance. So far, we're getting neither coordination nor contradiction in each story. Just a bunch of chickenshit name calling and bad mouthing, with each guy saying the other must've done it because he's such a sneaky, mean, low-down son of a bitch. Typical partners in crime, I guess."

"Maybe they didn't kill Andy," I said. "I've had the feeling for some time that these things from the USGS lab weren't worth murder. Maybe Paul was right the first time; maybe old man Hartzell did do it."

"That's what poor Boyd Cunningham thinks," replied Joe. "He keeps calling me, crying and blubbering about his son, saying he's sure Hartzell's the guy. He wants to know when we're gonna lock him up."

"Poor guy; I really feel for him. But the fact that there's no hard evidence to support it makes it hard to swallow."

"Don't I know it," said Joe, dragging on his cigarette.

"You know, speaking of Lionel Hartzell, it's a shame," said Mary. "It turns out he's another casualty of this whole business. Jack says that he's clearing out his office this weekend, getting ready to leave the MBL. I guess he was just caught in the cross-fire. Listen Joey: Bill Henderson's the guy. He did it, either with Chisholm or alone. Keep the pressure on; he'll crack eventually."

"I will, Mare. You know that. We'll get Jackie cleared. The way things stand now, too much has happened, too much is revealed for things to grind to a halt. We're at a slow spot, but it's not over. You watch: something's gonna turn up."

One hour later, after we'd done the dishes and were sitting in the living room, it did.

There was a muted crackle of crushed stone in the drive outside; the dogs jumped up, barking and raising hell. Joe got up from his chair, turned down the Bach on the radio, and lifted a corner of the curtain to peer outside.

"Well whadduyuh know," he grunted, "it's Moby Dick himself."

"Moby Dick? What're you talking about, Joey?"

"It's the great white whale. C'mere."

"You're right," Mary said, joining him at the window. "it *is* the great white whale!"

"What the —" I said, hopping up and peering out between them. They were right.

There it was: the big white Caddy Eldo, replete with smoked glass windows, wire wheel covers, continental kit, television, and broken phone.

It was our old pal, Slinky.

THIRTY

"NOW what the fuck's *he* want?" murmured Joe. "Shit, this makes my fuckin' day."

"*Tch! Tch!* Joey! You really should watch your mouth!"

Mary saying this. Right.

Eddie Falcone got out of the passenger's side. When the driver, Vinnie, came out from behind the wheel, the big Eldo eased up on its shocks about four notches. I could almost hear it sigh with relief.

"Hmmph! I see he's brought his gorilla with him," said Joe with a closed mouth. He sidestepped quickly over to the chair where his sport coat was draped and jerked it away. Underneath was his shoulder rig holding the Beretta. He withdrew the pistol from the holster and set it on the end table, put his sport coat on, then stuck the automatic inside his belt on his left side, butt forward. All this was done in a flash, with no sound and no wasted motion. Watching him, you knew he'd done it a few times before. Still, it always makes me nervous when anybody jams a loaded gun into their pants like that.

"Should we go somewhere?" asked Mary softly.

"Hell no. It's your house, isn't it?"

The front door chimed and the dogs put up a racket. Joe opened the door. Slinky stood in the doorway. He was wearing a modified zoot suit with wide, padded shoulders and pleated pants. An outfit you'd see on *Miami Vice*. Figured. But at least he didn't have a black shirt and yellow tie. Vinnie, clad in a bronze-tone silk suit that seemed stretched over his wide body, stood two steps behind him, off to his right. Just like Gunga Din in the Kipling poem, I thought, the regimental water boy who was always found waiting "right flank, rear." Only Vinnie was a hell of a lot bigger than poor old Gunga.

"Lieutenant Brindelli. I was told you might be here. I want to talk to the doctor."

"About what?"

"About Andy Cunningham," said Falcone.

Joe turned and looked at us. "Well? Shall we let him in?"

"Why sure, Joey," said Mary. "Hi Eddie. How are you, dear?"

Joe frowned at his sister, then stepped back from the doorway. "Okay, but tell Gloria Vanderbilt here to wait in the car, huh?"

Vinnie's jaw dropped at the mention of Ms. Vanderbilt.

"Get the name right, pal," he managed, rocking up and down on his toes.

"It's okay, Vinnie," said Falcone, crossing the threshold. "Wait out here." Vinnie turned sullenly and went back to the Eldo.

"Ah, Dr. Adams, it is indeed a pleasure," Slinky cooed as he entered the cottage. "And Mrs. Adams . . . so nice to see you again. I hope you are well. My, how lovely you look this evening."

"Cut the shit," snapped Joe in a quiet voice. "What's up Falcone? You're facing five to ten. I'm gonna see you get inside. Now you come in here and disturb my family; I'm gonna make it ten to twenty."

Slinky held up his hand in polite resignation. Held it up as if to stop Joe's unseemly references to incarceration. He was nice as pie, was Slinky, and polite as a debutante.

"See, what it is, I want to talk to you, Dr. Adams, on account of the kid. Everybody knows the kid owed me money. And like I said before, for some silly reason I have no paperwork on the loan."

"*Tch! Tch!* How careless of you, Eddie," Joe chided, wagging his thick, hairy finger at the young man. "I understand completely. You want maybe we should take it up with the Better Business Bureau?"

Falcone waved him off, and Mary offered him a seat at the

kitchen table. He sat down and accepted a cup of coffee, tasting it and smacking his lips.

"Wow, Mrs. Adams. You're as good a cook as you are beautiful."

"Aw shucks," she said, smoothing down her skirt. She was smiling. Falcone kept sipping his java and oooing and ahhing. Joe was drumming his fingers and glaring at the kid. He wanted to throttle him; I could tell. I just sat there, eager to hear about Slinky and the kid. Falcone's dark, thinning hair was blown back over his head, as if he'd been riding a motorcycle without a helmet. He wore a cream-colored shirt, no tie, and his upper chest was covered with gold chains over a rug of dark hair. I looked again at his head and saw the inevitable bald spot beginning to spread on the back of his crown. Happens every time; you got a hairy chest, you get a bald head.

"Okay, so here it is," he said, dabbing the corners of his mouth with a napkin. "Andy Cunningham wasn't paying me back. He said he didn't have the money. I pushed him a little on it. Once Vinnie and me made a big push. But he still couldn't come across, so I knew he just didn't have it. Lieutenant, I'm saying this voluntarily, and will say the same thing in court. But I hope you aren't taping this conversation. Are you?"

Joe shook his head, lighting a cigarette and looking out the window. He didn't want to look at Slinky, didn't wish to acknowledge his presence more than he had to.

"So I figured what the hey? Let him be a doctor, then he can pay me, you know? Basically, I knew he was a good kid, and not trying to pull any shit. Well, five, maybe six weeks ago, I get a call from him. He says he's going up to Eastham over the weekend with his friend Jack. Says they'll be staying at Jack's parents' cottage on the beach, right? He asks me could I come up there and meet him for a few minutes. Says he's got something for me that could be worth a lot of money."

Joe was leaning forward now, elbows on the table, looking hard at Falcone.

"Do you remember what day it was, exactly?" he asked.

"When he called? Sure. It was Friday. The day of the big storm."

"Andy was murdered that same night."

"Uh-huh. I found that out later. So I'm taking a chance telling you this. But believe me, I didn't kill him."

"Why should we believe you, Slinky?" asked Joe. "And why are you coming here to tell us this?"

Falcone stirred uneasily and ran his fingers through his hair. I asked him if he'd like a drink. He brightened at the offer, and asked for a vodka and tonic.

"Why am I here? Because, as you know, Lieutenant, I'm in a little bit of trouble. What I'm thinking is, I help you on this other business, you'll help me cut a deal later on. Okay?"

"Maybe," said Joe sleepily, "can't promise anything, but there's a chance."

"Well, what the hey. I mean, it can't hurt. That pile of shit he gave me isn't worth anything that I can tell. Just a notebook and bunch of papers. But maybe it'll help you guys find his killer, you know?"

"Stuff he gave you?"

"Yeah. Said I could hold onto it for him, for collateral, he said. And when he was ready, then we could sell it for a bundle."

"And this stuff he gave you was a bunch of papers? It wasn't rocks and graphs?" asked Mary.

"Rocks? Hell no, Mrs. Adams. There wasn't any rocks. Just a notebook and whole bunch of papers in one of those cardboard cases that tie up with a shoelace. Bunch of writing and numbers was all it was. I didn't even look at it hardly. You know?"

"And he gave you these? For you to keep? asked Joe, leaning over the table again.

"Yeah. I just said that."

"And you've still got this stuff?"

"Maybe."

Joe let out a long, soft sigh.

"Look," said Falcone, clasping his fingers together as if about to pray, "I know I got some time coming. I just don't wanta go to Atlanta on a federal rap. I get my ticket punched for Atlanta, I kill myself first. You get it?"

"Gee, I can't imagine why you feel that way, Eddie. Just because a young, cute guy like you, with all those delicate manners of yours, is gonna be in the slammer with all those scuzzbags who haven't seen a broad in half a lifetime. So you're gonna have to play drop the soap for all those —"

"*Stop it, Joey!*" snapped Mary. She was boiling mad, and I knew why. She was thinking about what could happen to her own son. Then she collected herself. "Go ahead, Eddie. Tell us everything."

"Thanks, Mrs. Adams. Hey, where's your family from?"

"Schenectady."

"No, I mean, where're you *from?*"

"San Mango, in Calabria."

"Ahhh, *calabrese!* Even Sicilians fear the Calabrians."

"For good reason," Mary answered. Eddie Falcone laughed. Little did he know . . .

"So c'mon, Eddie. What happened that night?" asked Mary.

"Well, let's see. He called me earlier that day, Friday. I think it was late in the morning, or maybe early afternoon. Wait. Yeah, it was afternoon, because he called me at a place I go to in Pawtucket. I remember sitting at the bar there when they brought the phone to me, and I remember looking at the clock. Well, I wasn't real anxious to drive up to the Cape then, you know? So I says, what is it? He says I can't explain it now, but you'll hafta trust me, and if you'll keep it for me safe and hidden, then at the end of the summer or whatever, I'll help you sell it for a lot more scratch than I owe you. That's what he told me. In a nutshell. And so then what I realize is, I realize I gotta go up there because you know why? Because him not paying me back, well, it looks bad, you know? Guy like me's got a rep to keep up. I mean, it gets around guys aren't paying Slinky back, it gets worse, you know?"

"Yeah. Or, you could always go to the authorities and complain, couldn't you, Eddie?"

"Hey yeah, right. Funny. So funny I should write it down. So we're talking and he tells me how to get here. You know, to this place, here. I says no, too obvious. I says name a place I can't miss, I'll meet you there. He says the windmill. Meet me at the Eastham windmill. I says where the hell is that? He says it's right off the highway, on your left. Can't miss it. So I says okay but it better be good. Can I have another, Mrs. Adams?"

Mary got him some more Destroyer and Slinky rattled right along, not missing a beat.

"So I leave the bar after dinner. First thing I realize when I go outside — Holy Christ! It's raining and blowing like crazy. I almost don't go. But then I figure what the hey; I'll have Vinnie drive while I watch movies in the back. So we're riding up here in the thunder and rain and I'm having a drink or two in the back, you know, watching some skin flicks. So finally Vinnie —"

"You were watching skin flicks all by yourself?" said Mary. "Poor baby."

"Lay off, Mare," said Joe.

"Anyway, so Vinnie, he spots the windmill. We stop the car and wait. Finally, here comes the kid, soaked through and lugging this case with him, which he's holding under his raincoat. He gets in the car with me; I offer him a drink. He says no; he feels like shit. Says he's feeling so bad he wants to go right back and crash. So I say okay, let's see. Well, like I said before, it was nothing I could dig. I says you better not be yanking my chain, kid. 'Cause if you are, it's bye-bye time —"

He paused suddenly in his narrative and looked up at Joe.

"Not that I woulda done anything. You know. Just an expression. So it winds up like this: I say let's meet in a coupla months and go over this together when we got more time. Meanwhile, don't get the idea you're off the hook because personally, I mean, speaking for myself, this don't look like shit."

"And?" said Joe.

"And . . . and so I drop the kid off at the bottom of this little road here, watch him walking back up to this house, and that's the last I ever saw of him."

"So where's the stuff he gave you?"

"You'll gimme a break?"

"I'll do all I can," said Joe. "That's my promise, and you've got two family witnesses."

Eddie Falcone slapped his two hands down on the table.

"That's good enough for me," he said. "But mind if I get my own witness?"

"Not him," I said. "Does it have to be him?"

"Who the hell else I got?"

"Okay," growled Joe, "but tell Tinkerbell to leave all his toys in the car, okay? And also, remind him not to eat the door on his way in."

So Falcone left and returned shortly with Godzilla, who stood near the table and nodded evenly at all that was said, sipping sullenly on a glass of red Mary had poured for him. How he was supposed to remember everything was beyond me, but then Falcone stood up, telling us to come along. We approached Slinky's mob-mobile as Vinnie raised the trunk and withdrew a brown cardboard file case and handed it to Joe. I looked over his shoulder as he opened it. He took the notebook out first, then bundle after bundle of papers. Some were typed, most were written in longhand. We saw crude diagrams, chemical and mathematical formulas, and miscellaneous scribblings and jottings. But no matter how apparently sloppy and haphazard the file appeared, there was no doubt as to what it was.

"Son of a bitch," said Joe. "The research notes of Lionel Hartzell."

"Good God. The kid was ripping off everything he could lay his hands on."

"Is it what we thought?" Mary asked.

"Yeah, it's what we thought. Jeeez, Mare, who'd ever think that a kid as charming and smart as Andy Cunningham would be trying to hold up everybody in his path. Maybe it's just as well he's dead. I know, I know, it's a shitty thing to say. But what kind of doctor would he have made?"

We said goodbye to Slinky. Joe told him not to get any bright ideas and take off. Mary gave him a hug, saying the dinner offer still held. Then she held up the paper bag he'd given her and thanked him.

"Aw, it's nothing," he said. "Hope you enjoy them."

"By the way, Eddie," I said, "how come everybody calls you Slinky?"

"Oh, well I'm not real proud of it. About six years ago, I got real drunk at my cousin's wedding? Well, the reception was up on the second floor of this big hotel in Providence? Anyways, I got so bombed I passed out as I was getting ready to go down the stairs? So what happened, I fell over and rolled, bump, bump, bump,

bump, you know, all the way down this wicked high staircase. Shit! Lucky it was carpeted thick. So anyways, afterwards they said I looked like a Slinky. You know, a Slinky is a kinda toy. It's a spring that goes —"

"Yeah yeah yeah," said Joe. "Take off, Falcone. And stick around for your hearing. As for Twinkletoes over there, get him to watch *Mister Rogers' Neighborhood.* Maybe it'll help."

The big white caddy rolled away from the Breakers, and we went inside. The first thing Joe did was to call Paul Keegan's office in Hyannis to tell him to reopen Lionel Hartzell's file.

"So you were right all along, Paul. It *was* the old guy. He looks better for it now than anybody. Our mistake was in assuming the burglaries and the murder were connected. Andy Cunningham was playing all sides against the middle, and lots of people had reason to kill him. What? Yeah. That's what I'd do; I'd start right now."

He hung up, and Mary went to the phone.

"I'm going to call Jackie and tell him," she said.

"Well, while you're at it, tell him to steer clear of old man Hartzell until Paul Keegan gets there," I said. "Joe, what'll he do tonight? Take him in?"

"Well where is he then?" said Mary into the phone. "Can you ask his brother? Is Tony there?"

"I doubt if he can arrest him. But maybe. Maybe he's having the paperwork started on a warrant right now. Who knows?"

"Tony, where's Jackie?"

"But I was just thinking. Is this folder of his papers enough evidence? Does it provide enough motive for a warrant? I mean hell, they cleared him once. Why —"

"Charlie! Joey!"

We turned to see Mary dancing in front of the wall phone, which was dangling on its cord, scraping the floor.

"He's gone with him! *With him!*" screamed Mary, collapsing on the floor. I reached for the receiver and grabbed it.

"Who's this?"

"Dad?"

"Tony, where's Jack?"

"That's just what I was trying to tell Mom. He went out to dinner with that Professor Hartzell. Hartzell called and said he wanted to take Jack out to dinner before he left to show there were no hard feelings. He picked Jack up about half an hour ago. Why? What's going on?"

THIRTY-ONE

JOE HAD HIS CRUISER'S dash beacon on, and we flew along the Cape Highway for Woods Hole. Mary was in the back seat, crying and carrying on. We had the radio going, and Joe was trying to raise Paul Keegan or his office on it. No luck. I sat there next to Joe with clenched teeth, closing and unclosing my fists. All I could think of was taking Hartzell's neck in my hands and squeezing.

The speedometer said a hundred and twelve on the straights, but it seemed to me that the road, lit up by the stabbing beams of our headlights, was moving underneath us as slow as molasses.

Joe's face was wet with sweat. One hand was on top of the wheel, the other clutched the microphone, punching down the call button, saying the same thing over and over: "Jack Adams, white male, age twenty-three, six foot two, hundred ninety pounds, blond hair, blue eyes . . . with Lionel Hartzell, white male, age sixty, five foot seven, weight, one seventy, thin white hair, glasses . . . request *all* local units in Falmouth and Woods Hole check eating establishments in area, including Coonamessett Inn. Do you read? Over . . ."

"Hurry, for Chrissakes!" I shouted, pounding the dashboard.

Joe punched the pedal down further. Hundred fifteen, hundred twenty, hundred twenty-five . . .

We shot past cars in the right lane. The exits whizzed by: Brewster, Harwich, South Dennis, Yarmouth Port, Hyannis, Barnstable, Marstons Mills . . .

Hundred thirty, hundred thirty-five . . .

"Joey! Joey! Joey! Not so fast!"

"Keep it to the floor Joe. Keep it right on the goddamn floor!"

I scarcely remember the drive south into Woods Hole. Along those twisty roads and tight turns, with thick woods all around, I remember mostly a continual blur of headlights sweeping past dark pine trees, the squeal of tires and shriek of brakes. And always, the white-hot hum of the big engine.

Then we were at the Coonamessett Inn, jerking to a halt in the parking lot behind a police car with lights flashing. Joe and I were out of the cruiser and running for the entrance when we were met by two cops who told us that Jack and old man Hartzell had left about fifteen minutes earlier.

There was some sort of brief conference, I guess, but I scarcely recall it. It was a dark, scary dream, punctuated with bright flashing lights cutting the air and reflecting off the badge of the officer we talked with, the night all bluish black, and cold. I think I was shouting; Joe told me more than once to be quiet. Then Mary came up and was crying. Next thing I knew, we were back in the cruiser again, all three of us, with Joe trying to calm us down, saying that three other police cars were cruising the area, looking for them.

"Have they gone to Swope? Have they tried Lillie Hall? What about the docks? Oh Christ, Charlie! The docks!" screamed Mary.

I wanted to jump out of the car and run in all directions. I wished there were twenty of me, running in all directions at the speed of light and calling Jack's name so he could hear me. Then I could find him and hug him and kill Hartzell. But there was only one of me and I was riding in a car — trapped in one place — and I couldn't get out and it was killing me. Mary was reaching her arm over the seat, holding on to my hand so hard her nails were digging into my palm, making me bleed. Charlie, oh Charlie! she was saying. We'll find him, we'll find him, God help us, we'll find him, I kept saying, and wishing it were true.

"A blue Ford Escort," Joe said. "Hartzell's got a blue Ford Escort, wagon I think. Look out for it."

Then we were screaming along Water Street and turning down School Street.

"Where the hell are you going?" I shouted to Joe.

"To Jack's place. Drop Mary off. Check Hartzell's house."

So we fishtailed to a stop in front of the boys' house. Joe leaned on the horn until Tony came running out, breathless, planting his hands on each side of Joe's window as he leaned inside the cruiser.

"The police phoned. So Hartzell's the guy?"

"Yeah, looks like. Take your mother inside and wait," said Joe. "Which way is Hartzell's?"

"Up that way, third on the right. We checked it though; nobody there. Uncle Joe, is there —"

"Gotta go kid," said Joe, opening the door for Mary and hauling her out. He dragged her out of the car like a rag doll and shoved her into Tony's arms.

"Watch the street here. They pull up anywhere, yell at Jack to bail out of the car. Now, you got an idea where they could be now? They left the Coonamessett already."

"Hell, they could be anywhere. Maybe check their lab in Lillie, then . . . I don't know."

"I'm coming too. Charlie! *Chhaaarrrlie!*"

We spun out of there and back onto Water Street. I glanced back to see Mary getting into Tony's car. Tony was already behind the wheel. Damn. We barreled right through town and slid to a halt in front of the big stone building.

Joe pulled a bull horn out from somewhere under his dashboard, right behind the twelve gauge pump that sits upright near the radio. He leaped from the car and pointed the horn up at the dark building.

"Jack! Jack Adams, you up there?"

A window flew up.

"They're not here; we just checked, Lieutenant. Maybe on the —"

BLAM!

He was interrupted by the sound of a gunshot. From the sound it made, I knew it was a large-bore pistol, and not far away.

BLAM! . . . BLAM! . . . BLAM!

Too late! Too late! Oh my God, my God! I was crying to myself as I ran down the street, guided by the noise. My throat was making a gurgling whine, and it ached. Jackie! Jackie!

A car door slammed off to my left. In the parking lot behind Water Street, Tony and Mary were getting out of the car. Next to it, I saw an empty blue Escort with a door left open.

"*Noooooooooo!*" she screamed. She ran after me and Tony after her. A lighted door was in front of me. It was the door to the supply shed, the Marine Resources building. I heard Joe yelling at Mary, then I was at the door, leaping full at it, bumping it open fast with my knee. An old man was inside, under the light, taking aim with a revolver, aiming at somebody on the floor.

BLAM!

I hit him full force, knocking him across the cement floor. But it was too late. Too late, too late, too —

I turned and looked at the man on the floor.

It was Lionel Hartzell. I turned again, and saw the old man trying to get to his feet. Then I recognized him; it was Boyd Cunningham, Andy's father.

"He killed him," Cunningham said sadly. "He killed him, Dr. Adams . . ."

"Where! Where's my son?" I screamed.

"He killed my boy . . ."

"Where's my son? You —" I grabbed him and shook him until my arms ached. He raised a trembling arm and pointed to the big brine tank.

I jumped over to the big tank and peered inside.

There, caught in the spray and bubbles, was Jack, motionless on the bottom.

THIRTY-TWO

I DON'T REMEMBER diving into that tank. I don't remember the eels, or the cold. I only became aware of the cold later when Jack came to and started shivering as he finished coughing up the brine that had almost killed him. I remember sitting on the concrete floor, holding him in my arms after we'd gotten most of the sea water out of him. He'd started to move during the mouth-to-mouth, then spat up a gallon or so of brine and began to shake all over. Mary was there, too, of course, and I'll never forget her change of tone from hysteria to warm thanks.

"Ohhhh, Jackie. It's okay, hon . . . Mommie's here . . ."

Somebody had brought a little green tank of oxygen, and we put the mask over his face for maybe twenty minutes. He tore it off when he came to completely, probably because it scared him. When you've gone without breathing for several minutes, you generally don't want anything in front of your face afterwards.

So he lay there while we covered him with blankets until the ambulance came. The only commotion was the kicking Mary and I heard behind us as we were reviving him. It was a flat, wet, hollow sound. It was Tony, kicking old man Hartzell's head. Kicking hard, as if it were a soccer ball, and shouting very bad things at the dead man.

They tried to pull him away; he slugged one cop, clipped another with a kick to the knee which sent him hobbling away on one leg, and then went back to kicking the prone body of the professor. Ugly thing to do, and I must say Hartzell's appearance wasn't improved by it. And I must also say that I really didn't give a damn, no matter if the old guy *was* sick. Couldn't have cared less. They got Tony under control and his Uncle Joe kept a huge, hairy paw on the kid's shoulder. Finally, Tony turned around and buried his dark head on Joe's beefy shoulder and cried his lungs out in relief.

They hauled Hartzell out of there in a plastic body bag, then put the bracelets on Boyd Cunningham, who stood meekly in the corner in the company of two officers until they put him in a cruiser. The other two officers who had tried to subdue Tony were discussing charging him with assaulting an officer (make that two), until Joe turned around and informed them in no uncertain terms that unless they canned that conversation immediately, put the notion entirely and permanently out of their heads, they were going to be very personal witnesses to an exceptionally barbaric example of assault on officers, and that they would be lucky to get out of the hospital within two weeks.

Joe, at around two hundred thirty pounds, is impressive when he gets steamed. Fortunately, it doesn't happen often. When it does, people sit up and take notice.

They put Jack on a gurney and wheeled him out to the ambulance. Mary, Tony, and I rode with him, with Joe following in his cruiser. They put a hot blanket over Jack, and when I saw his younger brother leaning over him, putting his head on his chest, crying, I came apart at the seams, and wept in that silent, strangled way men do all the way to the hospital in Hyannis.

The following Monday, September 25, I was driving Paul Keegan back down to the Cape. He'd ridden up to Boston with Joe the previous Saturday, the morning after the fireworks, taking Boyd Cunningham up to his arraignment for killing Lionel Hartzell, and now he needed a way back to Woods Hole to pick up his cruiser. There was no doubt that it was Boyd who killed Hartzell. The autopsy, in which I, as acting M.E., reluctantly took part, showed conclusively that death was brought about instantaneously by four .357 Magnum, 125-grain, semijacketed hollowpoint bullets, at close range. Two of these entered the chest, one the abdomen, with the final one passing through the shoulder region. Any but the last would have proven fatal.

Therefore, not much attention was paid to the other injuries induced after death — the massive contusions of the head, and the dislocated mandible, brought about by "post-mortem trauma" inflicted by an "enraged blood relative of the deceased's intended murder victim."

End of file. Thank God.

"Ten to one Cunningham gets two years, reduced to pro," said Keegan, looking out the window at the Columbia Point campus of U. Mass., as we headed down the constantly jammed Southeast Expressway — everybody's least favorite artery.

"Jury or no jury, but especially with a jury, there's no way they'll pin anything on him except involuntary manslaughter. Given what happened to his son, and the man's emotional state —"

"Not to mention the fact that he probably saved Jack's life —"

"Yeah. He'll walk, with probation. How's Jack doing?"

"He's fine. Totally fine. The last thing he remembers that night is walking with Hartzell into the supplies building and staring at the tank. That's when Hartzell sapped him from behind and flipped him into the water. He doesn't remember coming to in the shed, or the ride in the ambulance, either. The next clear memory is the hospital in Hyannis."

"Well, I'm glad he's okay. You got nice kids."

"Thanks; we've worked at it."

It wasn't until we crossed over the canal that he asked the question I knew was coming.

"So what's the big deal with Joe and marriage, Doc? I mean, I gather it's a sensitive subject."

"Yep. Rather sensitive."

There was a pause, and a nervous shifting of backsides on the car seats.

"I mean, can you tell me?" he asked.

"The reason it's hard for me to talk about it, Paul, is that I was involved."

"Oh . . ."

"Well, here goes: two years or so before Mary and I got married, Joe married his old high-school sweetheart, Jessica Baldi. What a wedding. And what a happy couple. Joe and Mary's dad was still alive then, and Joe went to work in the family business, Brindelli's. He'd just graduated from Syracuse with a business degree, and was more than happy to take over the management of the stores. They're home-improvement stores. You know, combination lumberyard and giant hardware store. It used to be a construction company, but when labor costs went sky-high in the sixties, old man Brindelli converted the construction company to three big home-improvement centers in Schenectady. Joe managed all of them, with his office in the central store. After his dad died, Joe became president. Soon afterwards, Jessica gave birth to their son, Peter. Joe was overjoyed. Business was doing well; things couldn't have been better."

"Uh-oh. Sounds too good to be true."

"It was. At that time, I was just beginning my practice, and Mary and I had just gotten married and moved to Boston, where I'd taken my first position, a staff physician in internal medicine at Mass. General."

"Yeah, I didn't think you were from around here," said Keegan.

" 'Course not. Can't you tell by my normal speech, my cautious driving, and my affinity for functional efficiency? I'm from Illinois and Iowa, places like that. Places that are essentially German and Nordic, as opposed to Latin and Celtic . . ."

"Well aren't you the lucky one."

"Anyway, Mary got pregnant and had our first son, Jack, just after we moved. Joe's little boy Peter was a little older than Jackie, but they toddled around together as kids. Joe, Jessica, and Mary and I used to rent a cottage together on the Cape during summer vacations. At Christmas, Mary and Jackie and I would drive out to Schenectady to see the Brindellis, and so on. Well, when Peter was seven, he came down with meningitis."

"I know that's serious," said Keegan.

"Yes, serious. And often fatal. As it happened, Joe and Jessica were visiting us at the time. So we rushed young Peter to Children's Hospital, where I, along with two other doctors, decided to administer a fairly new and quite successful antibiotic called chloramphenicol."

My hands had begun, ever so slightly, to tremble. I gripped the steering wheel tighter, but it didn't help.

"Results were what we expected; Peter shook off the meningitis and recovered. It wasn't until six weeks later, back in Schenectady, that Joe and Jessica noticed his declining health."

"So the meningitis came back?"

"No. That wasn't the problem. What happened was a phenomenon that eventually led to the recall of chloramphenicol from the market. It seems that in isolated cases — and the odds are figured at maybe one in fifty thousand — this antibiotic works against the recipient's bone marrow. The result is a condition called aplastic anemia, in which the patient's bone marrow shuts down completely. Both red and white blood counts plummet. The patient becomes progressively weaker, unable to fend off infection . . . and eventually dies. The progress and symptomology closely resemble leukemia, lymphoma, Hodgkin's . . . any of the catastrophic blood disorders . . ."

"Oh my God. Ohhhh, my God . . ."

"So what the two families had to do then was to rush young Peter, recently turned eight, back to Boston to Children's Hospital and watch him die."

"Jesus."

"And there wasn't a single, solitary, goddamned thing any of us could do about it. He just sank lower and lower. And all the latest medical advances, all the best care, all the best intentions, all the hours of prayers and oceans of tears, were of no avail, you see . . ."

I was having trouble holding the wheel now. I slowed down a bit.

"You okay, Doc?"

"No. No, I am not. I haven't been totally okay since it happened, which was, let's see, almost fourteen years ago. Anyway, that year was one I'd never be able to get through again. Little Jackie kept asking when his cousin was going to get well. Finally, on a cold fall day in October, we had to pull the sheet up over him. Joe and Jessica went back to Schenectady, and I was left with the knowledge that I had taken part in recommending the drug that set the whole ghastly thing in motion."

"But hell, Doc, you didn't know. It was an accident."

"I keep saying that. Mary keeps saying that. Even Joe keeps saying it. Sometimes it even helps. Anyway, the upshot was, I quit medicine. Now perhaps, if I'd had several years of successful practice under my belt, or if the kid was not a beloved, blood relative, or *something* . . . then maybe I'd have weathered it. But the fact that it was Joe's boy . . . Joe's and Jessica's, and that it happened at the very beginning of my practice, made it just too much."

"So you became a dentist."

"Right. I became a dentist for less than a year, then I quit that."

"But aren't you a dentist now?"

"No, I'm an oral surgeon, a doctor who works on people's mouths and jaws, and who removes teeth that are difficult. I quit being a dentist because it was boring and unpleasant. I couldn't stand being the guy nobody wants to see."

"So how's your current job better?"

"The teeth-pulling part isn't any better; that's why I hate that part of it. Too bad it's maybe eighty percent of what I do. But the remaining part is challenging, rewarding, fulfilling . . . all that good stuff. And also, I'm good at it. But back to Joe and Jessica. They had a real rough time, but then Jessica got pregnant again, business was booming, and it seemed they were off to a fresh start."

"And?"

"And then, seven months later, just before Christmas time, while she was waiting on a busy intersection on Pearl Street in downtown Albany doing her Christmas shopping, Jessica Brindelli was run down by a speeding car. She and the baby were killed instantly."

There was no sound from Keegan. I turned to see his jaw slack, his hands clasping the sides of his head.

"Well, as you can imagine, Joe went off the rails awhile. Always religious, he suffered a deep schism inside himself. Rather than denying God and religion, he came to believe that it was somehow his fault, that he was cursed . . . that everyone he reached out to was doomed . . ."

"Oh God. That must've been awful."

"Awful's hardly the word. The family business went to hell, and Joe quit his post before it went under and moved to Boston.

That was mostly Mary's idea, and I think it saved him. Then Joe became a priest."

"You're kidding."

"Not kidding. And he was good at it, too, until he got in trouble slamming young punks around in his parish. He was in a rough neighborhood in East Boston and he knew that it would take more than prayers and psalms to straighten these kids out. The neighborhood loved him, but not the Catholic brass. So he quit, drifted around a little, and became a cop. See, the car that ran his wife down wasn't driven by a drunk or a teenage hot rodder, but by two men who'd just pulled an armed robbery and were speeding away from the scene . . ."

"And so he's been trying to catch those guys ever since."

"In a sense, yeah."

"Well holy shit. Now I see why I shouldn't have —"

"The story's not over yet."

"Oh no. You gotta be kidding."

"Nope. Wish it were. Anyway, Joe was a great cop. Seemed made for the job, as you can see for yourself. His rise was fast; he became detective lieutenant quicker than anybody in the state's history. About three years after he moved to Boston he met Martha Higgins, who worked right in your headquarters building at Ten Ten Comm. Ave. They started dating, and soon Joe was in love again, and ready to begin his life all over."

"Ohhhhh, shit . . ."

"Oh shit is right, Paul. Four months into the relationship, Martha developed a lump in her left breast. A biopsy revealed a malignancy, and she had a mastectomy. It was all she could do to handle it, since she was barely thirty. But she could've hung in there, I think. But Joe came unglued and broke it off. He broke it off because he was by this time *convinced* that he was the cause of the cancer . . . that he was the world's greatest jinx."

"Christ almighty."

"And of course, Martha couldn't help but think he dumped her because she was disfigured. Anyway, it was a sad, pathetic thing. Martha was so crushed she left town, moved back to Pittsfield to live with her parents. She's never married. They still write now and then. Mary and I are convinced Joe still loves her. But he won't get near her — afraid he'll make her sick again."

There was a long silence. I wanted a cigarette.

"And so he just keeps torturing himself with this?"

"And so he just keeps torturing himself with it. Right. Mary and I tried to fix him up a few times. He'd meet these women, who always liked him a lot, but he'd manage to keep his distance every time and let the thing die. Joe was thin then, and very handsome. You can see his good looks in his face. Both he and Mary have the classic Roman profile. Mary's face is strong and fine, like the Statue of Liberty. Ever notice?"

"You kidding? A guy can't help but notice her, Doc."

"Yeah. Well, they're both good looking, as only Italians can be good looking. But then Joe began to gain weight. Of course he loves to eat, and he drinks like a fish now and then — as we can all understand, right?"

"Right."

"But Mary and I also think he got fat so women wouldn't be attracted to him. So he won't have to deal with it. And it's a goddamn shame, Paul, because there's nothing in this world that Joe Brindelli would like more than a wife and kids. Nothing in the entire world."

"Gee, if I'd have ever known that story . . ."

"Well, now you know it. And maybe you understand my brother-in-law a little more. It explains, for one thing, why he likes to visit us so much. And he loves his nephews. And boy, do they love him. He's spoiled the shit out of 'em since they were babies."

"Uh-huh. And maybe it explains a bit about you, too, Doc."

"How do you mean?" I asked. The question made me uneasy.

"Well, you know. Maybe you still feel guilty about Joe's kid. Even though there's no earthly, rational reason for it, you still feel responsible. And that's maybe why you like to get involved in these cases, especially when there's a kid like Andy Cunningham mixed up in it. That's maybe why you forget you're a doctor and go off —"

"Let's pull off a second, Paul. I gotta take a leak."

When I got back in the car, Paul suggested we just change the subject. I said that was just fine with me. Just absolutely, goddamn fine. We got to Woods Hole before ten.

THIRTY-THREE

A FEW WEEKS slid by, the way they seem to do, faster and faster with each passing year. Fall arrived. The leaves got bright and the nights got cold and clear. Jack missed his court appearance, of course. We could stand it. Paul Keegan was wrong; Boyd Cunningham didn't walk. He got ten years reduced to two, which meant he was eligible for parole in six months. Bill Henderson and his partners from OEI took the fall for the two B and Es. But their sentence was paltry. Joe said they'd be out and around within a year or so. To make matters worse, the smart money was betting that they'd be back in business then, hauling lengths of drilling pipe out to Tuckernuck Island. Where it would end, nobody knew, but the Woods Hole community wasn't exactly overjoyed.

As for Eddie Falcone, a.k.a. Slinky, he disappeared shortly before his scheduled arraignment. Dropped out of sight like an anvil in Lake Baikal. Joe was furious, thwarted at not putting another mobster behind bars. He speculated that Slinky unloaded his big white wagon, called in all his notes and markers and cashed them in, maybe did some last-minute scrounging and gouging, and took the loot and flew back to Sicily.

"Or else maybe he's gone undercover somewhere here, like Vegas, doing some low-level shit work for the Wiseguys. Who knows?"

"Well wherever he is, I hope he's fine," said Mary, unloading the dishwasher and putting things away. "He wasn't violent, was he? I kinda liked him, if you want to know. And are you guys forgetting that he was the one who saved our son's life?"

"Says who?" said her brother. "I think Boyd Cunningham saved Jackie's life."

"No, Mary's right. I think it was mostly Slinky. We were damned lucky he came calling that night."

"And while we're on the subject of young men gone bad, I hope you revise your soured opinion of Andy," said Mary, turning around and looking me in the eye. "I mean, it's easy as hell for you to condemn him for being money hungry, Charlie. You, who never had to worry in the least about it. But I've seen enough poor people to know this: poverty does *not* ennoble you. It does *not* give you character. It does *not* make you strong. It robs your self-respect and makes you scared as hell of every goddamn thing that comes down the pike. And I just, well . . . I just feel sorry as hell for both those kids."

She turned back to the sink and I saw her shoulders shaking. I went up and put my arms around her. She leaned back into me, wiped her eyes, and tried to smile.

"C'mon now," she said. "Hurry up you two; the party's at five, and we've got to meet the boys."

We finished breakfast and went up to Wellfleet Harbor in time to see *Ella Hatton* come storming around the breakwater. The sloop-rigged catboat came up to the wharf wing and wing, dropped sail, and made fast, with Jack, Tony, Tom McDonnough, Wayland Smith, and Art Hagstrom disembarking. They'd come around the outside of the Cape on a four-day cruise from Woods Hole, whale watching all the way. We drove them all back to the Breakers in two cars, stopping only long enough to buy yet more food and drink.

In early afternoon Moe showed up. He'd brought a carton of live lobsters and five bottles of first-class wine as his contribution. Jim and Janice DeGroot drove down from Concord, too, bringing two beef tenderloins, two bushels of butter-and-sugar corn, and a quarter-barrel of St. Pauli Girl.

A little later, Brady Coyne called to say he couldn't make it, but that he'd just received the split-bamboo fly rod I'd sent him from

Orvis. This was a token of thanks for help he'd given us in our darkest hour when Jack had needed the best legal help that influence could buy.

"God, it's great, Doc. Just great," he said over the phone. "How can I ever repay you?"

"You can't possibly," I sniffed, and informed him he'd have to live out the remainder of his lifetime under obligation to me. His reply to this was unfitting, if not downright rude, which only goes to show that when you go out of your way to be nice to people, they turn on you. Every time.

At four-thirty, after an hour of warm-up partying, Joe lighted two big stacks of charcoal, each sitting in its own wide grill. Down on the beach, people were frolicking in the surf with the dogs, coming ashore only to warm themselves in the sun and drink beer. Fall is tremendous on the Cape; the crowds are gone, the water's still warm, and you have a fire every night. Tony and Smitty were busy assembling a large pile of driftwood on the beach for that very purpose. Art Hagstrom had bought scallops in Wellfleet and he and Mary were wrapping them in bacon strips for grilling. Jim was filling the big lobster kettle and fiddling with the gas burner underneath. Moe was shucking corn, humming Haydn, reading a book propped up on the picnic table, and playing chess games in his head, all at the same time. Jack and I were leaning over the deck rail, drinking beer and just hanging out together, talking about whales again.

Paul Keegan and wife showed up just as Joe was pouring himself a large G and T. He'd been drinking beer all afternoon, but announced it was now time for the "heavy artillery."

"This party's gonna be a real shit-kicker, Doc," Joe said. "Just what I need."

"Don't we all."

Janice DeGroot, emerging from the cottage in a brand new, unbelievably brief bikini, walked to the center of the deck and pirouetted on her toes, spinning around like a model so all could see.

"*Ta dahhhh!*" she said.

"Wow!" said Joe.

"Can we talk?" said Mary, taking her firmly by the elbow and hustling her back inside. Janice reappeared moments later, pouting, wearing conventional swimwear.

"Killjoy," I said to Mary under my breath.

"Just you wait, pal. Just you wait."

"Hey Mary, how's your book?" asked Moe.

"Fine, Moe. I'm just about finished. I think they're gonna go for it. I just have to, you know, spice it up a bit."

Spice it up a bit. Give me a break, Mare.

Well, in capsule summary, the gala was one for the record books. We started in earnest around five-thirty, with cocktails and the grilled bacon-scallops in butter for appetizers, moving on to chilled gazpacho or steaming clam chowder — your pick of one, or both — followed by the surf-and-turf meal of lobster and filet mignon with corn on the cob, all washed down with vats of beer and wine, and topped with deep-dish apple pie, ice cream, and cappuccino. Then back to the keg again.

Everybody got totally out of line. It couldn't have been better. Sometime around nineish, as the gold faded to crimson over the bay and we were standing around the big, snapping beach fire, I felt an expert hand goose me from behind.

"*Ahhhhhh*, that feels great," I said, and turned to see Mary, giving me a hard, level gaze.

"Oh, it's you," I said.

She squinted at me; the jaw crept forward a fraction of an inch. Uh-oh. Never could take a joke.

But she put her face up to mine and gave me a long, wet kiss.

"C'mon, hunk. Time for the show ..." She led me up the beach, up the deck stairs, inside, and upstairs to our bedroom.

"But Mare, what'll the guests think?"

"Whatever they like. You know, Charlie, it's the strangest thing. I seem to get real horny after a couple of drinks ..."

By this time she was just about undressed and was working on me. Seeing there was no way out, I helped her remove the rest of my clothes and watched her go to the door and lock it. Then she flashed the wall switch off and on, off and on.

"What the —"

"Curtain time!"

Then she jumped into the sack, pulling me after her.

"Ohhhhh, Charlie," she said afterwards, and began tickling my back. "I'm so lucky."

"You said it."

She kept tickling and rubbing my back. The hoot and babble of merrymakers wafted up through the window. How sweet the sound.

"Mary, of all the things I've ever done, or dreamed of, marrying you and having our kids have been the greatest things of all."

She leaned over and kissed the back of my neck and said we'd better get dressed and rejoin our party. So we did. We got some catcalls and hoots and off-color comments from the crowd as we reappeared at the beach fire. The worst offender was none other than Number-Two Son Tony, who had a saucy young thing in tow. I noticed her blouse was buttoned all wrong. No telling where they'd been, but what they'd been up to was obvious. Ever notice how the people who give criticism about something are always the worst offenders themselves? It's true. Think about that the next time you see a TV preacher.

We sat down at the fire's edge and sang songs with our guests. The dogs lay at our feet drying off in the fire's glow. I noticed Mary gazing wistfully up the beach every so often. Perhaps she was hoping that Fuente and Company would appear on horseback over the nearest rise and come thundering up the sand looking for a little R and R. As for me, sitting on that cool sand, I hadn't thought about Patty Froelich at all. Hardly.

I was tired, so I lay down with my head on Mary's thigh. Jack sat down behind me and put his hand on my shoulder. I'm confident Tony would have done the same if his hands had been free. But it was all the thanks I needed. I was positive that there was no luckier man on earth than Charles Adams, M.D.

By and by I dozed off. Mary said later Jack just sat there in the firelight, watching me sleep. He didn't know it then, but his old man was dreaming about the whales.